THE STC
VEYLI

BOOK 1:
THE GOLDSTONES AND THE WAY

SUE WOOLLEY

SCIMITAR

EDGE

Published by Scimitar Edge

An imprint of Purple Unicorn Media

ISBN 978-1-915692-37-5

Cover design by Robin Stacey

www.scimitaredge.com

Dedication

For David – thank you for your inspiration, support and insights.

Author's Note

The following symbols have been used in chapter headings, to indicate the places they are set, or the peoples they concern. Their deeper meaning will become clear in the course of reading.

† Earth

Δ Talamdor

֍ The Commonweal of Veylindré

End Contents

GARÛNALOND
Ullmass
Mirûnan
Garûnashavn
LÈNIUM
RANU
Yrusian Sea
Mathwen
Ruslen
Nellenium
Ranusheim
Muillean
Fort of Ranu
Iascan
Sea of Lènia
Lèniashaven
Sea of Ranu
YRUSIAN
Poruspor
River Porus
Tarrin
Taellingsford
Néartanis
Néartanian Straits
Fenland
Ostfen
Virunen
Chorich Castle
Rouliris
Irnvein
Nordvein
Myndorian
NÉARTANIA
Nordkeep
River Cristail
Roilldon Fort
Cristail Keep
Ceardochis
Silvin
Talamunem City
Roillby
River Mistbourne
Mount Talamu
Mistbourne Keep
Central Plains
Caethniss Castle
TALAMDOR
South Plains Keep
Gulf of Dagàran
Luvodican
Crullfeld
Kalthund
Talmis
River Clearwater
Clearhaven
Smithsport
Saltis
DA GÀRAN
Deepwood Keep
River Roilldon
Caethwasim
Great Forest
Coèdnis
Fionnan
Nailach
N
Southern Sea
HAVIM
W
E
VEYLINDRÉ
Rorschak
S

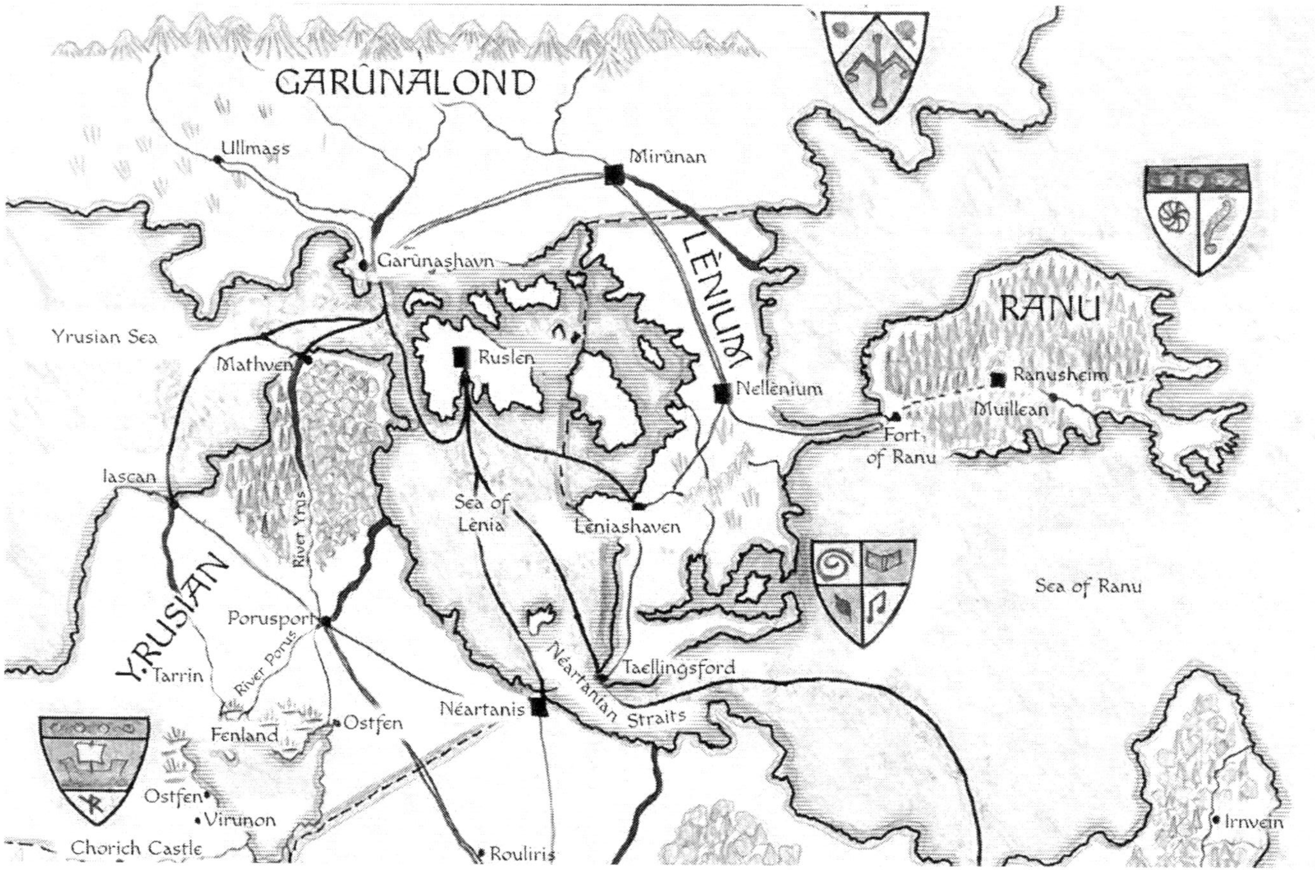
GARÛNALOND
Ullmass
Mirûnan
Garûnashavn
LÈNIUM
RANU
Yrusian Sea
Mathven
Ruslen
Nellènium
Ranusheim
Muillean
Fort of Ranu
Iascan
Sea of Lènia
Lèniashaven
River Yrus
Sea of Ranu
Y'RUSIAN
Porusport
River Porus
Tarrin
Taellingsford
Néartanian Straits
Néartanis
Fenland
Ostfen
Ostfen
Virunon
Chorich Castle
Rouliris
Irnvein

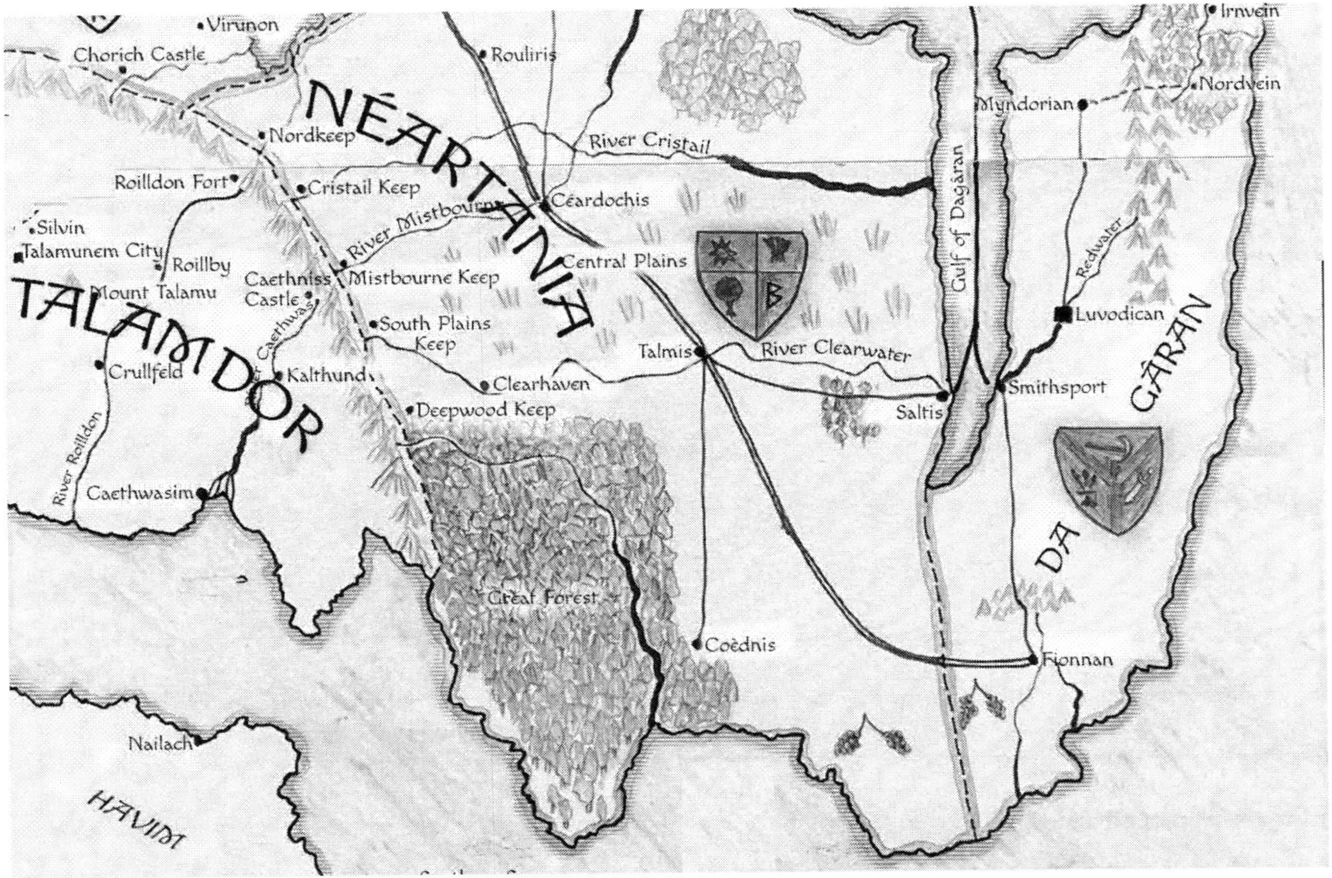
NÉARTANIA
TALAMDOR
DA GÂRAN
HAVIDI
Virunon
Chorich Castle
Rouliris
Irnvein
Nordvein
Myndorian
Nordkeep
River Cristail
Roilldon Fort
Cristail Keep
Ceardochis
Silvin
Talamunem City
Roillby
River Mistbourne
Central Plains
Caethniss Castle
Mistbourne Keep
Mount Talamu
Gulf of Dagâran
Redwater
Luvodican
South Plains Keep
Talmis
River Clearwater
Crullfeld
Caethwas
Kalthund
Clearhaven
Smithsport
Saltis
Deepwood Keep
River Roilldon
Caethwasim
Great Forest
Coêdnis
Fionnan
Nailach

† Chapter 1 ֍

"Abigail," her mother said, nudging her arm, "This is no time for daydreaming. Your father says that Captain Wood wants to catch the morning tide."

Abigail jumped – she had been miles away. "Sorry, Mother."

She had had no idea the ship would be so vast, at least to her eyes. Her heart began to beat faster as the raucous calls of the gulls wheeling overhead filled her ears, and the steep wooden sides of the *Sweet Sarah* loomed up in front of her, bobbing and tilting at the quayside. In spite of the resentment she still felt towards her father for uprooting all their lives, she could not help feeling excited now that their adventure was about to begin. It was the 6th of April in the year of Our Lord 1665, and their little band of pilgrims – twenty-eight men, women and children under the impassioned leadership of her father, Pastor Thomas Winters – were about to set sail from Southampton. Leaving England, leaving the security of the world they knew, because her staunchly Presbyterian father could not live under the tyranny of Charles the Second.

The *Sweet Sarah* was about seventy feet long from bow to stern and had three masts with square rigged sails. The crew, many of whom Abigail was secretly afraid, with their rough clothes and rougher ways, outnumbered the pilgrims by five to one. The greater part of the space below the deck was filled with a cargo of finished goods the New World settlers were crying out for. As she searched for the small cabin she would be sharing with three other women and her little sister, Faith, the thought crossed her mind that their inclusion on this voyage was very much an afterthought of Captain Wood's, to maximise his profit.

Abigail was proud of her father's status as one of the Ejected, the two thousand clergymen who had refused to conform to the tenets of *The Book of Common Prayer* in 1662.Even if it had led to this uprooting of their lives. Last year's Conventicle Act had been the last straw for him. She remembered him ranting about it as they sat around the supper table, in the little house they had now left behind – forever, she supposed. She could hear him now…

"That devil Clarendon means to make our lives and worship impossible," he had said, his face dark with anger. "This Conventicle Act makes it impossible for us to worship according to our consciences."

"What does it mean for us?" her mother had asked, her voice calm and soothing, as always.

Yet even her mother had been unable to pacify him – not that time. Abigail suspected it was no easy task to be married to her fiery father, but her mother generally knew how to manage him, how to lull him into complacency. As her father was the head of the family, her mother was their gentle guardian, to whom they all, her turbulent father included, turned with their troubles. Abigail adored her.

"What does it mean?" her father had shouted, trembling with the force of his emotion.

Even now, months later, Abigail could feel her stomach clench as she remembered her father's answer.

"It means that we, the Dissenting ministers, are forbidden to hold religious assemblies of more than five people outside the auspices of the Church of England. This will be the ruin of us. We have to leave. Soon."

"Leave?" her mother had said, dismay in her voice. "How can we leave everything and everyone we know?"

Abigail had been with her mother. She had spent all of her seventeen years in that house. Tears stung her eyes as she remembered the little bedroom in the eaves, which she shared with her little sister, Faith, with its sloping walls, its two narrow beds, its built-in cupboards, the scent of honeysuckle coming in through the window on summer evenings. And he had forced them to leave it all behind. Resentment burned in her chest. Until now, she had rarely even left their little village, only visiting the nearest town, Andover, on special occasions.

"The Pilgrim Fathers managed it," her father had snapped. "I don't see why we shouldn't do the same."

"As you say, my husband," her mother had said soothingly. "But it will take a good deal of organising."

Her mother had been right. It had taken her father months to find a captain willing to take them to the New World. But now Abigail – in spite of missing home – was beginning to relish the experience. She soon became accustomed to the privations of life aboard ship, and was relaxing into the novelty of the voyage.

Once she had got her sea-legs, which had taken a couple of days, she was enjoying the thrill of being at sea, watching the endlessly changing formations of the clouds and the waves buffeting the sides of the ship, sending spray high into the air. The invigorating scent of the ocean was always in her nostrils, promising adventures to come. If only she could do something which would make a difference, when they reached the New World. She wanted more from her life than home and family.

How she wished she could take off her confining coif and let her hair blow free. But her father would have a fit. He was very strict about seemly appearance, especially for women. One of his favourite quotations from St Paul was from the eleventh chapter of the *Epistle to the Corinthians*, "every woman that prayeth or prophesieth with her head uncovered dishonoureth her head." Abigail sighed – she knew that one off by heart. It was easier to fall in with her father's strictures than to defy him. She hoped the New World would mellow him. What was she thinking? That would never happen.

There was only one other fly in the ointment. In the confined area of the ship, it was difficult to avoid the attentions of Matthew Sanderson. He was at least ten years older than her, a thick-set man with a brutal face. Abigail disliked and distrusted him but knew her father had plans to marry her off to him. Never, never. Even if she and Jacob had to run away together, she would not marry Matthew Sanderson. Would not.

Jacob, tall, weather-beaten, his strong hands gentle when they touched her. Jacob, with his deep brown eyes, his dark curly hair, which she loved to run her fingers through. They had been meeting in secret for nearly a year now. In spite of her father's plans for her, she would not give Jacob up. Absolutely would not.

"You could stay here with me," he had said, as they had walked in the wood near the village one evening the previous autumn, safe from prying eyes.

"I can't, Jacob," she had protested. "My mother relies on me to look after the little ones."

"In that case, I'll have to come with you."

"Would you really do that, for me?"

"Of course I would, my little love."

The following Sunday, he had turned up at their secret meeting place in a friendly farmer's barn and, after attending a few meetings for worship, asked to join their band of pilgrims.

Abigail had held her breath, afraid her father would reject him. And yes, Pastor Winters had been suspicious at first, but the addition to their party of a strong young man with a useful skill had been too tempting to let pass. And Jacob was clever enough to seem sincere in his protestations of faith. Her joy was complete. She could face any trial, any deprivation, as long as she had Jacob by her side.

One day, when there were no other pilgrims in sight, they leaned against the weathered rail of the ship, revelling in the uncomplicated pleasure of each other's company. Jacob once more expressed the doubts she was beginning to share.

"Your father seems to think we will simply turn up in the New World and be accepted with open arms," he said, his hand over hers, warm and reassuring, "but I'm not convinced it's going to be as straightforward as that. Why should the established communities welcome us?"

The freshness of the air, together with the warmth of Jacob's lean body next to hers, were intoxicating. Abigail didn't want to think about future problems. "Surely they will not turn us away?"

"No, I expect we'll be allowed to stay, but I'm sure we will have to work for others, earn their trust, before we can set up our own place."

"I suppose you're right," she sighed. "Oh, why couldn't my father have been someone ordinary?"

"Cheer up, my dear. At least we are together."

She kissed his cheek. "I do love you, Jacob. I'm so glad you are here with me."

One evening, when they had been at sea for seven weeks, a late Spring storm blew up out of nowhere, turning sky and sea alike a dark, threatening grey. The small ship, its masts creaking, its sails bellied out, ran before it, helpless to do aught else. The waves were high and ferocious, sweeping over the deck, and Abigail fled to the comparative safety of the area belowdecks. Even here, she could hear the deep voice of Captain Wood, shouting hoarse orders to his crew. Down below, a sailor gruffly ordered them to close all the portholes, stow their belongings away and cling on to something solid. Then he swarmed back up the ladder out of sight. Sleep was impossible, so the rest of them, she, her family and the other pilgrims, huddled together, staying out of the way, sitting it out and in some cases, being violently sick. Abigail wrinkled her nose before burying it in her little brother Daniel's hair, which smelled only of slightly grubby small boy.

"Almighty God, preserve us poor sinners. Help us to remember the words of the Psalmist, 'Then they cry unto the Lord in their trouble, and he bringeth them out of their distresses. He maketh the storm a calm, so that the waves thereof are still. Then they are glad because they be quiet; so he bringeth them unto their desired haven.' Let us never doubt that the Lord's hand is over us and that we will come through this storm in safety and continue our voyage to the Promised Land. In Jesus' name, Amen."

Her father, so strong in his faith, spreading hope and reassurance to the miserable group belowdecks. "Have faith, my friends! The Lord will protect us and bring us safely to harbour."

"Abi, I'm hungry," Daniel said.

"Not now, Daniel," she whispered. "Maybe when the storm is over."

His small face crumpled in disappointment.

"Wait a moment," she said. "I think I have an apple in my pocket. Would that do?"

It was one of last year's crop, wrinkled, but still sweet.

The little boy beamed. "Thank you, Abi. I love you."

She cuddled him close. "I love you too, sweetheart."

"Holy Jesus," her father intoned, "bring us safely through this storm. Strengthen our hearts, we pray…"

His peroration was interrupted by a burst of lurid green, clearly visible through the portholes. No lightning Abigail had ever seen looked like that. She held her breath, wondering what fresh hell was round the corner. Then such a strange sensation – as though she was squeezing through a narrow hole, then coming out the other side. Daniel clung to her, bursting into noisy tears. What was happening?

Then the ship stopped pitching and tossing, the shriek of the wind died away.

"The Lord be praised!" her father proclaimed. "He has delivered us."

Really? But she had the sense to keep the question to herself.

Jacob, her dear Jacob, climbed the ladder to the deck above. Moments later, he was back, excitement blazing in his handsome face.

"Come and see! We have been delivered indeed."

They surged up the ladder and came out into… what? The sea, no longer grey, but a vibrant aquamarine, was calm, small white-capped waves rippling over its surface. Abigail looked up. The sun was shining, as though there had never been a storm.

Captain Wood strode towards them, his face pale under his seaman's tan. "I have never seen anything like it. One minute we were being driven before the storm and I feared for our lives. Then I saw a door – a great door standing on the waves.

We were swept through. And then, we were… here. It seemed like," and he lowered his voice, "magic."

Magic. Abigail had heard of witches and their evil powers. Surely not. And what was this about a door? A door on the waves? Impossible. She shuddered, a tremor of fear running through her.

"Hush, man. Do not speak of such things." Her father's voice was low and intense. Then he continued more loudly, "The good Lord has delivered us by the miracle of His grace, Captain Wood. Fear not. Let us continue our voyage unafraid. We are in His hands."

"But… the sea! That door! I fear we are no longer on the good earth."

"Nonsense, man! You must have imagined it. Where else could we be?"

"I do not know. But I like it not," the captain replied. "I will send someone aloft to see whether we are in sight of land."

As the sky darkened, stars started to appear, pinpoints of light blazing in the blackness above them. The night air was cool on Abigail's skin. She shivered, drawing her woollen shawl up around her shoulders. She looked in vain for the Plough, could not find any constellation she knew. As others did the same, a deep unease began to spread among them. Where were they? Where *were* they? Was it just that the storm had driven them far off course? She hoped so. She had heard that the stars were strange on the other side of the world. Yes, perhaps that was it.

Next morning, Abigail and Mercy, her best friend among the pilgrims, were in the cabin they shared with two of the other women and her little sister, plaiting each other's hair before covering their heads with the plain linen coifs they were required to wear in public.

"Honestly, Abigail, I was so frightened," Mercy said, her fingers gentle as she skilfully braided the thick mass of Abigail's blonde hair, before pinning it neatly into a great coil. "That green flash – it was so strange, so sudden... And then the storm just… stopped."

"I know," Abigail said, "and did you hear what the captain said about a door? It seems impossible, but… did you notice the stars last night? The constellations are strange. I fear we are no longer on the way to the New World."

"But how could that be? Surely there is no enchantment strong enough to transport us to another place?"

"Perhaps you are right," Abigail said. "Perhaps it is only our ignorance – after all, what do we know about the stars in the New World?"

The younger girl said nothing, but continued her ministrations. Abigail could feel her fingers trembling.

When she was done, Abigail smiled at Mercy before beginning to work on her friend's hair. The feel of Mercy's dark hair as it slid through her fingers had an everyday normality which calmed her. Now to soothe her.

"Do not speak of this to any other," she cautioned. "We must trust in the Lord, that He has not abandoned us."

"Thank you, Abigail. That helps. You are so strong in your faith."

If only she knew. But this was not the time to share her doubts, at least, not with Mercy. Not even to Jacob had she confessed the misgivings she was feeling about her faith. She was struggling with certain passages in the Holy Bible, finding it hard to believe that her loving Saviour, who had died to redeem them all, could also be so vengeful, smiting the enemies of the people of Israel. Her heart told her the holy scripture did not lie, but her mind was not at all sure she could respect the angry, vindictive God of the Old Testament.

Each time these thoughts crossed her mind, she pushed them back down, frightened by their intensity. If she shared them with anyone, and her father got to hear of it, the best she could expect was a whipping. Her father was not the gentle, forgiving type of pastor, like Jesus, but fierce and unforgiving of any spiritual doubts.

For three days more, they pushed their fears to the back of their minds, having no alternative. The little ship continued on her way, afloat on the turquoise ocean. Now that the weather was calmer, Abigail spent most of her time on deck, looking after Daniel and Faith, to give her mother a rest. She was telling Faith a story, cuddling her close, when she heard a shout. Daniel.

"Abi, Abi! Come and see!" he said, his four-year-old voice full of excitement.

Where had he got to? Why had she taken her eyes off him?

To her horror, he had somehow climbed up high into the rigging and was holding on with one hand, his expression rapt.

"Faith, don't move an inch," she told the little girl. Then to Daniel, "Come down from there directly."

Something in her voice made the little boy freeze. The joy on his face was replaced by fear. With an effort, Abigail stilled her trembling heart, and began to coax him down.

"Come on down, Daniel, and tell me all about it," she said, as persuasively as she could.

"I – can't," he wailed.

"Of course you can, dear one," she said, keeping her voice soft and even, although her heart was thumping in her breast.

"Or, I tell you what, I'll stand here and you can jump into my arms."

"All right," he said and, barely giving her time to brace herself, he let go of the rigging and leapt. She staggered as the solid weight of his body hit her, but managed to hold on to him.

"There we are," she said, hugging him to her before putting him gently down. Thank God she had caught him – her mother would never have forgiven her if anything had happened to him. "Now, what was it you saw?"

He opened his mouth to tell her, but was interrupted by a cry from the crow's nest. "Land!"

Everyone rushed to the ship's rails. They had done it. They had made it to the Promised Land.

Getting ashore was a wet and uncomfortable business.

Captain Wood put down anchor a couple of hundred yards out from the shoreline of a roughly oval cove with golden sands and a forest behind it. He lowered two small rowing boats to transport the pilgrims and their goods to dry land. It took many trips and several hours, and Abigail's father stayed on board to the last to oversee the unloading, deputing the organisation of the landing to Elder Sanderson.

By the time the sun was setting in a glorious display of yellow, orange, red and purple, the pilgrims and their stores were ashore. The men rigged a makeshift shelter for them towards the back of the cove, high above the tideline, using saplings from the nearby forest as a framework, with some rough sailcloth, purchased from the captain, thrown over it. It was basic at best, but at least they were out of the elements. Two of the men built a fire for cooking at the mouth of the shelter, and the women were bustling around, preparing a rich stew of salted meat and root vegetables.

Abigail sighed. It had not taken long for the usual division of labour to take place. She had hoped to do something morc meaningful in this new world. But maybe that would come. Captain Wood and his crew were going to share the meal with them before re-provisioning in preparation for the long voyage home.

When everyone had eaten, and the remnants of the food, together with the pewter plates, eating knives and spoons, had been cleared away, her father rose to his feet.

"Brothers and sisters! Under the good Lord's guidance, and through the beneficence of Captain Wood and his brave sailors, we have made this voyage to the New World. Never forget that we are the fortunate ones, who can now live free of persecution. Let any who doubt this, speak now, so that they may return to England on the *Sweet Sarah.* There is no room for people of little faith in this community."

His fierce blue eyes swept round the gathered pilgrims, sitting round the fire.

No-one spoke.

"Good. You are all strong in your faith. There will surely be trials ahead of us, but so long as we trust in the Lord, He will provide." Then, turning to Captain Wood, "Our thanks to you, good sir. We wish you plain sailing and calm seas, on your voyage home."

"Thank you, Pastor Winters. I will not hide that we will be glad to see England once more. We will stock up on necessaries on the morrow, then set sail for home."

Chapter 2

Jacob and the other men spent the next few days building two more permanent shelters, one for themselves, the second for the women and children. Fortunately, the local trees were easy to chop down, and the pilgrims had all the tools they needed – axes, saws, two adzes, hammers and nails. Some among them had carpentry skills and shook their heads over not giving the wood time to cure. But it couldn't be helped.

He delighted in using his body again – he had spent too long in the past few weeks being idle. And roofs over their heads were of paramount importance, as the weather was much cooler on this side of the Atlantic. If that was where they were. He was itching to explore this new world, But Pastor Winters was adamant – shelter first, exploration second.

From his position astride the roofbeams, Jacob spotted a ship with red sails. Was it Captain Wood returning? No, it couldn't be – the *Sweet Sarah*'s sails had been white.He shrugged, dismissing the question. The *Sweet Sarah* would be well on her way back home by now. Pastor Winters had prevailed on the sailors to stay for a couple of days to help them with the construction, but they had acquiesced with poor grace, and had left on the morning of the third day.

They had been fortunate in their choice of landing site. The deep cove of gorgeously blue water contained many fish, and Captain Wood had been happy to add to his profits by selling them one small boat, so they could have fresh fish to eat. As the men were working hard to finish building the two shelters, it fell to the women to turn them into homes, unpacking and arranging the family belongings, arranging areas to sleep, eat and come together.

Abigail's father was in his element, striding around at a great pace, issuing orders. Jacob was glad to be involved in the building work. Abigail and the other women had been set to making a detailed inventory of their food stores – salted meat, flour for bread, a few sacks of root vegetables and a limited supply of fresh water. It was clear they would not survive for long without relying on the land around them. Which meant they would have to make forays into the forest to hunt small game or gather fruits and nuts. Not to mention finding a source of fresh water – Captain Wood had only left them a couple of casks.

"Nobody must go alone," Pastor Winters decreed on the morning of the sixth day. "We do not know this land and must be cautious in our exploration, although I am certain that other settlers will soon hear of our landing and come and find us."

Really? Jacob was not so sure and knew Abigail shared his doubts. The man still believed they were in New England. They were equally sure they were not. She had told him of her belief that the flash of green at the height of the storm, the strange sensation they had both felt, had heralded their translation to a different world. But if it made Pastor Winters happy to think so, he, Jacob, was certainly not going to contradict him. The past weeks spent in close proximity to him had taught Jacob that opposition was met with anger. He shrugged, turned his attention back to what the man was saying.

"I want volunteers to make up foraging parties, four in each. You know what we need – grains, fruit, nuts and small game. And it is essential that we locate a source of fresh water. Elder Sanderson will issue each party with one firearm. The person holding it will be in charge of the party. The others must do as he says, without question, as though it were I asking them. Some will go north, the rest south."

Murmurs of assent arose. They knew better than to cross him and in any case, Jacob could not wait to investigate this new land. He made sure he and Abigail were as far away from Matthew Sanderson as possible, so they would not be in the same group. He was as domineering as his father, and Jacob had taken a strong and instant dislike to him.

By an adroit move through the waiting people, towing Abigail after him, Jacob managed to ensure that his small party was made up of himself, Abigail, Mercy, and Richard Forster, with Richard in charge.

He liked Richard, a tall young man a couple of years older than him, with a kind face and blue eyes, and he knew Abigail liked and trusted him. Richard was one of the less extreme members of the faith and had a keen sense of humour.

Jacob suspected that Mercy was sweet on Richard, and that this feeling was mutual. It looked as though he was not the only one with a little dalliance in mind. He smiled. It would be so good to get away from Pastor Winters and Elder Sanderson, if only for a short time.

As they stood waiting to be told where to go, he heard Abigail whisper to Richard, "Try to wait until Matthew Sanderson's party has left. Then we can choose a different direction."

Richard's eyes widened, then he nodded. Obviously, he disliked the man too.

A few minutes later, they set off. Each carried a pack with some food, a leather water bottle, a change of clothing and a blanket. Once they were safely out of sight and earshot, Richard slowed down. He caught Abigail's eye and grinned.

"Now we're safe for a while," he said. "No-one telling us what to do, how to think."

"Thank goodness," she said. "I don't know why I thought the voyage would change my father, because it really hasn't. He's the same strict and severe person he has always been, so sure of the rightness of his every action and statement."

Jacob drew her arm through his and held her close. "Just forget about him for a few hours."

"Let's take our time," Abigail said, smiling at Mercy, "so long as we bring back enough food to satisfy the elders."

"And find a stream or river," Richard said. "We mustn't forget that."

"I'm excited," Jacob said. "It's our first chance to explore this land. It's been so hard to stay in the cove all this time."

By this time, they were out of sight of the settlement, and walking into the depths of the wood with their foraging baskets. It was quite chilly, surprisingly so for early June, but so long as they kept moving, they were warm enough. The wood was deciduous with many broad-leaved trees. The going was soft underfoot and Jacob felt a bubble of contentment rising up in him.

"Does it feel like autumn to you?" Mercy said. "Look at the leaves. They're turning yellow and gold and orange already."

A small, grey squirrel scampered across the path in front of them, its cheeks bulging. It leapt up the trunk of the nearest tree with a whisk of its furry tail.

"Yes," Richard said, "he's gathering nuts against the cold season just like our red ones. It seems as though the year is further advanced here." He paused. "Wherever here is."

"Well," Jacob said, putting his arm around Abigail, "we're stuck here now, so we'd better make the best of it. I just hope any people we meet are friendly."

Richard turned, his face serious. "Hmm, I hadn't thought of that. They might not even share our faith in God." He shrugged. "Let's not worry about that now. Come on, we'd better start foraging."

Some of the trees were familiar – broad oaks, stately elms and slender birches – but others were strange to them. There were some magnificent trees with copper trunks and broad, star-shaped leaves, which none of them could identify. They moved with caution, unsure what creatures might live in this alien place. But fascinated to find out more about it, all the same.

"Look!" Abigail said, making a beeline for some bramble bushes. "Blackberries."

Jacob laughed at her enthusiasm. The four of them picked a good number and also ate some – they were deliciously sweet.

"Let's try and remember where these are and any other food supplies," Richard said. "We'll surely need to return another day."

They also found hazelnuts and chestnuts. But no game. Pastor Winters would not be pleased. And they had found neither stream nor river, which was the most urgent need of all.

"I think we had better split up," Richard said, "so that we can look in two directions at once."

"But what if we are benighted?" Abigail asked. "My father would not approve of a young couple being alone with each other."

Richard grinned at her. "What your father doesn't know, he cannot grieve over.Mercy and I will go north, I think. Jacob, you and Abigail go south. May the Lord be with you."

"And with you," Abigail answered.

With a wave of her hand, she and Jacob walked away.

"South it is," Jacob said, with a smile.

"Oh, it's so good to be on our own again," Abigail said, hugging him. "I've missed being alone with you."

A couple of hours later, she began to lag behind.

"Jacob," she called, as they came out of the trees into a sunlit glade, "can we rest here awhile? My back's aching from carrying the pack and my feet are sore. I hadn't realised how unfit I've become after the long weeks at sea."

Jacob glanced around. He felt fine himself, but it made a pleasant change to catch sight of a patch of blue sky.

"Surely," he said. "Let's sit over there, with our backs against that tree." He pointed to a giant of a tree, the kind they had seen earlier, its beautiful copper trunk rising into the canopy above.

She shrugged off her pack and sat down between two tree roots on the soft moss. Jacob sat beside her, putting his arm around her, and she snuggled into his embrace. She had removed her coif once they were alone, and he could smell the warm, sun-kissed scent of her hair.

As the late afternoon sunlight slanted through the trees, sitting with her in his arms, he was at peace for the first time in weeks.

"What are you thinking about, my love?" he asked.

She smiled at him. "I was wishing that this search for water would take some time. It has been so long since we have been alone together. I am so scared of Father finding out about us."

"Would it matter if he did? I love you and want to make you my wife."

Tears welled up in her eyes. "Oh, Jacob! That's what I want too. But I'm afraid Father has other plans for me."

"What other plans?"

"He has spoken of marrying me to Elder Sanderson's son."

She started to cry, turning her face into his shoulder.

"Matthew Sanderson? But he must be ten years older than you."

"Yes, he is," she said, her voice muffled. "But that is Father's plan."

"That is not going to happen," Jacob said, anger licking through his veins, gripping her tightly in his arms. Another reason to hate the man. "Even if we have to run away together, I'm not losing you, not now."

"Oh, my love! Where would we run to in this strange land?"

"I care not. Anything would be better than seeing you with that… oaf."

At that, her tears fell faster. "If only I could believe there was somewhere to run."

He heard a rustling further off. "Hush! I can hear something coming through the trees."

They hurried to their feet, shouldered their packs, and hid behind the tree they had been sitting against. Whoever or whatever it was, kept on coming. He could feel Abigail's heart beating, hear her breath coming ragged and uneven. He took her small, cold hand in his own large, warm one, squeezing it in reassurance. Then held his breath, praying they would not be seen.

A large animal with a thick, black pelt lumbered into the clearing. It had long, sharp claws, a thick snout, tufted ears and small, wicked-looking eyes, set deeply into its skull. He guessed it was some kind of bear. Then, behind it, two miniature versions, which had to be its cubs. He squeezed Abigail's hand in warning. Their survival depended on their stillness and silence.

The adult bear paused, raised her head and sniffed the air. Jacob held his breath, his other hand dropping to the knife at his belt. He knew it was a futile gesture – they would have little chance against such a large beast even with a firearm. And Richard had that.

Then he stooped, picked up a stone and flung it over to the opposite side of the glade. It made a satisfying crash as it landed. The bear's head came up and she moved off in that direction, followed by her young. Jacob and Abigail stayed where they were for another few minutes, until the sound of the animals' passage died away.

He took Abigail in his arms, hugged her close. She collapsed against him, trembling, clearly unable to believe the danger had passed.

"God was with us, my love," he said, stroking her hair. "Let's wait awhile, then continue with our search."

She took a deep breath and smiled up at him.

"You're right. And that stone was good thinking. Let's find another route. One encounter like that is more than enough for me."

In the early evening, as the light was fading, they found a stream. They reckoned they had come about twenty miles, no mean achievement given the terrain they had covered, mostly uneven forest floor. They were too tired to start back that night, and also afraid of losing their way in the tree-shadowed darkness. So in spite of Abigail's misgivings about what her father would say, they ate the greater part of their remaining food, wrapped themselves in their blankets and fell asleep in each other's arms.

The next morning, they explored some way upstream. Abigail could not help worrying about her father's response to their long absence, so they turned back when the sun was yet high in the sky. The return journey to the cove was uneventful, for which she was profoundly grateful. She had had enough adventure for the time being. They dallied along the way, unwilling to bring their time alone to an end, sleeping out for a second night. By mid-afternoon of the third day, they were recognising landmarks. She would even be glad to see her irascible father again.

She was about to walk down the last hundred or so yards of path, when Jacob grabbed her arm.

"Wait!" he said in a low, urgent tone. "Can you hear anything?"

They stood and listened. Nothing broke the stillness, except for the sound of their breathing, the distant beating of the waves on the shore, and the chirping of some birds. But at this time of day, the settlement should have been humming with activity. Her stomach clenched, her heart beat faster.

"You stay here," Jacob said in the same, quiet voice. "I will go ahead and look."

Ten minutes later, he returned, his face ashen, his dark eyes full of unshed tears.

"What? What has happened?"

"The camp has been attacked. I fear… I fear there are no survivors."

Abigail broke from his grasp and ran down the path. Then stopped dead, horrified by what she saw.

The settlement they had left bustling with life and vigour was now a place of death, a place of slaughter. There were bodies everywhere, of men, women, and children. Of people she knew. She saw Daniel, her little Daniel, his childish body cast aside, a gaping wound in his chest, a look of terror on his face. Her mother and the other women violated and then murdered. She looked for Mercy and Richard, praying they had not yet returned. But in vain. Both were there, both dead.

They were all dead. Every last one. Even her indestructible father. Flies were crawling around and over the bodies, enjoying the unexpected feast. Their arrival disturbed some carrion birds who were tearing at their flesh with their sharp beaks. The stench of so much blood and death made her feel sick to her stomach. It was beyond her worst nightmare.

But she was awake. Her mind could not encompass the horror of it. It looked as though the menfolk had put up quite a fight – there were three strangers among the dead – but they had been no match for the killers. Then she noticed the final gory detail. Each broken corpse had a rough H with an extra line across the top cut into their foreheads. She fell to her knees, retching and weeping. Who could have done this? And why?

Jacob knelt beside her, his arm around her shoulders. "Look," he said, pointing.

Far out to sea, she could see a ship with red sails.

"I saw one like it before," he said, "but thought nothing of it."

"How could you have known? No-one could have foreseen this."

She turned her face into his shoulder, wetting his shirt with her tears. Jacob stroked her hair, which soothed her a little, his own eyes wide with shock, tears sliding down his cheeks.

"Come back up the path," he said, "I'll find somewhere safe for you to hide, then I'll check the stores to see if I can find anything we can use. We are going to have to get away from here, find help."

"No," she said, the panic rising in her throat, "I want to come with you."

He shrugged. "Come, then."

Most of the settlers' stores had been ransacked or ruined. But they found one small cache of food that had escaped the raiders' despoiling. They loaded their packs with as much as they could carry – a couple of long, flat loaves, some salted meat, half a sack of carrots and a small pot for cooking. Some clothing, set to dry on distant bushes at the edge of the settlement, had also escaped, and they gathered it all. They had no idea how long it would take to find help, and the nights were growing colder.

Abigail was shivering, from reaction not cold. "Should... should we bury them?" she asked between chattering teeth.

Her mind was all over the place; flashes of dead and mutilated bodies, all the blood – so much blood, terror at their predicament, and a bottomless grief for all she had lost.

Jacob frowned. "We cannot afford the time – it would take days for me to dig a grave large enough for all. How do we know the ship will not return?"

"Then what can we do? We cannot just leave them. Those horrible birds..."

Jacob stood awhile in thought. "We must carry them into the men's dwelling and then set fire to it, once the ship is out of sight."

"But if we do not give them Christian burial, how will their souls find their way to God?"

Jacob shrugged. "When the martyrs of old were burned alive, didn't they go straight to Heaven?"

"I suppose so. Oh, I hate this! We were doing no harm, why did they have to kill them all?"

"I don't know. But I do know we have to get away from here, as soon as we can."

"What about the strangers?"

Jacob's face hardened. "We leave them. But I will search them in case they are carrying anything that will help any people we meet believe our story."

Abigail shuddered. How could he bear to do that? But she knew he was right. Rather him than her. She hugged herself, her hands clasping both elbows, struggling to fight off the horror and sickness that were overwhelming her.

When he returned, he was carrying a small, red pouch of soft buckskin. "I found this on a leather thong around one of their necks," he said. He opened it and drew out a red, triangular stone. "It may be a clue. Keep it safe."

He put it back into its pouch and passed it to her. She put it in the linen pocket around the waist of her gown.

Then Abigail set her teeth against her incipient nausea and began to help him with the gruesome job of separating the tangled bodies and carrying each one up from the beach into the men's dwelling. By the time they were done, her back was aching fiercely. But there was more to do. They began to arrange each body in a seemly manner, each pair of hands clasped at their breasts. It was a more difficult job than she had expected, as the bodies had begun to stiffen in death. She hoped and prayed that what they were doing would be acceptable to God. She worked with tears burning in her eyes, her hands shaking, fixing each loved face in her memory. Even those she had disliked in life were sanctified for her in their deaths.

They stopped when the sun set, washed in the sea to get rid of the blood, forced themselves to eat a quick meal and then went to sleep in the women's dwelling, taking what comfort they could from the warmth of each other's bodies. She woke more than once during the night, crying and shaking. Without Jacob, she was sure she would have lost her mind.

The next morning, they re-entered the men's building to say one last farewell. Abigail said a brief prayer over them, then wiped her sore eyes. She had cried more in the past twenty-four hours than she could remember ever doing before, and her head was aching. Jacob fashioned a rough cross out of two stout branches tied with twine and thrust it deep into the earth in front of the building.

Then, as the afternoon waned, they gathered twigs and branches from the nearby forest, more back-breaking work. But Abigail was glad to do it – concentrating on her physical aches and pains helped her to forget the horror of the cove. Once Jacob thought they had enough, they arranged it in piles around the outside of the dwelling. Then Jacob used his tinder box to set the fires. Soon, all too soon, the building was alight.

Abigail faced the flames and recited the 23rd Psalm, then prayed aloud, "Dear God, receive the souls of these your people. May they be with you in Heaven. Amen."

Jacob echoed, "Amen," then said, "Come, Abi. We need to go now."

"It breaks my heart to leave them," she said, trying to dam the insistent tears. "What are we going to do? How can we survive on our own?"

"They are known unto God," Jacob said. "And, I don't know, but we must leave now. That fire will be seen from afar. We need to be nowhere near it."

They took one last look round, shouldered their packs and left the cove. From now on, they were on their own.

Chapter 3

Exhausted though they were, Jacob and Abigail forced themselves to keep on walking, until they were well away from the cove, from the betraying smoke of the fired building, rising thick, greasy and black behind them. When darkness fell, they took it in turns to rest fitfully for a few hours, one of them always on the alert for pursuit, and set out again as soon as the sun rose. They reached the stream they had found before by late evening and turned west to follow it. Fortunately, the moon was nearly full, so they had a little light to see their way through the shadowy trunks of the sheltering trees.

Once they were out of sight of the threatening coast, they relaxed a little, breathing deeply, taking in the bosky scents of the woodland around them, but still wary of encountering any wild creatures, like the bear they had seen a few days before.

By this time, there was a distinct nip in the air – it definitely felt later in the year here. They were both stumbling with weariness, and the need to find somewhere to spend the night was becoming urgent.

Then Abigail tripped over a hidden tree root, fell to the ground, and cried out in pain.

"Abigail, are you all right?" Jacob said, both concerned and alarmed.

"It's my wrist. I twisted it underneath me when I fell."

Very gently, Jacob felt along her wrist. He could tell she was in pain and would be able to go no further that night.

"I don't think it's broken," he said. "Bide here a while, and I'll find somewhere for us to lie up until morning."

He helped her to stand, then pointed to a mossy rock. "Sit there. I won't be long."

He did not like leaving her, but what else could he do? Then he spotted it, a deeper patch of darkness. On investigation, it proved to be a small cave. He entered it cautiously, knife in hand, his eyes, ears and nose alert to any hint of another living creature, but it was empty, and seemed to be uninhabited. He'd have to risk it.

He hurried back to her. "I've found somewhere for us to shelter. It's not much, but at least it's out of the weather."

She stood up. "Thank goodness!"

The cave was small and cheerless, with rough, rocky walls, cold and damp to the touch, yet warmer than the chill night air outside. Abigail sank to the earthen floor, clearly at the end of her endurance. He'd better do something, fast.

He rummaged in his pack. "I'm going to start a fire at the mouth of the cave," he said, bringing out tinder box and flint. "We need warmth and something hot to eat. There are twigs aplenty round here."

"But what if somebody sees it?"

"I think it's worth the risk. We're both tired and cold and hungry. At least if we have a fire, we can solve the last two before we sleep."

When they had eaten, Jacob fetched some water from the stream using their cooking pot and set it to heat over the fire. He insisted on bathing her sore wrist, which by now was red and swollen, then bound it up with a woollen stocking from her pack, being as gentle as he could, using its pair as a rough sling.

"Thank you, Jacob, that feels much better. I think I'll be able to go on tomorrow."

"Tomorrow will be here before long. We'd better try to sleep."

Abigail awoke from a nightmare of blood and bodies, tears pouring down her face, shaking with the force of her grief. The fire had died down to grey ashes and she felt cold and stiff. She sat up, smothering a cry as pain shot through her injured wrist. This was going to be a nuisance. But they couldn't stay here.

She turned to look at Jacob, still fast asleep beside her, his dark hair curling every which way. He had been so kind the previous night – finding the cave, cooking their meal, tending her wrist. She felt so loved, so cared for. What would she have done without him?

His eyes opened and he smiled up at her. Then his face changed. "Abi, what's wrong?"

She shuddered. "I had a nightmare. I was back there in the cove, seeing them all again."

He sat up, took her in his arms. "You're safe now."

"Thanks to you."

She kissed him. For a moment, they clung together.

Then Jacob said, "How is the wrist this morning?"

"Better than it was, but it still hurts when I move it."

"D'you think you're going to be able to walk today?"

"Of course I will," she snapped. "It's my wrist that hurts, not my legs." Then blushed. "I'm sorry, Jacob. You didn't deserve that."

"That's all right. I love you, Abigail Winters."

"I'm so glad you're here," she gulped down a sob. "At least we have each other."

He kissed the tip of her nose. "Nothing can part us now."

They ate some of their remaining food as breakfast, then Jacob said, "Give me your pack. I'll take some of the heavier stuff so that you can sling your pack over one shoulder and rest that injured arm."

"Thank you, Jacob."

In less time than it takes to tell, he was done. He stood up, then reached out a hand to help her to her feet.

"Come along, Abi, time to go."

They followed the stream westward for the next couple of hours. Abigail looked around her – she could recognise most of the trees; ash, oak, beech, and elm – but others were unfamiliar, like the big trees with thick reddish-brown trunks, and broad, coppery, star-shaped leaves, which she and the others had noticed a few days earlier. Mustn't think about that. The season was well-advanced here, the leaves in their full autumn glory. Which was a great contrast to the early June they had left behind during the storm. She shivered. Where were they?

They were not talking much. Jacob was ahead of her, blazing the trail and she was content to follow his lead. She took every step with care, anxious to avoid another accident, for there were tree roots aplenty snaking across their path. She gritted her teeth, determined to keep going. But by noon, her wrist was throbbing, and she was starting to feel light-headed. She was relieved when Jacob stopped.

"Let's rest and eat," he said, turning back to look at her. "Oh, love, are you all right? No, of course you're not. Come and sit down."

He took a blanket out of his pack and spread it on the ground. She sank down on to it in relief.

"When do you think we will find some people?" she asked.

"I don't know. I have no idea where we are. We can only pray they aren't related to the pirates who murdered our kin."

A shaft of horror went through her. All this time, she had thought they were fleeing away from danger, but he was right. They might be rushing towards it.

"Oh, Jacob! What are we going to do?"

"Keep on travelling, I suppose. There's not much else we *can* do. We can only hope that not all the people in this world are evil."

"Oh, surely not," she said.

They were packing up their belongings in preparation for departure, having no further idea of where to go apart from following the stream, when they heard the sound of hoofbeats in the distance, heading their way. Jacob put her behind him and drew his knife.

Aidren and Ellyn were out riding in the woods some miles south-east of Nordvein. It was a cold, crisp afternoon, and the sun was shining through the canopy of trees, dappling the path before them with light.

Aidren grinned. "It's good to be out on a day like this."

If only he dared to tell her… but it was no good. Why would she, niece of the Waymage, look at him, the son of a miner and a weaver?

Ellyn smiled, tossing back her glossy black curls, her face lighting up in the way he loved. "We'd better make the most of it. There won't be many more chances once the weather closes in as the Season of Completion takes hold. Wait a moment, what's that?" She pointed to a dark spiral of smoke clearly visible against the sky.

"We'd better take a look. But keep your eyes and ears open."

They slowed their horses to a walk and followed the direction from which the smoke was coming. On the way, they came to a clearing, into which the afternoon sun was shining through the dappled shade of the trees, and saw two young people standing there. They were white, tired. Aidren had not seen many pale-skinned people before – only a few Yrusian traders or a stray Garûnalonden Watchman. Which was not surprising – he had never been outside Dagâran. The sun made the girl's hair look like spun gold. He noticed that the young man had a knife in his hand. As he and Ellyn rode up to them, Aidren saw with a shock that neither bore Waymarks.

"Who are you?" Ellyn demanded. "Where have you come from?"

Her fearlessness worried him sometimes.

The young man drew himself up. "We mean you no harm," he said, sheathing his knife. "We are travellers from the coast. Our community was attacked by pirates while we were away finding water. We are the only two left alive."

Aidren looked to Ellyn, wondering what to do.

She shrugged.

So it was up to him. One thing was clear. They must be taken back to Nordvein, where the Council could decide what to do with them. They looked harmless enough. Or at any rate, the girl did. Apart from having no Waymarks.

"You do not look evil," he said. "Come with us."

"Is it far?" the young man asked. "My companion is injured. She has hurt her wrist. We cannot walk much further today."

"Ellyn," Aidren said in a low voice, "you ride back to Nordvein. Fetch the Waymage and some others. I will stay here and guard these strangers."

"Are you sure?" she murmured. "They have no Waymarks and may be dangerous."

"What else can we do?" It was a chance to prove himself as a Warrior of Dagâra.

As she nodded, her mouth twisted in a grimace. He could tell she was worried."All right… But keep a sharp eye on them."

He turned to the strangers. "I will stay here with you. Ellyn," he nodded at the young woman, "will return to Nordvein to report your coming."

Ellyn wheeled her horse and cantered off.

Aidren dismounted, loosened his horse's girth then tied the reins to a nearby tree stump.

"My name is Aidren," he said. He was shorter and leaner than the other man but had the self-confidence that came from being a trained warrior. He took a deep breath, then smiled at the strangers and extended his right hand, palm open. "It will be some hours before Ellyn returns. Let us sit and talk awhile. I would know more of you."

The young woman seemed unafraid. She was exotically beautiful, with her mass of blonde hair, fair skin and blue eyes, so different to any woman he had seen before.

She smiled back. "I'm Abigail and this is Jacob. We are strangers here."

"I know," Aidren said. "You have no Waymarks."

"Waymarks?" the young man – Jacob – said. "What are they?"

Aidren couldn't believe his ears. He pointed to his own forehead. "This is my Waymark," he said. It was a red circle about an inch across, with the symbol of Dagâra at its centre. "It shows that my affiliation is to Dagâra, and that I am a warrior. Every person in Veylindré has one."

"We have never heard of these," the young woman – Abigail – said. "Where we come from, no-one has one. Is Veylindré your country?"

Aidren hissed an intake of breath. His hand shot to the sword at his belt. "By the Six!" he exclaimed. "It is as I thought. You are not from our world. I will have to report this to the First Waymage in Luvodican."

The two strangers glanced at each other, obviously uneasy.

He forced himself to relax his stance. "How did you come here?" He would have the truth from them or die in the attempt.

"There was a storm," Abigail said. "Our ship was set to founder in the turbulent waves, and we feared for our lives. Then there was a flash of vivid green and I felt the strangest sensation, as though I was being squeezed through a narrow space. Then we found ourselves on a quiet, calm sea, about three days out from your coast. We mean no harm."

Aidren gnawed at his lower lip. "I have never heard of this," he said, "but mayhap the Waymage will know more."

"How long must we wait?" Jacob asked. "We fled from our camp with only the supplies we could carry and they are running low."

"You are hungry? That at least, I can remedy," Aidren said, walking over to his horse, being careful to keep them in sight. He opened his saddlebags and brought out three small loaves of *feolin* and a flask.

"Here," he said, passing a loaf to each of them, "eat these."

"Thank you," Abigail said, before biting into it.

"What do you call this?" she asked. "It is delicious."

"*Feolin*. We use them as travel provender."

They ate in silence. Aidren's flask held a thin, bitter, red wine, and they shared it among them. The girl, at least, seemed to relax.

"You say we are in… Veylindré?" she said. "Is that the name of your country?"

"Do you really not know?" Aidren said. "The Commonweal of Veylindré is wide. There are six lands, each under the care of one of the Six."

"Who are the Six?" Jacob asked.

"The Six Goddesses of Veylindré," Aidren said, wondering at their ignorance. "Ranu, Dagâra, Lènia, Néarta, Garûna and Yrusia. Is it possible you do not know this?"

"We only know one God," Abigail said.

Aidren leapt to his feet and drew his sword. "You are followers of the Prophet of the One?"

Instantly, Jacob's knife was in his hand, his eyes narrowing.

Abigail stepped between them. "No," she said, her voice soft and even. "Our God is from our world. Please, Jacob, Aidren, put down your weapons. Our God is a god of peace."

Jacob's nostrils flared. "Stay out of this, Abigail."

"Jacob, please, don't," she said, taking his arm. "We need their help."

Slowly, breathing deeply, he lowered his knife.

Then, and only then, Aidren did the same. "If you are not followers of the Prophet, who is this God of yours?" he said, his voice still sharp, his sword still in hand. "We know only the Six in Veylindré." Who were these people? He was out of his depth here. Hopefully Ellyn would return soon with reinforcements. The Waymage would know what to do with these strangers.

"Aidren, Jacob, please… sit back down," Abigail said.

She was brave, this yellow-haired girl, he had to give her that.

"Let's talk about something else," she continued. "You said you lived in Nordvein, Aidren? Please, tell us about it."

Scowling, Aidren sheathed his sword before sitting down. He kept his hand on the pommel. Jacob also sat, his knife beside him.

"All right," Aidren said, still on his guard. "Our village is called Nordvein, because it is one of the most northerly settlements east of the Dagâran Range. We are a mining community. There are lodes of gold and silver and iron nearby."

"But you are not a miner?" Abigail said.

"My father is, but I am a Warrior of Dagâra. I have nearly completed my sword training and am waiting to be posted wherever Lord Lesym and Lady Bélia send me."

"Who are they?" Jacob asked. "Are they the rulers of your land?"

"Yes, they are the rulers of Dagâran. And they will want to see you."

"Do they live in Nordvein too?" Abigail asked.

Aidren laughed aloud, then felt a little ashamed. "No. They live in Luvodican, the capital city of Dagâran, on the other side of the Dagâran Range."

Abigail's face fell. "We do not know how to get there."

"When we get back to Nordvein, arrangements will be made for your escort," Aidren said. "Now, rest while you may. It is a long walk back. I will keep watch."

"And make sure you do not escape," he added under his breath.

"Sleep, love, I will keep watch," Jacob said.

"Wake me when Ellyn returns," she said, "I am sure they mean us no harm."

"I am not as trusting as you."

Aidren knew the feeling.

Abigail awoke to the sound of hoofbeats echoing up through the earth. The sky above them was dark. She was positive, now, that they were no longer in their own world. She had never seen anyone as dark-skinned as Aidren, and his talk about Waymarks and Veylindré seemed to prove it. How would they get on here? She hoped the people Ellyn had gone to fetch were as friendly as Aidren seemed to be.

She sat up, rubbing her eyes. Jacob helped her to her feet, then stood close, his hand once more on the pommel of his knife. She could sense his wariness.

In the bright moonlight, she could see the new arrivals, Ellyn and three strangers, with six horses. Relief swept over her – they wouldn't have to walk.

Aidren strode over to a woman who appeared to be the leader of the group. She was wearing leather riding clothes, like Aidren's, but had an air of quiet authority. Her hair was iron grey, drawn back from her face in a tight bun. Her eyes were dark, her glance wary.

Although Aidren spoke in low tones, Abigail caught some of his words, "… and they say they know nothing of our world."

The woman dismounted and approached them, her right hand extended, palm open, the same gesture Aidren had made earlier. It seemed to be a sign of friendship, so Abigail copied her. Jacob stood silent beside her.

"We are Abigail Winters and Jacob Wallingford," she said. "Our community was killed by pirates, back on the coast, and we have nowhere to go. Will you help us?"

"In the name of the Six, welcome," the woman replied, inclining her head in acknowledgement. "My name is Shaunan. I am Waymage of Nordvein. You must come with us now. Can you ride?"

"Yes," Jacob said.

"No, I'm sorry," Abigail said. "My wrist is injured."

Shaunan nodded. "I will tend it before we leave," she said. "We will ride slowly. One of us will lead your horse, if necessary."

The Waymage undid the rough bandage and felt along her wrist gently. "Can you move it?"

Abigail tried but gasped as pain shot through it. "I'm sorry," she said, biting her lip, "it hurts so much."

"It is not broken," Shaunan said. "This I can help without waiting to reach Nordvein. Grunen!" she called. One of the strangers approached. "Fetch my bag, please."

He hurried off, returning with a large, leather bag, beautifully decorated with beads, and the quills of a bird or animal. Shaunan delved into it and brought out a small jar. Abigail noticed that she, like Aidren and Ellyn, wore a soft leather pouch around her neck. It was attached by three leather thongs of subtly different shades of brown, plaited to form a necklace, which set off her dark skin and long neck to great advantage. Shaunan untied the strings of the pouch, and brought out a pale, golden stone shot through with veins of darker gold.

"Hold out your wrist," she said.

Abigail did as she was told, supporting her outstretched arm with her other hand.

Shaunan opened the jar and applied the salve in it to the sore wrist. Then to Abigail's surprise, she took the golden stone in her hand, murmuring some words under her breath, "*Belannath Ranu, gal lo bynn wellwich*".

Abigail could sense the power of the words. "What do those words mean?" The pain in her wrist had vanished. It was like magic.

"I am calling on Ranu to heal you."

Ranu? Abigail watched as the veins in the golden stone shone out brightly.

Then the Waymage put the stone back into its pouch before binding up her wrist deftly.

The abrupt cessation of pain was astonishing. "How… how did you do that?" she said. "It feels so much better already."

Shaunan looked at her, eyes twinkling like amber in the moonlight. "I am a healer," she said, "and it was not a great hurt."

"Thank you so much. I am grateful."

"Come!" the Waymage said. "Let us ride. It is late and the way is long. When we reach Nordvein, you can sleep. On the morrow, we will meet again."

Jacob sat on the edge of his bed, biting his fingernails. He had hardly slept, not knowing whom to trust. When Abigail opened her eyes, he smiled at her, glad to see her looking rested.

She was lying on a low bed like his own, well-padded beneath, with a soft, woollen blanket over her. She stretched luxuriously, then sat up and looked around her.

They were in a small, white-washed room with two beds, a small table, and a wooden chest against one wall, with pale sunlight streaming in through the window.

"Good morning, sleepyhead," he said. "I thought you were never going to wake up. It must be nearly noon."

"I was tired," she said. "Where are we?"

"Don't you remember? We are in Nordvein, wherever that is. The Waymage, whoever *she* is, is waiting to speak with us."

He saw her face change as memory came flooding back. Would there ever be a time when her eyes were not filled with sorrow?

"I'm so hungry," she said. "I hope we can eat something first."

Jacob reached across to the table. "Here is another of those meat and bread loaves, *feolin*, I think he called them, to break your fast. I ate mine a while ago. They've also given us some water to wash with."

She ate with a good appetite, using both hands freely. "My wrist!" she said. "She's healed it."

"Yes, she seems to have some power. We will need to tread carefully here."

Abigail looked at him. "I don't think they mean us any harm. We must be as strange to them as they are to us."

"It's not natural," Jacob growled, rising to his feet and beginning to pace. "It's like witchcraft."

"Oh, surely not," Abigail said. "She's healed me, not harmed me."

Jacob shrugged, not convinced.

When she had finished eating, he waited while she washed her face and hands, drying them on the cloth provided. Then she rummaged in her pack and brought out the coarse-toothed comb she used for her hair. After taking the hairpins out, she tugged it through the blonde mass, which he loved to run his fingers through, then pinned it up again neatly. It gleamed in the sunlight, soft and golden.

"There, that's better," she said, smoothing down her skirts. Her every movement fascinated him. "I feel I can face the world now."

Chapter 4

They walked out of the house, braced for… they knew not what. Abigail took Jacob's hand, comforted by his closeness. Whatever happened, they were together.

She looked around curiously. Nordvein had two main streets, actually unpaved tracks, which met in a large, central square. All the buildings, including the one they had been staying in, fronted on the square and most had two storeys. From what she could see, she guessed that the ground floor of each dwelling was dedicated to crafts and trades, with the people living upstairs. She noticed a smithy, a bakery, a tavern and a leather goods shop, among others, and was reassured by the familiarity.

But one building was different. She had never seen anything like it. It was neither square, nor rectangular, but had more than the usual four sides. The side facing the square had two large, wooden doors with metal studs. It was built of a pale gold stone, which glittered with hints of many other colours in the sunlight, unlike the other buildings which were mainly of brick, or a darker stone she couldn't identify. She guessed it might be their church. Or whatever they called their place of worship. A tall pillar made of the same stone stood in front of it.

In the centre of the square was a large tree, of the kind she had noticed in the forest, its thick trunk dividing into sturdy branches, each with many star-shaped leaves, which shone copper-gold in the sunlight.

She could feel unseen eyes watching as they crossed the square. The people out and about avoided their gaze. She shrank closer to Jacob. Where was the Waymage?

Then the doors of the unusual building opened and the woman, Shaunan, emerged. She walked towards them and smiled. "I hope you are rested. Come with me."

She turned back the way she had come. They followed her. When they were through the doors, both Abigail and Jacob stopped dead.

As Abigail guessed, it was Nordvein's place of worship. It was high and austere, and the golden stone from which it was built glowed gently in the sunlight, which streamed in through arched windows set high in all the walls – seven of them. Below each of the six windows not above the doors was an altar of the same golden stone, and above each altar was an unfamiliar symbol, each one different. Tall candles in silver sconces stood on the altars. None of the symbols was a Christian cross.

"What is this place?"

"This is the Temple of the Six," Shaunan said. "Our most holy place, where we worship the six goddesses of Veylindré." She pointed to each of the symbols in turn. "Néarta, Lènia, Garûna, Yrusia, Dagâra, and, most important of all, Ranu."

"Please forgive me if I seem rude," Abigail said, her mind reeling with the strangeness of this revelation, "but if Ranu is the most important goddess, why do you worship the other five? In our world, we have only one God."

"So," Shaunan said, "what Aidren reported is true. Where do you come from? What is your purpose here?"

Jacob told their story again. When he mentioned the peculiar H symbol carved into the foreheads of the slain, Shaunan sighed.

"The Havimi," she said. "They are becoming bolder and more troublesome, raiding our coasts, killing, looting, and burning. Your story rings true."

"There is something else," Abigail said, with a proud lift of her chin. "Our men fought bravely to defend our people, even if they fell and failed. Among our dead were three of the strangers. Two had swarthy skins, and long hair in braids, gaudy red clothing, and leather boots, with blood-stained cutlasses in their hands.

"But the other was different – perhaps their leader. He was tall, thin and pale, with dark hair and eyes. He wore a black jacket and breeches, buckled shoes on his feet and a dark cloak lined with red. He had a dark red triangle on his forehead, like the mark on yours.

"Then, because Jacob said our story would not be believed without any proof, he searched them… and he found this hanging on a leather thong around the neck of the third man."

She delved into the pocket of her dress, brought out the red buckskin pouch and produced the red triangular stone with flecks of other colours in it. A black triangle was carved deeply into one facet.

When the Waymage saw it, the colour drained from her dark brown face, leaving it a muddy grey. "Ranu herself must have guided you," she breathed. "May I examine it more closely?"

Abigail passed it to her and Shaunan received it with shaking hands. "Had I not seen this with my own eyes, I would not have believed it."

"But what is it?" Jacob asked. "Why does it frighten you?"

"It is a sign of approaching darkness," the Waymage replied. "The Wayzenmoot must be told. I must take you to Ranusheim as soon as possible." She handed the stone back. "Put it away and show it to no-one. Keep it safe. I must take you to the Council now. Do not mention this stone when you speak to them."

"Who are the Wayzenmoot and where is Ranusheim?" Abigail asked.

Shaunan ignored the question. "What is your purpose here?" she said.

The intensity in her voice made Abigail shiver. "We do not have a purpose," she said, her voice wobbling. "We are fugitives, unable to return to our world. Your world is the only one which remains to us. Have mercy on us."

The Waymage's face softened. "Do not fear," she said. "I can hear you have told the truth. I will answer your question. We worship the Six because each played a part in creating our world, so all are worthy of reverence. Ranu, goddess of wisdom and lore, is the mother of all, including the other goddesses. She mated with the spirit of the universe and conceived the other five. The Six joined their hearts and powers to create our world. Ranu gave each of her daughters dominion over one of the lands, and also over those who bear their Waymark."

"Aidren mentioned Waymarks," Abigail said, "and showed us his. But yours," she looked at Shaunan's forehead, "is different. I don't understand what they mean or how they work."

"It is well you have asked me, rather than any other inhabitant of Nordvein, for they fear the unknown, or the unfamiliar, such as you," Shaunan said. "I am Waymage, so my affiliation is to Ranu. I have powers which affiliates of other Waymarks lack, including the ability to discern the truth of a question." She paused. "I hear you have asked in good faith, so I must answer."

"When the Six created the world, they also created the Way of Veylindré, and the Golden Stones which enable us to access the powers of the Way. When I healed your wrist, I used the power of my Goldstone to aid me."

"I noticed that the golden veins in your stone shone out brightly," Abigail said, "was that the… 'power of the Way'?"

She tasted the phrase delicately. Everything about this world was so very… different. She was fascinated by it, but also uneasy. It seemed they had no option but to make their home in this world. But how would she keep faith with God? Would she even be allowed to?

The Waymage nodded. "Every child born in Veylindré is given a baptismal Waymark by the Waymage of their town or village. These baptismal marks are for protection only – they confer no power. When they reach puberty, each young person undergoes a Time of Testing, to discover which Goddess is calling them. Then, at the Ceremony of Assignment, held at each of the six Festivals, their final Goddess affiliation is revealed, and their baptismal Waymark changes to that of their Goddess. They are then given their own Goldstone, through which they may access their powers."

"What are the Goldstones made of?" Abigail asked. "I've never any stone like it."

"They are made of *ranusfelsen*," Shaunan replied. "When the Ceremony of Assignment takes place, the presiding Waymage calls on the power of the Way to bring out its latent power to form veins of the appropriate colour. As you saw last night, the veins in my Goldstone are a deeper gold, which is Ranu's colour."

"We have nothing like this in our world," Jacob said, his brows furrowed. "We are taught that magic is evil, and that its power comes from the devil."

Shaunan frowned. "In Veylindré, we know nothing of this 'devil' you speak of. But," and her voice grew stern, "you would be wise not to speak of the Way as evil. It is the centre of our lives and works only for good."

"I'm sorry," Jacob said, bowing his head, "I only spoke as I've been taught. Forgive me."

After an awkward pause Shaunan said, "Tell me of your faith."

"I'm not sure where to start," Abigail said. "We worship one God, who is also three, Father, Son and Holy Spirit. We believe that our Lord Jesus, the Son, died more than sixteen hundred years ago to save us all from sin."

"Your god died?" Shaunan said, her eyebrows shooting up. "How can that be?"

"He came down to earth and took on human form, so that He could be crucified in order to pay the blood price for the sins of all mankind," Jacob said.

Shaunan gasped. "Your people put their own god to death? I find that hard to understand."

Jacob's face darkened. "It is what we believe," he said. "Do not doubt us."

"I meant no disrespect," the Waymage said. "It is just so different from our faith. Our goddesses have never been mortal."

As Jacob nodded at her, Abigail let out an audible sigh. He was going to have to learn to be less defensive.

"You will find it difficult to live in our world without Waymarks of your own," Shaunan continued, "because your unMarked foreheads reveal you as aliens, who do not belong here. We must travel to Luvodican to consult the First Waymage of Dagâran. It may be that she has the power to assign a Waymark to each of you, even though you are strangers."

Abigail glanced at Jacob uneasily. They knew nothing of this world, and now they were marooned here and could never go home. Events were moving too quickly. Was it only a few days ago that they belonged somewhere? Now they were strangers indeed, rootless and alone. In a world with a different religion, different customs and… magic. She shuddered. How were they going to cope with it all?

"Fear not," the Waymage said, as though she could read Abigail's thoughts. Perhaps she could – who knew what powers that Goldstone of hers gave her?

"We will eat now, then I will take you to speak to the Council of Nordvein, of which I am a member. We will start our journey on the morrow."

Shaunan led the young people across the square into the village hall, a large building right across from the temple. They climbed some stairs, through an antechamber, into the Room of Meeting. Its walls were panelled, as was customary, in the rich, dark wood of the Ranus tree. The other five members of the Council of Nordvein were waiting for them, seated in high-backed, carved chairs around an oval table, also made of Ranuswood.

Shaunan watched the strangers closely. The girl, Abigail, seemed to be openly curious, if a little afraid, but she could sense hostility radiating from Jacob. That one would bear careful watching.

The other five members of the Council were waiting for her to speak, their dark eyes fixed on her, their expressions stern. She would have to persuade them that this was beyond their jurisdiction.

"Members of the Council, these are Abigail and Jacob. They come from a distant land. Their companions were slaughtered by the Havimi, who seem to have allied themselves with the Talamdorians. Although Abigail and Jacob are strangers to Veylindré, and do not know the Way, I have spoken with them and believe they are not evil."

"With the Talamdorians?" Bodan said. "That is ill news."

"It is," Shaunan said. "Which is why I have brought them here."

"I trust your judgement, Waymage," Brann said. "But they cannot stay here. What is your will for them?"

"I wish to take them to the First Waymage in Luvodican," she answered. "Marinden is wise in the Way and will be able to discern what their arrival in Veylindré portends."

"It is late in the year to be travelling," Brann said. "You must not go alone. The Myner's Gap is treacherous in this season."

"May we speak of this in private?" Shaunan asked.

"Wait without," Bodan said to Abigail and Jacob. "We will discuss this matter, then call you in to hear our decision."

Abigail curtsied. "Thank you, sir," she said, "we are in your hands."

Shaunan waited until the door had closed behind them, then turned to the other five Council members.

"How do you know they are telling the truth?" Bodan asked.

"I have opened my mind to them and can discern that they have not lied."

"You know our law, Shaunan," Brann said, his dark eyes flashing. "These strangers are not from our world – that much is clear. We should imprison them, then send word to Lord Lesym and Lady Bélia in Luvodican."

The other members of the Council nodded.

Shaunan drew herself up. "I think this decision is beyond us, my friends," she said quietly. "I have spoken to them both and have healed the girl. I sense great power in her. As I have said, I believe it would be wiser to take her – to take them both – to Luvodican straight away, to consult First Waymage Marinden." And to tell her about the Bloodstone, she added in the silence of her own mind.

"But as Brann said," Bodan protested, "it is getting late in the year to be travelling so far."

"Nevertheless," Shaunan sighed, "we must chance it. I ask for two to go with us, and horses to ease our journeying."

"You ask much, Waymage Shaunan," Brann said.

"Trust me, Brann, I have a strong feeling about this. I believe the girl has an important part to play in Veylindré's future."

He looked into her amber eyes for a long moment, then nodded. "Members of the Council, I believe we must concede to the Waymage's request. Who shall we send to accompany her and the two strangers?"

Shaunan bowed her head in acknowledgement. "Thank you, Brann. May I suggest Aidren and Ellyn, who found them in the first place? It would be good practice for Aidren as a young Warrior of Dagâra and, when we reach Luvodican, he might be able to train at the Hall of Warriors for a time. And I do not wish to leave my niece behind."

"How long do you think you will be away, Shaunan?" Lyma asked. "You are our Waymage. How shall we manage without you?"

Shaunan smiled. "None of us is indispensable," she said. "I will ask Waymage Findoran of Myndorian to send you the Ranusian adept she has been training. The young man is skilled in healing and wise beyond his years. His name is Hedwin, and I will vouch for him."

Brann's smile transformed his stern face. "You seem to have thought of everything, Shaunan. Very well. Let us summon the strangers and tell them our decision."

He nodded to Bodan, who was nearest the door.

"Come within," Bodan said.

The young people stood in front of the table.

"You are not people of the Way," Brann said, his face stern, his lips compressed. "Our law states that you should be imprisoned."

Abigail's eyes widened as she took Jacob's hand. Shaunan sensed her sudden fear.

"But," he continued, "the Waymage has persuaded us that this decision is beyond us. We have agreed you will travel to Luvodican, and the Waymage with you. We will spare two of our people to guard you, five horses and provisions for the journey. When you reach Luvodican, it will be up to the First Waymage to decide your fate. It is out of our hands."

"Thank you, sir," Jacob said, bowing.

The next day, the inhabitants of Nordvein gathered in the square to see these strangers and the Waymage on their way. Their dark faces were closed, revealing nothing of their thoughts, but Abigail sensed they would be glad to see the back of them. She was heartened to see Aidren and Ellyn riding up, ready to travel – at least they were not complete strangers.

Once they were all mounted, Brann stepped forward.

"Farewell," he said. "Ellyn and Aidren have agreed to travel with you as far as Luvodican and will then return to us. The

Waymage will make her own decisions. May your journey prosper, and may the Way be your guide."

Their horses were small, but sturdy. Abigail had only been on horseback once or twice in her life and had never ridden astride. Fortunately, her dark bay mare seemed fairly docile, content to follow the others. On Shaunan's advice, she had exchanged her gown for the leather riding clothes worn by the Dagârans, with a warm, woollen cloak. It seemed indecent to be wearing breeches rather than skirts, and the breeches were like none she had ever seen before, fitting closely to the legs and going right down to the ankles. But they were snug and comfortable. She shrugged; she'd have to get used to it. Her own clothes were in her pack, now fastened to her horse's saddle. It was a relief not having to carry it herself.

Once the village was left behind, Shaunan explained what lay ahead.

"Our road lies through the Myner's Gap and on to Myndorian," she said. "As Brann said, this is not a good time to travel. We will have to hope the Gap remains open. If the weather worsens and the snow comes, our path may be fraught with danger. If the Way is with us, we should reach Myndorian in three days or, at most, four. Then, after resting for a day, we shall take the road to Luvodican, which will take at least another seisdag."

"Seisdag?" Abigail repeated, "what does that mean?"

Shaunan laughed. "I forget you are such strangers," she said. "Our year is divided into six seasons, one for each Goddess. Each season is sixty days long. So we divide each of them into ten seisdags. Today is Dagârsdag, the fourth day of the second seisdag of the Season of Completion."

"Ah," Abigail said, "now I understand. Thank you, Shaunan. So your world has…" she did a swift calculation, "…

three hundred and sixty days in the year? Ours has five more, and we have four seasons, Spring, Summer, Autumn and Winter. Each season has roughly thirteen weeks, like your seisdags, of seven days."

"That sounds complicated," Aidren said.

Abigail sensed his interest.

"It is, in comparison with yours," Jacob said. "Our year is also divided into twelve months, three for each season, but they are not all of equal length. Most have either thirty or thirty-one days, but one, February, has only twenty-eight."

"Why is it called the Season of Completion?" Abigail asked.

"Because," Shaunan said, "it is when all the crops have been harvested and the land starts to slow down in preparation for the Season of Dormancy. Our new year starts at the beginning of that season."

"That makes sense," Jacob said. "What are the other seasons called?"

"The Season of Awakening, the Season of Growth, the Season of First Fruits and the Season of Thanksgiving," Ellyn chimed in.

"If all goes well," Shaunan said, "we will arrive in Luvodican in good time for Dagârastide, the Festival of All Souls, which marks the end of the Season of Completion."

They rode on. The narrow, rocky path began to climb as the mountains of the Dagâran Range loomed over them, high, grey, and austere, with snow on their peaks. Abigail breathed in deeply; the air was crisp and invigorating. She was wondering how they were going to get over these formidable mountains when Aidren, in the lead, made a sharp right turn and entered a narrow defile marked by an ancient upright stone, carved with unfamiliar markings.

"The Myner's Gap," he said over his shoulder. "This is the only safe route through the mountains. We use it to transport our mined ore to Myndorian."

"I would never have guessed it was there," Abigail said. "It is well hidden."

"It is not generally known," Aidren said. "Until recently, we believed that only the people of Nordvein and the other mining settlements knew of it on our side and the traders of Myndorian on the other. But in the past few seasons, two ore caravans have been attacked by robbers, living wild in the mountains. Which is why I ride with you. For protection."

Abigail exchanged a dismayed glance with Jacob. How dangerous was this journey going to be?

The path of the Gap was wide enough for only one horse, which made further conversation impossible. Abigail sat her mare as best she could, relying on her to follow Aidren's.

By the time the sky darkened and Shaunan declared a halt, she was exhausted and stiff. Unused to riding, she needed help to dismount and could not suppress a cry of pain as she stumbled towards the Waymage.

The other three hobbled the horses, then scattered to collect wood for the fire, if any could be found at this altitude. The trees had become rarer as their path had meandered upwards.

"Here," the Waymage said, passing Abigail a small, glass bottle and a metal spoon. "Drink a spoonful of this. It will help."

Abigail downed the bitter drink in one gulp, then sat down, wincing. "I'm sorry," she said. "As I told you, I am not a rider."

"The potion will help," Shaunan said, "and your body will get used to it in a few days. Try to move with your horse, rather than resisting. Rest now. Once we have a fire, our meal will not take long."

Abigail shivered. A fire and food could not come soon enough for her.

After their meal, Abigail, Jacob, Ellyn and Shaunan wrapped themselves in their blankets and settled down to sleep, leaving Aidren to take first watch.

But tired as she was, Abigail could not drop off. Shaunan's draught had banished the worst of her aches and pains, but she was still not used to sleeping on the ground and could not get comfortable. And Aidren's talk of robbers had frightened her. What if they were attacked while they slept?

She stood up and tiptoed over to where Aidren was standing watch. She liked what she had seen of the young man, who seemed to be about the same age as she was, admiring his air of quiet competence.

"What are you doing here?" Aidren asked softly.

"I cannot sleep," Abigail whispered, "and I didn't want to disturb the others. May I stay and talk awhile?"

Aidren shrugged. "If you wish."

"Your world is so new to me," Abigail said. "Tell me about your life, how you came to be a warrior."

"In Veylindré," Aidren said, "our Waymarks dictate our lives. At the Ceremony of Assignment, my Waymark was revealed to be that of a Warrior of Dagâra. I have spent years honing my skills with the sword."

"What happens if someone is unhappy with the Waymark they've been given? I mean, what if you had really wanted to be… a weaver or a farmer?"

Aidren frowned. "My own mother is a weaver, my father a miner. So I suppose I might have been called to either of those. But I've never heard of people being dissatisfied with their

Waymark. Surely the Six know the hearts of their people and would not assign a Waymark that didn't suit them. Perhaps you had better ask the Waymage, who knows more of these things."

"Thank you. I will do that." She yawned.

"You need to sleep now, Abigail. We have a long day ahead of us."

Δ Chapter 5 ֍

A knock on the door.

"Open in the name of the Prophet."

Portak hastened down the hall. He had been anticipating this summons for seisdags. Opening the door, he saw one of the Prophet's own guards. One he hadn't encountered before.

"You are Portak, agent of His Holiness, the Prophet?"

"I am."

The guard reached out to test his Bloodmark, suffered his own to be tested, then said, "His Holiness requires you to read this," a letter was thrust into his hand, "and report to the Great Temple for further instructions."

Portak accepted it with a brusque nod, unwilling to show this youngster the mixture of joy and apprehension running through him.

"As the Prophet commands."

The guard saluted, turned on his heel and marched off.

Closing the door, Portak padded into his living room, dropped into a chair near the fire and broke the seal with trembling fingers, eager to learn what his master required of him.

> "Portak,
>
> A message arrived last night from *The Reaver,* one of the Havimi ships in our service. The news it brought is of great import, not only to us, but also to Holy Talamu.

> Three days ago, the crew of *The Reaver* raided a settlement on the north-east coast of Dagâran. To their astonishment, none of the two dozen or so settlers bore a Waymark.
>
> They killed them all, but left two of their own behind, as well as one of our agents.
>
> Assume your normal disguise and place a glamour over your Bloodmark. Report to the Great Temple to pick up what you will need and to hear what your mission will be. Then be ready to travel within the hour.
>
> Do not fail me."

He would not fail.

He had carried out this kind of covert work for the Prophet before. His widely despised red hair and pale blue eyes, inherited from his dead mother, who had Garûnalonden blood in her veins, with clothing to match, was the normal disguise his master alluded to. They came in useful when he needed to move around in the Commonweal without raising suspicions. It was almost worth the mockery he got at home, to be able to serve his master in this way.

Portak sped to the Great Temple, joy giving his feet wings. He had a mission once more and could not wait to get started. Yet even in his haste, he paused to admire its magnificence, cleansed and restored since Talamdor had won free from the Havimi oppressors, back in service for the worship of Holy Talamu after decades of heathen rites. His eyes followed the columns of black basalt that flanked the bronze doors up, up, to the twin spires, which towered high above him.

Once inside, he hurried up the central aisle to pay his respects to Holy Talamu at the high altar before he left Talamunem City. Her dark eyes bored into his soul.

He bowed his head in prayer. "Holy Talamu, give me the strength and good fortune to fulfil my mission as your Prophet requires. Be with me on my long journey. So may it be."

Then through a side door to the left of the high altar, into the corridor which led to the Prophet's private apartments, to pick up the aids he had been promised.

As he entered the Prophet's audience chamber, he felt the familiar sense of being in a presence that was not quite human.

His master was seated on his throne of black basalt, clad in his customary black, fiddling with the Bloodstone he always wore on a silver chain around his neck. He looked weary.

"Master, I am here."

"Portak. Yes, I sent for you."

The Prophet frowned, as if trying to remember why.

"Are you well, master? Should I fetch someone?"

As Portak watched, a cold, almost inhuman expression came down over his master's face, leaving only a semblance of life.

"You are insolent, Portak. I am perfectly well. Your mission is two-fold.

"First, to visit the cove the Havimi raided, to discover whether there were any survivors, and what sort of people they were, that they had no Waymarks. If there are any yet living, you must bring them here, to the Great Temple.

"Second, and equally important, to recover the Bloodstone from the body of our agent. It must not fall into the hands of the Veylindréan witches. Use your Bloodstone to keep me appraised of your success. Do you have sufficient supplies of blood?"

"Only one vial, my Lord."

"Then ask the High Priest for more. I will need to hear from you regularly."

"Yes, my Lord," Portak said, bowing. "Is there anything else?"

"Yes, these." He passed three bangles of control to Portak. "Use them to subdue any survivors to your will, before returning here with them. You are familiar with their operation?"

"Of course, my Lord. Thank you."

"Good. Then take a fast horse out of the stables and ride to Caethwasim with all speed. When you reach there, speak to Lavim, our factor at the harbour. He will have organised passage aboard an Havimi ship for you. Here is a purse of Veylindréan money and a token to show Lavim you are on my business. You will find him on the east side of the harbour complex."

"Yes, my Lord," Portak said, accepting the metal coin, carved with an intricate triangle on both faces with tiny, bevelled triangles around its edge. "I will not fail you."

He would have to say farewell to Balmak first. It was the only drawback to travelling in the Prophet's service. He would miss his dear friend so much.

Walking rapidly through the streets of the city, he found his way to Balmak's apartment and let himself in.

Balmak limped out of his study, his face alight with welcome. Portak hugged him, pressing his friend's long body against his own, trying to imprint the sensation on his memory. Who knew how long it would be before he would see him again?

"There is news in your face," Balmak said as Portak released him. "Is the Prophet sending you away again?"

"He is. To a cove on the coast of east Dagâran, to investigate the death of an agent."

"When do you have to leave?" Balmak's voice was steady and Portak appreciated his friend's kindness in making this leave-taking easy. Which it was not, for either of them.

"As soon as possible, I'm afraid. Oh, Balmak! I'm going to miss you so much."

"As I will you, my dear. But if the Prophet calls, you have to obey."

Portak's chest tightened. He loved his work for the Prophet, loved the trust his master had in him. And would never forget what he owed him. But he loved Balmak too. And if the Prophet ever found out about them, there would be trouble. His master had outlawed love between men nearly thirty years before, so he and Balmak had to be careful.

But he would not give him up. They had been through so much together.

"I must go now, my love."

"Look after yourself. I will be waiting for you."

Portak kissed him on the lips, hard and long, then tore himself away.

Half an hour later, Portak was on his way, riding south-east from Talamunem City towards Caethwasim. It was a journey of a hundred and forty miles. If he could change horses every night, he reckoned it would take five days.

He travelled light, two changes of clothing enabling him to pass as Garûnalonden; a map of north Dagâran; a water bottle; a small amount of food. He would rely on staging posts for food and rest.

He kept his Bloodstone and the bangles in an inside pocket of his jerkin, buttoned down for security. The Veylindréan coins and the token were in a linen money belt around his waist under his tunic and the precious vials of blood were in a padded leather pouch to keep them safe. He didn't want to have to open a vein to send a message. His stout felt cloak and leather gauntlets kept him warm.

By the end of the second day, he had reached Crullfeld, an old stamping ground. He wended his way through the crooked streets until he reached the mean alley in which his safe house stood. He knocked on the door; three loud knocks, followed by three soft ones. The old crone who looked after the place in his absence answered the door.

"My Lord Portak!"she said, curtseying low. "I am honoured by your visit."

"I will not be here long," he said. "Tell your grandson to stable my horse, then fetch me something hot to eat."

He strode up the narrow stairs and entered his usual room. It was spartan, holding only two narrow beds, a small table and a couple of chairs. No fire was laid in the grate. He wrenched the door back open and shouted down the stairs, "Bring some firing. It is freezing up here. And then supper."

The following morning, Portak crossed the River Roillon, flowing smooth, fast and pale green beneath the town's bridge, then took the southern highroad to Caethwasim. He had entered the most fertile region of Talamdor, where most of the food for the whole country was grown. He rode past already-harvested fields, and orchards with their trees heavily laden with fruit. The land had recovered well since the liberation. If this fine weather and good going continued, he would be there by the middle of the third day.

It would be a new experience to sail from Caethwasim. All his other journeys for the Prophet had been overland, via the secret pass. He knew the town was situated on the western side of the Caethwas delta. It had been the main port for slaver ships, crossing to and from Nailach in Havim, back when the tyrannical Havimi controlled Talamdor. Trueblood Talamdorians like himself had avoided the place for decades. Even now, the bay at the mouth of the Caethwas delta was known colloquially as 'The Bay of Slaves'.

Was it only thirty years ago? It felt like a lifetime. Thirty years since the Havimi held the whip hand over all followers of Holy Talamu. Now it was they who were eager to trade with the newly prosperous Talamdorians, a sea change of which he was proud, for it had been achieved by his master, the first and only prophet of Holy Talamu.

Even while a deep and hidden part of him questioned its wisdom.

Fortune favoured him and he reached Caethwasim shortly after noon on the third day since leaving Crullfeld, as he had hoped.

It was loud, raucous, and teeming with people, like all trading ports. At this time of year. the farmers and growers traded their surplus goods to the Havimi, and he passed overflowing carts and wagons aplenty. There would be more than one unwary farmer who returned home minus his purse; the local pickpockets did a thriving business in the poorer areas near the harbour. He checked again. Yes, the Bloodstone and bangles were still safe in his inside pocket.

He followed his nose to find the harbour – the stench of fish grew stronger as he approached. Overhead, the gulls wheeled and squabbled. Pushing through the throng, he made his way towards some buildings at the east side of the harbour.

The factor's office was in small, nondescript premises, set apart from the others. He knocked, and a gruff voice shouted, "What?"

"I am looking for Lavim."

"Who's asking?"

The man was of mixed race – part Talamdorian and part Havimi. He was swarthy like the Havimi, with a hooked nose and crooked teeth, yet he bore a Talamdorian Bloodmark. And he was big – not fat, but a wide, solid, well-muscled man, who looked more like a prize fighter than a factor. Not a man to be trifled with.

"I am Portak, trusted lieutenant of the Prophet."

"Show me your proof."

Portak fished the metal token out of his money belt and handed it over. "Here."

Lavim examined it closely, grunted, then returned it. "Come into my private office."

When he stood, he towered over Portak. He led him into a small, windowless office.

"I conduct the Prophet's business here," Lavim said. "There is a Havimi ship, the *Red Raider*, which leaves on the next tide. I have prevailed on the captain to take you, as a special favour."

"My thanks," Portak said. "Would you stable my horse while I am gone?"

Lavim laughed, showing flashes of gold. "No stables here. You will have to sell it."

This was a blow. Portak had hoped to return the same way he came.

"Very well. Tell me which jetty the *Red Raider* is berthed at."

"Come with me."

The sea journey to north-east Dagâran took two long, tedious seisdags. It was Portak's first voyage and, he hoped, his last. As soon as the ship was clear of the harbour, he started to feel queasy and threw up his lunch over the side. The following days passed in a blur of misery and nausea.

At long last, they reached his destination. He was weak and tired and felt ill-prepared to achieve his mission. But the Havimi had brought him here and now it was up to him to do the job. He would doubtless feel better on dry land.

As the *Red Raider* put down anchor a couple of hundred yards out, a small boat was lowered over the side. Portak climbed awkwardly down the rope ladder, his pack on his back. A sailor rowed him to shore and held the boat steady while he scrambled out. Then skilfully turned the boat round and rowed back to the waiting ship.

From now on, Portak was on his own. He looked around and saw what looked like bodies further up the beach. But there should have been more… he counted only three. Stumbling on the uneven sand, he hurried towards them.

Even from a distance, he could smell the stench of rot and putrefaction. A wave of nausea swept over him. Then he noticed a layer of grey ash cloaking the bodies. What was going on? That could wait… examine the bodies first. Two of the dead were Havimi sailors – that much was clear from their gaudy, red clothing, long, braided hair, and red leather boots. But the clothing of the third looked Talamdorian. This must be the agent the Prophet had spoken of. But apart from the clothing, he would not have recognised them – the carrion birds and insects had been busy stripping the corpses and after three seisdags they were a gruesome sight.

He steeled himself, pressing his lips firmly shut to stop his gorge rising. The Havimi were irrelevant, as was the agent himself; he was here for the Bloodstone. Gingerly he searched the man, shuddering at having to touch his bloodstained clothing, his ravaged flesh.

No Bloodstone.

His heart sank, his mind raced. What would his master say? And where were the rest of the bodies? According to what he had heard from the Prophet, there should have been many more. He would have to search the rest of the site. At least he had solid ground beneath his feet once more.

As he moved away from the beach, the reason for the ashes and for the lingering smell of burning became clear. There were two buildings, one of which was a blackened shell. It looked as though the Havimi had done a comprehensive job of stripping the other. But why had they only burned one? Or had it been torched by others? He jumped to a curious conclusion – was this ruined structure a funeral pyre? Two sticks bound together in the shape of a cross, one vertical, one horizontal, were thrust into the ground in front of it. What did that mean?

It meant there had been survivors. People who had perhaps been away from the settlement at the time of the attack and had returned to find their companions dead. But they must be long gone. What to do? He dared not return empty-handed. Somehow he would have to find them. Should he send a message back to the Prophet now or wait until he had found them?

Now. It was fortunate he was one of the few Talamdorians who could communicate with the Prophet using his Bloodstone. He fished the red buckskin pouch out of the inner pocket of his jerkin and took out the Bloodstone. Opening the padded leather pouch containing the vials of blood with his other hand, he extracted one, pulling out its stopper with his teeth. After dripping a few drops onto his Bloodstone, he re-stoppered it, before returning it to the pouch. Then, closing his eyes, he visualised the face of the Prophet's Chief Messenger, Tamin. Focusing all his attention on the Bloodstone, he sent the words, "Found cove. Only dead Havimi and Talamdorian agent remain. Regret, no Bloodstone. The rest burned. Will search for survivors. Portak."

Which way would the survivors have gone? He guessed they would have been looking for a stream of fresh water. He took the map out of his pack and scrutinised it. If he was where he thought he was, there were two streams marked, one to the north, the other to the south. He'd have to choose one, then follow it inland. He shrugged, shouldered his pack, and turned north.

How had the Havimi known which cove to raid? Had it been random luck, or something more?

֍ Chapter 6 ֍

As Shaunan expected, the next day dawned cold and bright. They were soon on their way towards the top of the pass with the morning sun behind them. The path was wider here with high rock walls encrusted with lichen on either side.

Abigail drew her horse in alongside her. "Waymage Shaunan, may I ask you something?"

"Of course, Abigail." Good. She was curious.

"I was talking with Aidren last night and he explained how he came to be a warrior. And I was wondering… what happens if a person isn't happy with the Waymark they have been assigned? He said he'd never heard of that."

"It is a rare event," Shaunan said. "Most Veylindréans find that the revelation of their Waymark feels right and matches the desires of their hearts.So they accept it and learn to use their powers for the good of the community. But the Wayzenmoot long ago recognised that, very occasionally, a revealed Waymark will be contested by its bearer."

"What is the Wayzenmoot?"

"The Wayzenmoot is the Council of the Way, and comprises twelve senior Waymages, two from each land. They dwell in Ranusheim, on the Isle of Ranu, and make all decisions concerning the enactment of the Way in Veylindré. If a young person is discontented with the Waymark revealed, they have the right to appeal to the Wayzenmoot at Ranusheim within a calendar year of the Ceremony of Assignment. The members of the Council are the only ones who have the power to change an assigned Waymark."

Aidren and Ellyn, riding just in front of them, were listening with interest. Abigail's fascination with all matters Veylindréan would be good for them.

"I never knew that," Ellyn said. "I thought once your Waymark had been assigned, that was it. I would never have dared to contest mine… and in any case, it felt right. I love working with leather."

"That is the usual pattern," Shaunan said, nodding. "But the Wayzenmoot knows it is better to offer the right of appeal, rather than allow someone to grow in resentment and deviate from the Way."

"And we have to go through this?" Jacob said from behind them, his voice wary. "I can't understand how it would work with us. After all, we're not from here."

Shaunan reined in her horse and turned to face him. "You do not *have* to undergo the testing, Jacob, but I strongly urge you to do so. Without a Waymark, you will find life in Veylindré challenging, as you will always be seen as an outsider, an alien."

"But would that mean accepting your goddesses as ours?" Abigail asked.

"Of course. You would be unable to access your Waymark's powers without following the Six."

"But we don't know anything about your faith," Abigail said, frowning. "We are strong in our own."

It was Shaunan's turn to frown. "I did not realise that," she said. "Perhaps we should put off your testing until you have done some studying and decided for yourselves to accept the Way of Veylindré."

Abigail relaxed. "Thank you. I do not rule out being baptised into your faith, but I need to learn so much before then."

"That is fair," Shaunan said. "We will talk more when we reach Luvodican." Whatever happened, Abigail must be persuaded.

Abigail dropped back to speak to Jacob. They dawdled until they were out of earshot. "What are we going to do? How can we deny our Lord Jesus?"

"We can't," Jacob retorted. "It's as simple as that. If they want us to join their… religion," he almost spat the word, "they're going to have to accept that. I cannot simply start worshipping female gods. It isn't right."

Abigail stared at him. "So it's worshipping goddesses that makes you uneasy?"

"Well, doesn't it stick in your craw?" he said, his voice rising.

She thought about that for a moment. "No. That's not what troubles me. In fact, I rather like the idea of worshipping the Divine as feminine. Apart from the Catholics calling Mary the Mother of God, the whole of Christianity is about worshipping God the Father, and God the Son. I'm not sure what gender the Holy Spirit is, but I'm sure most priests and ministers think he is male. And all the clergy are men too. Shaunan being a religious leader gives me hope." She smiled at the thought.

It was Jacob's turn to gape. "Are you serious?"

Her smile faded. "Yes, I am, as long as they allow me to continue worshipping Jesus, I don't mind thinking of God as female. In fact, seeing God as my divine Mother seems right to me."

"Then it's me against all of you."

Her heart was beating loudly in her ears. This couldn't be happening. "No, Jacob! I'm not against you, never that."

"You are if you deny God as Father."

"I'm sorry you see it that way. I still love you."

He scowled at her, dug his heels into his horse's sides and re-joined the others, leaving her desolate and confused. Why was he so angry?

By evening, the company had reached the top of the pass. It was freezing cold and a few desultory snowflakes were whirling through the air. Ellyn shivered.

"The snows come early this year," Shaunan said. "We will have to find somewhere to shelter. Ellyn, Aidren, see if you can find a small cave."

They searched for a while and Ellyn was beginning to doubt they would find one, when Aidren pointed to a dark shadow high on the mountain wall ahead of them. "Look."

She followed as he scrambled up the mountainside. He was right. It was a cave. She noticed a narrow path leading down to where they had left the others. So the horses would be able to make it, too. Thank goodness for that. "Well spotted! Let's tell the others."

The cave, a cheerless hole with rough walls that sloped down towards the rear and an earthen floor, was barely large enough for the five of them and their horses. But they entered it gratefully. It was a relief to be out of the wind and snow which had begun to fall more heavily. Shaunan sent Ellyn and the other three back out into the elements to collect some firewood. They were shivering when they returned – even their leather clothing and thick woollen cloaks did not keep out the bitter cold.

Shaunan brought out her Goldstone. "*Leumin*," she said. A warm yellow light radiated from the stone. Then she turned her attention to the firewood. "*Tanem.*"

As the firewood caught, Abigail jumped backwards, nearly bumping into Ellyn's horse. It was as if she hadn't seen magic before.

"How did you do that?" she asked, shocked.

"Through the power of the Way," Shaunan said.

Once they had removed the horses' tack, they gathered around the fire, the snow dripping off their cloaks and hissing as it hit the flames.

"I feared this," Shaunan said. "If this snowstorm sets in, we could be trapped here for days. How much food do we have, Ellyn?"

Ellyn could see the fear in the strangers' faces and had to suppress a snort of contempt. Did they expect their lives here to be easy? "Enough for four more days, five or six, if we are frugal."

"Then frugal we will have to be," Shaunan said. "I do not like the feeling of this storm. I have a hunch it may be serious."

Aidren looked sombre. He was taking his role as their protector seriously. Ellyn hid a fond smile. "Does your weather sense tell you how long it will last?" he asked.

"No," Shaunan said, "but I feel it will be a bad storm."

So their supper that evening was half the size of previous meals. The fire was dying down and there was nothing else to do but roll themselves up in their cloaks and try to sleep.

Some hours later, Ellyn awoke, feeling as though she could not breathe. She sat up in panic, opening her eyes to total darkness. Where was she? Then she remembered. They had taken shelter in a cave. But where was the cave mouth? Surely there should be some light coming in?

"Aidren, wake up!" she said, shaking him. "We're trapped in the cave."

The sound of her voice roused the others. It was clear what had happened… there must have been a snowfall, which blocked the mouth of the cave. It felt warmer, with no wind whistling round, but they knew they had to get out, and quickly, before more snow fell to trap them completely.

Shaunan conjured some light using her Goldstone.

Aidren moved towards the cave's entrance. He drew his sword and poked it through the snow, some of which plopped down on top of him. He jumped back with a startled cry.

An eddy of fresh, cold air and a thread of light entered the cave. Ellyn sighed quietly. She would not have shown it for the world, but she had been so afraid of being trapped in the darkness, of dying there.

Aidren withdrew his sword from the hole he had made. "It isn't that deep," he said. "But we will have to be careful how we clear it. We don't want the whole lot to fall in on top of us."

Shaunan nodded. "This is your knowing. How can we help?"

"The main problem is that we don't have anything to dig with," Aidren said. "I have my sword, and Ellyn and I have our Goldstones, which we can use to give us strength. But this snow is soft and difficult to control."

She and Aidren took out their Goldstones, closed their eyes, then said together, *"Gal ma bynn dreit."*

"What does that mean?" Abigail asked.

"They are asking for the strength they need to complete this task," Shaunan replied.

"That was harder than it should have been," Aidren said, grimacing. "We're getting too close to Dagârastide. My Goldstone will soon need recharging."

"Do what you can," Shaunan said. "I am sure Jacob and Abigail will help you."

It took the four of them most of the morning to clear a passage through the snow to the outside world. By which time, they were all freezing cold, wet and shivering.

"Now that we have some air, I will light a fire and cook us something hot," Shaunan said. "We need to be dry, and warm inside before we venture out into that."

"Has it stopped snowing?" Abigail asked.

"Yes, for now," Ellyn said. "Aunt Shaunan, do you think it is safe for us to carry on?"

"I believe so," Shaunan said. "Mayhap my foreboding was about being trapped. I think we need to press on for Myndorian with all speed. That sky has more snow in it. I feel it in my bones."

"How long will it take?" Jacob asked.

"If the lower reaches of the pass are not blocked on the Myndorian side, we should be there by late afternoon tomorrow."

Ellyn saw Jacob shrug. Why did he doubt her aunt's word?

Jacob's doubts were misplaced, but the final part of the journey was difficult. As the wind had blown the snow into deep drifts, they relied on the horses to plough their way through. No further snow fell, but the going was not easy. They kept their horses to a walk, always wary of plunging down the steep and slippery path from the Gap, which headed west into the setting sun.

Abigail asked, "Waymage Shaunan, would you tell us about Myndorian?"

Jacob saw the Waymage smile. "Shaunan will do. You need not call me 'Waymage' all the time. Myndorian is the main trading centre for the miners and smiths of Dagâran because most of the lodes of iron, silver and gold in Veylindré are in the north-east of this land. Raw ore from the mines is transported to Myndorian by mule trains from the mining villages, and the smiths smelt it and turn it into useful and beautiful objects. The traders of Yrusian travel right across Néartania to collect the finished goods to sell on. It is also the home of the Hall of Metalworking, where the smiths receive advanced training in the Way."

"So are all the people of Myndorian smiths and metalworkers?" Jacob said, suddenly interested. "I am a smith myself."

"By no means, although there is a larger concentration of them there, because of the Hall. But, like every community, there are people with all six Waymarks living in Myndorian. And if you are a smith, Jacob, perhaps you will end up with a Dagâran Waymark."

Jacob frowned. "Perhaps," he said.

It was nearly dark by the time they reached the outskirts of Myndorian. Jacob could see that it was a much bigger place than Nordvein – a proper town, with walls around it.

"Jacob, Abigail," Shaunan said, "put your hoods up to cover your foreheads. We do not want your unMarked state to deny us entry."

They rode up to the East Gate, a stout wooden door studded and banded with iron, set between high walls of a stone Jacob couldn't recognise in the dim light. Aidren knocked with the pommel of his dagger.

A small hatch opened in the gate. "Who goes there?"

"Waymage Shaunan of Nordvein, with four companions. May the Way guide you."

"Welcome, Waymage Shaunan," the gatekeeper said. He was dressed in leather breeches, a dark orange tunic bearing a blazon of crossed hammers, a mail shirt beneath, a sword at his side."I am Oltan, guard of the East Gate. You are known in Myndorian and are welcome among us. Who are your companions?"

"Thank you, Oltan," Shaunan said, dismounting, and gesturing to the others to do the same. "My companions are Aidren and Ellyn from Nordvein, and two strangers, Abigail and Jacob. We are on our way to Luvodican and require shelter for the night before we continue on our journey."

"I must test your Waymarks."

Jacob's eyes widened. What was going to happen now? Now he understood why Shaunan had insisted that he and Abigail put their hoods up. Were they going to be thrown back out?

Shaunan sighed. "You may test the Waymarks of myself, Aidren and Ellyn. But as I said, Abigail and Jacob are strangers from a distant land and do not have Waymarks."

Oltan's sword was in his hand in a flash. "No Waymarks? Then we cannot admit them."

"Oltan," Shaunan said, drawing herself up to her full height and fixing her amber eyes on him, "please send someone for Waymage Findoran, that I might explain matters to her."

Jacob looked at the Waymage in astonishment. Her usually soft voice had taken on the cadences of command. He was not surprised when the guard bowed his head and retreated to the guard house. A couple of minutes later, a younger guard scurried out and set off at a run into the town.

"Please wait here, Waymage Shaunan," Oltan said. "I have sent for Waymage Findoran. Now, if I might test your Waymarks?"

As Jacob watched, Oltan touching the middle fingertip of his right hand to each of the three Veylindréans' Waymarks, and had his own Waymark touched in return. Jacob had no idea what that proved.

"May we take shelter out of the cold?" Shaunan asked, although it sounded more like a command than a question to Jacob's ears.

Oltan gestured toward the guard house, bowing his head. "Of course, Waymage. Please join us within. Your horses can stay in the stables."

The guard house was a small, stone building, and dark inside, except for a couple of oil lamps and a blazing fire in the hearth. Anxious to get warm, Abigail made a beeline for it. Before Jacob could stop her, she threw back the hood of her cloak.

He heard a harsh intake of breath.

Oltan's hand leapt to his sword hilt, and the other two guards jumped up and drew their own weapons.

"Peace," Shaunan said, raising her hand. "I would not bring danger to Myndorian. Although these strangers do not bear Waymarks, they are not evil folk. I will vouch for them."

Slowly, too slowly for Jacob's liking, the guards returned their swords to their sheaths.

He sighed with relief. He was beginning to understand what a hindrance not bearing a Waymark in this world could be. And, looking back to when they had first met, he wondered at Aidren's trust of them. The way these guards had reacted, it was a marvel Aidren had not slain them out of hand.

"May I offer you a drink?" Oltan said. "The wait may be long, if Waymage Findoran is busy."

Shaunan bowed her head. "Thank you, Oltan. That would be welcome."

Soon they were sipping hot, spiced wine from pewter goblets. Jacob could feel it warming him inside. But the unease remained… how long would they have to wait here? As he moved closer to Abigail, she smiled up at him.

He reckoned about thirty minutes had passed when the young guard burst in. "Waymage Findoran is on her way."

A couple of minutes later, Waymage Findoran entered the guard house. "Waymage Shaunan! It is good to see you, my old friend. When was the last time we were together?"

"Waymage Findoran," Shaunan responded formally. "I bring visitors to Myndorian and ask for the hospitality of the Temple for the night. These are Abigail and Jacob. They are strangers to Veylindré."

"So I see," Findoran said drily. *It seems as though you have a tale to tell, my friend.*

"I will vouch for them," Shaunan said. *I do indeed.*

"That is well. We want no renegades in Myndorian. Come with me, all of you."

She swept out of the guard house, leaving them to follow. Aidren offered her a ride behind him, which was graciously accepted.

They rode through the dark, narrow streets towards the Temple, the horses' hooves echoing on the cobbles. Fortunately, there were few people about at this time of night, for which Shaunan was grateful.

Even with the hoods of Abigail's and Jacob's cloaks safely back up, their unWaymarked state, not to mention Abigail's blonde hair, blue eyes and pale skin in their dark-haired, dark-eyed, dark-skinned country, made them conspicuous.

The Temple of Myndorian was much larger than Shaunan's own in Nordvein, and behind a gate. A Temple servant came towards the gate bearing a torch, whose flame guttered in the cold wind.

"Who wishes to enter the Temple of Myndorian?"

"I, Waymage Findoran, with five guests."

Good. Findoran was smoothing their path.

"Brunan, these horses need stabling," Findoran said. "Waymage Shaunan and her companions will be housed in the Visitors' Hall."

The little man bowed his head. "Yes, Waymage."

The travellers removed their packs from their horses' saddlebows and followed the Waymage through a courtyard to a large, shadowy building.

"The Visitors' Hall," Findoran said. "Be welcome in the Temple. We will speak tomorrow."

"My thanks, Waymage Findoran," Shaunan said. *Be gentle with them, Findoran. They are new to our world.*

Which is why they need to be questioned.

Shaunan shrugged. Her friend was right, of course. She hoped Jacob would be able to control his anger.

Another Temple servant was waiting within to show them to their rooms. Shaunan noticed that Abigail and Jacob were careful to keep their hoods up until the servant had left. The sooner they were Waymarked, the better.

Abigail and Ellyn were given one room, Aidren and Jacob another, and Shaunan, as Waymage, was given a room to herself.

"Aidren, Ellyn, look after Jacob and Abigail," Shaunan said, "and call me at need."

She walked into her own room and shut the door.. It was small and plainly furnished, like all Temple accommodation, but a bright fire burned in the hearth, making it blessedly warm. There was a low table over to one side with two chairs drawn up to it and a tray with bread, cold meats, cheese and a flask of wine. Food would be welcome indeed.

As for tomorrow… it would come soon enough. At least she had got them this far.

Feeling refreshed after a sound sleep in a decent bed, Abigail washed and dressed. She turned to Ellyn. "I'm looking forward to breakfast, aren't you?"

"Yes, but I need to do my Immersion practice first."

"What is that?"

"It's part of having a Waymark," Ellyn explained. "Every morning, we're supposed to sit in silence with our Goldstones and commune with the Way. I haven't done it for a few days, while we've been on the road. You're welcome to stay, if you wish, but please be quiet."

Abigail watched in fascination as the other girl lowered herself into a cross-legged position on the rug beside her bed, took out her brown-veined Goldstone from its pouch around her neck, closed her eyes and started to breathe deeply and evenly.

Abigail held herself quiet, knelt down, closed her eyes, clasped her hands together and began to pray in silence. First she said the Lord's Prayer, then repeated the prayer her father had taught them to begin each day. She had missed this – she hadn't realised how much. It soothed her soul to be back in communion with the Lord.

Devotions done, they joined the others and enjoyed a welcome breakfast of fresh bread, soft cheese and cold meat, washed down with a smoky herbal tea, before awaiting Waymage Findoran.

“I will introduce you and tell your story,” Shaunan told Abigail and Jacob. “Then the Waymage will question you. Whatever you do, tell the truth. She will detect falsehood.”

“Yes, Shaunan, we will,” Abigail said.

Jacob said, “I’ve got nothing to hide. She doesn’t frighten me.”

“Jacob!” Abigail whispered. “We need to walk softly here.”

He shrugged. “If you say so.”

Shaunan made no comment, but Abigail saw her lips tighten.

When Waymage Findoran entered the Visitors’ Hall, Abigail got her first good look at her. The light in the guard house had been poor and then they had travelled to the Temple in darkness.

The woman was as tall as Jacob and was statuesque and beautiful. Her long, dark red hair was braided intricately, then woven around her shapely head. Her skin, in contrast, was as pale as fine linen, which made her dark blue eyes stand out. She wore a floor-length gold-coloured robe, banded at the waist with an intricate golden belt, and wore a silver brooch with a faceted yellow topaz at it centre on her left shoulder. She exuded the air of effortless authority that being a Waymage seemed to confer.

“Come with me,” she said. “We will speak in the privacy of my chambers.”

“Thank you, Waymage Findoran,” Shaunan said. “That is gracious.”

“I have known you long, Waymage Shaunan. I trust that you would not bring evil to Myndorian.”

֍ Chapter 7 ֍

The Myndorian Waymage's chamber was a large, circular room, with rich tapestries depicting scenes from what Abigail supposed was Dagâran history on the walls and low, cushioned seating around an oval table. A fire blazed in the stone hearth.

Findoran gestured to the seats.

"Tell me, Shaunan, what has transpired to cause you to attempt the Myner's Gap at this time of year?"

Once more, Shaunan told the story of how Abigail, Jacob and their community had been attacked by Havimi pirates, that now the pair of them were alone and friendless in Veylindré.

"I have spoken long with them and hear no falsehood in their words," she concluded. "It is my thought that they should be taken to First Waymage Marinden in Luvodican to determine their future."

As Abigail watched Findoran's face, she prayed she would understand, be on their side.

"Thank you, Shaunan, that explains much," Findoran said. "Now," turning to Abigail and Jacob, "I will ask you some questions."

Abigail's stomach tightened. She was afraid of this stately woman who wore her authority like a cloak. When she looked up and met Findoran's deep blue eyes, they pierced her with their clarity. She also feared what Jacob might say, if the questioning went ill. She nodded, her hands moving automatically to smooth down the skirts she was no longer wearing.

"You say you are fugitives, quite alone in Veylindré?"

"Yes," Jacob said. "We have nowhere else to go."

“We know we are ignorant about your world,” Abigail added. “Shaunan has shared much with us since our arrival in Nordvein, but we are still finding things to perplex us each day.”

“You wish to learn about our world?” said Findoran. “Why?”

“Because we are here and have no home to return to, even if we wished, so it makes sense to learn all we can.” Abigail said with what she hoped was dignity.

“That is a wise response,” the Waymage said with a smile which transformed her stern face.

She turned to Jacob. “Do you also wish to learn about Veylindré?”

He shrugged. “I don’t see that we have a choice if we are to survive. But your religion is very strange to me. We believe in only one God.”

Findoran’s breath came out in a hiss. “I… see. Then you are followers of the Prophet of the One?”

“People keep asking us that, “Jacob said angrily. “We’ve never heard of him. Our God is from our world.”

“Gently, Jacob,” Shaunan said. “There is no need for anger.”

Findoran nodded at her, before continuing her examination. “I hear no falsehood in your words, but much resistance. Are you open to learning otherwise, as your companion here seems to be?”

Jacob looked at the Myndorian Waymage for a long moment before replying. “Yes.”

The Waymage frowned but said nothing. Abigail feared Findoran had sensed the untruth in Jacob’s affirmation. As the pause stretched, Jacob’s cheeks flushed red.

"Very well," Findoran said. "We will make arrangements for your onward journey to Luvodican. May the Way guide you."

"Thank you," Abigail said.

"Put your cloaks back on and your hoods up, before you leave," Findoran said.

Even here in the Temple, they had to hide their true identity.

Shaunan led the way back to the Visitors' Hall.

Abigail was worried by her silence. "Shaunan, is all well?"

"I hope so, Abigail," Shaunan sighed, "but I am afraid Waymage Findoran caught the lie in Jacob's words."

"I said what she wanted to hear," Jacob said.

"Yes," Shaunan said, "but you did not mean it, and she knew that."

"So what happens now?" he asked.

"I think we will be allowed to leave Myndorian and travel to Luvodican. But Jacob, I implore you, try to open your heart to the Way. If you do not, I fear for you."

"I cannot lie about how I feel."

"And I am not asking you to do so. Merely to open your heart to the alternative."

"Please, Jacob," Abigail said, tears in her eyes. "I need you with me."

He stroked her cheek with his callused thumb. "For you, Abi, I will try."

Shaunan led them back to their rooms. Once there, the question burst out of Abigail, "Shaunan, why does Waymage Findoran look so different to the rest of you? She is so pale, and you are all so dark."

Shaunan laughed. "She is Garûnalonden by birth – that is in the north of Veylindré. She comes from a small village near

Ullmass, which is where the annual Wool Fair is held – the Garûnalonden are famous for their fine wool. When her Waymark was revealed as Ranusian, she did her initial training at their capital city, Mirunan. We were called to be Waymages at the same time and are old friends. We met at the Fort of Ranu, the only entrance to the Isle of Ranu. I'm not sure which of us was more apprehensive." She laughed again.

"Once we had completed our training at Ranusheim," she continued, "we were sent to the Hall of Healing in the Vale of Berlysian, which is in Lènium, to learn healing. While we were there, she met a Dagâran warrior from Luvodican, Petan, who was recovering from a bad wound. They fell in love and wished to marry, so she asked to be assigned somewhere in Dagâran. She was sent to Myndorian, and I returned to Nordvein."

"Waymages are permitted to marry?" Jacob said. "I thought you all had to be celibate or something, like Catholic priests."

Such a strange question. "I know nothing of these Catholic priests you mention," Shaunan said, "but of course Waymages are allowed to marry. Otherwise, we would be cutting ourselves off from an important part of life."

"Are you married?" Abigail asked.

A surge of remembered grief. "I was, once," she said, "to a fine man called Donan, a Masterminer in Nordvein. He was killed a few years ago in a mining accident which also claimed my brother. My sister-in-law died in childbirth shortly after. Ranu did not see fit to give me any children, so I am alone in the world now, apart from Ellyn, my brother's daughter. My work is my life."

"Oh, I'm so sorry," Abigail said. "I didn't know."

"How could you? It is an old grief, long accepted."

There was silence for a little while, then Abigail asked, "How do Veylindréans marry?"

"It is a simple ceremony. When a couple fall in love, they are required to wait for a few seasons so the elders of their community can ensure there are no hidden sadnesses or conflicts in the relationship. Then, at the next festival, they and any other couples who have completed the Season of Proving are hand-fasted by the First Waymage of their land, vowing to share life in the Way, and are accepted as a new couple by their community. There is a marriage feast, at which new songs are sung, and new dances learned.

"The new couples then have the choice, to live with the woman's community, or with the man's. Often, these are the same, but sometimes one of them is required to move away. Which is why the Season of Proving is so important. It is vital that the young people know each other well so they may support each other throughout their lives."

"That sounds lovely," Abigail said. "I wish…"

"What do you wish?" Shaunan asked.

"I wish Jacob and I could get married here," she said. "It would make us feel that we belonged somewhere."

"That will have to wait until you have your Waymarks," Shaunan said. "Now, I must speak with Waymage Findoran once more, to ask her to send her adept, Hedwin, to look after the people of Nordvein while I am away."

And tell her about that Talamdorian agent. And the Bloodstone he carried.

The following morning, they rode through the town towards the South Gate. In daylight, Jacob noticed that the tall houses had shaped and patterned gables. "Do the shapes of the roofs have any significance, Shaunan?"

Shaunan glanced upwards. "In Myndorian, it has long been fashionable to indicate the family's trade or Goddess affiliation by the shape of the roof. If you look carefully, you will see the crossed hammer shape, which is the symbol of Myndorian, atop many houses. It is also the sigil of the Hall of Metalworking. Others, like that one," she pointed to a gable shaped like an inverted W, "show that the owners are craftspeople with an affiliation to Néarta."

"But what happens if the house changes hands?" he said. "It must be expensive to change the roofline every time."

"You're right, Jacob," she said, her eyes twinkling. "It would be. But the houses in the centre of the town tend to belong to established families, passed down the generations. As we move towards the outskirts, the houses become smaller, less ornate."

"So if your family are smiths, your Waymark will be a smith's?" Abigail said.

"Not necessarily, but often. It is unusual for none of the children in a family to follow their parents in their Goddess affiliation."

"It's so complicated," Abigail said. "I'm never going to understand it."

"Give yourself time," Shaunan said. "You have only been in our world for a few seisdags, after all."

They rode on towards Luvodican. This side of the Dagâran Range, the countryside was gentler. They rode past brown fields with dry stone walls, dotted with tidy farm buildings, basking in the late autumn – no, Season of Completion – sunshine. This side of the mountains was more like the Hampshire Jacob and Abigail had left behind. As Jacob started to relax, he saw Abigail doing the same. He noticed that her seat on her horse was becoming more secure, as she was learning to move with the animal.

They made good progress on the first day, stopping at a small village to spend the night in the tavern. Once more, Shaunan bade Jacob and Abigail to put their hoods up before they went in. Would there ever be a time when they were not outsiders?

A man in an apron came bustling up to them. He had a Waymark Jacob had not seen before on his forehead, shaped like a pointed P with a diagonal line through it against a blue background.

"Good evening, Waymage. Barlan's my name. What can I do for you?"

"Good evening, Barlan," Shaunan replied. "We need three rooms and stabling for five horses. Then supper, please."

"That will be three guilders for the rooms, plus five florins for the stabling. There's a fine mutton stew on the hob with fresh-baked bread and home-brewed ale to go with it," Barlan said. "Will that content you?"

"That would be excellent, thank you. We will eat in our rooms."

Raising his eyebrows, he said, "I'll get Norin to stable your horses, then show you to your rooms. You'll want to wash before supper, I expect."

"That is kind, thank you."

The rooms were small, clean and neat. As the taproom was directly below them, they could hear many voices coming up through the floorboards. It sounded like the Black Bull back home. Jacob was missing home so much.

"I think we will stay in here and not join the company," Shaunan said. "It would look odd if you kept your hoods up in the warmth of the taproom and we need to avoid awkward questions."

"Aidren and I could go down," Ellyn said. "It might be useful to catch up on any local gossip."

Shaunan nodded. "After we have eaten."

Their meal was served by a young girl, who flicked nervous glances at Abigail and Jacob, still cloaked and hooded. Jacob worried she would report this to Barlan.

When she left the room, they removed their cloaks with relief. "I was getting so warm in here," Abigail said.

Ellyn smiled at her. "Once you have a Waymark of your own, you will belong here."

Abigail smiled back a little sadly, which roused all Jacob's protective instincts. "Once we have Waymarks, we will no longer be so conspicuous," she said. "But I fear it will be a long time before we belong."

"That will be up to you," Shaunan said. "If you embrace the Way and learn to follow our customs and our faith, you will come to truly belong."

That sounded like a warning. Jacob frowned, not at all sure that he wanted to embrace this strange Veylindréan faith. He could not understand why Abigail was so open to it.

Abigail sat with Jacob and Shaunan by the fire in the Waymage's room, watching the dancing flames, while Ellyn and Aidren went to join the company in the taproom below.

Abigail was sleepy, the flames were mesmerising. But she wanted to learn more about the Way. "Could you tell us more about the Time of Testing?"

"It usually takes place after a Veylindréan's twelfth birthday," Shaunan said. "They learn about the different Waymarks, about the powers they confer, and begin to discern a calling toward one of them. Then, a seisdag before the next festival – we have six during the year – they are tested by the Waymage or Master who has been mentoring them, and two others, which will reveal their Waymark. This is confirmed at the festival, when the Waymark is assigned by the senior Waymage present."

"But how will that work for us?" Jacob said. "We are long past our twelfth birthdays and know so little of your world."

"For you, the time of learning will be more intense because you will have to also learn about Veylindréan customs and traditions."

"What does the testing involve?" Abigail asked.

"The candidates are questioned about their knowledge of the Way and their skills in particular areas are tested. How they respond to the questions and tests gives the Waymages and mentors who oversee the process a good indication of which Waymark will be appropriate."

"When do you think we will be able to do this?" Abigail said, "because every day I'm seeing the disadvantages of not having a Waymark."

"We will have to arrange for it to take place in Luvodican," Shaunan said. "I will speak to First Waymage Marinden about it when we arrive. We may be too late for your Waymarks to be assigned at Dagârastide because I am unsure how long it will take you to truly understand our ways."

"How long is it until Dagârastide?"

"Another seven and a half seisdags. We will be at least another five days on the road, and I do not think six seisdags will be long enough for you to learn what you need to know to be tested."

"I suppose not," Abigail said, crestfallen. "When will the next festival be?"

"Another ten seisdags after Dagârastide, so sixty more days."

"Sixty days?" Abigail said. "That seems a very long time."

"Fear not," Shaunan said. "You will find the time passes quickly. You both have so much to learn."

"So," Jacob said, "does that mean we will have to sit in classrooms with children?"

Abigail winced. His distaste for the idea was obvious.

"No," Shaunan said quietly. "I will undertake your training myself. It would not be appropriate for you to share the learning with young Veylindréans."

"Not appropriate? What do you mean?" he said, his voice rising in anger.

"Gently, Jacob," the Waymage sighed. "It is because your questions and learning needs will be quite different to theirs. I am seeking to protect you from ridicule, not to belittle you."

"I'm sorry," he said, flushing. "I'm finding this all very difficult."

"I know, my friend, but anger will not help you on the Way."

He frowned and pursed his lips.

"Thank you for offering to teach us, Shaunan," Abigail said, rushing in to fill the silence. "That would be wonderful. Could you give us a moment alone, please?"

"Of course." The Waymage moved over to the far side of the room.

"I'm so worried," Abigail whispered. "We're here for good now, so we need to learn all we can about Veylindré and the Way. But you seem so angry. Help me to understand." She reached out and touched his arm.

He shook her off. "And why shouldn't I be? This is not our choice. We are being forced to do this."

"Do you really think that?" she said, surprised by his vehemence. "Shaunan's trying to help us. Would you rather spend the rest of your life as an outcast?"

"Of course not!" he snapped. "But I don't understand why you are so willing to go along with all this."

"I'm going along with it, as you call it, because when there is no alternative, it makes sense to go with the flow, not fight it. If we are to become Veylindréan, we need to be open to the Way."

He shrugged, frowned, then reached for her.

Gratefully, she walked into his arms. "I do love you, Jacob. We can do this, together."

"Help me, Abi. I feel so… angry, so alone."

"You're not alone. I'm here with you. Somehow, we'll make this work."

"So long as you're with me."

Aidren and Ellyn came back upstairs.

"There is much talk about Abigail and Jacob downstairs," Aidren said. "People are wondering who the mysterious strangers are and why they are not mingling."

"Yes," Ellyn added, "and why they want to keep their faces hidden."

Shaunan sighed. "I expected this. We will move on in the morning and find quieter places to stay. I hope we will be permitted to leave in peace."

Chapter 8

Despite Shaunan's hopes for a quiet departure, many of the villagers were lining the muddy track leading south to catch a glimpse of these mysterious strangers. Word had spread fast. She led the way with the quiet dignity Abigail admired and those she made eye contact with looked away.

Although Abigail had made sure her forehead was hidden, her face was burning. She wondered miserably whether, to avoid hostilities, she and Jacob would have to be kept in seclusion in Luvodican. Only when they were well clear of the village did she let her hood fall back.

"It's so awful being treated like some kind of pariah," she said. "Is this going to happen everywhere we stop?"

"I am afraid it may," Shaunan said. "We cannot risk showing your unMarked state, so it is only natural that people make up stories about why your heads are covered. It does look secretive, after all."

"I suppose so," Abigail sighed. "And you say we may have to wait until Lèniastide to get our Waymarks. So this... hounding is going to continue for a long time yet."

"Do not worry," Shaunan said. "Once we are in Luvodican, we can keep you and Jacob out of harm's way. We will find some lodgings where you can be hidden from the sight of strangers."

"Thank you for all you are doing for us. We would be lost without you."

The Waymage's face softened. "I could do no less," she said. "If I were in your world and being singled out because of my Waymark, I would expect no less of you."

Abigail hadn't thought of that. "Oh! I see what you mean. Yes, in our world, your Waymark would make you as unusual to our people as we are to yours. That helps, thank you." But you'd be lucky to find someone as accepting of strangers in our world. We are not as open to anyone different.

"But where are we going to stay for the other four nights?" Aidren said, concern furrowing his brow. "It's getting too cold to sleep out."

Shaunan thought for a moment, then said, "We will tell people that Abigail and Jacob have a rare disease and we are taking them to Luvodican for treatment. Then we will ask for shelter in a farmer's barn and you and Ellyn will be the only people who go near the farmer and his family. Yes… that should work."

"But won't they be afraid they'll catch it from us?" Ellyn asked.

"You must tell them you are immune," Shaunan said. "That is the best I can come up with. The sooner we reach Luvodican, the better."

"Amen," Jacob muttered.

"What was that, Jacob?"

"I said, 'Amen'," he said, "which means I agree with you wholeheartedly. This skulking around like a footpad is getting tiresome."

"We'll be there soon," Abigail said, "and I'm feeling… excited!"

"Excited?" he said. "Well, I'm glad one of us is. I feel more apprehension than excitement."

"I will not allow any harm to come to you," Shaunan said.

In the afternoon, a fine rain started to fall and soon grew heavy. Before long, the company were soaked through – not even their woollen cloaks could keep the rain out. The countryside they were riding through was sparsely populated with only a few farmsteads, the only sound the splash of their horses' hooves as they walked through the many puddles. They scarcely saw a living soul, apart from the odd flock of sheep, huddled together against the rain. Abigail guessed that most of the inhabitants were sensibly indoors, out of the weather. When a farmhouse loomed up in the grey gloom, they were all relieved. It would be good to have a chance to get dry and warm again.

"Remain here," Shaunan said. "I will go and speak to the farmer."

A few minutes later, she returned. "He is not happy," she said, "but he will allow us to stay for the night in a disused barn, over there." She pointed to a low stone building across the yard. "He will not let the rest of you anywhere near the farmhouse, but he knows that no Waymage would lie. I will fetch us some food."

By the time Shaunan returned, carrying a large, lidded pan and five bowls and spoons, Abigail and the others had managed to clear a space for them to eat and to pile up some straw for beds, which they covered with their blankets. The pan contained a warming broth, which took the edge off their hunger but not much more.

"At least we have eaten and are out of the rain," Ellyn said.

Jacob scowled. "I'm glad one of us is happy."

Why did he have to be so grumpy? "Jacob! It's not Ellyn's fault." Abigail said.

"I never said it was," he snapped.

"Enough, Jacob," Shaunan said. "Arguing amongst ourselves will not help."

He hunched his shoulders.

Once Shaunan had returned the pan and bowls, there was little else to do but sleep, which was difficult enough on the prickly straw.

The next four days followed the same pattern: cold, wet riding through a grey-brown landscape, under a grey-black sky, with churned up mud underfoot which made their horses slip and slide, followed by a reluctant welcome and uncomfortable, intermittent sleep. Not how Aidren had imagined setting off on a quest would be.

He was getting heartily sick of scant rations and could not wait to reach Luvodican. If only he had been coming here to train at the Hall of Warriors instead of escorting these two young strangers. Abigail seemed nice enough, but Jacob's thinly disguised hostility was setting his teeth on edge. If it hadn't been for the Waymage's presence, he would have had something to say about it by now. Shaunan was taking a route which kept them away from villages. Which made sense, given the unMarked state of the strangers, but it also made the journey take longer. Which was getting tedious.

"Is it going to take much longer?" Abigail asked Shaunan, her teeth chattering with cold.

"We ought to reach Luvodican by nightfall."

"Well, thank God for that," Jacob said.

Aidren frowned, but as the Waymage seemed content to let it pass, it was not his place to comment.

It was dark by the time they reached the North Gate of Luvodican. The city was as big and grand as he had dreamed – the gate was set in high walls of granite, and he could see the roofs of some tall buildings behind them.

Once again, after the Waymage told Abigail and Jacob to cover their heads, they gained admittance.

"I am Waymage Shaunan, from Nordvein. The five of us have travelled here to consult First Waymage Marinden. Please send for her while we wait within."

"I must test your Waymarks first," the guard said. "These are uncertain times."

Aidren listened as Shaunan explained that Abigail and Jacob were strangers to Veylindré and had no Waymarks.

"I'm sorry," the guard said. "You will have to wait outside. I cannot risk allowing unMarked strangers into the guard house."

"In Nordvein you would not be treated so harshly," Aidren said. How dared they challenge his Waymage? But Shaunan shook her head at him, and he closed his mouth.

"Their mistrust is misplaced," she said, "but we must bear it as best we can." Then, to the guard, "May we at least shelter in your stables?"

The guard thought for a long moment before nodding. "Yes. I will inform you when the First Waymage has arrived."

And with that they had to be content. The stables were cramped and draughty, with little light. At least he was with Ellyn. Aidren would put up with any amount of deprivation to be in her company. The First Waymage arrived forty minutes later, by which time they were cold and weary indeed.

"Waymage Shaunan, it has been a long time since we have seen you in Luvodican," First Waymage Marinden said. "What brings you here, so soon after Néartastide?"

Shaunan inclined her head. "First Waymage Marinden, I am here with Aidren and Ellyn of Nordvein, and two strangers to Veylindré, Abigail and Jacob. Their ship landed on the coast to the north-east of us, and their community was murdered by Havimi pirates. They are alone in our world. They do not know the Way but are willing to learn. It is my hope that we can stay here awhile, so that I can teach them what they need to know."

"Very well, Waymage Shaunan," Marinden said. "They may stay in the Visitors' Hall of the Temple for the present."

"Thank you, First Waymage Marinden," Shaunan said. "We are grateful for the hospitality of the Temple."

At least they hadn't been turned away.

When she had settled the young people in at the Visitors' Hall, Shaunan went to find Marinden. As she expected, the First Waymage was awaiting her in her chambers, a spacious suite of rooms next to the Temple, richly decorated with tapestries depicting Dagâran life.

Marinden rose as she entered, her hand outstretched in welcome. "Come within, sit, eat."

Marinden was in late middle age, with dark skin and deep brown eyes. Silver threads had begun to invade her dark hair. She looked tired, as though the responsibilities of being First Waymage of all Dagâran lay heavy on her shoulders. But she wore the golden topaz brooch of her calling proudly on her left shoulder.

Shaunan removed her cloak and set it to dry by the fire, then gratefully sat. "Thank you for taking us in, Marinden," she said, taking up a goblet of wine. "I am glad to have arrived here safely."

"You were right to bring them here, Shaunan," the older woman said. "I wonder what their coming portends. Please, eat. You must be hungry."

Before answering Marinden's question, Shaunan ate for a while in silence. "That concerns me, also," she said. "According to their story, they sailed here through some kind of portal in the Eastern Sea at the height of a storm with their families and friends. Then, while the two of them were away looking for a source of fresh water, Havimi pirates raided their settlement, leaving all dead. Marinden, there was a Talamdorian agent with the Havimi. The boy searched him and found a Bloodstone in a pouch around his neck. The girl has it now. I've told her to show no-one."

Marinden's face drained of colour. "A Bloodstone? And the Talamdorians working with the Havimi? That would explain much."

"I know," Shaunan said. "It seems the Prophet of the One has discovered a means of creating personal Bloodstones for his agents. No wonder we have felt the power of the Way waning. Which is why I need to take them to the Wayzenmoot as soon as possible. This ill news is too important to trust to the Messenger Service." She paused. "Coming back to our visitors. Their grief is deep. The girl, Abigail, has promise – she has asked many questions about the Way and seems to accept her fate here among us. When I healed her, I could sense great power within her. The young man, Jacob, is another matter. He is struggling with his situation and is resistant to learning more."

Marinden frowned. "Resistant? In what way?"

"They have explained that in their world, they only worship one God, and he, male. I think Jacob's main issue is accepting the Six as real, and worthy of worship."

"They follow the Prophet of the One?" Marinden asked.

Shaunan shook her head. "They say not," she said, "and deny all knowledge of him. I wonder whether they might have come from the same world as the Prophet did."

"That would be ominous indeed," Marinden said. "Let us hope it is false." She frowned again. "What is it you want of me, Shaunan?"

“A safe space in which to teach them the Way. It is my hope they can be initiated at Dagârastide. I believe they need to be under the protection of the Six. Especially Abigail.”

“You ask much. Dagârastide is less than seven seisdags away. You say the young man is unwilling to acknowledge the Six?” She paused. “Then I do not see how he can be accepted.”

Shaunan had been afraid of this. How could she make Marinden understand? The girl’s power was too great for her initiation to be delayed and Shaunan knew full well she would not allow the boy to be left out. “Give me a chance to bring him round,” she said. “He is not a bad person, just very confused. And his reaction to that is aggression. But the girl loves him, which I believe may change his mind and heart in the end.”

“I will have to consult with Lord Lesym and Lady Bélia,” Marinden said. “If they agree, which I think they will, I will find you rooms within the Temple grounds to teach them.” Her voice changed. “What of the other two? The young people from Nordvein? Do they wish to return home now their task is done?”

“I think they may wish to remain,” Shaunan said. “They are young, enjoying the adventure of travelling abroad.” She smiled. “It is their first time in Luvodican. You know Ellyn is my niece? They may wish to undertake further training with the Warriors of Dagâra and a Master Cordwainer. I believe their continued presence may help Abigail and Jacob.”

“Very well. Let us leave it there. Go now, Shaunan, get some rest. You look weary, my friend.”

The following morning, Jacob and Abigail were sitting talking to Aidren and Ellyn when Shaunan walked in.

"I have spoken with First Waymage Marinden, my young friends," Shaunan said, "and she has kindly agreed to house us in the Temple grounds while I teach you the Way. Depending on how you progress, it is our hope you will be initiated at Dagârastide."

"Does that mean," Jacob said, looking up, "we will not be allowed into Luvodican?"

"That is correct, Jacob. But it is for your own protection. Without Waymarks, you would attract unwelcome attention."

He frowned. "I suppose you're right. But I'm fed up with being treated like a leper."

"A leper?" Ellyn said. "What's that?"

Jacob turned to her in amazement. "Someone who suffers from leprosy. Don't you *have* leprosy in this world?"

"I've never heard of it," Ellyn said. "Is it a disease?"

"Yes," Abigail said. "It's terrible – it rots the skin and makes people blind and disfigured. Some people believe it is a punishment from God. Lepers are shunned by normal folk and have to live apart in lazar houses."

"Can't your healers cure it?" Aidren asked.

Abigail shook her head. "There is no cure. It is a living death. Nobody knows what causes it, so healthy people do not risk going near lepers in case they catch it."

"Who looks after them?" Shaunan asked. "Surely someone has to?"

Jacob nodded. "You're right. In the Middle Ages, they were looked after by monks. But since Henry the Eighth did away with the monasteries, lay people have cared for them. Leprosy is less common these days but there was a lazar house outside Andover, the nearest town to our village."

"There are so many things I don't understand," Ellyn said, her expression puzzled. "What are the Middle Ages? Or monks? And who was Henry the Eighth?"

Jacob and Abigail looked at each other. Where to begin?

"The time we call the Middle Ages was between three hundred and five hundred years ago," Abigail began. "Nearly everyone in Europe – that's like your Veylindré – was Christian, following our God, the Lord Jesus Christ, through the Catholic church. Monks were men who wanted to worship God full time by taking vows to live apart from ordinary people in monasteries. Then, about a hundred and fifty years ago, a man called Martin Luther came along and broke with the Church in Germany – that's another country in Europe – and translated the Bible – our holy text – into German, his native tongue, so everyone could read it, not just the priests. Many people in other countries followed his example and became Protestants – people who wanted to read the word of God for themselves. Henry the Eighth was the King of England, which is our country, a hundred years ago, and it was he who set up the first Protestant church in England. Since then, many other denominations have been founded, including ours. We are Presbyterians."

"Which is why we are here," Jacob chipped in. "Since our new king, Charles the Second, came to the throne five years ago, Presbyterians and other Dissenters have been persecuted by our government, and many have chosen to flee the country. I guess it was an eye for an eye – after all, the Nonconformists had been persecuting ordinary Christians for the previous twenty years. We were sailing across the Atlantic Ocean, to join other Protestants who have settled in the New World. Abigail's father was a Presbyterian minister, and I chose to join them because of her."

Shaunan shook her head. "Each explanation you give leads to more questions. If I understand you rightly, what you call Christianity is the equivalent of our Way, but there is disagreement about how to follow it. Is that correct?"

Jacob thought before answering. "Ye-es, I suppose that's right. But at least our people are allowed to read the Bible for themselves. The Catholic services are in Latin, a language only the priests – like your Waymages – understand, and the people have to take what they are told on trust."

"But what if the priests are corrupt?" Aidren asked.

"Exactly," Abigail said, "there was no way for ordinary people to know. But our ministers preach the Word in our own language, that we might hear and understand."

Aidren nodded. "That makes sense," he said. "But your… Christianity?" He looked at Abigail for confirmation and she nodded. "It seems very different to our Way. Is there a link with what you do in the world?"

"Not really," Jacob laughed. "Unless you work for the church, it's enough to attend services on Sunday. My being a smith has nothing to do with my faith."

"Yes," said Abigail, "your Way seems a lot more… comprehensive than our Christianity. It touches your whole lives. Of course, we are supposed to live our lives in Christ Jesus, as Saint Paul tells us, but in reality, our faith can be quite separate."

Shaunan nodded. "The Way *is* our lives," she said. "I am beginning to understand how different your faith is to ours. It may take a while for you to fully comprehend our Way – what it means to be a Veylindréan."

"I hope that doesn't mean you're refusing to teach us?" Jacob said, on the alert straight away.

"Of course not, Jacob," Shaunan said. "I have said I will teach you, and I will. It simply means it may take longer. You have so much to unlearn."

"Unlearn?" Abigail said. "Are you expecting us to renounce our faith? Because I don't think I can do that. I have worshipped God through our Lord Jesus all my life."

"I didn't say that," Shaunan said quietly. "But if you are to be accepted by Veylindréans, you will have to embrace our Way also."

Abigail frowned. "All right," she said, "I think we can do that. So long as we do not have to stop believing in God."

Jacob said nothing, pressing his lips together.

"Jacob," Shaunan said, "are you going to be able to adopt the Way of Veylindré?"

He was silent. What should he say? He was somewhat afraid of this Waymage, however much Abigail seemed to like her. "I will try," he said, "but what I have learned of it so far runs counter to my own beliefs. For me, God is one, and male."

"Then it is our worship of the Six which is your main problem?" Shaunan asked.

He nodded. "Yes, or at least, one of them. My whole life I have worshipped God, our Father, Jesus, his Son and the Holy Spirit, three in one."

"We are never going to be able to go home, Jacob, back to our world," Abigail said. "Please try to be open to the Way. You don't want to stay unMarked forever, do you? We need to find a place for ourselves in Veylindré, and the only way we're going to do it is by following the Way. Shaunan has said we don't have to renounce our own faith."

He frowned, then shrugged. "I suppose you're right. All right, I will try."

Why didn't she understand his reasons for rejecting the Six? Was it because she was a girl and liked the idea of a female deity? Would he have accepted the Six more readily if they had been gods? Surely not. To worship more than one God was blasphemy. Back in their own world, he hadn't thought about his faith much. But here, he clung to it fiercely. He knew in the deepest part of himself that this… Way, this belief in female goddesses, was wrong. He couldn't understand why Abigail had accepted them so easily? He'd have to talk to her, bring her round to his way of thinking.

At least they'd be here for a while. He was heartily sick of the incessant travelling, not only here, but also the long weeks at sea. Now they'd be able to stop, reflect, find out more about this world. Not that he believed they would change his mind. He knew what he believed and saw no reason to do otherwise. Abigail would just have to be persuaded.

Chapter 9

Abigail changed back into her familiar worsted gown with some relief. The Dagâran riding clothes were comfortable, but she had found the experience of wearing trews rather than skirts unsettling. It seemed all wrong, somehow – almost indecent. But she was pleased that the Veylindréans allowed women to appear in public bare headed. She shook herself; she'd have to get used to these new and different customs. She had a shrewd idea that this journey wasn't over yet, not by a long way.

The five of them had been assigned a suite of rooms in the Visitors' Hall – three bedrooms, each with two beds, and a comfortable space for sitting, eating and learning. As before, she and Ellyn, Jacob and Aidren shared a bedroom each, with Shaunan taking the third. These rooms would be their home until their learning was complete.

It was the first time they had stayed still for more than a few hours, since leaving England, all those months ago. Abigail was relieved to be done with travelling, at least for the next few weeks… no, seisdags. Would she ever get used to this?

She looked around the room she was sharing with Ellyn: its whitewashed walls, two narrow beds, plump with blankets and pillows, a couple of upright chairs, a wooden chest for each of them to store their belongings, and a window to the outside world. Or at least, into the Temple gardens.

She carried a chair over to the window and gazed out, admiring the neatly trimmed hedges and well-dug beds, ready for the following year. It reminded her of their garden at home, which her mother had tended so lovingly. Her mother…

When Ellyn returned from her first exploration of Luvodican, Abigail was stretched out on her bed, sobbing heartbrokenly.

"Abigail? What's wrong?"

She shook her head, unable to speak.

"I'll fetch Aunt Shaunan."

"Abigail," Shaunan said, sitting on the edge of the bed, "what is grieving you?" Abigail felt the Waymage's gentle hand on her shoulder.

Abigail raised her head. "Oh, Shaunan," she wept, "I'm missing my mother and my family so much."

Shaunan took her in her arms. "Of course you are," she said in a gentle voice. "Tell me about them."

Ellyn was hovering near the door. "Do you want me to leave?"

"No, Ellyn," Abigail said between sobs, "you can stay. It's just… it's really come home to me for the first time that I'll never see any of them again. While we were travelling, I had other things to think about, and could push their… deaths to the back of my mind. But now we're here… I looked outside and started thinking about my mother – she loved to tend our garden at home so much, and then…" A fresh wave of grief shook her.

"Let it all come out," Shaunan said. "You have suffered a huge loss. It is not surprising you're grieving. Tell us about your family."

Abigail strove to dam the scalding tears long enough to speak. She drew herself out of Shaunan's arms, plumped up the pillows and sat back against them, her legs folded underneath her. "My father was a minister," she began. "A devout man, fierce in his faith. Like we said before, he's the reason why we're here. He wasn't allowed to preach his beliefs at… at home, so we all agreed to travel to the New World, where people are allowed to follow their faith without persecution."

"New World?" Shaunan said. "Do your people travel between worlds?"

"Oh, no," Abigail said, "I meant America. It is a far country in our world, across the Atlantic Ocean from Europe, which is where England is. It was only discovered recently, so we call it the New World."

"You were talking about your father…"

"Yes. I loved him but I was also afraid of him. He was so absolute in everything he did, so sure he was right, all the time. I never dared to question anything he said."

"But you had questions?" Shaunan asked.

"Oh, yes, so many questions. He taught us all to read the Bible, our holy text, and there were many stories in it which puzzled me, because they showed God not as a loving, merciful Father but as a capricious tyrant who condemned anyone who didn't follow the faith of his people to eternal damnation. I couldn't understand how that could be." She sighed. "But it doesn't matter now. He'll never rebuke me again." She bit her lip as more tears welled up in her eyes.

"What about your mother?" Ellyn said. "I can hardly remember mine. Aunt Shaunan has been the only mother I've really known."

"You're lucky to have someone as kind as Shaunan to care for you. My mother…" she dug her fingernails into the palms of her hands, fighting for control, "my mother was the same. She protected us children when my father was angry and wasn't afraid to stand up to him if she disagreed. Most of the time, she could calm his anger with a word. I adored her and would do anything she asked me. Which mostly meant looking after the little ones."

"You had brothers and sisters?" Shaunan said.

"Yes, three. Isaac, who was three years younger than me and as strong in his faith as my father. Then the two little ones, Faith, who was seven, and Daniel, who was four. They were so young, so innocent… why did they have to die?" She scrubbed at her sore eyes with the sleeve of her gown. Unwanted, unasked for, a vision of their little bodies, mutilated and bloody, with no life in them, flashed into her mind. She shuddered, the tears leaking down her cheeks.

Shaunan reached into her pocket and passed her a handkerchief. "The Havimi are an evil folk," she said, her face stern. "I do not know why they slaughtered your family and your friends, but there will be a reckoning. This has been happening all too often in the past few years."

"A reckoning?"

"Yes. When your training is complete and you have received your Waymarks, we will travel to Ranusheim to tell your story to the High Waymages. I have a feeling that the Prophet of the One is behind the new boldness of the Havimi. If this is true, we will need to take action to stop them once and for all."

Abigail saw Ellyn's eyes sparkle. "We're going all the way to Ranusheim?"

Shaunan looked at her niece with a twinkle in her eye. "I said nothing about you and Aidren," she said. Then she smiled. "If Lord Lesym and Lady Bélia agree, you may come with us."

"Oh, thank you, Aunt Shaunan!" Ellyn said, hugging her. "I never dreamed I'd visit Ranusheim."

"There is much to be done before we get that far," Shaunan said. "Abigail, would you like me to find Jacob and send him to you?"

"Yes, please. He knew my family. But thank you for understanding, Shaunan. I feel… so tired." The tears had finally stopped. She felt drained, but more peaceful.

"Come, Ellyn," Shaunan said. "Let us find Jacob."

"Abi, what's wrong?" Jacob said. "Shaunan and Ellyn said you were upset."

She sighed, a deep sigh from the heart. "I'm missing my mother so much."

He walked over, sat down and put his arm around her. She turned her face into his shoulder and started to weep again, silently, hopelessly.

"Why did they have to die?" she said, her voice forlorn.

He stroked her sunlit hair. "I don't know." What else could he say?

"Oh, Jacob, what are we going to do? Everything and everyone we knew has been taken away. I feel so confused, so alone."

He gathered her in and felt her relax against him. "I don't know," he said again. "But as long as we are together, we'll cope somehow."

She wound her arms around him. "I'm so glad you're here with me," she said. "I would be lost without you."

"I am with you," he said. "We are together. We will get through this."

"Thank you, my love. You mean so much to me."

When Abigail and Jacob walked into the shared room after lunch, hand in hand, her eyes were still sore and her head ached, but she had cried herself out. When she saw Shaunan, her eyes widened in surprise. Now the Waymage was at Luvodican and in the Temple of the Six, she had discarded her Dagâran riding clothes and wore her Waymage robes – a golden-yellow ankle-length robe gathered at the waist by a golden belt, and a similar topaz and silver brooch to Findoran's. Abigail guessed it was the badge of a Waymage. The robes made her look more imposing, less… approachable, somehow.

"Shaunan! You look so different."

"I only wear riding gear for travelling. I am a Waymage. These clothes go with my calling. I'm going to give you and Jacob the rest of the day to settle in, then we will start our studies tomorrow morning."

Still the same, kind Shaunan. Thank goodness.

"What about me and Aidren?" Ellyn asked.

"We are in Luvodican, home of the Hall of the Warriors of Dagâra," Shaunan said. "I thought Aidren might like to do some further training. We need all the trained warriors we can get in these troubled times."

"Thank you, Waymage Shaunan," Aidren said, bowing. "I am grateful for this opportunity."

"I have already spoken to Master Gildon on your behalf," Shaunan said. "He is expecting you tomorrow."

"What about me?" Ellyn asked.

"I have arranged with Master Markhan of the Guild of Cordwainers for you to train with him. He is a dab hand at bringing on young apprentices."

Ellyn's face lit up like a sun. Abigail admired her dark, exotic beauty. "How wonderful! Thank you, Aunt Shaunan."

"So we'll all be learning together," Abigail said.

The next morning, Abigail and Jacob waited for Shaunan in the warm, wood-panelled common room, enjoying the pale winter sun shining in through the windows. They were sitting on two low chairs in front of the fire and had drawn a third chair up, ready for the Waymage. Abigail was so excited – today they would be starting to learn more about this strange world. But she was worried about Jacob, who was sitting with his arms folded across his chest, a grim expression on his face. She opened her lips to ask him what was wrong, but just then, the Waymage came in.

"Good morning, my friends," Shaunan said. "Today your learning begins. My task is going to be both simple and complicated. In one way, it will be simple, because you are strangers to Veylindré, so I do not have to worry about what you already know. On the other hand, it will be complicated because I cannot take for granted that you know basic things about our world which our children learn at their mothers' knees. I will also need to learn about you and your world so that I can judge how best to teach you. I have brought paper for you to write on, and quills and ink, so you can make notes, if you wish."

Abigail smiled, as she took hers. "Thank you, Shaunan. You've taught us so much already," she said. "But may we start by learning about the Six? So far, I know only their names, that Ranu is the mother of the other five and that each of them has a land under their special care."

Shaunan nodded in approval. "You have listened well, Abigail. Very well, let us start there. Our Way is closely linked with the Six, because each of the guilds which are responsible for passing on learning and skills in Veylindré also have an association with a particular goddess. Their guild halls are located in her land. I have brought a map with me, so you can begin to understand the shape of the Commonweal."

"The Commonweal?" Jacob said.

"That is what we call the federation of the six lands which make up Veylindré," Shaunan said. She unrolled the map. "We are here in Dagâran," and she pointed to a long, narrow land to the south-east of the map. "And this," pointing to a large island in the east, linked to the mainland by a narrow strip of land, "is the Isle of Ranu."

Abigail looked closely at it, fascinated by the unfamiliar outlines of the different countries. It brought home to her, as nothing else had, that they were no longer in their world. Jacob's harsh intake of breath told her he felt the same. She brought her attention back to Shaunan as the Waymage began to explain that the inhabitants of the Isle of Ranu were supported by the other lands of the Commonweal.

"Like tithing, then," she said.

"Tithing? What is that?"

"It is how the church works in England, or at least the Church *of* England. Each person has to pay a sum of money according to the rent value of their property to support the Anglican clergy. It wasn't fair," Abigail added hotly, "that we Presbyterians had to pay it. Our own ministers didn't benefit from it at all."

"I see," Shaunan said. "Our system works rather differently – as I said, the peoples of the other lands support those on Ranu because they recognise their importance to the life of the whole Commonweal."

"That does sound fairer," Abigail said. "I'm sorry, Shaunan, please go on."

Shaunan smiled, accepting her apology, and continued. "Aside from the members of the Wayzenmoot, the only other residents are members of the Hall of Papermakers, at Muillean, as I said, and the Hall of Scriveners and Printers, which is also in Ranusheim. And their families. These two halls are on Ranu because the lore of the Way needs to be sent out from the Isle to the other lands."

"You have printing here?" Jacob said. Abigail was surprised too – this world seemed to be more advanced in some ways, but more old-fashioned in others.

"I hadn't expected that," he continued. "In our world, we have had printing for only the last two hundred years. It has made a huge difference to the learning of ordinary people. But…" and he blushed, "I don't read very well, myself. I only had a couple of years of schooling before I started learning my trade under my father."

Abigail could sense how much it had cost him to admit that. She squeezed his hand.

"You said you are a smith, Jacob," Shaunan said, kindly ignoring his discomfort. "Is that right?"

"I am," he said with obvious pride, "I can turn my hand to any form of smithing."

"Then I expect your Waymark will be Dagâran," Shaunan said. "Dagâra is the Goddess of War and Metalworking, We passed the Hall of Metalworking in Myndorian, which is located there to be near to the most important mines. The Halls of Weaponcraft and of the Warriors of Dagâra are here in Luvodican, our capital city." She smiled. "Once you have your Waymarks and can go out and about, you will see many people from other lands here, learning to make weapons or advance their training as warriors."

"Why do you need so many warriors?" Jacob asked. A good question – what were they getting into?

"Because our world has changed in the last thirty years, since the Prophet of the One came to power in Talamdor. The people of Veylindré must be ready to defend the Commonweal."

"Why? Jacob asked again. "Is he going to invade it?"

"We do not know," Shaunan said. "But we fear he may. But that is a lesson for another day. I was telling you about the Six."

Jacob frowned, but said nothing.

Abigail rushed to fill the silence. "What about the other goddesses?"

She listened in fascination as Shaunan told them about Néarta, the goddess of agriculture and crafts, and Lènia, the goddess of musicians, storytellers and healers.

"Waymages also have healing skills," she said, smiling at Abigail, "as I think you know."

Abigail returned her smile. "Yes, that was when I first truly realised we were no longer in our world."

"Where are the Halls in Lènium?" Jacob asked.

"The Healer Hall and the Hall of Apothecaries are in the Vale of Berlysian, where most of the herbs are grown. The Hall of Tradition, where the musicians and storytellers learn the songs and stories which explain our history and customs, is in Taellingsford, at the south-west tip of Lènium, to make it easy for them to travel to other lands."

"Ranu, Dagâra, Néarta and Lènia," Abigail said. "That leaves… Garûna and Yrusia. Is that right?"

Shaunan nodded before telling them about Garûna and Garûnalond, whose chief city was Mirunan, which was also the secular capital of Veylindré, for some reason.

"I don't understand," Jacob said. "I thought Ranusheim was the most important place."

Abigail agreed – she had thought that too. This world was so confusing, so very different to their own. But maybe Ranusheim was like Rome used to be – the centre for the church.

"And so it is," Shaunan said, "as the principal centre of learning for the Way of Veylindré."

Exactly like Rome then. But for six goddesses, not one God. Abigail shivered – this world was so different, so very strange. Would they ever feel at home here?

The Waymage continued, "But Mirunan is where the Hall of Justice is located. The laws for the whole Commonweal of Veylindré are debated and decided there. Each land has six representatives, Lords and Ladies of Justice, who are elected every six years."

"It must be complicated," Abigail said, "having two centres making laws."

"I see what you mean," Shaunan said, "but in reality, it works fairly well. The Hall of Justice deals with mundane matters, the Wayzenmoot with spiritual ones."

By the time Shaunan had finished telling them about the guilds which looked to Garûna and Yrusia, and something about the inhabitants of Garûnalond and Yrusian, Abigail's head was aching. It had been so much to take in, in one sitting.

"My head is reeling," Jacob said. "How are we going to remember all this?"

"You are not expected to remember it all. My purpose is to help you to understand how the Commonweal works, and about the Way, so that you can be Waymarked at Dagârastide."

"Thank you, Shaunan," Abigail said. "I'm feeling a bit overwhelmed, myself."

"We will leave it there, for today," Shaunan said. "I have given you much to think about all at once. When we start to study the Way of Veylindré, and as you experience more of our world for yourselves, it will begin to make sense to you."

She smiled and left them.

"That was fascinating," Abigail said, looking through the notes she had taken. "I think it's wonderful how the whole of Veylindré fits together, each land contributing to the good of the whole… what did Shaunan say? …Commonweal. It sounds a bit like our Commonwealth before the King returned."

"Yes, I understand a bit more now," Jacob said. "But I really want to study that map again. At the moment, I've no idea how big Veylindré is. I've got a feeling it's much larger than England. But it's difficult to tell from what she said."

"And *I've* got a feeling we've only seen one tiny corner of it so far," Abigail said. "I wonder how far we will travel in the coming months."

"Who knows?" Jacob said. "As far as I can see, we are here for the next few weeks at least, while we learn more about this world."

"Listen to us," Abigail said, with a smile. "We're still talking about weeks and months. It's going to be hard to get used to thinking about time in terms of seisdags and seasons instead."

He grunted. "That will be the least of it, I'm afraid. Everything is different here, not only the way they talk about time." He sighed. "There's so much we don't know."

"Yes, it all seems so strange to me, so different to everything in our world. How do you feel about the learning, Jacob?"

He frowned. "I'm not that happy about it, to be honest. It's all right for you – you can read anything. I…" he hung his head, as though reluctant to meet her eyes, "… really struggle with it. I can learn anything that involves working with my hands, but book learning… And I'm still uneasy about their goddesses. It's all so… different."

"Don't worry, Jacob, I'll help you with the reading," she paused, "if you want me to..."

He nodded, his face clearing a little.

"And the rest of it is as new to me as it is to you," she continued. "At least you have a craft skill. All I've ever done is look after the children and help my mother harvest and dry the herbs in our garden. It seems as though here everyone is expected to contribute to the work of the world in some way, depending on their Waymark. I've no idea which Waymark will be mine, but it's going to be a steep hill to climb, whichever."

He hugged her. "That makes me feel a bit better," he said, "and at least we're together."

֍ Chapter 10 ֍

Jacob and Abigail were in their shared living room in the Hall of Visitors, talking quietly together. The pale morning sun, still low at this time of year, was slanting in at the windows, adding a lustre to the dark wooden furniture.

Shaunan walked in. “Ranusdag is our rest day,” she said, “so Aidren, Ellyn and I will be attending worship at the Temple. You are welcome to come with us, if you wish, but I think it would be better for you to wait until you have learned more of the Way.”

Abigail glanced at Jacob, her eyebrows raised, then answered on behalf of them both. “Yes, perhaps we’d better wait a while. From what I saw of the Temple at Nordvein, your worship is quite different to ours, and I think we’d feel awkward.”

Jacob nodded.

“I have brought you a book to look through while we are gone,” Shaunan continued. “*Veylindré: Our Commonweal*. We use it to teach our children about our world, so I think you might find it interesting.”

Jacob watched Abigail’s face light up. “That sounds like exactly what we need. Thank you, Shaunan. When will you return?”

“I will be back in time to share lunch with you, unless First Waymage Marinden wants to talk to me. You are welcome to wander in the Temple gardens if you wish, but please remember to keep your hoods up and your foreheads covered.”

She smiled at them and left.

Jacob watched Abigail sit down in one of the low chairs near the fire, made comfortable with thin cushions, and open the book. He did not share her passion for learning about Veylindré. Admittedly, the map Shaunan had brought them the previous day had been fascinating, but he was beginning to realise they had only seen one minute corner of the Commonweal, which seemed to be easily ten times the size of England, and he was feeling overwhelmed. She smiled at him in clear invitation, but he glowered down at her.

"She's treating us like children."

She stood and put her hand on his arm. "You're wrong, Jacob. We know so little about Veylindré. I want to learn as much about it as I can, and a children's book is a good place to start." She paused, then asked, "Why are you so angry?"

He flung her hand off and began to prowl around the room, the soles of his leather boots loud on the tiled floor, stopping now at the window, now near the fire, but keeping his distance from her. For some reason, her willingness, her downright eagerness to learn about this place made him feel worse. He was sick of being indoors, sick of going along with all this. She sat back down, a look of sadness on her face. He had disappointed her, again. She held out her hands to the flames.

"Why shouldn't I be angry?" he burst out. "It wasn't my choice to be stuck here, away from everything and everyone I know. Back home, I had a place in the world – I could work with my hands and belonged in my craft. Here, I'm helpless. But you…" he paused, "… I don't understand why you seem so eager to embrace all this. I… I want to go home." He sat down opposite her, scowling.

"Oh, my love," she said, kneeling on the rug in front of him, putting one hand on his knee. "I'm so sorry. I don't know what to say to you. I'd love to go home too, but I honestly don't believe we can. I think our only choice is to accept that we are here and do the best we can to find our feet in this world."

He met her gaze, infuriated by the very mildness of her words. “That’s no choice at all. And I’m sick to death of being cooped up in here. I feel like a prisoner… nothing to do but eat meals and listen to lectures. I want to get out, walk around, feel free.”

“But we’re being kept here for our own good,” she said. “Don’t you remember how awful it was when people stared at us because we don’t have Waymarks? And the only way we’re going to get them is by doing the learning.”

“What if I don’t want a Waymark?”

Abigail gaped at him. Why didn’t she understand? “You don’t want a Waymark?”

“No, I don’t. I’m a Christian. Like I thought you were. I don’t follow their Way and have no desire to, either.”

He saw the shock in her eyes. Good. It was about time she woke up, realised that he was not with her in this.

“You’re beginning to sound as fierce in your faith as my father,” she said.

“Well, one of us has to.” She was a minister’s daughter. She ought to be as wary of this Way as he was.

“Please don’t be angry with me.”

She put her hand on his arm. It was hard to resist her, but he had to make her understand.

“I’m still a Christian,” she continued. “I still follow our Lord Jesus. I still pray to God every morning. No-one has said we can’t continue to do that. Shaunan has only asked us to be open to the Way, to learn about and accept the Six.”

“God! You even sound like her,” he growled, standing up again, flinging himself back into motion, stalking around the room. “Accept the Six. Accept the Six. Well, *I* can’t.”

She sank back into the chair. “Then… what do you plan to do?”

"I don't know. Get out of here, for a start, then find someone willing to sail me back home."

"But what about me? What about us? Don't you love me anymore?"

"Of course I do," he continued, glaring at her. "You're the one who doesn't care... Have you any idea how difficult I'm finding all this? I gave up *everything* for you, Abigail," slamming his hand down on the table, "my home, my family, my trade. I even converted to your father's faith, so I'd be able to come with you. Because I believed we could make a new life together, and that was the most important thing for me. For *us*, I thought. But now we're here and none of that seems to have meaning for you anymore. I can't understand why you've accepted this Way of theirs so easily. Doesn't your father's Christianity matter more than that? Don't *I* matter more than that?"

Abigail sat on her chair by the fire, looking lost and alone, plaiting her fingers, not meeting his hot, angry gaze. The silence was only broken by the crackling of the flames.

"Well?" he snapped. "Nothing to say for yourself?"

"Oh, Jacob, I love you so much. But you're frightening me. Please," she reached out her hand, "come and sit down here, by the fire. Let's talk about this and see what can be done. What do you need to make you happier?"

"What do I need?" he echoed. Why did she even have to ask? Why didn't she understand? "What I need is you at my side. You *on* my side. I love you, Abigail, but I feel so alone. I feel as though you're so keen to become a Veylindréan, that what I think doesn't matter to you anymore. That *we* don't matter anymore."

She stood up, flushing. "That's not true," she said, her voice rising. "Of course I care about what you think. But *you* don't seem to understand why I find Veylindré so… so refreshing, so marvellous. At home, I was a loyal daughter, expected to do as I was told. All I had to look forward to was marriage and children. Whereas here…"

"What do you mean, *all* you had to look forward to? Isn't that enough? Isn't marriage with me enough for you? What more do you want?" He was pacing again, unable to contain his feelings.

"Of course I want to marry you, to share my life with you. But here in Veylindré I could also do something useful in the world, make a difference somehow. My life at home was so narrow, so confined. Here, I can learn a skill and use it to make life better for other people. Can't you see how exciting that is for me?"

He stopped dead and turned on her. "So marriage with me would be narrow and confined, would it? Thank you very much."

"That's not what I meant, and you know it," Abigail said, and he could hear real anger in her voice. "But I've been given a glimpse of the possibility of a richer, fuller life here and," she met his gaze, lifting her chin, "I want to find out more about it, to be a part of it."

"Then there's nothing more to say," he said, striding towards the door.

"Jacob, please, don't go…"

He turned his back on her, marched out of the room, slamming the door behind him.

When Shaunan returned with Ellyn and Aidren, she found Abigail sitting alone on the broad, low window seat, leafing listlessly through the book, her eyes red. The fire had died down to glowing embers, the room was dark. After stoking up the fire and putting on more wood, Shaunan crossed to the dresser and lit the two oil lamps.

"Where is Jacob?" she said. "I am sensing some discord between you."

"He's gone out for a walk, I think," Abigail said. "Oh, Shaunan! We've had the most awful argument."

"Aidren, Ellyn, go and look for Jacob, please." Shaunan said, fear flooding her mind. Blessed Ranu, keep him safe.

"Now, Abigail," as the young people bowed and left, "come over to the fire and warm yourself." She took the young woman's hands between her own and began to chafe them. "Tell me," she said gently, "what has happened between you two that Jacob has felt the need to bolt?"

Abigail did as she was told, scrubbing at her eyes with her knuckles, so endearingly childlike. "I don't know," she wailed, "…let me think. First of all, he was angry with you for giving us this book. He said you were treating us like children. Then, when I defended you, and said we needed to start learning somewhere, and this was as good a place as any, he turned on me. Oh, Shaunan! It was awful. He accused me of betraying him, of taking your side against him. He hates being mewed up in here so much. He feels trapped."

"Trapped?" Why would he think that? "That is not the intention. It is for your own protection that you are secluded here."

"I know. That's what I told him. I reminded him how awful it was having to hide our foreheads all the time, and that we'd have to wait until we had our Waymarks. And then… then, he said…" She faltered, and Shaunan could sense her resistance to sharing his words with her.

"Yes?" she said gently, tilting Abigail's chin up with her finger, so that the young woman was forced to meet her gaze.

"What did he say that distresses you so? I will not be angry. But I need to know."

"He said…" and Shaunan could sense how the words had burned into her memory "… he said, 'What if I don't want a Waymark?' He said he was a Christian and didn't want to follow the Way."

She met Shaunan's gaze. Shaunan broadcast feelings of openness, non-judgement, hoping the girl would pick them up. And sensed when she did.

"He just wants to go home. He's really struggling with being here and can't understand why I'm liking it so much. He accused me of caring more about Veylindré than about him. When I tried to explain why I'm happy here, he got angry again, and left. He said he was going for a walk and marched out. And… and, that's all."

"I… see," Shaunan said. "I knew he was resistant to learning about the Way but had not realised the force of his feelings. How long has he been gone?"

Abigail shook her head. "I'm not sure, for a while… I don't know."

"Let us hope he has not left the Temple grounds. If he has, alone and unWaymarked, I fear for his safety. Wait here. I am going to check his room to see whether his belongings are still there."

"I'm coming with you."

The two of them hurried down the narrow hall to the small bedroom Jacob was sharing with Aidren. His pack was still by the side of his bed. Such a relief. But where was he?

"Oh God," Abigail said. "I hope Aidren or Ellyn find him."

"So do I, child. Come back to the fire."

When Jacob had stormed out, it had been with the intention of leaving for good. But he couldn't leave her. He loved her too much, in spite of everything. So he left his pack where it was, threw on his cloak and strode out into the Temple Gardens. He kept walking until he was out of sight of the Visitors' Hall, then stopped, breathing deeply. It felt so good to be outside again, and without any Veylindréans by. They must all be in the Temple. He started to explore the gardens, enjoying the cold air in his lungs. He glanced around, then threw back the hood of his cloak. It was marvellous to feel the wind in his hair.

He walked fast for a while, without a destination in mind, needing to use his body to work off his anger. Ahead of him were a pair of beautiful wrought-iron gates. He walked closer to examine them. Whoever had made them was a master of the smithcraft's art.

"Jacob!"

A voice behind him, Ellyn's. He whirled, his hand going to the knife at his belt.

"What are you doing here?"

"I've come to find you. When we got back from Temple, Abigail was beside herself with worry."

"She needn't have bothered." He glared at her, all his hard-won peace vanishing in an instant. "I was only taking a walk. No need to send you after me."

"Please, Jacob, come back with me and," she paused, "better put your hood up."

He shrugged. There was nothing else to do.

When they walked in, Abigail sprang to her feet, her eyes red, her face pale.

"Jacob! Thank goodness you're back. I was so worried!"

"Thank you, Ellyn," Shaunan said. "Where did you find him?"

"Near the West Gate of the Temple gardens."

"I can speak for myself, thank you," Jacob snapped. "I went out for a walk, to clear my head. You *said* we could walk in the Temple gardens, and I needed to be out of doors, by myself. I was admiring the scrollwork of the gate when Ellyn found me and marched me back here." He turned to Ellyn. "I didn't know you were my gaoler."

Ellyn flushed but stood her ground. "I do as the Waymage commands."

"So I see," Jacob sneered. Then, to Abigail, "I suppose you blabbed everything to Shaunan?"

"Oh, Jacob, don't be angry with me," Abigail said. "Of course I told Shaunan. I was so scared you'd get into trouble. I didn't know where you'd gone."

Aidren walked in.

"So," Jacob said, "you've been out looking for me as well, have you?"

"Jacob," Shaunan said, "what is wrong?"

"I told you," he said hotly, "I wanted to think, to try to decide what to do. I've done nothing wrong, and I'm fetched back here like a wayward child. But if you really want to know," he paused, "I feel as though my life means nothing here. In our world, I had a place, a trade and hopes for the future. I could have worked on gates like that one. Here…" he paused again, "here, I don't count for anything. My faith is dismissed, my skills don't matter, and Abigail…" his voice trailed off.

"And Abigail?" Shaunan said softly.

Jacob faced his love, almost hating her in that moment. "You've given up any hope of going home. You seem happy to stay here, to learn about Veylindré, about the Way, forgetting our God and all that Christianity stands for. I can't do that, Abi. I can't."

She reached out a hand to him, but he ignored it. Turning to Shaunan, he said, "I want to go back to our world. If your magic, your 'Way', is so wonderful, I'm sure you can make it happen." He folded his arms across his chest. "I've had enough. I want to go home."

Shaunan looked at him in silence.

"Well?" he said. "Can you or can't you?"

"I am sorry, my friend," the Waymage said quietly. "I do not believe that what you ask is possible. Even if we knew exactly where you came through to Veylindré, I do not think I could find anyone willing to risk losing their way home to take you there."

"You see?" Abigail said. "That's what I said, Jacob. We're here and we just have to make the best of it."

"Abigail," Shaunan said. One word, but Jacob heard the warning in it.

She flushed. "I'm sorry," she whispered.

Turning back to him, Shaunan continued, "I understand why you feel trapped, Jacob. You feel as though the power of choice has been taken from you. That you are no longer the agent of your own destiny."

He nodded, his lips pressed together, his arms folded. "We haven't had any choices since we landed here. Ever since we met Aidren and Ellyn in the forest outside Nordvein, we've not been free. We've done what you asked, gone where you told us to, like sheep. And nobody has asked us what *we* want to do."

Shaunan asked Abigail, "Do you feel this too?"

For a moment, Abigail didn't answer. Then she said, "Oh, Jacob! I think I understand now. Why you've minded this so much more than I have."

She turned to Shaunan, her face bright with comprehension. "You see, in our world, men are the dominant ones, the ones who make all the decisions. Women follow the men, do what they're told. So it's been much easier for me to go along with what you've asked us to do. But for Jacob, it's as though his right to decide for himself has been taken away."

Jacob nodded fiercely, then reached out a long arm to bring Abigail to his side. "Finally, you get it," he said, his anger subsiding a little. "I thought I would never make you understand."

"Is this truly how matters are arranged in your world?" Shaunan asked.

"Yes," Abigail said, "but I've never thought about it before. I've always accepted that my father had the right to dictate what I did… It's the way things are."

"There was one time when you went against his wishes," Jacob reminded her, "otherwise we would not be together."

Abigail blushed. "That's true," she said. Then she explained, "My father wanted me to marry a man older than myself, Matthew, the eldest son of Elder Sanderson, his second in command. But I had met Jacob and fallen in love with him."

Ellyn looked horrified. "Your father had the right to decide who you would marry?"

"Yes," Abigail said, "but Jacob converted to our faith, so that he could come with us to the New World. I think my mother would have persuaded my father to let us marry in the end." Her eyes filled with tears at the thought of her mother.

"He must really love you," Ellyn said, "to leave everything he knew to be with you."

He saw the impact of Ellyn's words on Abigail. Her face paled and her hand flew to her mouth.

"I'm so sorry," she said, biting her lip. "I didn't realise until this morning how strongly you felt about our situation. I've been so excited by all these new ideas that I didn't stop to think that you might feel differently... Can you forgive me?"

"Of course I can," he said. "Don't you know I love you?" The words were almost a slap; he saw her flinch. "But I'm still not happy."

"What can we do to make you happier, Jacob?" Shaunan asked.

His head jerked up in surprise. Abigail had asked the same question. "I… don't know. At the moment I feel like I have no control whatsoever over what happens to me. And I can't stand it."

Shaunan nodded. "I realise that, my friend. But can you at least trust that I have your best interests in mind?"

He gazed for a long time into her amber eyes, then sighed. "Yes, I suppose I can."

"I think we need to speak more about your own faith and about how society works in your world, as it is so important to you," she said. "Maybe if I understood these matters better, I would be able to comprehend your resistance to the Way."

Jacob looked down, considering his response. "Yes, all right. That would be a start. But I need to have something to do. I can't sit around doing nothing. It makes me feel as though I don't count."

"What would you be doing now, if you were at home, in your own world?" Aidren asked.

Jacob looked out of the window, gauging the time of day by the angle of the sun. "I'd be at work in my father's smithy, making and repairing tools or shoeing horses," he said. "And if we'd reached the New World, instead of coming through to here, I'd have been apprenticing myself to a smith out there. I need to work with my hands. I'm a doer, not a book-learner, not like Abi. I hate being cooped up in here, with nothing to do."

Shaunan's expression softened. "You love your work. I can hear it in your voice."

"Yes. Looking at the scrollwork on that gate reminded me how much I'm missing the feel of the tools in my hands, the joy of creating something new. And here, I can't approach anyone. They'd take one look at my forehead and report me to the Watch."

Shaunan nodded. "That is true, my friend. Which is why you need to be patient, learn what you need to know, so you can get your Waymark and find a place here."

"But I can't get a Waymark unless I accept this Way of yours. So we're back where we started." His shoulders slumped in frustration.

"I do not think so," Shaunan said, with a gentle smile. "You have shared your mind and heart with us and that is an important advance. It is now up to me to help you to discover a path towards accepting your presence here, so you learn enough about our Way to be Waymarked. Does that sound reasonable?"

"That sounds fair," he said slowly, "but I need to be doing something too. I can't sit around, doing nothing."

"I will see what I can manage."

Chapter 11

After the tumult of the morning, Abigail was glad for some time alone. She was sitting by herself in the common room, her legs curled up underneath her, watching the flickering flames. Shaunan had taken Jacob off by himself, to start making good her promise of discovering more about their world. Aidren and Ellyn were off somewhere.

She was feeling guilty about not understanding how strongly Jacob felt, and also irritated by his stubborn refusal to embrace the Way. What could she do to make things right between them? How could she reach him? She cudgelled her brain, but no ideas came. She sighed a deep sigh from her heart. Leave it for now. Shaunan would sort it out…

She picked up *Veylindré: Our Commonweal.* The book fell open to a rhyme about the Six.

First there was Ranu,
Great Mother of all,
Goddess of Wisdom,
Who gave us our lore.

Lènia, healer
Through story and song,
Goddess of Healing,
Who helps us belong.

Néarta, Goddess
Of crafts and of crops,
Who helps us to fill
Our barns and our shops.

Garûna who serves
Both justice and laws,
To help us keep straight
And manage our flaws.

Dagâra the strong,
Stern Goddess of War,
Mining of metals
For smithies and more.

Yrusia shrewd,
The travellers' friend,
Who aids all traders
To deal and to spend.

On the page opposite was a fine woodcut engraving, showing the Six in a group, each goddess holding an item indicating her attributes.

The one in the centre must be Ranu, holding a scroll. The other five were arranged in little vignettes around her.

As Abigail pored over it, she used the rhyme to help her distinguish each figure.

Lènia was sitting on a rock, tiny, printed words issuing from her mouth, surrounded by a group of listening children. Néarta was pictured in a field with a sickle. Garûna held a set of scales. Dagâra was shown with a sword in her hand, and a quiver full of arrows on her back. Yrusia carried a pedlar's pack, obviously full of trade goods.

And there were details in each vignette about the lands too.

Some mining tools and weapons for Dagâran, some beautiful plants for Lènium – they must be herbs. A tiny ship, sailing on a miniature ocean, for Yrusian and a broad landscape planted with crops of all kinds for Néartania.

Abigail noticed a tiny sheep in one corner of the Garûnalond one and remembered that Findoran had come from the wool centre there. And a printing press in Ranu's.

The more Abigail studied it, moving nearer to the oil lamp to examine it more closely, the more details she noticed, and the more she learned about Veylindréan society.

Then she looked at the border, which comprised some intricate scrollwork and six symbols resembling the ones she had seen above the altars in the Temple at Nordvein.

So each must stand for one of the Six.

She recognised Dagâra's, which looked like a capital Y with an extra line in the middle of it, because Aidren had it on his forehead, and Néarta's, a pointy B, which was Ellyn's. And Ranu's, the circle with eight swirling divisions, because it was Shaunan's. But she couldn't work out which of the other three belonged to Garûna, Lènia and Yrusia.

She read the rhyme again and decided to learn it off by heart. It had a lovely rhythm to it, which made it easy to remember.

She started chanting it to herself, "First there was Ranu, Great Mother of all…"

The next day, their learning resumed. Abigail hoped that Jacob would be more open to it this time, but resolved to say nothing which might upset him. One row like yesterday's was more than enough. She had never meant to hurt him.

"This morning," Shaunan said, "I'm going to start teaching you about the Way – what it is, how it works and about the powers of the different Waymarks."

It was colder today, and the rain beat on the windows, its staccato drumming a counterpoint to her voice. Abigail was glad of the fire, burning merrily in the grate.

"The first thing you need to understand," Shaunan said, "is that the Way is all around us and works through us. When we are assigned our Waymarks at the Ceremony of Assignment, we take our places in Veylindréan society. Each Waymark confers different powers and the Goldstones we receive at the Ceremony help us to access those powers. You have already seen mine," she nodded to Abigail. "What you may not know, each Goldstone is different."

"I noticed," Abigail said, "that Ellyn's had brown veins running through it."

"That's right." Then Shaunan turned to Jacob, "Ask Aidren to show you his sometime."

"I am a Waymage with a Ranusian Waymark," she went on, "so the veins in my Goldstone are a deeper gold. But the other Goldstones have different coloured veins running through them to symbolise the Goddess affiliation of their bearer. Néarta's are brown, Lènia's lilac for healers, purple for musicians and storytellers. Garûna's are green, Yrusia's are blue for traders, aquamarine for mariners and fisherfolk. And Dagâra's are red for warriors and orange for smiths and miners."

"What's to stop anyone stealing someone else's Goldstone and using its power?" Jacob asked.

"It does not work like that. Both Goldstone and Waymark are necessary parts of the power. Only a Veylindréan with a Dagâran Waymark can access the powers of a Dagâran Goldstone. And most people would find it difficult to use any Goldstone but their own, although it can be done. We become attuned to our own Goldstones."

"How does that happen?" Abigail said. "I don't understand 'attuned'."

"I am glad you asked that," Shaunan said. "One of the important learnings every young person undertakes is training in Immersion in the Way."

Jacob's eyebrows shot up. "Immersion in the Way? What's that?"

"You may have noticed that Aidren and Ellyn spend some time each morning in silent meditation, holding their Goldstones, as do I," Shaunan said. "That is our practice of Immersion in the Way. We try to empty our minds to allow the power of the Way to come into our hearts."

"Yes," Abigail said, "Ellyn told me about it when we were in Myndorian. I've been joining her in prayer most mornings since."

"Your people practice Immersion too?" Shaunan said, her eyebrows shooting up.

"It's not quite the same thing. We pray to God through Jesus. It's more wordy than this practice of yours, I think."

"What words do you use?"

"I always start with the Lord's Prayer, the prayer that Jesus taught his disciples, then I say a prayer that my… my father taught us, to begin each day."

"I would love to hear them. They would give me an insight into your faith."

"The Lord's Prayer," Abigail began, blushing, "is the original Christian prayer. As I said, it was taught to the disciples by our Lord Jesus himself. These are the words. 'Our Father, which art in heaven, Hallowed be Thy name. Thy kingdom come, Thy will be done on earth, as it is in heaven. Give us this day our daily bread, and forgive us our debts, as we forgive our debtors. And lead us not into temptation but deliver us from evil. For Thine is the kingdom, the power and the glory, forever, Amen.'"

"And the other prayer, the one which your father taught you?"

"I've always loved it." Abigail took a deep breath, clasped her hands together and closed her eyes. "'Eternal God, as you cause the sun to rise, bring the light of Christ to dawn in our souls, and drive out all darkness. You call us to adventures of which we cannot see the goal, by roads as yet untrodden, through dangers unknown. Give us faith to step out with courage, not knowing where we go, but only that your hand is leading us, and your love is ever with us. Give us grace to reflect Christ's glory, and may his love show in our deeds, his peace shine in our words, and his healing in our touch, through Jesus Christ our Lord, Amen.'"

Jacob's voice echoed the 'Amen.' "I'd like to learn that one, Abi. Although I don't think the adventures it talks about included ending up a different world..." The corners of his eyes crinkled as he smiled at her. He seemed to have forgiven her. Thank God for that.

She smiled back. "No, I don't suppose it did, but I find it comforting. As though God is with us, even here."

"That is a beautiful prayer," Shaunan said. "It sounds as though the presence of your God is similar to the presence of our Way. All around us, but also within us, supporting us on our journeys through life. But perhaps our Way is even more present as we can connect with it directly through our Goldstones."

"Mm, maybe," Abigail said, exchanging a glance with Jacob. It didn't sound the same at all to her. "But tell us about the powers of the Way, please, Shaunan. You've said that each Waymark gives its bearer different powers."

"The powers a Waymark confers," Shaunan said, "are intimately connected to a person's role in society. The only power which all Veylindréans share is Augmentation, the ability to enhance your own or someone else's powers."

As Abigail and Jacob listened, she explained that Augmentation could strengthen everyone's powers, in different ways. It sounded like magic to Abigail. Which of course, it was. She shifted uneasily in her chair.

"How can they affect someone else's powers?" Jacob asked.

"Enhancing another's powers always requires direct physical contact, hand to flesh. And there are also ethical limitations, which are enforced by the Wayzenmoot."

Ethical limitations. How did they work? But at least it meant that the Veylindréans weren't allowed to do their magic regardless of the consequences. Which was comforting.

Shaunan continued, "Then there is the power of Location or Finding, which is the ability to find someone's mind by using a personal belonging to increase connection, or to keep track of where they are on a journey.

"Only those with an Yrusian or Garûnan Waymark have this ability, and not all of them. It is considered a great asset, as it enables traders, guides and messengers to find their way across unknown territory, so long as they have a clear picture of the destination in their minds."

"Does that mean they can find people who are lost?" Abigail asked.

"That's right, Abigail," Shaunan said, smiling. "Let me see, the next power is Elemental, which is the power to influence the elements, such as water divining and weather working. Adepts can use it to find water underground, to make fire and light – you have seen me do that on our journey – and to foretell and influence the weather. Although influencing it is a last resort, as in the hands of the unskilled, who do not understand the complexities involved, it could be disastrous."

"Which Waymarks have this power?" Abigail asked.

"Those of Ranu, Néarta and Yrusia. The next power is Empathy, the power to read or sense another person's emotions or to control their emotions or feelings."

Jacob shot to his feet. "Does that mean people here can read our minds?"

"Peace, my friend," Shaunan said, her voice warm and reassuring. "Not your thoughts, but only your feelings. Its use is strictly regulated. People with empathic powers cannot just dip into people's emotions at will. The Wayzenmoot punishes abuses of Empathy severely. But, used for good, it can save lives in the hands of a Lèniumen healer by strengthening a person's will to live, or enchant an audience in the hands of a Lèniumen musician or storyteller, ensure justice in the hands of a Garûnan Officer of the Watch, or smooth the trading process in the hands of an Yrusian trader. Again, close proximity to the person or people being influenced is necessary."

It still sounded intrusive to Abigail. But Shaunan was speaking again.

"The next power, Healing, you have experienced already," she continued, smiling at her. "People with the Waymarks of Ranu and Lènia can heal. Every settlement in Veylindré has a healer, and in larger communities, there is usually a Hall of Healing. Its use requires direct physical contact – you remember I had to touch you to heal your wrist. It is more physically and mentally exhausting than some of the other Waymagics and, in times of widespread sickness, some healers can burn themselves out. It is one of the powers least open to abuse, as all healers take an Oath of Healing when they become adepts, the breaking of which is instantly known to the Wayzenmoot."

"The last two powers are limited to those with a Ranusian Waymark – the Sight, or perceiving the future – and Mind Reading, the ability to read another person's thoughts or to communicate mind to mind over distances. "The Sight is the rarest power and is highly prized. The High Waymages of the Wayzenmoot use it to guide their advice to the secular rulers of the lands. There are two types of Seeing: Precognition, which is where the Ranusian concerned has a vision in a Truedream, whether they are asleep or awake, and Scrying, which is where the future is discerned by looking into the heart of the Golden Stone of Ranu. But the visions can be imprecise, or deceptive, and much skill is required to read the future truly."

"Can you do it?"

"No, not in its fullest form, and I think I am thankful for that. I sometimes have forebodings of the future, but they are usually vague and nebulous. But I am a mind reader. I can communicate with other Waymages, mind to mind, although not over great distances. The best mind readers can communicate across the whole Commonweal."

The colour drained from Jacob's face. "So you *can* read our thoughts?"

Shaunan met his gaze. "Yes, but I have chosen not to. Used wrongly, mind reading is an abuse of a person's privacy, and I would not do that to you."

Clearly uneasy, he settled back in his chair. Abigail touched his hand – they would need to talk about this later. He nodded, understanding.

"So the powers are Augmentation, Empathy, Finding, Healing, the Sight and Mind Reading?"Abigail asked.

"That's right. And Elemental."

"Oh, yes, I forgot that one. What training is needed to use the powers?"

"The revelation of your Waymark at the Ceremony of Assignment is but the beginning of your journey. Each kind of Waymagic has three levels of skill – initiate, adept and mage. Which are linked to the Guild system of apprentice, journeyman or woman, and master or mistress. But sometimes, a person might have an innate natural talent greater than their Guild ranking. Immersion is used to hone all seven Waymagics, which is why the symbol of the Way and of Ranu," and she pointed to her own forehead, "is a circle with eight divisions."

"It all sounds so complicated," Jacob said. "How do people learn to use their powers safely?"

"Training in the use of your Goldstone is done locally in the early stages, but as a person becomes more skilled in accessing the powers of their Goldstone, they will need further training, which may mean moving to a larger town or city where adepts of the particular craft or profession gather in the Guild Halls. The Chief Guild Hall of each trade or craft provides advanced training in the Way. Which is why Aidren is going to the Hall of Warriors each day, and Ellyn to Master Markhan. Had we not been on this journey, she would have been travelling soon to Céardochis, to the Hall of Clothiers, to complete her training there. In fact, she probably will, when all this is over.

"The other thing you have to learn is how to access the Way through your Goldstone. By holding it in your hand, focussing your mind and heart on the task at hand and using special words, which you will be taught by your mentor later on, when your Waymark has been revealed."

She paused. "There are other factors involved, of course. How well you can use your powers will depend on your innate mental strength, on the regularity of your Immersion practice and on how much you have to draw on the power of your Goldstone.

"Each Goldstone needs recharging once a year, at the festival of its Goddess. And you may have noticed a pillar made of the same substance in each settlement we've been through. These pillars are called Waystones and form a network of power throughout the Commonweal. Over most of the Commonweal, no-one is more than ten miles away from a Waystone. There is a First Waystone in each capital city, and they in turn are linked to the Golden Stone of Ranu in Ranusheim."

Shaunan stood. "That is quite enough for today. I will leave you to talk it over, and we will meet again tomorrow."

"Which Goldstone are you hoping for?" Abigail asked Jacob, once they were alone.

"That's easy. A Dagâran one, of course, to help me become a better smith. How about you?"

"I don't know… most of my life so far has been spent looking after the little ones and helping my mother, so perhaps I'll end up with a Garûnan one. Or perhaps a Lèniumen one – I used to love learning about herbs and their uses from her."

"I suppose we'll have to wait and see," Jacob said. "But I don't like the sound of some of their powers – what right has anyone to read another person's thoughts or feelings?"

"I know. That makes me uneasy too. But Shaunan did say that their use was regulated."

"That's easy for her to say," he scoffed, "but I bet they can bend the rules fast enough if they need to."

She looked shocked. "Surely not. If I've learned one thing about Shaunan, it's that she keeps her word."

"Yes, but Shaunan is only one Waymage. I wouldn't be at all surprised if some of the other Veylindréans are not as scrupulous as she is."

"We'll just have to be patient. We'll find out soon enough."

"Not soon enough for me."

"But I do like the idea of having some power to make a difference," Abigail said. "I had practically none at home."

Jacob's hackles were raised. "Why do you want power?"

Abigail shrugged. "I just do," she said. "I want to be able to make my own decisions, to help other people."

There was a determined set to her lips, which he hadn't seen before. This world was changing her and he didn't like it, not one bit. But he had the sense not to say anything. He didn't want another argument like yesterday's.

"I'll see you later," he said. "I'm going back to my room."

When Jacob returned to the room he shared with Aidren, he found him lying on his bed, one arm flung over his eyes.

"You look exhausted."

"Yes, it's been a hard day. Master Sanderon has been teaching us a new technique for sword fighting, and I ache all over."

"I'd like to learn how to use a sword. I have a feeling it may be useful here."

Aidren looked at him. "I could give you a few tips, if you'd like?"

Jacob felt a rush of gratitude. "That's very good of you. But I have only a knife."

"I'll see whether Master Sanderon can lend me a pair of practice swords. It would do me good, to be able to practice outside the Hall of Warriors."

How kind. Jacob felt the first stirrings of friendship towards the young Dagâran. "Thank you, Aidren."

Chapter 12

When Abigail and Jacob entered the common room a couple of mornings later, Shaunan was waiting for them. Three chairs were arranged around a low table on which a tall, yellow, beeswax candle stood.

"Come, join me," she said. "Today I am going to lead you through your first experience of Immersion."

"But how can we do that?" Jacob asked. "We don't have any Goldstones."

"Immersion is a spiritual practice to invoke a calm, meditative state of mind, which you can practice without a Goldstone."

She lit the candle with a single word, *tamen*, then sat back, a serene expression on her face. "Find a position that is comfortable for you, with your feet planted firmly on the floor, your backs straight, your hands in your lap, and close your eyes. I am going to invite you into the time of stillness and connection which we call Immersion in the Way. Then we will sit in silent contemplation for a few minutes. Do not worry if your mind fills with thoughts. Acknowledge them and let them go."

Abigail sat upright, closed her eyes. This was going to be interesting.

"First, concentrate on your breath… Each breath in, a breath of life… each breath out, a breath of love."

Abigail sank down into the silence. She had never thought about breathing before; it was something her body did with no help from her conscious mind. So nice, *each breath in a breath of life*. Wonder how Jacob's getting on… no, concentrate on the breath. *Each breath out, a breath of love.*

Shaunan spoke, slowly, quietly, leaving a period of silence between each short phrase. "The Way is all around us, and deep within us... It nourishes our souls… and helps us to grow into our best selves…. How should we live in the Way? … In our living, may we be grounded… In our thinking, may we be simple, leaning to the straightforward… In our conflict, may we be fair and generous, seeing the other person's viewpoint… In our work, may we do what feeds our hearts, to the best of our abilities… In our lives with family and friends, may we be completely present… In trusting the Way, may we find ourselves content, and not compete with, or compare ourselves to others."

Abigail began to understand what Shaunan meant, when she'd said that the Way was similar to God's presence in her life. The Waymage's words reminded her of the prayer her father had taught her… *each breath in, a breath of life.*

"…and now, come back to your breath, come back to yourself and, when you are ready, open your eyes."

Abigail sighed, then opened her eyes. She smiled at Shaunan. "That was wonderful – thank you. It felt so much like my father's prayer."

"Yes, hearing that gave me hope that you would be able to access the power of the Way."

Jacob shifted in his seat. "My mind was all over the place. Every time I tried to be still, another thought popped into my head."

"That is usual, at first. Do not be harsh on yourself, Jacob. These things take time. With regular practice, it will come."

He shrugged. "If you say so."

"I do say so," Shaunan's voice became a little sharper. "Please, Jacob, try not to resist it."

Abigail held her tongue, knowing that if she said anything, it would only antagonise him more.

"Jacob, I have some good news for you. An old friend of mine and Donan's from Nordvein is a master smith in Luvodican. His name is Kalen, and he is willing to let you work at his smithy for a couple of hours each morning. Luckily for us, he lives not far from the Temple. I will take you there in a moment and collect you later."

Jacob beamed, the first real smile she had seen on his face for far too long. "That is marvellous, Shaunan. Thank you! You have no idea what this means to me."

Abigail smiled at his enthusiasm. "See you later," she said. "I hope it goes well."

"How could it not? I can't wait."

Shaunan led Jacob, cloaked and hooded, through the streets of Luvodican. Jacob strode out, happy to be outside the confines of the Temple.

"Here we are," the Waymage said, as they turned into a narrow street, lined with shops and workshops. "I will introduce you to Kalen, then return to Abigail."

"Thank you."

They walked into the smithy. Jacob breathed in the familiar smells of fire and hot metal and felt at home straight away. A tall and broad man, his face ruddy from the heat of the forge, his leather apron marked with old burns from flying sparks, turned and nodded at them.

"Master Kalen," Shaunan said. "This is Jacob. He was a smith in his old life and would like to learn more from you."

Kalen's face split in a friendly smile. "Welcome, young man," he said in a deep voice.

"Thank you, sir," Jacob said, smiling back. He was itching to feel the tools in his hands once more.

"I will leave you now and return in a couple of hours," Shaunan said.

"Thank you, Waymage."

As soon as she had gone, Kalen spoke, "Let us see what you know. The Waymage says you are a smith?"

Jacob nodded. "Yes, sir."

"Master Kalen will do," the man said. "What experience do you have?"

"My father is the smith in our village," Jacob said. "I have been his apprentice for the past few years. We mainly worked with farming tools and shoeing horses."

Kalen nodded. "Here we work more with crafting weapons, and metal items for use in the home. Have you done that?"

"Not weapons, si… Master Kalen. But I'd like to try."

Kalen clapped him on the shoulder. "Good. I have been working on a carving knife for the kitchens of Lord Lesym and Lady Bélia. I have done the first shaping, but it needs refining. You start," and he handed him the knife," and I will watch you."

Jacob's heart was racing – he couldn't wait to hold smithing tools in his hands again.

"You'll need this," Kalen continued, giving him a spare leather apron, "and some tools. What would you choose for this work?"

Jacob grinned. Kalen's questions reminded him of his father testing his knowledge. "The hammer and anvil first, tongs, of course, then a file."

The man gave him an approving nod. "I will stoke the fire with the bellows."

Jacob picked up the hammer lying by the anvil and set to work. It felt wonderful to be working at his craft once more.

“Abigail,” Shaunan said when she returned, “it is time to test your powers.”

She noted the girl’s look of surprise. But now was the time, with Jacob out of the way, to see whether Abigail had the powers she, Shaunan, suspected she did.

“Sit at ease and let your mind drift. I am going to put a picture in your mind. Tell me what you see.”

Abigail closed her eyes. Blessed Ranu, help her to see. Shaunan projected a picture to her, mind-to-mind.

“There is a beautiful tree, tall and broad,” Abigail said, “with a copper trunk and golden-green star-shaped leaves, like the one we saw in the centre of the square in Nordvein. I think you call it the Ranus tree. It is in the centre of a courtyard surrounded by tall, white buildings with many windows glinting in the sun. Each building has a flag flying out front, flapping in the wind, with a symbol on it in gold on a dark background. I think it is the symbol of Ranu. And… wherever it is, you love it.”

“Good, Abigail, very good. You saw clearly.”

“But how could that happen? I’m no Waymage.”

Sensing the girl’s unease, Shaunan transmitted reassurance. “Fear not. I had hoped for this. As soon as I touched you in the forest at Nordvein, I suspected you might have great power. There is a reason you are here, Abigail, although it may not yet be clear to you.”

Shaunan watched her think about it, plaiting her fingers in her lap. She sensed the moment when the girl’s resistance began to fade. “Do not worry. It will all make sense, in the end.”

"Are you reading my thoughts?" Abigail said, suspicion in her voice, "I thought you said you weren't going to do that."

"I am not," Shaunan assured her. "Your body language shows your unease. Please try to accept this power. It will work only for good."

A deep and searching look. Shaunan kept her mind open, radiating trust and calming thoughts. She saw the girl's shoulders relax.

"All right, but what does it mean?"

"It means your Waymark will probably be Ranusian. Only those with Ranusian powers are able to read the minds of others. Now try to share a picture with me."

"I'm not sure I want to…" Panic unconsciously transmitted from the girl flooded the Waymage's mind. She was strong, this one.

Shaunan kept her voice soft and even. "There is nothing for you to fear. I promise you, by the Six and by the Way."

Abigail took a deep breath, then closed her eyes. An image came into Shaunan's mind, fuzzy at first, then sharper as the girl began to settle down, to relax into the process. "It is a medium-sized room, with a table laid for a meal at its centre. The cupboards and dresser around the walls are made from a light brown wood. There are people sitting around the table – a tall man with fire in his eyes, choler in his countenance. This must be your father. At the other end of the table, a woman with gentleness and clarity in her expression – your mother. And at the sides, three children. The eldest is his father in miniature but without his anger. The little ones are sweet and untouched by cares."

Abigail burst into tears. "Yes, my family, as I remember them. Why did they have to die?" She buried her face in her hands and sobbed.

Shaunan took the weeping girl into her arms. When her grief had run its course, she gently released her.

"Oh, Shaunan! It hurts so much to think about them."

"I know. Losing those we love always hurts so very much. But you will come through this. You are stronger than you think."

Abigail blew her nose and sat back. "I hope you're right. At the moment, it is hard to bear."

"That is natural. It has only been a few short seisdags since you lost them. Now, my dear, I ask you to keep the revelation of your new power to yourself for the present. The proper time for sharing it will come soon enough at the Ceremony of Assignment. But we will work together in the meantime to bring it out."

"Why do I have to keep it a secret?"

"Think about it. Imagine how Jacob might react to knowing you have the power to read his mind."

Abigail's face drained of colour, her hands flew to her mouth. "Oh, God! I hadn't thought of that. He wouldn't trust me anymore."

"I fear not. We will have to think of a way of persuading him to accept it before the Ceremony. It is time for me to collect him now. I will leave you to reflect on all you have learned."

Abigail's mind was in a whirl. Her Waymark would be of Ranu. *First there was Ranu, Great Mother of all.* If all went well, she would become a Waymage, like Shaunan. But how could that be? She wasn't even from Veylindré. How could she, an English girl from another world, become a Waymage? Would they accept her? She had so much to learn.

Hiding it from Jacob seemed wrong. Like a betrayal. But she could understand why Shaunan was advising discretion. At home she would have been burned as a witch. Yet she could sense no evil in this power. Oh, this was so confusing.

Her faith and upbringing were telling her one thing, her lived experience another. And Jacob was having enough trouble accepting the Way as it was, without finding out that she was going to have power in this world – more power than him, probably.

That wasn't going to go down well. She put her head in her hands. Why had this happened to her? Breathe, Abigail, breathe. She sat upright, as Shaunan had advised, and began once more to follow her breath. After a few minutes she was calm, ready to see him again.

Jacob burst into the room, full of excitement. "It was brilliant, Abi! It was wonderful to be working with my hands again."

She smiled. "Tell me all about it."

"Master Kalen is a really skilled smith. After asking me some questions to test my knowledge of the craft, he let me work on a carving knife he's making for the kitchens of Lord Lesym and Lady Bélia. Then he showed me some of his prize pieces. I've never seen work that good before. I could learn much from him."

He was so much happier, better than he had been for ages. Working with his hands again obviously agreed with him. He walked over to her, gave her a big hug.

She hugged him back and smiled. "When will you be seeing him again?"

"Shaunan is going to take me back tomorrow. All being well, I'm going to work there for a couple of hours every day, except for Ranusdag, which seems to be like their Sunday."

"I'm so pleased for you. I know how much you've missed practicing your craft."

He beamed. "You're right there. I feel… whole again."

"That's good."

"What were you doing while I was away?"

"Oh, Shaunan shared some more of the lore of Veylindré with me."

"Rather you than me," he grinned. "I've enjoyed this morning so much more, having got out of here. I was so fed up with being cooped up in these rooms."

"That is so beautiful," Abigail said, admiring the soft, dark brown leather, which Ellyn was burnishing to a shine. "What is it going to be?"

"Aunt Shaunan has asked me to make a new healer's bag for her. Hers is getting shabby. Master Markhan is allowing me to do it as my journeywoman piece. I've spent the last couple of seisdags designing it, then choosing the leather and cutting it out. I'm planning to include a number of compartments inside so Aunt Shaunan can find everything more easily."

"I'm sure she'll love it. What are you doing at the moment?"

"I'm using beeswax to make it both shiny and waterproof. It takes a lot of work to apply it evenly so that the colour is uniform."

"It's going to be gorgeous. Shaunan is so lucky."

Ellyn blushed.

"This morning," Shaunan said on her return from Kalen's workshop the next day, "I am going to explain some of the limitations of using Waymagic."

"Limitations?" Abigail said. "I thought you could do practically anything with it."

"Far from it. Although our Goldstones give us certain powers, there are physical, mental and ethical limitations to using them."

"I know the powers of the various Goldstones differ, so I'm guessing that's why people need training after the Ceremony of Assignment…"

"Yes, but there is far more to it than that," Shaunan said. "You remember I told you there are three levels of training for each power – initiate, adept and mage? The Ceremony of Assignment unlocks the innate power of the initiate but training, regular Immersion and a great deal of practice are required if the initiate is to progress to becoming an adept and later a mage."

She watched Abigail think about this. "So unless new initiates are properly trained and practice regularly, things can go wrong?"

"Absolutely," Shaunan nodded. "The practice of Immersion in the Way helps the new initiate to attune themselves to their Goldstone and to access its powers. Mental strength is necessary to use Waymagic and regular Immersion helps to cultivate this. It also helps if our bodies are feeling strong and well-rested. You will find it more difficult to call on your powers if you are tired or stressed."

"I remember you saying something about Lèniumen healers burning out if they try to do too much healing, all at once."

"That is right, and that applies to all forms of Waymagic. You should also know that your Goldstone will need re-charging once a year at one of the First Waystones. So towards Ranustide – if your Waymark is Ranusian, as I think it will be – it will be more difficult for you to use your powers effectively. Do you remember Aidren saying something like that in the cave at the top of the Myner's Gap?"

Abigail shook her head. "I'm sorry, no. Why do they have to be re-charged?"

"Have you heard of the Bloodstone of Talamu?"

"No, only of Goldstones. What is the Bloodstone? And who is Talamu?"

"When Ranu and the other Goddesses created the world and the Way and the peoples of Veylindré, they also caused the Waystones and Goldstones to be made and placed the Waystones at intervals all over the Commonweal, to allow their people access to the Waymagic."

She paused. Perhaps it was time.

"I had not told you this before, but in the beginning, there were seven Goddesses, not six. The seventh was Talamu, the eldest of the six daughters of Ranu. She was jealous of the power of her siblings, wanting to be first and greatest in Ranu's heart. But Ranu loved her daughters equally.-

"Talamu could not understand that Ranu's heart was big enough to love them all. Her own heart grew dark, and she turned against her mother and her sisters. She pitted her will against them, seeking to control everything and everyone. Eventually the Six pooled their own powers and banished her to Talamdor. In the heart of Mount Talamu, she fashioned a Bloodstone to use against the Six and against Veylindré. With its aid, she began to suck the power from the Golden Stone of Ranu and from the Waystones.

"Many centuries ago, all the peoples of Veylindré rose up to defeat her and it was thought that the Bloodstone had been destroyed during the conflict. So for long centuries, it was only necessary to re-charge our personal Goldstones once a decade.

But about thirty or so years ago, the Prophet of the One came to Talamdor and we fear he may have found the Bloodstone.

"In the last three decades, the power of the Golden Stone of Ranu and the First Waystones, and hence of the whole network of local Waystones, has begun to wane, in spite of all the efforts of the Wayzenmoot. This decrease in the power of the Way has become so severe, we have to re-charge our Goldstones once a year during the festival of our Goldstone's goddess. The power of the Way, on which we rely, has become more difficult to draw on. It is vital the Bloodstone is found and destroyed."

"Where is it now?"

"We believe it is in the possession of the Prophet of the One in the far land of Talamdor."

"Wait a moment," Abigail said. "Wasn't the stone Jacob found on that man's body a Bloodstone?"

This girl from another world was quick.

"I fear it might be. I had no idea there was more than one, that it was possible to make Bloodstones for individuals. But it seems the Prophet of the One has found a way. This means the original Bloodstone of Talamu is now a Master Bloodstone. It has similar power to our own Golden Stone of Ranu. Which is why you should tell no-one about it. It means the Talamdorians are moving against us."

"Where is Talamdor?"

"It lies to the south-west of Néartania," Shaunan said. "After the ancient war, the Néartanians and Yrusians, who share a border with it, built a series of forts at strategic locations. They linked these locations with a wall on our side of the Talamdor Range. The Range forms the border between Néartania, Yrusian and Talamdor.

"I believe that once the Wayzenmoot have heard your story and seen the Bloodstone you bear, they will mount an expedition to destroy the Master Bloodstone. If they do not, the power of our Goldstones will continue to wane until we can no longer work our Waymagic for the good of all Veylindré."

"Why are you telling me all this?"

A wave of certainty rolled over Shaunan, like a message from Ranu herself. Her voice rang out in the quiet room, taking on the cadences of prophecy, even in her own ears. "I also believe that your coming to the Commonweal of Veylindré is no accident. I believe you have been given special powers by the Six and will play a central role in the destruction of the Master Bloodstone."

Abigail went white. "But… but how can that be? I'm not even *from* your world, from Veylindré. I'm not anyone special…"

"I sensed your power when I healed you in the forest near Nordvein. I will be with you, to help you. Once the Festival of Dagâra is over, we must travel to Ranusheim to discover the will of the Wayzenmoot."

"But what about Jacob?"

"He will come too. I would not separate the pair of you."

Abigail relaxed. Good. Time for a change of subject. "I have not yet told you about the ethical limitations of using Waymagic."

"Ethical limitations?"

"Since the power of our Goldstones has begun to diminish and they have needed re-charging more frequently, it has become easier for the unscrupulous to abuse the system. For example, some people choose to make significant purchases in the seisdags immediately before Yrusiastide, when the

Yrusians' Waymarks are at their weakest, which makes the traders easier to bargain with.

"Abuse of the Waymagic of Empathy can lead to undue influence on another. And although Lèniumen healers take an Oath of Healing to prevent abuse of their powers and are the most ethical of our people, Veylindréans dread falling ill or having an accident in the seisdags leading up to Lèniastide, when the powers of the healers have diminished."

"What happens if they are found out?"

"If misuse of Waymagic is suspected, the miscreant is tried in a special courtroom in the nearest City Watch House, which is shielded using the wood of the Ranus tree. This not only prevents the illegitimate use of Waymagic, but also strengthens the powers of the Watch officers to discern the truth."

"It all sounds so complicated," Abigail said. "I'm not sure I'll ever get it clear in my mind."

"It takes time, yes, but I'm sure you will be strong in the Way."

Chapter 13

One evening, when Shaunan was away on Waymage business concerning the upcoming Festival, Abigail and the others were relaxing around the fire in their common room. Abigail felt warm and comfortable, and surprisingly at home here. She could sense the beginnings of real friendship between the four of them – the two young Veylindréans, herself and Jacob.

"Tell us about your training," she said to Aidren. "You know what we've been doing, but you haven't told us much about what you've been learning."

"All right," he said. "If you really want to know."

"Yes, I'd be fascinated," she said.

"Me, too," Jacob agreed.

"As Jacob knows," Aidren began, "I've been training each day with Master Gildon's sword-master, Master Sanderon. To look at him, you wouldn't think he was anyone special – he's small, quite thin, and old – older than my father. But by the Six! He can fight." Aidren's dark eyes were glowing with enthusiasm. Abigail had never seen him so animated. "I have never known anyone like him. He's taught me new fighting techniques – not only with the sword, but also how to watch my opponent, so I can read their next move before they make it. It's hard work and I spent more time on my back than on my feet at first. But I can feel I'm improving. And it will be easier once my Goldstone has been recharged at the Festival. It's hard to draw on its power at the moment."

"That sounds wonderful," Jacob said. "I almost wish I could go with you, but I wouldn't miss my hours with Master Kalen for anything."

"Oh, it is," Aidren said. "But at least I'll be able to carry on honing my skills on our journey, thanks to you, Jacob. Master Sanderon gave me the practice swords today."

"That's excellent news," Jacob said, to Abigail's dismay. "I'm looking forward to learning how to use a sword as well as craft one."

"How about you, Ellyn?" Abigail said, hurriedly changing the subject. "What have you been learning?"

Ellyn smiled. "It's been marvellous being apprenticed to Master Markhan. Master Raimun, back in Nordvein, had covered the basics of leatherworking with me, but Master Markhan has been teaching me some more advanced skills, like how to stamp leather with patterns, and special stitches for sewing Dagâran riding clothes together. Like Aidren, I've learned heaps. I'm going to miss my time with him."

They all looked at each other and sighed. Whatever happened after Dagârastide, these quiet seisdags of learning and training would be over soon.

And so the time passed. Each morning, Abigail and Jacob practiced Immersion with Ellyn and Aidren. Then, once Jacob had left the Temple, cloaked and hooded, to learn more smithcraft from Kalen, Abigail was inducted into the lore of Veylindré by Shaunan. As she began to grow in confidence, and to learn more about the Commonweal and the Way, Abigail began to feel more at home.

"Shaunan," she said one day, "I'm beginning to understand how I will be able to follow the Way but still remain a Christian."

"That is good to hear. Tell me more."

"The key to accessing the power of the Way seems to be Immersion," she glanced at her mentor and received a nod of approval, "and I've found I can still pray to God through Jesus, but also revere Ranu." She paused. "I can't believe I'm saying that. If I was back home now, I'd be put to death for witchcraft. But I cannot discern any evil in the Way."

"I am glad to hear it, Abigail, because there is none. Ranu would not expect you to relinquish your faith – it is part of what makes you, you. How is Jacob getting on?"

"I'm not sure. He seems to be willing to use the power of the Way to help him become a better smith, but I'm not sure he reveres Dagâra or any of the Six."

Shaunan frowned. "Then let us hope his faith in the power of the Way will suffice. I must fetch him now."

When she returned with Jacob, Shaunan said, "The Festival of Dagârastide will commence on the evening of this coming Dagârsdag, continue all the way through Néartasdag and finish in the evening of Ranusdag. It is time to prepare you both for what will happen. It is clear that Jacob's Waymark will be that of a Dagâran smith – I have had a good report of your work from Kalen," she smiled at him, "and Abigail, I am sure your Waymark will be of Ranu."

"I hope so, Shaunan," Abigail said, blushing. "That's what I want, more than almost anything."

"Almost anything?"

"What I want most of all is to be with Jacob."

Dagârastide, the Festival of All Souls, began when the moon rose on the tenth Dagârsdag of the Season of Completion. Abigail was both nervous and excited. Ellyn and Aidren took her and Jacob to the huge Square of Dagâra, outside the imposing palace of Lord Lesym and Lady Bélia, to watch the lighting of the ceremonial fire in front of the tall First

Waystone of Dagâra. Shaunan, naturally, was with the other Waymages.

"The fire will be lit when the moon and the Six are visible in the night sky," Ellyn explained. "It marks the beginning of Dagârastide and will be kept alight until moonrise on Ranusdag, the last day of the year."

"What?" Abigail exclaimed. "The Six appear in a vision?"

Ellyn laughed. "No, it is a group of stars we call the Six – five stars grouped around one very bright one."

"Now I understand."

Ellyn scanned the darkening sky, then pointed, "There. Do you see them?"

Abigail followed her friend's pointing finger by standing behind her right shoulder. It was hard to spot a particular group of stars if you didn't have a known shape to look for, like the Plough at home. Then she had it. "Ah, yes! I see them."

She gazed at them in fierce concentration, trying to fix their configuration in her memory. And felt the by-now familiar swoop in her stomach. Another reminder of how very far from home she and Jacob had come.

She was so glad he was there with her.

Folk from outlying villages and towns crowded into the city of Luvodican with their friends and families. Every inn, every lodging house was full. The company were grateful for their rooms in the Visitors' Hall of the Temple.

"Do all the people of Dagâran come to Luvodican for Dagârastide?" Abigail said, as the crowd milled around. She had never seen so many people in one place at the same time.

"Many will make the journey," Aidren said. "It is considered lucky to celebrate the Festival at Luvodican, but most will observe it in their nearest city or large town. So there will be festivities in Myndorian, for example, at Fionnan in the far south of Dagâran and in other towns."

It was a cold evening with a light wind. Abigail was shivering in spite of her warm cloak.

"We'll be warm enough soon," Ellyn said, smiling at her, "and witnessing the lighting of the ceremonial fire is worth a few shivers."

"You've seen it before?" Jacob said. "I thought this was your first visit to Luvodican."

"It is, but Aunt Shaunan has often taken me to the festivals at Myndorian."

"Here they come," Aidren said, pointing across the square to a procession of Waymages, wearing their topaz-yellow robes and belts of interwoven gold, their brooches glittering in the moonlight.

"I can't see Shaunan," Abigail said.

"There she is, the third from the front," Aidren said. "Shush now, they're about to begin."

Once the Waymages had positioned themselves in a great circle around the stack of wood waiting to be lighted, arms outstretched, heads bowed in silent respect, First Waymage Marinden raised her arms. A hush fell on the assembled people.

"Holy Dagâra, Goddess of War and Metalworking, we gather at the end of the Season of Completion to honour you. All year long, you have given us your aid and enabled us to follow the Way of Veylindré with faith and courage. May your Festival be a time of remembrance, rejoicing and renewal."

In unison, the other Waymages responded, "So may it be."

Everyone present echoed their words. A thrill ran through Abigail's body.

Marinden took an unlit torch from a temple servant, pronounced the words of fire summoning, "*Belannath Dagâra, gal lo bynn tanem,*" and the end of the torch burst into flame. She thrust it into the heart of the gathered wood. The fire kindled swiftly and sent flames and sparks high into the night air.

A sigh compounded of awe and wonder went up from the waiting people. Then what seemed like a thousand conversations broke out at once, the air humming with the sound of human voices.

"That was… special," Abigail said. "What happens now?"

"Now we feast!" Aidren said, his eyes gleaming.

He led them to an adjacent square, filled with trestle tables with long wooden benches on each side of them. Around the edges, there were stalls serving food and drink.

"Jacob, come with me" Aidren said. "Ellyn, you and Abigail find us somewhere to sit."

Ellyn nodded. "Come along, Abigail."

The tables were filling up fast, so the girls were lucky to find four seats together. A man in a weather-beaten cloak was sitting at the table next to them. His clothing and bright red hair marked him as Garûnalonden but the expression on his face was sour. He did not seem to be with the other people at the table.

Abigail shivered; she didn't like the look of him at all. Turning to Ellyn, she said in a low voice, "Do you see the man on the next table? I wonder what he's so fed up about?"

As Ellyn glanced over, the man drew up his hood, and Abigail got the strong feeling he wanted to evade notice.

"I see what you mean," she whispered, "but he seems harmless enough."

At that moment, Jacob and Aidren returned, laden down with four plates, four goblets, a jug of mulled wine, and platters of food. There were roasted meats, bowls of fragrant rice and vegetables, and smaller dishes containing red, orange and green sauces. And a platter of small honey cakes, a festival treat.

Aidren handed out the pewter plates. "Help yourselves. Tonight we feast in honour of the Goddess."

"What are the sauces?" Abigail asked, filling her plate.

"The red," Ellyn said, "is a mixture of tomatoes and roasted peppers, the orange is carrot, flavoured with ginger and turmeric, and the green is hot, chock-full of spices from southern Néartania."

"Apart from carrots, I've never tried any of those," Abigail said. "Maybe I'd better have a small taste first."

Soon each of them had a laden plate of food and a goblet of mulled wine.

"Is the training still going well?" Jacob asked.

"It's been fantastic," Ellyn said. "I've learned so much from Master Markhan and the other apprentices."

"Yes," Aidren said, "it's been an education, learning how to use the power of my Goldstone in new ways and how to fight more effectively. How about you? Are you ready for the Ceremony of Assignment?"

"Like you," Jacob nodded at Aidren, "I've learned so much from Master Kalen. I can't wait to have a Goldstone of my own so that I can apply what I've learned to my craft."

Thank goodness. Jacob was finally accepting the Way. Abigail squeezed his hand.

"How about you, Abigail?" Ellyn asked.

"Oh yes, Shaunan has taught me so much about the Way and about Veylindré. But I still feel nervous about the Ceremony. What if the First Waymage finds us unworthy?"

Aidren's brow furrowed. "I've never heard of that happening before. But there again," he grinned at them both, "I've never known any people from a different world."

"Oh, I'm sure Aunt Shaunan would not let that happen," Ellyn said. "She wouldn't allow you to undertake the Ceremony unless she thought you were both ready."

Even so, Abigail could not help feeling anxious. Shaunan had explained the Ceremony to her, and it sounded simple enough. But she was glad it came at the end of the Festival. She wanted to experience the rest of it first. Maybe then she would feel more ready to become an initiate of Ranu. She was looking forward to being able to walk around with the hood of her cloak down. The necessity of concealment had become burdensome.

"Let's find the storytellers," Aidren said. "You are in for a treat."

Abigail, Jacob and Ellyn followed as he threaded his way through the crowds towards an amphitheatre a little way out of the city centre. As they approached, Abigail could hear the resonant sounds of musical instruments and the hum of voices, rising and falling.

When they reached the place, they saw a large stage set up in the centre, on which stood a group of people in bright, multi-coloured costumes. Some were playing instruments – Abigail could see a zither, a guitar and pipes of various kinds. Others were declaiming a story, acting it out as they went along. A couple of minutes later, the crowd in the tiered seats surrounding the stage applauded – the story had finished.

"Thank you, my friends!" said a striking man in a purple and red striped costume with a tall, fantastically decorated hat on his head. "Thank you for listening to our tale. If it moved you, please give generously on your way out. We will now take a short break before our next story."

"Do you want to wait for the next performance?" Aidren said as the people made their way out of the square. "If we stay now, we'll get good seats."

"Yes, please," Abigail said. "I've never been to anything like this before. My father," she paused, remembering once again all she had lost, "my father did not approve of such things. So we were never allowed to go."

"Whyever not?" Ellyn asked.

"Oh, he thought they were frivolous, and distracted people from the worship of God."

"How strange," Aidren said. "Here, we listen to the storytellers to learn about the Six and the world we live in."

They found seats half-way up the tiers, facing the front of the stage.

"I wonder which story they'll tell," Ellyn said.

"What kind of stories do they tell?" Jacob asked.

"All kinds," Aidren said. "About the Six, about the history of Veylindré, about glorious quests and daring deeds, that sort of thing."

"I'm looking forward to it," Abigail said.

A few minutes later, the man in the red and purple outfit came back on to the stage. "Ladies and gentlemen! Welcome to our show. The Dagâran Players are proud to present *The Tale of the Seventh Goddess.*"

"The *seventh* Goddess?" Jacob said over the crowd's applause, "I thought you only had six?"

"We do," Aidren said. "Wait and see. This tale explains why."

"Long ago, when our world was young, Great Mother Ranu gave birth to six daughters. She gave to each a people – farmers and crafters to Néarta; smiths and warriors to Dagâra; healers, musicians and storytellers," and here he bowed, "to Lènia; those who wished to serve others, to Garûna; traders, travellers and seafarers, to Yrusia; and governors and stewards to Talamu, her eldest daughter. She kept for herself those who followed the paths of wisdom and lore."

Abigail watched, fascinated, as players representing each Goddess came on to the stage and bowed low to the audience. They wore beautiful painted masks on their faces and were dressed in long, flowing robes of various colours. Néarta's were every shade of brown, from amber to darkest mahogany. Dagâra's were rich, warm hues of red and orange, scarlet, crimson, maroon, tangerine, flame and apricot. Lènia's were every kind of purple, from lavender and lilac to mulberry and dark amethyst. Garûna's were all the shades of green, from those found in nature to brilliant emerald and dark malachite. Yrusia's were every tone of blue, from darkest navy through ultramarine and sky-blue to palest aquamarine. Ranu's were yellow and gold, from palest primrose to the deep gold of honey.

But the robes of Talamu, the seventh Goddess, the one Shaunan had told her about, were of one shade – a dark, midnight black. Abigail's gaze seemed to fall into it. The robes reflected nothing back. She found the contrast with the brightly coloured robes of the others uneasy.

"Each Goddess bestowed particular powers on her people to help them to use their gifts wisely and well," the narrator continued. "In time, all people came to be marked with a special symbol on their foreheads and were given Goldstones to enable them to access their powers."

As the story unfolded, the various players enacted it on the stage. Abigail was entranced. She wondered whether they were using Empathy to enchant their listeners. Probably.

"And so the years passed, and Veylindré grew in peace and contentment. The inhabitants were diligent in learning to access the power of the Way and to serve their Goddesses. The results were prosperity and peace.

"Talamu alone was not content. The power given to her people to rule and govern others did not satisfy her ambition. Darkness grew in her heart, and she was jealous of the power of her mother, Ranu. She desired to rule the whole world of Veylindré and to strip away the powers of her sisters and mother. Quietly, in secret, she laid her plans and gathered an army of those who were likewise discontented with their places in Veylindré in the remote land of Talamdor.

"And in the deepest forges of Mount Talamu, she shaped a Bloodstone, a weapon to leech the power from all the Goldstones and Waystones of Veylindré.

"When the time seemed right to her, her army marched to the border of Talamdor and invaded Néartania. The Néartanians were unprepared. The slaughter was immense. One brave Waymage sent a despairing message to the Isle of Ranu. The Wayzenmoot called on all the peoples of Veylindré to rise up and expel their enemies. After a long and bitter war, a seasoned Dagâran warrior named Balon led his troops to the very borders of Talamdor. There the forces of evil were vanquished. And it was thought that the Bloodstone had been destroyed. Talamu herself was diminished and fled to her mountain fastnesses to lick her wounds.

"The Six combined their powers to raise the Mountains of Talamdor, to keep her out of the Commonweal. The people of Veylindré, sadder and wiser, built a series of forts in Néartania and Yrusian along the length of these mountains, to keep watch on this new border. They withdrew their worship from Talamu, vowing to worship only the Six. The people of Garûna, those who lived to serve others, were given governance in the stead of the Talamdorians. And they have ruled wisely and well, seeking to serve and enable, rather than to dominate the hearts and minds of others. And so the centuries passed, and our world recovered.

"If my tale has pleased you, give generously on your way out."

As he gave a florid bow, the audience burst into applause.

Ellyn turned to Abigail. "Wasn't that amazing?"

"Yes, it really was. Thank you for taking us." But she wondered why people didn't seem to know about the finding of the Bloodstone by the Prophet. Perhaps it was a secret only known to the followers of Ranu. She must ask Shaunan.

The second day of the Festival started with a more solemn purpose.

The people of Luvodican gathered in reverent silence at the First Waystone to remember and to pay their respects to the family members and friends who had died during the previous year. Abigail's eyes flooded with tears as she remembered her fellow pilgrims, who had set out from England with such high hopes, only to be slaughtered by the Havimi.

Jacob stood beside her, his face grim, his own eyes wet. He put his arm around her. "We will avenge them, my love."

"I do not see how. We do not know who killed our people."

His other fist bunched in frustration. "There must be a way."

They returned to the Temple to eat some lunch.

Ellyn said, "Would you like to watch the handfasting of all the couples who have come through the Season of Proving? It is a joyous occasion."

Abigail smiled at her. "Yes, I would." She was curious to see how the actual ceremony would compare with what Shaunan had told her in Myndorian.

The four of them returned to the amphitheatre where they had watched the storytellers the previous day. It was already more than half full. By the appointed time, there was not a seat empty.

After a musical fanfare, a group of Waymages, clad in their fine topaz-yellow robes, each with a golden circlet on his or her hair, came out onto the stage.

"Look! There's Aunt Shaunan," Ellyn whispered.

Abigail nodded, her eyes on the spectacle below, her hand clasping Jacob's.

First Waymage Marinden raised her hands. The crowd became quiet. Into the silence, she said, "Friends and followers of the Way! We are met here at the Festival of Dagârastide to celebrate the handfasting of seventeen couples who have completed the Season of Proving in the last ten seisdags. You are here to witness this happy event. Hold them in your hearts as they share their vows."

The first couple came out through two doors at the base of the amphitheatre – the woman from one, the man from the other. The woman was wearing a beautiful dress which had long sleeves and a fitted bodice, then hung from just below her breasts and dropped to mid-calf in graduated shades of green.

The man wore a white tunic, dark red breeches and highly polished boots.

"The colour of the dress means she has a Garûnan Waymark," Ellyn whispered, "and the man's breeches mean he's a Warrior of Dagâra, like Aidren."

Abigail nodded her thanks for the information and returned her attention to the young couple.

They came together in front of the Waymages.

Waymage Findoran from Myndorian stepped forward. She smiled. "Haldor and Janissan, you have completed the Season of Proving. Do you wish to be handfasted in the presence of this company?"

"I do," said, Haldor, the young man, in a gruff voice.

Janissan's clear, high voice rang out across the space: "I do."

Moving forward, Findoran joined Haldor's left hand to Janissan's right with a golden cord, then she stepped back.

"As the sun brings light to our world of Veylindré, do you, Haldor and Janissan, vow to bring the light of love and joy to your union?"

"I do," they said in unison.

"And do you vow to honour each other as you honour the Way which we all hold sacred?"

"I do."

"Repeat the Vow of Handfasting after me."

They nodded.

Turning to the young woman, Findoran led her through the words.

"I, Janissan, promise to love you, Haldor, to honour you, comfort you and keep you. I promise to be by your side in sickness and in health, in times of want and times of plenty, for better, for worse, for the rest of our lives. I vow to share my life and the Way with you, now and always."

Then Findoran addressed the young man. When both had completed their vows, she raised her eyes to the assembled gathering, and said in a loud, clear voice, "Let all bear witness that Haldor and Janissan are joined in love and joy and freedom, and in the power of the Way. May their love be secure and true, and may they grow together in wisdom, peace and harmony."

The crowd rose as one and shouted, "So may it be, today and always."

Once everyone had sat down, Findoran waited for silence, then turned back to Janissan and Haldor, and raised her hands in benediction. "My own blessing, and the blessing of all those assembled here be with you. The blessing of the Six be with you and with all that flows from your union. May their peace be with you, may their spirit live within you, may their love wrap around you, today and always."

Then, turning once again to the gathering, she said, "Haldor and Janissan have been joined in the presence of you all. May their union be blessed."

And again, the crowd answered, "So may it be."

The newly-handfasted couple moved to one side, and it was time for the next couple to be joined.

Abigail turned to Ellyn, with tears in her eyes. "That was so beautiful," she breathed. "I hope Jacob and I can be handfasted one day."

As the various Waymages worked their way through the couples, Abigail whispered to Ellyn, "What happens next?"

"There will be a marriage feast this evening, hosted by all the couples involved and their families. New songs will be sung, and the couples will teach new dances."

"It sounds so much more fun than our marriage rites," Abigail said.

Ellyn hushed her. "Tell me later. The next couple are coming through the doors."

To Abigail's and Jacob's astonishment, the next two to be handfasted were men. Abigail was bursting with questions but had to wait until the ritual was complete.

"Are men allowed to be handfasted in Veylindré?"

"Yes," Aidren said, "and women too."

Jacob gaped at him. "You don't consider it sinful, for two people of the same sex to lie together?"

"Why should we?" Aidren said, his brow furrowing. "So long as they love each other, why shouldn't they share their lives?"

"Our Bible teaches that it is a sin," Abigail said.

Jacob said nothing, his mouth set in a straight line.

Aidren shrugged, then turned his attention back to the ceremony.

When the last couple had been handfasted, the horns rang out again and the newly joined couples processed around the amphitheatre to the applause of all.

"Now we feast!" Ellyn said.

Chapter 14

The final day of Dagârastide could not come soon enough for Abigail.

In the morning, she watched as the hundreds of Veylindréans with a Dagâran Waymark, Aidren included, lined up at the First Waystone of Dagâra, glittering golden in the morning light, to recharge their personal Goldstones. According to Ellyn, it would take all morning and into the early afternoon.

By which time, the three of them had returned to their lodgings in the Temple, to meet Shaunan.

"You must change," Shaunan said, "into your Ceremony of Assignment outfits as soon as you have eaten."

"I'm so glad I've earned enough guilders from Kalen to buy them for us," Jacob murmured to Abigail. "I've had enough of relying on the bounty of others."

"Thank you, Jacob. Hopefully we'll both be earning soon."

"Hmph," he said.

The clothes were laid out for them in their rooms. Abigail admired the long-sleeved white dress, fitting tightly to her elbows, then flowing out to her wrists. It had a demure neckline, for which she was grateful, fitted to the waist, and then a full skirt, dropping to mid-calf. The buttons were all at the back, so she asked Ellyn to help her. Fine woollen hose, also in white, and a pair of soft leather shoes completed the outfit.

"You look lovely," Ellyn said. "Would you like me to help you with your hair? You should wear it up for the Ceremony."

"Yes, please, that would be kind of you. There's so much of it, I find it hard to do alone."

Ellyn brushed the golden mass until it was smooth, then plaited it into two long braids, which she swept up and pinned into a neat coronet on Abigail's head. It reminded her of all the times she and Mercy had done a similar service for each other. Don't go there.

"There," Ellyn said, "you look beautiful."

Abigail hugged her. "Thank you, my friend."

The girls returned to the living-room where Shaunan, Jacob and Aidren were awaiting them.

Jacob's eyes glowed when he saw her. "This looks like a bridal," he said, hugging her, his eyes full of love.

He looked so handsome. A dark brown jerkin, with tight breeches in the same shade, a simple white linen shirt open at the neck and a pair of knee-high boots of russet brown leather.

"Abigail, Jacob," Shaunan said, "you will be the last to have your Waymarks assigned. We thought it best to allow the younger candidates to go first."

"Why?" Abigail asked.

"Because your vows will be slightly different from theirs, as they will include allegiance to the Christian God as well as the Six. We do not want to risk upsetting the rest of the Ceremony by this innovation."

"Thank you, Shaunan," Jacob said. "You have no idea what that means to me, to us."

Abigail nodded. How good of Shaunan. She must have had to do some fast talking to persuade the other Waymages.

"Make sure you keep your cloaks on and your hoods up until it is time."

Shaunan led them to the amphitheatre, which was half-filled with the families and friends of the young people participating in the Ceremony. She showed them where to wait, in an anteroom behind the double doors which led into the arena, then left them.

There were about thirty children there already, dressed in their ceremonial best – the girls in white dresses like hers, the boys in outfits like Jacob's..

"What are you doing here?" a tall, thin boy asked.

"We are strangers to Veylindré," Abigail said, "who are receiving our Waymarks today."

The more timid youngsters retreated, wary of these unWaymarked strangers. But the boy who had asked the question walked over to them and smiled. "I'm Lymon. Where are you from? I'm from Myndorian."

Abigail looked at Jacob. How much should they tell? "I'm Abigail and this is Jacob," she said. "We're from... somewhere else, but we came through Myndorian on our way here."

Lymon opened his mouth to ask another question, but they were saved from answering by a fanfare of music.

Silence fell in the amphitheatre.

"It's about to start," one of the girls whispered. "I'm so nervous."

"Shula of Myndorian," came a voice, resonant and commanding. Abigail recognised it as First Waymage Marinden's. "Come forth."

The girl gulped, smoothed down her skirts and walked out into the arena. Abigail and Jacob joined the others at the entrance to listen. No candidate was allowed to witness the Ceremony before going through it.

"I wish we didn't have to wait until last," Jacob whispered to Abigail.

"Me too," she whispered back, "but I can understand why Shaunan planned it that way."

One by one, the candidates for Assignment were called into the arena. Eventually, as the light began to fade from the sky, she heard Marinden's voice. "Abigail Winters, come forth."

Jacob squeezed her hand and she walked out, her head held high. The amphitheatre seemed to have doubled in size since her last visit. She felt very small and insignificant. So many faces were looking at her. The first one she focused on was First Waymage Marinden's. The tall, stately woman smiled and beckoned her forward.

"Abigail Winters is a stranger to Veylindré," she announced. "But she has expressed a desire to become one of us and has received the requisite training. Today, she presents herself for the Ceremony of Assignment. Let any who object speak now."

Abigail held her breath. There was a subdued rumbling of voices in the crowd, but none spoke out.

Marinden nodded. "Who is Abigail's sponsor?"

"I, Shaunan, Waymage of Nordvein, am Abigail's sponsor," Shaunan said, stepping up beside her. "She has learned much of our world in her seisdags among us and is a worthy candidate. I believe she has great potential."

"Thank you, Waymage Shaunan."

The First Waymage turned to Abigail. "Abigail, if you are ready to become one of us, repeat the words of the Vow of Assignment after me."

"I am ready," Abigail said, trying not to let her trembling show.

"Repeat after me. I, Abigail Winters –"

"I, Abigail Winters," she said –

"– swear that I will do my utmost,

to be true to myself
and to the Waymark that is assigned to me,
to follow the Way of Veylindré with my whole heart,
to serve the people of Veylindré,
and live by the Law of the Way.
In the names of the Six and the Christian God,
this is my vow."

There was a murmuring among the assembled at this innovation, but the First Waymage raised her hands and they fell silent. She turned her attention back to Abigail.

"What is the Law of the Way?"

Abigail took a deep breath and recited the words Shaunan had taught her.

"To follow the Way, I must have integrity,
to follow the Way, I must live simply,
to follow the Way, I must be compassionate toward others,
to follow the Way, I must be open to its truth,
to follow the Way, I must continue my training,
to follow the Way, I must respect my mentor,
and to follow the Way, I must live in its flow."

"Abigail Winters," Marinden said, "you have completed your initial training and taken the Vow of Assignment. Do you wish to have a Waymark assigned to you?"

"Yes, that is what I want more than anything," she said, looking into Marinden's eyes.

The First Waymage gestured to a low, padded stool. "Then kneel before me and I will reveal your Waymark."

As Abigail knelt, she strove to let go of her fears, to trust in the process.

Marinden reached out the index finger of her right hand and pressed Abigail's forehead above and between her eyebrows.

Abigail closed her eyes. She felt a burning sensation and fought not to flinch. Then, it was as though a hitherto unknown door in her mind had opened. She felt different, full of new possibilities. Marinden raised her to her feet.

"Your Waymark is that of Ranu," she said. "Here is your Goldstone and some money to start you on your journey." She pressed a soft leather pouch into Abigail's hands, which jingled as she took it.

"Thank you."

Smiling at her, Marinden continued, "May you follow the Way faithfully and serve the people of Veylindré for the rest of your days."

"I will try," Abigail whispered.

Shaunan took her hand and drew her to one side. "Welcome, Abigail," she said quietly. "This is the beginning of our journey together."

"Thank you so much, Shaunan, for everything."

Then, as Marinden called Jacob's name, the two of them fell silent. Abigail hoped with all her heart that nothing would go wrong, that Jacob would be able to say the words of the Vow and repeat the Law. His sponsor was Kalen, the smith he had been working with, these past weeks, no, seisdags. She wondered how he would feel about kneeling before Marinden. She held her breath.

But all went well. As she had expected, Jacob's Waymark was that of a Dagâran smith. Accompanied by Kalen, he walked over to where Abigail and Shaunan were waiting. Then he noticed the Waymark on Abigail's forehead.

"That's the same Waymark as Shaunan's."

"Yes, my Waymark is Ranusian," Abigail said. "I thought you knew."

"Hush, now," Shaunan told them. "First Waymage Marinden is about to close the Ceremony."

"People of Veylindré, once more we have welcomed new initiates into the Way of Veylindré. They are now adults with a responsibility to serve Veylindré and its people through following the truth of their Waymarks. Now is the time for feasting and celebration.

"It is also the end of this Festival of Dagârastide. Until we meet again at the next festival, may you all follow the Way in truth and dedication. May you live in peace."

People left the amphitheatre and made their way back to the central square, where the ceremonial fire would be extinguished and the final feast take place.

At last, she and Jacob belonged somewhere.

The following morning, Shaunan came into the living room as the four young people were finishing their breakfast. She was dressed once more in her Dagâran riding clothes of soft leather.

"Today, we move on," she said. "Please pack up all your belongings. We will be visiting Lord Lesym and Lady Bélia later this morning before heading to Ranusheim."

She had to suppress a laugh at their various reactions. Ellyn – dear Ellyn – was full of excitement and jumped up immediately to start packing. Aidren was no less upbeat but suppressed it behind a polite nod before hurrying to his room. Jacob looked wary – he still did not trust her completely. And

Abigail… Shaunan felt a frisson of fear in the girl's mind and sent soothing thoughts to her. It was still so new to the girl.

Within the hour, they were ready. Before leaving the Temple for the last time, they sought out First Waymage Marinden to thank her for her hospitality.

"So you are leaving us today," Marinden said.

"Yes, we must see Lord Lesym and Lady Bélia later this morning, then we will be on our way."

"Where are you bound?"

"To Smithsport first, then we'll take a ship up the Gulf of Dagâran to Taellingsford."

"May the Way be your guide. The blessings of the Six be with you on your journey." *Are you sure you need to go to Ranusheim?*

"Thank you, First Waymage. We leave in peace." *Yes. The Wayzenmoot need to hear about the Havimi being allied with the Talamdorians, about the Bloodstone, about the Portal in the Eastern Sea and to meet Abigail.*

"May the Way guard and guide you all." *Go well, my friend.*

Shaunan led them through the streets of Luvodican towards the palace of Lord Lesym and Lady Bélia.

"May we visit Master Kalen first?" Jacob said. "I would like to thank him and to bid him farewell."

"Yes, Jacob, we have time for that." The boy was going to miss his mentor.

"Master Kalen," he said, "I'd like to thank you for all you have taught me."

The big man smiled at him. "You have been a good apprentice, Jacob. I have a parting gift for you."

He went back into his workshop and came out, carrying a long sword in a leather sheath. "It is made of finest Luvodican steel and carved with runes for strength and protection. Look after it well."

Jacob was visibly affected by Kalen's generosity. "Thank you so much, Master Kalen. I will take great care of it."

"Don't forget all I have taught you," Kalen said gruffly. "I will expect a full report on your return."

He held out his hand to Jacob. "Go well, my friend."

Jacob shook it. "Thank you, Master Kalen."

Shaunan could sense the conflict in his heart, torn between staying with Kalen and following Abigail. She would have to watch over him.

It was so good to be able to walk through the streets unremarked. Poor Jacob. At least her mentor was going to be with them. Abigail squeezed his hand.

Then she sensed she was being watched. She looked around. A figure in a dark, ragged cloak darted into an alley. Where had she seen him before – for she was sure it was a "him". Then she remembered. That odd man at the ceremonial feast three nights ago. Was he following them? Should she mention him to Shaunan? Surely it was a coincidence.

When they had arrived at the Temple of Luvodican, they had been amazed by its grandeur. But it paled to insignificance beside the palace of Lord Lesym and Lady Bélia, the secular rulers of Luvodican. It was enormous, built of a warm, golden brown sandstone, which glittered in the pale sunlight. The flag of Dagâran flew above the ramparts – a rich brown with the split Y symbol of Dagâra in red. Two guards in the livery of Dagâran, standing at the main entrance, barred their way with crossed spears.

"Who are you and what is your business with the Lord and Lady?"

"I am Shaunan, Waymage of Nordvein, and these are my companions – Ellyn and Aidren of Nordvein, and Abigail and Jacob, who come from distant lands."

"And what is your business?" the guard asked, in a more respectful tone.

"We come from First Waymage Marinden. It is essential that we speak with Lord Lesym and Lady Bélia."

"I will test your Waymarks."

The five of them stood as he tested their Waymarks. Abigail sensed Shaunan gently nudging the guard's mind and was not surprised when he lowered his spear and gestured to his fellow guard to do likewise.

"Pass, friends," he said. "I will send for someone to show you the way."

"No need," Shaunan said quietly. "I am no stranger here."

She led them across the courtyard, through a tunnel under the twin towers which came out to an inner quadrangle. Without hesitation, she strode towards a high door set in the east wall. It opened at her touch. How was she so familiar with these rulers?

"Come," she said.

A servant bustled up to them. "Who are you? And how did you get here?"

Patiently, Shaunan repeated her explanation. The servant turned with a swish of her skirts and led them through another two very grandly appointed rooms, threw open a set of double doors and announced, "The Waymage of Nordvein and her party, seeking an audience with the Lord and Lady."

Abigail gasped.

Before them was the largest room she had ever been in, long and wide and high, the size of a large church. Its walls were decorated with brightly coloured tapestries, the elaborate vaulting of its wooden roof lost in shadow. The floor was paved with dark red and deep orange tiles. Stone ovens were set in recesses, keeping the space warm. Finely dressed people were milling around the side walls. Dagâran warriors stood to attention at spaced intervals. At one end, on a raised platform, were two people, sitting on what she supposed were thrones, which were intricately carved.

Shaunan paced steadily down the room, then came to a halt a few feet in front of the thrones. She bowed her head in respect.

The woman on the left-hand throne rose to her feet. She was tall and full-figured, with dark skin, and eyes which looked dark enough to be black. Her gleaming black hair flowed loose down her back but was held away from her face by an elaborate, golden coronet. Her gown was the colour of flame with a deep crimson overskirt. She was beautiful, regal, imposing.

Shaunan gestured to the others to bow.

"Lady Bélia, Lord Lesym," the Waymage said, "thank you for granting us an audience."

"You are welcome in our court, Waymage Shaunan," Bélia said in a voice that was deep for a woman's. "Tell us what you seek." She sat back down, her eyes bent on Shaunan.

"You are gracious, Lady," Shaunan said. "May I introduce my companions?"

Bélia nodded.

"These are Ellyn, my niece, an apprentice cordwainer, and Aidren, a young Warrior of Dagâra. They have accompanied us from Nordvein. These others," she indicated Abigail and Jacob, "are strangers to Veylindré, but have been accepted at the recent Ceremony of Assignment. It is on their behalf I am here."

Lord Lesym leant forward on his throne. He was as tall as the Lady, but older, with greying hair and beard, and a lined face. His eyes, like hers, were very dark. "Strangers to Veylindré, you say? From whence do they come?"

"If we might speak privily, my Lord?" Shaunan said. Abigail felt the smallest push at the Lord's mind.

"Very well." He raised his voice to address the assembled court. "Leave us. We would speak with the Waymage and her party alone."

"Thank you, my Lord."

Once the room had been cleared, Shaunan shared the by-now well-rehearsed story of Abigail's and Jacob's arrival in Veylindré, and of the slaughter of their community by the Havimi.

"They come from another world?" Lesym said, clearly surprised.

"Yes, through a portal in the Eastern Sea."

"I have never heard of this before," Lesym said, staring at Abigail and Jacob, "but I know that as Waymage, you must be telling the truth. How very strange." He looked down at them, his face stern.

Bélia put her hand on his arm and he sat back. "When did this happen?" she asked.

"So far as we can understand it, the community landed on the east coast of Dagâran in the last seisdag of the Season of Thanksgiving. Ellyn and Aidren came across Abigail and Jacob in the forest south-east of Nordvein during the second seisdag of the Season of Completion. When the Council of Nordvein heard their story, it was agreed I should bring them to Luvodican. We arrived here during the fourth seisdag and have been lodged in the Temple while they underwent the training needed to be accepted as Veylindréans. I have brought them to you."

"*Why* have you brought them to us?" Lesym asked.

"We ask for the boon of a ship from Smithsport to sail us to Taellingsford in Lènium. From there, we will make our way overland to the Isle of Ranu."

"Why do you need to visit Ranusheim?" Bélia asked, leaning towards her.

"Because the news of the Portal," Shaunan said, "and of the Havimi raiders needs to be shared with the Wayzenmoot."

She hasn't mentioned about the Talamdorian, nor that she wants the Wayzenmoot to see me. Why?

"Very well, Waymage Shaunan," Lesym said. "I will give you a letter under our seal to present to a sea captain at Smithsport."

֍ Chapter 15 ֍

It had taken Portak far too long to find them. His master would not be pleased.

He had eventually picked up their trail in Nordvein, having drawn a blank at the villages further north. He'd used his favourite false identity, posing as a Garûnalonden Watch officer named Kormak, which meant he could carry a sword openly and would not raise suspicion by asking questions. He had given out that he was on the trail of two reindeer pelt smugglers, having been tipped off that they had fled to north Dagâran. And he'd bought a horse from an old miner in Irnvein, a bit of a screw, but it would do for his purposes.

Why had a comparative newcomer like Gomlak had been trusted with the job of finding the cove, rather than him? A shaft of jealousy quickly suppressed. After all, the Prophet had trusted him with this mission. Surely his place was secure… surely? Don't think about it.

It had been a journey fraught with mishaps. He had nearly died in a snowstorm on the path of the Myner's Gap and had only been saved by finding a dense thicket of evergreen trees in which he and the horse had sheltered for three long days.

He finally reached Myndorian near the end of the Talamdorian Season of Remembrance – the middle of the Season of Completion to the heretics. He carried an almanac which translated the sensible four seasons of Talamdor into the six of Veylindré so he wouldn't get caught out. There, he had managed to ingratiate himself with Oltan, one of the guards at the East Gate, and took him for a drink when he came off duty at eighth hour. He hadn't been hard to persuade, particularly once he realised Portak was paying.

He had chosen the inn carefully – not too busy, not too quiet. He guided Oltan into a remote corner and started plying him with drink. And now the man was well sozzled, swaying back and forth and garbling his words. Time to pick his brains.

He leaned in more closely, not wanting anyone else to hear what he was about to say. "Have you seen anyone strange recently, Oltan?"

Oltan gazed at him owlishly, trying to bring him into focus. "Other than you, heh?" He swayed towards Portak, eyes alight in drunken friendship. "You're all right for a Garu-na-londen, you're all right."

Forcing a laugh, Portak mimicked the guard's slurred speech. "An' you're all right too. I heard a rumour there was people with no Waymarks on them seen in these parts. Am I right?" He lurched towards Oltan, pantomiming drunkenness.

"Ho, them. Yeah, I know all about *them*." Oltan said, pushing back his shoulders in self-importance. "You should've seen 'em, good Kormak. The pair of 'em without a Waymark between 'em. It made me fair shiver in my boots, I can tell you."

"No Waymarks? How very odd. When did these strangers arrive?"

Oltan pursed his lips, swaying in his seat, gazing into space as he tried to remember. "Lemme see… must of been three or four seisdags ago. The Waymage, Shaunan of Nordvein, I knew her all right, so no reason to keep them outside. It was a cold night… cold enough to freeze the balls off you." He went to take another drink, but his tankard was empty. "Le's get another drink. Thirsty work, this remembering."

Grinding his teeth in frustration, Portak got another round in. He'd been sure to take the antidote before the session started, so the alcohol would not affect him.

"You were saying about these strangers?" he prompted.

"Was I?... Oh, yeah, the strangers."

Portak wanted to throttle the man. Would he ever come through with the goods? But he bit his tongue, bided his time. He sensed the man would tell what he needed to know, given a bit of patience.

"Yeah. We let them in, and then," Oltan pushed himself upright in indignation, "then she told me two of them was strangers to Veylindré, no Waymarks! That gave me such a chill, I can tell you. And the girl's skin was 'most as pale as yours, Master Kormak, an' she had long yellow hair, not like our dark Dagâran beauties." He paused to lick his lips in appreciation. "The young man looked more like a Lèni-umen, with a fine head of curly brown hair. But no Waymarks, like I said. An' while we was waiting for our Waymage to arrive, the girl heads straight for the fire and throws back the hood of her cloak. It gave us all a shock, I can tell you. So I took meself back out to the Gate sharpish. Didn't want to see 'em no more."

"I can imagine," Portak said. "What happened next?"

"Well, our Waymage, Waymage Findoran, you know, came and took 'em all off with her. An' that was the last I saw of them."

"And the last you heard of them, I'll warrant," Portak said, trying to sound casual.

"Not a bit of it," Oltan replied. "The whole town was buzzing with rumours. We heard they'd moved on a couple of days later, heading for Luvodican, I think."

"What a fascinating story."

"I need a pee…" Oltan stood, swaying on his feet. "You're a good man, for a Garu-na-londen, a good man."

Portak watched him stagger out the back, waited a few moments, then followed. He waited until the man was emptying his bladder, swaying on his feet, singing loudly and tunelessly, stepped up behind him and broke his neck, quietly and efficiently. He had the information he needed, and his drinking companion had outlived his usefulness. He felt a twinge of regret – Balmak would not approve. But he knew the Prophet would. He felt so torn sometimes, between the gentle love of Balmak, which he hated having to keep secret and his fierce devotion to the Prophet.

He arranged the body to look as though the man was asleep, then climbed over the back wall and walked innocently back to his lodgings.

Saddling his horse, he left by the South Gate, trotting until he was out of sight, then galloped towards Luvodican.

A bit of skulking around in Luvodican had taught him that they were staying in the Visitors' Hall of the Temple. No prospect of winkling them out of there. He took some lodgings nearby and kept his ears and eyes open. But saw no sign of either of them. He'd have to wait until the Festival of Dagârastide, see if he could spot them then. Surely they wouldn't stay mewed up in the Temple then.

And he had been right. It had been a stroke of luck sitting near the girl at the ceremonial feast.

He was sure she was the one, and the young man with her, looking just as the drunken oaf had described them. At least, they were the only two he had seen who kept their hoods up like they had something to hide. Now all he had to do was to follow them and find out where they were going next.

For the next two days, he tailed them closely. He watched the Ceremony of Assignment and saw them receive their

Waymarks. Everywhere they went, he followed, a silent, observant shadow. He watched them leave the Temple after the Festival, heading for the palace. He'd taken far too long to fulfil his mission. He couldn't lose them now, or the Prophet would never forgive him. He'd bide his time and wait until he caught one, or preferably both of them, alone. He checked the inside pocket of his jacket – the Bangles of Control were still there. Good.

Chapter 16

At that moment, someone pounded on the door of the audience chamber, which made Abigail jump.

"Come," Lesym said.

A guard burst in, followed by a weary man dressed in dark green, his clothing spattered with mud.

"My Lord, my Lady," the guard said, "here is a messenger from Smithsport. He has urgent news."

Bélia gestured to an upright chair near the thrones. "Sit down before you fall down, man."

The man bowed low, before collapsing gratefully into the offered seat. "My thanks, Lady Bélia. I am Jaradol, of the Messenger Service. I bring ill tidings. Havimi pirates have been sighted in the Sea of Ranu near the mouth of the Gulf of Dagâran. Trade Master Torlin sent me to warn you and to ask you to send messengers across the Land of Dagâran to alert all."

"Thank you, Jaradol," Lesym said. "We are now forewarned. Rest now. I will contact the Messenger Service Master in Luvodican and instruct him to spread the word."

Jaradol stood, bowed and left. Bélia turned to Shaunan and her party.

"Well, my friend, this will put a spoke in your plans."

Shaunan smiled ruefully. Abigail felt a shaft of apprehension from her mentor, quickly suppressed. "It will indeed, Lady Bélia. It seems as though we will have to cross the Gulf of Dagâran from Smithsport to Saltis, then travel through Néartania to Néartanis. A long road, with many dangers."

"I think you should not go alone," Lesym said, stroking his beard. "It so happens we have an Yrusian trader at our court presently. I think she should join your company, to guide you on your way, at least as far as Néartanis."

Shaunan inclined her head. "Thank you, my Lord. That would be a boon indeed."

"She shall be found. In the meantime, go with our steward, and take some refreshment."

Jacob looked around curiously. This room, although smaller than the throne room, was as richly furnished, with finely carved furniture and tapestries on the walls. These Dagârans did well for themselves.

"So much for my plans," Shaunan said once they were alone. "The journey through Néartania will take much longer than the sea route would have. But there is no help for it. We must keep you," here she nodded at Abigail and Jacob, "out of the hands of the Havimi and the Talamdorians at all costs."

"Why do we need a guide?" Jacob asked. "Don't you know the way, Shaunan?" He was not happy about the idea of admitting a stranger to the company.

"I've only made that journey once, Jacob, when I was called for advanced training to qualify for my Maging, and that was more than twenty years ago."

"Oh." He frowned, unable to pick a hole in her reasoning. "Well, I hope we can depend on whoever it is."

"I am sure," Shaunan said, her amber eyes glinting, "Lord Lesym and Lady Bélia would not saddle us with someone untrustworthy."

He bowed his head. Slapped down again. He felt Abigail slip her hand into his and pull him gently aside, into a corner of the room out of earshot of the others.

"What? What is it?"

"Don't worry so, Jacob. If Shaunan doesn't know the way, we'll need a guide. Let's see what she's like."

He looked down at her, saw determination in the set of her lips. "You," he said, "are getting too like her." He nodded in Shaunan's direction.

"That's not surprising. She is my mentor, after all."

"I liked you better the way you were before."

"The way I was before? Subservient? I'm sorry, Jacob, I'm not that girl anymore. All of us change and grow."

The shock was so great, she might as well have struck him. How could someone alter so much in such a short time?

Her face softened, "I still love you."

"Do you?" It was a valid question. She seemed to be so different now, so much more sure of herself. And that Waymark… did it mean that she could read his thoughts?

"Of course I do. Why wouldn't I?"

"That Waymark," he said. "It means you've got all sorts of powers, doesn't it?"

"Yes, but I've got long weeks, no, seisdags," she corrected herself, "before I'll be able to use them properly. Shaunan will continue my training on our journey."

He frowned. "You're so lucky. I wish I could stay here and be apprenticed to Master Kalen." He took a deep breath, then voiced his deepest fear. "I'll be a dead weight on this journey. My smithing skills won't be any use to anyone."

He could see the pain in her loving eyes. She embraced him fiercely. "How can you say that?" she demanded. "You're Jacob, the only person I know from our old world and I love you. I may be an initiate of Ranu, but there are things I can share with you that I couldn't say to anyone else."

"Such as what?" he scoffed.

She drew back, gave him a straight look. "My fears, she said quietly, "and my ignorance of Veylindré. I *need* you, Jacob."

She was telling the truth. He relaxed, pulled her back into his arms. "I love you too, Abi."

He bent his head and kissed her, his tensions dissolving as she kissed him back.

Then the door behind them opened. A stranger strode in, her hand on the pommel of the knife at her belt.

The woman glanced around the room, then made a beeline for the Waymage. "The Lady Bélia says you require my services." Her voice was light and she spoke briskly, all business.

"Yes, my friend," Shaunan said, "I see you are Yrusian."

"My name is Ylonya, daughter of Guildmaster Brickon and Guildmistress Margera of the Hall of Traders. If you need a guide, I am one of the best."

"That is good to hear," Shaunan said, "for we have a long way to go. We have heard that Havimi pirates have been seen in the Ranusian Sea, near the mouth of the Gulf of Dagâran, so we need to travel overland from Saltis to Néartanis, then north through Lènium to the Isle of Ranu. Are you willing to travel so far?"

"I am."

A short response, full of certainty. Good.

Shaunan looked at the younger woman and liked what she saw. In her early thirties, she was of middling height and, like most Yrusians, had mid-brown hair, which threw off glints of red in the lamplight, brown eyes and deeply tanned skin. Around her neck, she wore a leather thong with a turquoise stone bearing the sigil of Yrusia. Beneath her white linen shirt and tunic, she wore black breeches and black knee-high boots, and carried a sheathed knife at her waist. Her hands were long and slender with silver rings on every finger and both thumbs. Her turquoise blue leather coat was soft and well-used.

She held herself well, had an air of competence which Shaunan immediately trusted.

"Then be welcome to our company. This is my niece, Ellyn, who is a Néartanian cordwainer, and Aidren, a Warrior of Dagâra. These others are Jacob, a smith of Dagâra, and Abigail, a Ranusian initiate whom I am mentoring. Jacob and Abigail are strangers to Veylindré. It is mainly on their behalf that we are making this journey."

Ylonya's eyes widened at that but she made no comment. "When do we leave? I will need to settle up at the inn and take my leave of the lord and lady."

"As soon as possible. I would like to get to Smithsport by evening tomorrow."

"Very well. I will return as soon as I may."

She nodded to Shaunan and left.

"So that is Guildmistress Margera's daughter," Shaunan mused aloud. "We are fortunate indeed to have her as our guide. I have heard tales of her exploits. Her knowledge of Veylindré is both wide and deep."

"Her coat was beautiful," Ellyn said. "I never dreamed I'd ever meet her."

"Why?" Abigail asked.

"She is famous throughout Veylindré, as both trader and guide," Shaunan replied.

They were on their way by mid-afternoon.

Lord Lesym and Lady Bélia had been generous. Each member of the company had a pack well filled with gifts of food for the journey, as well as their clothes, blankets and other necessaries. The horses they had ridden from Nordvein were well rested and raring to go. Ylonya's mount was a graceful and fiery grey mare.

"Farewell, Waymage Shaunan," Bélia said. She had come out to the courtyard to say goodbye to them, a dark brown cloak falling from her shoulders. "Farewell, all of you. May your journey be easy and may the Way guide and guard you."

"Thank you, Lady Bélia," Shaunan said, inclining her head. "May the Way be with you also."

The six of them mounted and rode out through the gates of the palace. The streets of Luvodican were emptier now. Most of the festival goers had already left.

The weather had turned colder, and a fine drizzle was falling, so Abigail was grateful for her warm cloak and hood. It was exciting to be back on the road again, although she was sad to be leaving Luvodican. She had learned so much here, about Veylindré and about herself. She was no longer the timid girl who had set out from Southampton, all those months ago. Now she was an initiate of Ranu, with a purpose in life.

Ylonya drew her horse up beside Shaunan's. "The quickest route to Smithsport is to take the road that runs alongside the River Redwater."

"I agree," Shaunan said.

"Why is it called Redwater?" Abigail asked.

"The water," Ylonya said, "is fed by run-off from the fields hereabouts and the soil is rich in minerals, which gives the river its reddish tinge."

"How much did the lord and lady tell you of our mission?" Shaunan asked Ylonya.

The younger woman shrugged. "Not much. Only that it was imperative for you to reach Ranusheim as quickly as possible."

"Now you are a member of our company, I can tell you our true purpose," Shaunan said. "We," she indicated Ellyn, Aidren and herself, "met Abigail and Jacob in the forest south-east of Nordvein. They were fleeing from their settlement, which had been raided by the Havimi, leaving the rest of their community dead. The Havimi are getting ever bolder, as we have seen by the news which Jaradol brought. It is vital that the Wayzenmoot hear of this as soon as possible so a plan may be made to make our coasts safe. And there is more. There was a Talamdorian agent on that ship."

Ylonya's response was unexpected. "Finally. The proof I needed."

"Proof?"

"I have suspected an alliance between them for some time but could never find any solid evidence. Thank you." She paused. "But wouldn't it be quicker to send messengers?"

"Probably as quick," Shaunan agreed, "but it is also important for the Wayzenmoot to meet Abigail."

"Why?" Ylonya glanced at Abigail, who met her eyes squarely. She was not going to be intimidated by this woman, however sure of herself she seemed.

"Because," Shaunan said, her voice taking on the cadence of prophecy, "her coming to Veylindré at this time is like the rolling of a small stone at the top of a slope of scree. There is purpose in it, which is hidden from me."

She had spoken of this "purpose" before. What did she mean? Abigail shivered and drew her cloak more closely around her.

Ylonya nodded. "Yours is the knowing. I will lead you well."

"Thank you. How far will we be travelling today?"

"It is about forty miles from Luvodican to Smithsport. I am hoping we can cover fifteen miles by nightfall and the other twenty five tomorrow. A village called Claymont a few miles down the road has a good inn. We can stay there overnight."

By the end of their ride, Abigail was glad to reach the village. All her clothes were damp and she felt as though she would never be warm again.

Shaunan bespoke three rooms for them and stabling for the horses. They dined well on a rich, meaty hotpot, which warmed them up. It felt so good to be able to show her face, to know she belonged at last. So different from their previous journey, when she and Jacob had to hide away for fear of discovery.

The next morning, after they had done their Immersion practice, she asked Ellyn, "What do you think of her?"

"Ylonya?" Ellyn shrugged. "She seems pleasant enough to me. Aunt Shaunan trusts her and I trust Aunt Shaunan's judgement. I've never known her to be wrong about a person. Why?"

"I've never met anyone like her. She seems so… sure of herself."

Ellyn grinned. "She has a right to be. Even in Nordvein, we've heard of Ylonya. She has been on many dangerous journeys for the Guild of Traders and others. Some of them have been made into tales by the storytellers."

"Really? She is that well known?"

"Yes. She seems to lead a charmed life, full of adventures and narrow escapes." Ellyn's eyes glowed. "I'd love to have adventures like that."

Abigail looked at her friend. "Do you think we will be in danger on this journey?"

"Who knows?" Ellyn said blithely, "but I'm looking forward to it."

Cheered by Ellyn's optimism, Abigail swallowed her doubts.

As soon as they had broken their fast, they mounted up and were on their way. The weather had not improved, and Jacob was already getting fed up with riding in the rain, splashing along muddy tracks. But there was no alternative – they had to get to Smithsport by evening. After that, who knew where they'd be heading.

He wished he knew more about the geography of Veylindré. He'd ask Shaunan for another sight of that map. He had been slowly getting used to Dagâran and its people, and now they were leaving it. He didn't know much about the inhabitants of the other lands. If Ylonya was a typical specimen, he wasn't sure he wanted to. However, as ever, he didn't have a choice. Whatever happened, he was going to follow Abigail wherever she went.

He frowned. How had this come about? When they had started their journey, it had been he who had taken the lead, he who had made the decisions. And that was how he liked it, if he was honest. But now he was reduced to a supporting role, going where Shaunan decreed. He liked Shaunan, even respected her, but it still felt profoundly unnatural to be following a woman. He wondered how Aidren felt about that.

But the young Dagâran warrior seemed to be content to tag along. He shrugged. There was not much he could do about it.

He looked around him. The land they were riding through seemed orderly and well looked after. They passed through a couple of small villages, stopping at one for a quick meal and to refresh the horses. Then it was back in the saddle for the final leg of the journey to Smithsport. The sound of the wind was loud in his ears. Despite his leather gloves, his hands on the reins were getting cold.

Finally, the walls of Smithsport came into view. They quickened their pace a little, glad to be near their journey's end. At least for that day. He must ask Shaunan for that map.

Content with the progress they had made, Shaunan gave the reins of her horse to Aidren and walked into the inn Ylonya had chosen – a stout building near the harbour, with wattle and daub walls and two storeys.

The innkeeper, tidying up behind the bar, looked up. "Good evening. How may I help you?"

"We would like three rooms, and stabling for six horses, please."

"Have you come far? It's gloomy weather to be travelling."

"From Claymont. And yes, it is."

"I see you are a Waymage. Who are the other members of your party?"

It might be natural curiosity. It might be something else. "Four young people and an Yrusian guide. We are hoping to catch tomorrow's ferry across the Gulf to Saltis. What time does it leave?"

"At the fourth hour, if the weather lets up." He looked out of the inn's front window. "I doubt it will be running if the wind doesn't die down."

He came out from behind the bar and showed her upstairs to three well-appointed rooms.

"My thanks," she said. "Would you let the other members of my party know where our rooms are, please? And we would appreciate some supper as soon as you can."

The man louted, then left. Shaunan removed her wet cloak with a sigh of relief and set it to dry in front of the fire. Soon she heard the sound of the others on the stairs and opened the door.

"Abigail and Ellyn, your room is there," pointing to her left, "Aidren and Jacob, yours is there," pointing to her right. "Ylonya, you're sharing with me. I will see you all downstairs for supper presently."

After a meal of fish stew and dumplings – "the speciality of the house" the innkeeper assured them – the six of them sat around the table with drinks in front of them, content for the moment to be warm and dry and fed.

"Ylonya," Shaunan said, "the innkeeper tells me that the ferry is due to leave at fourth hour tomorrow morning. Would you organise passage for us as early as possible?"

"Surely," Ylonya nodded. "Although," and she looked at the rain battering the windows, "I'm not sure it will be running in this weather."

"So the innkeeper said." Shaunan frowned. "I suppose there is no other way?"

"Not unless we ride another three days' south and west around the bottom of the Gulf."

"I do not want to lose that much time. Let us hope the weather is kind."

"Shaunan," Jacob said, "d'you have that map you showed us in Luvodican? I'd like to learn more about where we're going."

"Yes, it is in my pack. I will fetch it."

"I'll go up for you, Aunt Shaunan," said Ellyn.

"Thank you, Ellyn. It is in the rear pocket."

A few minutes later, Ellyn returned, waving the map in triumph. "Here it is."

"Thank you." He unrolled it carefully and spread it out on the table in front of him.

"What do you want to know?" Ylonya said. "I could probably tell you."

Jacob's shoulders stiffened and he frowned. So, he had taken a dislike to Ylonya. This would bear careful watching. Shaunan saw Abigail touch his hand, as though warning him. So she had felt the young man's animosity too.

"Yes, please," Abigail said. "Jacob and I have never been out of Dagâran, and we don't know very much about Néartania."

The guide nodded at Abigail. It was clear that she hadn't missed the interplay between the two young people. Shaunan sensed a shaft of amusement, hastily suppressed.

"If the ferry runs," Ylonya said, smiling at Abigail, "we'll be crossing to Saltis, which takes between four and five hours, depending on the wind. Then we'll pick up the road to Talmis, on the edge of the Central Plains, and join the Great South Caravan Route there. It will probably take us another seisdag to get that far. After that, we'll travel faster. The Great South Caravan Route is well-maintained, as it is one of our most important trade routes."

"Thank you," Abigail said. She too was looking at the map, seeming a little daunted by the distances involved. *Do not worry, we will be safe with Ylonya.*

The girl looked up, startled. Then she smiled. *I'm not worried, just a little overwhelmed. I didn't realise this journey was going to take so long.*

Shaunan smiled in her turn. Her initiate was getting used to her new powers. Good. She would have to make sure she gave her opportunities to use them.

Chapter 17

"Wake up, sleepyhead!" Ellyn said, shaking Abigail's shoulder. "The storm is over, we'll be leaving soon. I'm so excited! It's the first time I've travelled outside Dagâran. I wonder what Néartania is like?"

Abigail sat up, rubbing her eyes. "What time is it?"

"About second hour, I think. We've got time to do our Immersion practice and pack before breakfast."

When they were done, they headed down the stairs to the inn's common room where Jacob and Aidren were waiting.

"Where are Shaunan and Ylonya?" Abigail asked.

"Ylonya's gone to book our passage on the ferry," Aidren said. "I haven't seen the Waymage."

"We've had our breakfast," Jacob said. "You'd better have yours too. We'll be off soon, I expect."

They heard footsteps coming down the stairs and Shaunan appeared. "Good morning, my friends. Are you all ready to travel?"

Ellyn smiled. "Nearly. We," she indicated Abigail and herself, "haven't eaten yet, but the others have."

"Nor have I. Let us break our fast now so we can leave in good time."

"Come on, Jacob," Aidren said, "There's time for a bit of sword practice."

The two young men left. Soon, Ellyn could soon hear the clash of their practice swords from outside.

They had just finished eating when Ylonya returned. "I have booked our passage on the ferry," she said. "We need to be there half an hour before it leaves."

"Thank you, Ylonya," Shaunan said. "We are nearly ready to go. Ellyn, please collect our lunch from the innkeeper. It will be mid-afternoon before we reach Saltis."

Aidren and Jacob came back in, their faces flushed with the exercise.

"Good, you are done," Shaunan said. "We are ready to leave. Abigail, Jacob, be sure to keep your hoods up. We cannot risk you being recognised by an agent of the Prophet."

Abigail shrugged and did as she was told, but Ellyn noticed Jacob's scowl. Why did he have to question everything Aunt Shaunan said?

In a very short time, they had mounted up and were walking the horses towards the harbour.

Ellyn breathed deeply, gazing around. She could hear the squawking of the sea birds, squabbling over scraps, their calls strident in the cold morning air. She was thrilled to be on this journey, determined to prove herself as an adult and travelling with Shaunan and Aidren, the two people she loved best. Maybe he would eventually realise how she felt about him. She sighed. Abigail was so lucky to have Jacob. Wonder how they got together.

The ferry was not what she had expected. It was a long, wide, flat-bottomed vessel, more of a large boat than a small ship, with banks of oars on either side and a single square sail.

The captain was waiting for them on the wharf. "Come along, come along! We need to set sail straight away while there is still some wind."

They dismounted and walked their horses on board. A member of the crew led them to some railings where they could tie them up. Ellyn loosened her horse's girth, patted him, and turned to Shaunan.

"How long will this take, Aunt Shaunan?"

"Between four and five hours," the crewman answered, overhearing her question. "It depends on the wind. If we have to row, nearer five."

"Thank you." She smiled at him and he grinned back.

There were only a few other passengers beside themselves, and they on foot. For a moment Ellyn thought she recognised one of them, the man they had seen at the ceremonial feast on the first night of the festival. But that would be such an odd coincidence. She shrugged, dismissing it from her mind, followed her friends into the long, low cabin, and sat on one of the hard, wooden benches.

Abigail smiled at her. "I never thought I would be sailing again so soon."

"Yes," Jacob agreed. "This is very different to the *Sweet Sarah.*"

"Who is sweet Sarah?" Ellyn asked.

"Not a who, a what," Abigail said. "It was the ship we sailed from home in, the ship which brought us to Veylindré. It was much bigger than this, with three square-rigged sails, and holds and cabins below for the cargo and passengers."

"Not so loudly, Abigail," Shaunan cautioned her.

Abigail flushed. "I'm sorry. I forgot."

"Tell me about your journey," Ellyn said in a low voice.

Once again, Abigail shared the story of their arrival in Veylindré – the long tedium of the sea voyage, the storm, the flash of green light which had heralded their translation, then the landing in north-east Dagâran.

She sighed. "I wonder what's happening in our world, now."

After a pause, she continued. "Then, while Jacob and I were away from the camp looking for a source of fresh water, the Havimi came and slaughtered our families and friends." She wiped a tear from her cheek. "After we had buried them, our only thought was to get as far away from the settlement as possible." She looked at Jacob with love in her eyes. "I wouldn't have made it without Jacob."

"And then," Ellyn said brightly, "Aidren and I found you and brought you back to Nordvein."

Then shrank back as Jacob glared at her.

Abigail touched his arm and he bit down on whatever else he had been going to say.

"And the rest you know," Abigail finished. She smiled at Ellyn. "Now we're off on another adventure."

As the long crossing continued, Abigail became bored. She left the cabin and walked to the prow of the – boat? ship? – to see whether the Néartanian coast was in sight. It was good to feel the wind in her hair. She heard footsteps behind her, firm and precise. Expecting Jacob, she turned with a big smile on her face, but it was Ylonya. She nodded to her and made space for her to stand alongside.

"It is not wise for you to be alone, especially in these troubled times," the Yrusian said. "May I talk with you awhile?"

Abigail blushed. She supposed Ylonya was right. When would she be able to walk around unafraid? "Of course."

"I was fascinated by your tale. You have had more adventures in your short life than most of us manage in a lifetime."

"Not really. My life was most *un*adventurous until we sailed for America. Since then, it has been nothing but adventure, but that is only the last few seisdags." She was proud of herself for remembering the correct word.

"You landed on the north-east coast of Dagâran, I think?" Ylonya continued. "I have only visited that corner of Dagâran once before. What was it like?"

"We landed on the beach of a deep cove, with a forest behind it. It was when Jacob and I were away trying to find a source of fresh water that the Havimi paid their little visit." She pressed her lips together, unwilling to show Ylonya how much it still hurt to talk about it.

"Then Jacob and I returned to the stream we had found and followed it inland. Aidren and Ellyn found us in the forest and took us back to Nordvein. They and Shaunan took us first to Myndorian, then to Luvodican, where we learned enough about Veylindré to become one of you."

"One of you? I don't understand."

"In our world, we don't – didn't – have Waymarks. And knew nothing of the Six. Our God is one, and he, male."

She watched Ylonya process this information. Unlike everyone else she'd told, the Yrusian did not immediately jump to the conclusion that she and Jacob were followers of the Prophet of the One. Which was refreshing. "Tell me about yourself. Ellyn told me you have had many adventures too."

As Ylonya smiled, an unexpected dimple flashed in her cheek. It made her seem more approachable, more friendly, somehow. Perhaps she was not as formidable as she seemed on first sight. Although Abigail noticed the Yrusian was always on the alert for anything unusual, her eyes roving back and forth as she leant against the rail.

"A good question. If we are to travel far together, it would be as well for you to know something of me. Where should I begin?" she mused. "I am the eldest daughter of Guildmaster Brickon and Guildmistress Margera, of the Hall of Traders – that's in Porusport, at the northern end of the Great South

Caravan Route, which goes all the way through Néartania to Fionnan in south Dagâran.

"My family have been traders for generations, so it is no wonder my Waymark is Yrusian. When I was growing up, my mother took me with her on her trading journeys. So I've got to know the lands of Veylindré as well as anyone alive. The only one I haven't yet visited is the Isle of Ranu. And Talamdor, of course. But that is no longer part of the Commonweal."

"Tell me about Yrusian," Abigail said. "I know very little about it – only what I've read in a book Shaunan gave us in Luvodican, to help us with our learning."

"What was it called?"

"*Veylindré: Our Commonweal.*"

Ylonya sighed, a reminiscent smile on her face. "I had that book as a small girl," she said. "It's years since I've seen a copy. Do you have it with you?"

"Yes, it's in my pack."

"I'd love to see it again. But for now, perhaps it would be best if you asked me questions and I answered them."

"Thank you. From what I remember, Yrusian shares borders with most of the other lands," Abigail began. "I suppose that's why you became traders?"

Ylonya nodded. "You are right. We have direct borders with Néartania to the south-east, Garûnalond to the north and Lènium to the east. The north-western end of the Talamdor Mountains forms our border with that land. But we do not go there. And of course the Great South Caravan Route gives us a link to Dagâran. Garûnalond is a short sail from Mathven to Garûnashavn. Most Yrusians are sailors, merchants or traders. We are willing to go wherever the business calls us."

"That sounds like an exciting way to live. What do you do, if you don't mind my asking?"

"Of course not. In the years since my majority – you know we are considered adults at eighteen? – I have made a living as a guide. I have criss-crossed five of the six lands of Veylindré many times, on foot, riding and by sea. I know not only the major routes but also the side roads and by-ways. Which is why Lord Lesym asked me to go along with you all." She laughed. "And you seem to have the best adventure going, at the moment, so I'm more than happy to be part of it."

"It sounds like a lonely way to live."

"Not at all. I would far rather be involved in what is happening in the world than stagnating in a single village or town." She shuddered. "Which is why I have never married – I value my freedom too highly. This way, I have no-one to rely on or who relies on me."

Abigail smiled. She had never met anyone like Ylonya – at least, not any woman like Ylonya – but she was warming to her ebullience. "I'm glad you are with us."

The short day was nearly done by the time they reached Saltis, a small seaside port, its white-painted houses bathed in the light of the setting sun.

Shaunan decreed they should stay the night there and set off early the next morning.

"If I remember rightly," she said to Ylonya, "Talmis is more than a hundred miles away?"

"Nearer a hundred and ten, I should think. And the condition of the road is not good, particularly at this time of year. We should allow a whole seisdag to reach it."

"Are there places to stay along the way?" Shaunan asked.

"Not many," Ylonya said. "A few farms, and a couple of small villages, no more. And we will be travelling through the Saltiswoods some of the time. No-one lives there."

"Ah, well, I am sure we will be able to find shelter." If anyone could find somewhere to stay, it would be Ylonya.

The weather was getting colder, with a thin wind which blew right through them, stealing the warmth from their bones. The road to Talmis was indeed more of a track than a proper road, rutted by the passage of carts, and very muddy.

On the first day, they travelled less than twenty miles, including a short stop for lunch, eaten standing up, because there was nowhere dry to sit.

Shaunan was relieved to see a farmhouse looming up in the gloom.

"We will stop here," she said. "Aidren, please knock and ask for shelter."

Aidren returned with the farmer and a young lad, who was surely his son.

"Good even, Waymage," he said, "Rodis is my name. Be welcome among us."

"Thank you, Farmer Rodis," Shaunan said. "My name is Shaunan, and I am Waymage of Nordvein, in north-east Dagâran. These others are Aidren and Ellyn, also of Nordvein, Ylonya, an Yrusian guide, and Abigail and Jacob, lately of Luvodican. We ask for your hospitality for the night."

"Welcome, all of you," Rodis said. "My wife is cooking a fine beef stew, which will go around easy, and we can offer you floor space to sleep on. Are you content?"

"Thank you, we are more than content," Shaunan said. "Do you have somewhere we can leave the horses?"

"There is room in my barn, if they do not mind bedding down among the cattle," Rodis said, a broad smile on his face.

Like most Néartanians, he was short and stout with a face made for laughter. His blue eyes twinkled as he surveyed the bedraggled riders. "You'll be glad of some time in the warm, I'm sure," he said. "Jordis here will show you where to settle your horses, then come away in."

Gratefully, they followed the boy to a substantial barn. He showed them where to tether the horses and helped them feed and water them.

"My thanks, Jordis," Shaunan said.

The boy blushed bright red. "This way, Waymage."

It was Jacob's first sight of a Néartanian farmhouse. He was impressed by the neatness and order within.

Jordis led them into the substantial kitchen, which had a large hearth in which a fire was burning cheerily. In the centre of the room was a long table, set with enough chairs to seat all of them and to spare. Around the walls were stout cupboards, and a fine dresser, filled with plates and dishes. The light came from an oil lamp which hung from the ceiling. The furniture was of a light wood he did not recognise. There was still so much about Veylindré he didn't know.

A short, middle-aged woman, dressed in a long, mid-brown gown with an apron over it, and with a kind face with many laugh lines, bustled forward. "Welcome, Waymage Shaunan. Welcome, all. I am Alaine, wife of Rodis. Are you travelling far?"

"We hope to reach Talmis in a few days," Shaunan said.

Why hadn't she told the woman where they were going? He shrugged. She must have her reasons.

"Such weather to be travelling in!" Alaine said. "You must be freezing. Come, warm yourselves by the fire. Supper will be ready soon."

He and the others clustered around the fireplace, water dripping off their cloaks. Soon a delicious stew and fresh-baked bread were brought to the table, and a light beer to drink with them. He was famished. He was about to tuck in when Abigail gave him a nudge. He realised that Alaine had put her hands together and was saying grace.

"Beloved Néarta, thank you for the gifts of this day, for food and warmth and fellowship. May we follow your Way with diligence and gratitude. So may it be."

"So may it be," the others echoed.

"Eat, friends!" Alaine said. "The evening is for fellowship and sustenance."

After the meal, Alaine led them through to the family parlour, in which a loom took pride of place.

"You are a weaver?" Jacob asked.

"My wife is the best weaver in the district!" Rodis proclaimed. "Alaine, bring them some of your work to admire."

Alaine blushed but did as she was bid. The finished cloth was intricately patterned and wonderfully even. The craftsman in Jacob admired the skill.

"This is beautiful work," he said. "Have you always been a weaver?"

"I learned at my mother's knee," Alaine said. "I love it."

She was so lucky, to be able to spend her days practicing her skill. He so much missed working with his hands. It felt like a constant itch that he was unable to scratch. His hours spent with Master Kalen were like a distant dream. When would he be able to work again?

The next morning, Alaine rose early to give them a hearty breakfast of bacon, scrambled eggs and fried mushrooms and pressed some loaves of bread and a round Néartanian cheese on them "for the journey".

Abigail joined her thanks to those of the others. As they left, she asked Shaunan, "Are all Néartanians so jolly and hospitable?"

"Jolly and hospitable. That is a good way to describe them," Shaunan smiled. "Yes, most of them are. They spend their days in close companionship with the land, working with their hands to produce the food we eat and crafting many of the everyday items we use. It is a good way of life. Their land is broad and kindly and they live in close harmony with it."

A little further on, the wood closed back in around them, although the track was broad, with room for two to ride abreast. The winter trees which lined it were elegant in their spare beauty. And the rain had stopped, for which Abigail was grateful.

Ylonya was leading the way, followed by Abigail and Ellyn. Shaunan came next, and rode with absent ease, seemingly lost in her thoughts. Jacob and Aidren brought up the rear. Abigail was glad to see they were getting more friendly, although she fretted each time they did their sword practice – what if Jacob were injured?

"Rodis and Alaine reminded me of the farmers in my village at home," Abigail said to Ellyn with a pang of sadness. "They, too, live simply and close to the land."

"Tell me about your village," Ellyn said.

Her clear voice carried in the still air. Ylonya dropped back to listen.

Abigail shrugged. "It was a village, like any other. Squire Petty lived in the big house and he owned much of the land, which was worked for him by tenant farmers. But some of the farmers worked the land for themselves. There was a potter and a blacksmith's forge," here she smiled, thinking of Jacob, "and some of the village women spun wool and wove it into garments or made lace. We had a parish church, St John the Baptist, where most people worshipped. Because of the new laws, we Presbyterians were not allowed to meet for worship."

"What were the houses like?" Ellyn asked.

"Some were still made of wattle and daub, like some I've seen here. But others were built of brick or stone. And most had glass in the windows. Our house," she paused – it was still difficult to talk about her home without the remembrance of all she had lost sweeping over her – "our house was one of the better ones. It was brick built and had two storeys with two rooms downstairs and three upstairs. We mostly lived in the kitchen during the day and gathered around the fire in the parlour after supper. My father…" her voice wobbled, "…my father would read to us from the Bible most evenings."

"What is the Bible?" Ylonya asked.

"It is the holy text of our faith, Christianity," Abigail said.

"Then you do not follow the Six?" Ylonya said, her eyebrows shooting up in surprise.

"We do now, since we came to Veylindré" Abigail said, "but we are also still Christian and follow our Lord, Jesus Christ."

Ylonya opened her mouth to question further but, at that moment, a small animal scurried across the path, right under the hooves of Abigail's mount. Startled, the horse reared, then bolted, Abigail clinging on for dear life. As the horse passed under a low branch, she was swept off its back.

Blackness.

"Abigail!" Shaunan cried. She vaulted off her own horse and rushed to examine the girl lying unconscious under a tree.

"Aidren, go after Abigail's horse and bring her back," she said. "Ellyn, fetch my healer's bag from my saddlebow."

Jacob was kneeling beside Abigail, his face white. "Is she badly hurt?"

Shaunan shook her head. "I think not, but I will not know until I have examined her."

Anxiously, she felt along the girl's limbs, but nothing seemed to be broken. She put her hands gently on Abigail's temples. Using her healing sense, she explored more deeply. Then opened her eyes and smiled at Jacob.

"She has just been knocked unconscious," she said. "I can perceive no deeper harm."

"Then why isn't she coming to?" he asked, gnawing his lower lip, anxiety radiating out from him. Shaunan blocked it off; she needed to concentrate on Abigail.

"Give her time. She has knocked her head on this tree root. Come, my friend, help me to move her so that I can see more clearly what damage it has done."

Jacob lifted the girl gently and put her on her side. Her blonde hair was in disarray. There was a deep cut near the crown of her head.

"Ah, this is where the problem is. Fetch me some water, please. I will bathe it."

He ran to his horse and returned with his water bottle. By then, Ellyn and Ylonya were crowding around, worried.

Shaunan smiled up at them. "Do not fear, it is not as bad as it looks. I will clean it up and apply some healing salve. She will have a bad headache when she comes round, but nothing worse."

Opening her bag, she brought out her Goldstone, a pair of sharp scissors and a small jar of ointment. "I will get this done while she is still unconscious." She held her Goldstone quietly for a moment, communing with Ranu, snipped the hair away from around the wound, cleaned it gently, then smoothed on the healing salve with light fingers. She was pleased to see that a lump was already forming around the wound – better out than in.

Ten long slow minutes passed before Abigail began to stir and then to moan.

Jacob knelt down beside her and took her hands in his. "Come on, Abi. Come back to me."

Her eyes opened. "What happened?" mumbled. Then turned on one side and spewed up her breakfast.

Jacob helped her into a sitting position, then held her close. "Oh, thank God, thank God! You're all right."

"It is all right, Abigail," Shaunan said softly. "Your horse bolted and threw you off. Do you remember?"

The blue eyes were still glazed but there was a spark of recognition in their depths. "Oh… yes… I remember. My head hurts." She leaned against Jacob, seeming to take strength from his proximity.

"You banged it on this tree root," Shaunan said. "We will rest here until you feel up to riding again." She laughed. "Not that we can go anywhere at present. Your horse bolted and Aidren is away after her. Drink this," she said, holding a spoon to her lips, "it will help with that headache."

Turning to Ylonya, she said, "How far are we from the nearest habitation?"

"I'm not sure, a few miles in either direction, I think. No-one lives in Saltiswoods."

Nodding to herself, Shaunan made her decision. "Then we had better stay where we are. Can you find somewhere for us to shelter? I do not think we will be travelling much further today."

Chapter 18

Aidren found Abigail's horse more than a mile away, her sides lathered with sweat, her mane and tail tangled with briars. He led her back to the others. As he'd never been outside Dagâran before, he had no idea how far through Saltiswoods they were. Such a Six-forsaken place. He doubted Ylonya would be able to find any refuge for them. He fought down his apprehension – no Warrior of Dagâra should show fear.

After a few minutes, Ylonya returned. "We are fortunate. There's a charcoal burner's hut not far from here. No-one is living there at this time of year, but at least we'll have a roof over our heads."

The company followed her, grateful to find some shelter. Jacob rode slowly and carefully, cradling Abigail drowsing in his arms. Behind him, Aidren led the mare, who would need some attention when they reached this hut, wherever it was.

They came into a clearing, with a crude shack in its centre and, around it, some paler areas of grass, which showed where the wood-stacks had been. The wood had long since been burned and the charcoal collected to feed neighbourhood fires.

The hut was built of wooden planks, nailed together in overlapping slats, with a turfed roof. Inside was a bare earth floor, cold and damp in this season. The only furniture was a wooden platform, which served as a bed, a wooden press for possessions, a low table and one chair. There was a small hearth along one wall, a long-handled rake propped against another.

Aidren shivered. This would be a lonely way to live. He dismounted, passed the two horses' reins to Ellyn and Ylonya, then strode over to Jacob, who was still mounted with Abigail in his arms. “Give her to me. I’ll take her inside.”

“Thank you, my friend.”

Inside the hut, Shaunan had laid a thick blanket on the low platform. Aidren carried Abigail in and gently placed her on it.

Jacob followed him in, his face anxious.

“Thank you, Aidren, Jacob,” Shaunan said. “I need to be alone with Abigail now.”

Aidren saw Jacob draw in breath to protest and took him by the arm. “The Waymage needs to do her healing in private. Come with me. We’ll see to Abigail’s mare.”

Frowning, Jacob followed him out. They took off the mare’s tack, then Aidren produced a stiff brush from his pack. “We’ll need to give her a good grooming. It will help her to calm down.”

“I know horses,” Jacob said shortly.

The pair of them worked in silence for some while, Aidren brushing the dried sweat and mud from her coat, Jacob patiently untangling the briars from her mane and tail. Having something to do had a calming effect on them both.

“We had better see to our own mounts now,” Jacob said.

Ellyn and Ylonya had tethered all the horses, removed their tack and left them to graze.

As Aidren strode up to them, he heard Ylonya say, “This delay could be costly. I smell fog in the air.”

“What does fog smell like?”

Ylonya looked at him. “Fog,” she said unhelpfully.

He looked up at the sky, which was almost grey, as though it was nearer day’s end than noon. He feared she was right.

“Come,” he said, “we need to get our belongings into that hut, out of the weather.”

As predicted, the fog began to swirl around about forty minutes later and, in a short time, they could not see for more than a couple of feet in any direction. Inside the cramped quarters of the hut, the company laid out blankets to sit on, and Shaunan used her Goldstone to start a fire and make light. Abigail was asleep on the platform. The colour had begun to return to her cheeks.

"I fear we will be here at least until the morrow," Shaunan said. "I have tended Abigail, but she needs to sleep herself out. The morning should bring better tidings."

"Is she going to be all right?" Jacob asked.

"Yes, Jacob, the worst is over. By morning, she should be much better."

He smiled at her, visibly relaxing. "Thank you. If anything had happened to her…" He shuddered.

"Peace, my friend. All is well."

There was a pause, then, "This feels like a bad fog to me," Ylonya said. "I'm afraid we may have to stay here until it clears."

"You have the weather sense, then?" Shaunan asked, smiling at the younger woman. "I thought you might, being Yrusian."

"I do, and my heart is full of foreboding."

Ellyn looked up at this, and Shaunan hastened to reassure her. "Worry not, Ellyn. We have food and drink enough to last us some days."

"What about the horses?" Aidren asked. She could sense his concern.

"I think we will have to tether them among the trees, where they will get at least a little shelter," Shaunan said. "Let us hope it disperses sooner rather than later."

"Can you influence it?" Ellyn asked.

Jacob looked up, surprised. “No-one can influence the weather.” His face paled. His eyes filled with apprehension. “Can you?”

“If there is great need, yes,” she replied. “But it is something I would not do lightly. There are far too many interconnected factors to consider, and if I made a mistake, I could devastate a wide area. Foretelling the weather is one thing, trying to change it quite another. It would take several Waymages working together to do it safely.”

His shoulders slumped. “Then we have no choice. We’ll just have to sit it out.”

Shaunan touched his shoulder, soothed him. “Let us see what the morrow brings.” She stood up. “In the meantime, let us eat and drink before we rest. Aidren, Jacob, please move the horses to a more sheltered spot.”

Abigail woke to the sound of murmured conversation. As she started to sit up, a dull pain made itself felt at the back of her head.

“Where on earth are we?” she said, moving slowly and carefully.

Jacob rushed over to her. “Abi! You’re all right!” He gathered her gently in his arms and kissed her long and fervently.

She returned his embrace, then asked again, “Where are we?”

“In a charcoal burner’s hut in Saltiswoods,” Shaunan said. “Are you feeling better?”

“Better? What’s wrong with me?”

“You remember nothing?” Abigail shook her head, immediately regretting it as pain shot through it. “Your horse bolted, you were thrown off and hit your head on a tree root. We brought you here late yesterday morning."

"Yesterday morning?" Abigail wished she could think straight, rather than echoing what others said. "How long have I slept?"

Shaunan chuckled. "Nearly a night and a day. But you needed it. I have examined you. No lasting harm has been done. I expect you have a headache?"

Abigail nodded, then winced. Her head really hurt.

"I will give you something for it. We need to move on once you have eaten. Come, sit here."

With Jacob hovering next to her, for all the world like a mother hen with one chick, Abigail swung her legs off the cot and walked over to join Shaunan.

"Where's everyone else?" she asked.

"Outside, preparing the horses for the onward journey."

Abigail drank the potion Shaunan gave her, grimacing at its bitter taste, then ate the offered bread and cheese ravenously, washing it down with long swallows from her water bottle. Smiling at Shaunan, she said, "I'm sorry to have been such a trouble."

"It was not your fault. A small woodland creature burst out of the undergrowth under your mare's hooves. She took fright and bolted. You were swept off her by a low branch."

Abigail frowned, then memory returned. "I remember now! It happened so quickly. I was afraid I would never be able to stop her… Is she all right?"

Jacob hastened to reassure her. "Aidren caught her about a mile away. Once we got here, the two of us checked her over and gave her a good grooming. She soon got over her fright."

"Ah, that's good. Then how did I get here?"

"I carried you," Jacob said.

She smiled at him, her heart full of love. "You always seem to be around to save me."

"And I always will be," he said fiercely.

The going was slow through the eddying fog which, although less than it was, was still dense in patches. Only Ylonya's knowledge of the trail and the power of her blue-veined Goldstone kept them on track. Jacob watched in fascination as she held it aloft, and said, "*Ganasa mi y peuran ir Talmis cenfen.*"Whatever that meant. He could still not get used to the Veylindréans' casual use of what seemed to him to be magic, although they called it "the power of the Way".

It was full night by the time they reached the next village, which emerged abruptly out of the fog as they left Saltiswoods behind. Weary, stiff and cold, they dismounted outside the local inn.

"Ylonya," Shaunan said, "please bespeak three rooms for us, and stabling for six."

Ylonya slid off her grey mare, giving her to Aidren to hold. Moments later, she returned, followed by the innkeeper. Although Néartanian in appearance – short, stout and with a round, friendly face – Jacob noticed his Waymark was Yrusian, like Ylonya's. He must ask Shaunan why. Or perhaps Aidren. He didn't like betraying his ignorance to the Waymage.

While the women took the baggage inside, he and Aidren stabled the horses.

"Aidren," Jacob said, "why did the innkeeper have an Yrusian Waymark, even though he is Néartanian?"

"He is an innkeeper," Aidren said. As though that explained everything.

"So what?"

Aidren gave him a quizzical look. "Surely you know that our Waymarks show who and what we are, not where we are from. So although I am Dagâran and also have a Dagâran Waymark, Shaunan and Ellyn are Dagâran, but their Waymarks are of Ranu and Néarta."

"Of course." Why hadn't he remembered that? "But the innkeeper is neither traveller nor trader. Why is his Waymark Yrusian?"

"But he is a trader. All innkeepers and shopkeepers have Yrusian Waymarks because they buy and sell goods."

Put like that, it seemed obvious. Jacob flushed, angry with himself. How could he be expected to know all this? He was glad he had asked Aidren, rather than the Waymage.

The rest of the journey to Talmis took another four days. Each day was a long, tedious slog along the muddy track, often through driving rain, wet, cold and miserable. Each night, Ylonya's skill managed to find them somewhere to shelter – there were several small hamlets dotted along the route. But Jacob was heartily thankful when the walls of the town came into view up ahead.

"Will we be staying here long?" he heard Abigail ask Shaunan.

"It is Ranusdag tomorrow, so we will stay at least a day. We were in the charcoal burner's hut last Ranusdag, and I would like to spend some time in worship. Would you like to join us this time?"

Abigail's face lit up. "Yes, please. But I don't know what to do, how to act."

"Do not worry. Just follow our lead."

Veylindréan worship. In spite of all he had experienced, Jacob was not sure he was ready for that. Sighing, he followed the women as they approached the gates.

After they had done their daily Immersion and eaten breakfast, Shaunan led them through the streets of Talmis to the temple. The town reminded Abigail of Myndorian, with streets of houses and shops, surrounded by sturdy walls. The style of the buildings was quite different – the Néartanians used more wood than the Dagârans, which gave the town a warm and welcoming feel. The Temple of the Six was on one side of the central square. Its doors were open, welcoming worshippers to the service.

The temple reminded Abigail of the one at Myndorian. Like all Veylindréan temples, the imposing central building, built of the sacred golden stone – *ranusfelsen,* Shaunan had called it – had the customary seven sides. She now knew the lesser buildings clustered around it were for learning and to accommodate the temple's Waymage and other staff.

But the only temple she had been inside had been the small one at Nordvein. Although they had stayed for long seisdags in the Visitors' Hall of the Temple at Luvodican, neither she nor Jacob had ever attended a worship service. She couldn't wait to experience Veylindréan worship, to see how it compared to the faith she had been brought up in.

They walked in through a small vestibule to the main worship area.

Abigail looked around curiously.

Like the temple in Nordvein, there was no formal seating – no pews, like there would be in a Christian church or chapel. Instead, three rows of long, low benches which tilted forwards slightly, stood in front of each of the six altars. The centre of the worship space was covered with brightly coloured woven mats, on which many people were already seated. Great ceramic stoves stood at intervals around the walls, which made the air pleasantly warm.

As Shaunan gestured for them to sit, she lowered herself to the floor, adopting a simple, cross-legged posture with her back straight, like the one Ellyn used in her Immersion practice.

A bell rang.

An elderly Waymage walked slowly in from a side door Abigail had not previously noticed. As he was the first male Waymage she had seen, she studied him with interest. Instead of a full length robe, he wore wide-legged ochre trews, with a long tunic of the same shade over them, which was intricately decorated with beads, but had the brooch of a Waymage pinned to his left shoulder. His grey hair was still long and thick, and his brown eyes below spectacular bushy eyebrows sparkled with life. As he was shorter than any of the female Waymages she had seen – Findoran, Marinden and Shaunan – she guessed he was probably Néartanian.

He made up for his lack of inches by an intense presence. He had the same air of effortless authority as other Waymages she had met.

He made his way to a shallow platform in the centre of the congregation – she supposed she should call them – then stood and waited for silence to fall.

Which it did, with an uncanny suddenness.

He raised his hands in blessing and started not to speak, but to chant softly, in a language Abigail did not understand but which sounded similar to the language she was learning to access the Way. Old Veylindréan, Shaunan had called it.

His voice was deep, rich and sonorous. The language was musical and expressive. She caught the names of various members of the Six and the occasional phrase of blessing. But that was all. Every so often, after each – section? verse? – everyone joined in the refrain, reciting in fervent tones. Only she and Jacob did not know the words.

She glanced across. He was sitting between her and Aidren, who was listening with rapt attention. Not Jacob. Although he remained silent, she knew him well enough to read his feelings. His lips were pressed tight together, his nostrils flared in disgust, and his eyes, usually a deep brown, were almost black. Oh dear. She reached out, took his hand.

He turned his head to face her and mouthed, "I want to leave."

She felt a twinge of dismay and clutched his warm fingers. "No," she whispered, trying to plead with him with her eyes. "Please don't."

Because Shaunan was seated in front of them, Abigail tried to keep her emotions private, knowing the Waymage would sense them.

Not Jacob. He was broadcasting his violent feelings – of rejection, almost abhorrence – and Abigail's heart sank when she felt Shaunan's and the Talmis Waymage's attention focus on her beloved.

Clutching her Goldstone in her right hand, she thought as clearly as she could, *There is nothing to fear. I will deal with it,* then sent feelings of soothing and calm to Jacob.

And was mostly successful. Shaunan nodded slightly and returned her attention to the service.

Abigail saw the Néartanian Waymage's eyes widen and meet hers. Then, on the heels of the last words of the chant, she heard his voice in her head. *Thank you, young lady. We will speak anon.* Shaunan had silently communicated with him.

Aloud, he addressed the assembled people, this time in the common tongue. Apparently the other language was only used for liturgy. Fascinating.

"My friends! When the Six breathed life into our world, the Season of Dormancy played a crucial role in the turning of the seasons. Which it still does. In the first half of the season, the days become ever shorter, with our sun rising later and setting earlier each day. This time is a gift from Mother Ranu – nature falls into its annual sleep phase and the pace of our lives slows. Instead of protesting the limitations of this season, we should take them as a sign from the Six that it is time to rest, for our fields to lie fallow and for us to make the transition from our sunlit outdoor lives to finding light and warmth by our hearths. This is the season when we have time to spend on indoor crafts long neglected by our participation in the agricultural cycle.

"It is the season when most of us will stay close to our homes, only travelling if it is absolutely needful." He paused, glancing round the congregation, his eyes twinkling. "Not that we Néartanians do this much anyway."

This comment was met by rueful laughter.

"It is time for us to appreciate our community. To help each other with our crafting. To bring the young children of our community on in their skills, so they may in their turn take their places in our society. The craftspeople in the town will be hosting workshops to facilitate this in the next few seisdags. Details are on the board in the vestibule.

"Our time of communal worship is over. Our time of individual devotions is about to begin. May the Way protect and guide you all, until we meet again."

"May the Way protect and guide us, so may it be," the congregation responded.

This was evidently the signal for the people to rise and approach the six altars, waiting patiently to make their individual prayers to their own goddess.

Not surprisingly, the line in front of Néarta's altar was the longest, as most of Talmis's inhabitants were craftspeople. But all six goddesses had their adherents. Ylonya walked over to the Yrusian altar, while Aidren took Jacob to the Dagâran one.

As Abigail watched, people lit candles on the altars, then sat on the benches, folded their lower legs underneath and prayed to their goddesses. That was why the benches tilted forwards – how clever. This way of worship was alien to her, but also attractive. It was clear that in Veylindré, people could speak to their God – goddess, she corrected herself hastily – without mediation from a priest. She approved wholeheartedly.

"Come with me," Shaunan said, touching her shoulder, "I would like you to meet Rewald, the Waymage of Talmis."

"But…" Abigail started, "I need to check that Jacob is all right."

"Aidren is looking after him."

Abigail shrugged and followed her. Rewald was waiting for them by the altar of Ranu, the only one there.

"Waymage Rewald, I would like you to meet my young initiate, Abigail."

Rewald took her hand and looked deep into her eyes. "The young lady who soothed that young man during the service," he said. "Welcome, Abigail." Then he turned to Shaunan. "And what brings you here so early in the year, Shaunan, my friend?"

"The six of us are on our way to Ranusheim, with news for the Wayzenmoot."

As she re-told the story of Abigail and Jacob's arrival in Veylindré and the Havimi raid, Abigail's attention wandered.

She looked over to the Dagâran altar, where Jacob seemed to be arguing with Aidren and Ellyn. Abruptly, he spun on his heel and stalked out, Aidren following. She wanted to run after him, to make sure he was all right, but Shaunan was now deep in conversation with Rewald. It would be rude to disturb her.

Ellyn did it for her.

"Waymage Shaunan," she said, plucking at her aunt's sleeve, "I'm sorry to interrupt you. Jacob has left the temple. He's very upset. Aidren's gone after him."

The Waymages' attention snapped on to Ellyn.

"My apologies, Waymage Rewald," Shaunan said. "The young man is still, in many ways, a stranger to Veylindré. I fear we must follow him."

"I understand, my friend," Rewald said. "May the Way guard and guide you all." His hands sketched a blessing over them.

As they walked towards the entrance, Shaunan said, "Ellyn, fetch Ylonya, then return to the inn." When Ellyn had gone, Shaunan stopped, turned to Abigail. "Tell me what is wrong with Jacob."

֍ Chapter 19 ֍

Jacob threw himself out of the temple, so furious he could hardly think straight. That had not been worship – it had been a mockery. He couldn't go along with this any longer.

His footsteps pounding on the uneven cobbles of the narrow streets, he thought of nothing except getting the most space he possibly could between himself and the temple.

He heard running feet behind him. And a voice.

"Jacob! Wait for me!"

Aidren. What did he want? Couldn't he ever have some time alone? But no, that wasn't fair. Aidren was a decent young man – he was even starting to think of him as a friend. But now, he wanted to be on his own.

He felt a hand on his arm. "What? What do you want?"

"Come and have a drink with me. Tell me what's bothering you."

He shrugged, guessing that if he refused, Aidren would follow him just the same. "All right. Where?"

"There are plenty of inns in Talmis. Let's find one that serves food."

The word "food" reminded his stomach he hadn't eaten since an early breakfast. Which must be hours ago. He shrugged again. "Lead on. But," he warned, "nowhere the Waymage could find us."

They found a small tavern in a back street, under the sign of the boar. Jacob ducked his head as he entered. The light was dim inside, so he stood for a moment, waiting for his eyes to adjust.

It was a small, dark taproom, with a few tables scattered around the walls, at which a variety of Néartanians were quietly drinking. It smelled the same as all the taverns he'd ever known, of beer and sawdust.

"You find a table," Aidren said, "and I'll get us something to eat and drink."

Jacob nodded. "Thanks. But I'll pay for the next one."

As he made his way over to a table in a far corner, the eyes of the drinkers followed him. He guessed this was an inn mainly patronised by locals, so of course they were curious. He sat down and waited for Aidren, keeping his eyes on the table in front of him. He was sick of being an object of interest, tired of feeling like an outsider.

A couple of minutes later, Aidren returned, carrying two large mugs of beer. "I've ordered bread and cheese," he said, putting the mugs down on the table. "The barman will bring them over in a few minutes."

Jacob took a long drink. It was a deep, rich, dark brew, which went down nicely. After a moment, he looked up and saw Aidren's dark brown eyes on him.

"What is wrong, my friend?"

Jacob sighed. How could he explain how uneasy the Veylindréan service had made him? Aidren would never understand – why would he? He was Veylindréan, after all. But as the young man held his silence, Jacob realised he would have to give some explanation for his abrupt departure.

"Ach, I don't know. It's just… your worship service was so different to anything I've ever experienced. I'm used to another style altogether, where the minister preaches to the congregation and the people listen. The only time we participate is to sing hymns or join in with the prayer of Jesus. Individuals praying at different altars seemed so… so strange to me."

"Strange?" Aidren asked, looking puzzled. "What do you mean, strange?"

"Well, not right, somehow. I'm still struggling with the whole idea of the Six. My whole life, I have worshipped one God and one God only. Trying to worship six different ones is… difficult." Jacob knew he had better not describe worshipping the Six as an abomination. He didn't want to offend his only friend. And anyway, Aidren wouldn't understand.

"I don't know what to say," Aidren said. "I know nothing other than the Six. Tell me about your faith. How is it different from ours?"

"You'd be better off asking Abi. Her father was a minister."

"But Abigail's not here," Aidren said, "and you are."

Jacob gave him a wry smile. "Good point. Where do I start? You remember we told you that our God is one, but in three persons – God the Father, our Lord Jesus, the Son, and the Holy Spirit?"

Aidren wrinkled his forehead. "Ye-es, I think so. But doesn't that mean that you worship three gods, not one?"

"No!" Jacob yelped. The people around them turned their heads. "No," he repeated more quietly. It wasn't fair to take his anger out on Aidren, who was trying so hard to understand. "It is one of the mysteries of our faith that our God is three and one at the same time. In the Bible, our holy text, God spoke to Moses out of a burning bush. And he gave him ten commandments for all to follow. The most important one says, 'Thou shalt have no other gods before me.' So you can see why I'm really struggling with believing in the Six."

Aidren looked at him, doubt written all over his face. "I suppose so. But you're in Veylindré now. Everyone here follows the Six and the Way."

Jacob's head fell into his hands. "I know, but it's so hard for me. Abi doesn't seem to have any problems following both our Lord Jesus and the Six, but although I can accept the Way – I could see how using his Goldstone's power helped to make Master Kalen such a skilled smith," and here he lowered his voice, "I'm still trying to get my head around the idea of six goddesses."

Aidren patted his arm. "But can you at least try? It's going to be very difficult for you to get on here, if you can't accept the Six at all."

Jacob sighed and looked at his friend. "I know. And now I suppose I'm going to have to go back and apologise to Shaunan. Again."

"Let me go to the privy first," Aidren said. "I won't be long."

As Jacob sat finishing his drink, a stranger came and sat across from him. "I couldn't help overhearing your conversation, my friend."

Jacob looked at him warily, wondering why he kept his cloak on and hood up in the warmth of the tavern. What did he have to hide? The man had a Waymark he hadn't seen before, a vertical line with two Vs like wings on either side, on a green background. He thought it might be Garûnan. "Who are you?"

"A friend to any who do not follow the Six," the man said in an undertone.

Jacob didn't know what to think of that. Where was Aidren? He looked over in the direction which his friend had disappeared. There was no sign of him.

"Why not come with me? I'll introduce you to some… others, who feel as we do."

The man's voice was soft, sibilant, hypnotic.

Jacob shrugged, his mind quiescent. It was a reasonable request. After all, there was no-one here to miss him. He followed the stranger out of the inn.

"Where's Jacob?" Abigail's voice was sharper than Aidren had ever heard it. He felt his cheeks flush red.

He drew himself up to his full height, wishing it was more, and met her stormy eyes. "I'm sorry, Abigail. I don't know."

"What has happened to him?" Shaunan said.

Gratefully, he turned his attention to the Waymage. "I followed him out of the temple, caught up with him and took him for a drink. We talked about how he is struggling to follow the Six. Then I needed to go to the privy in the back yard. I wasn't long, but by the time I got back, Jacob had vanished.

"I asked the barman if he knew where Jacob was. A man sitting at the bar said he'd seen him talking to a cloaked and hooded stranger. He said the man had a strange accent, not one he recognised, like he was almost hissing. And that he'd slipped something into Jacob's drink. He'd been about to draw it to the barman's attention, when they had stood up and walked out together."

He paused. "I rushed out into the street, but there was no sign of them. So I thought I'd better come back here and tell you. I'm so sorry."

He glanced over at Abigail, who had turned white.

"Jacob!" she whispered. "How could you leave me? You promised you'd always be there for me."

His heart sank. He hung his head. He should never have left Jacob alone. He had seen Shaunan's face change when he had told how the man at the bar had described the stranger. What had he done?

"You are not at fault, Aidren," Shaunan said gently. "I fear an agent of the Prophet of the One has abducted Jacob. It has long been rumoured that his servants are abroad in the Commonweal, preying on those who are vulnerable to their lies."

"That's not the point," Abigail burst out. "How are we going to find him? That's the only thing that matters." She sat down abruptly and burst into noisy tears.

Shaunan sighed. "Ylonya, can you use your finding powers to locate Jacob? Aidren will take you to the place they were. Ellyn and I will stay with Abigail."

Ylonya nodded. "I'll need something of Jacob's to help me locate him."

"Aidren, please fetch Ylonya something from Jacob's pack, then go with her to the place you left him."

There was something he could do. Relief washed over him in waves. "Thank you, Waymage. I won't let you down again."

He took Ylonya to the tavern and watched with fascination as she took her blue-veined Goldstone in one hand and Jacob's shirt in the other, intoning, *"Belannath Yrusia, gal em bynn cenfent."* Then she closed her eyes, moving her head from side to side as though searching for something. He held his breath.

As she opened her eyes, her shoulders slumped. "How odd. I can sense no trace of him. Let us search some more."

For the next hours, he followed her as she paced the streets of Talmis, visiting every road that led out from the town and every tavern they passed. Each time she used her finding spell, her energy levels lessened. He admired the way she kept on trying, pushing herself to the limits of her strength.

In the end, he called a halt, worried that she would burn herself out. "Come, let's go back now. You've done your best. Some dark force must be preventing."

It was full evening by the time Ylonya and Aidren returned. Shaunan only needed one glance at their unhappy faces to realise their search had been unsuccessful.

"You could not find him?"

Ylonya shook her head. "I am sorry. Aidren and I have tramped along every road leading out of Talmis, and on most of the ones in the town, and asked in every inn and tavern we passed, but I could find no hint of his mind anywhere, nor anyone who had seen him. I don't understand. I should have been able to discover *some* trace of him." She sat down, her elbows on her knees, her whole stance one of dejection and exhaustion from prolonged use of her power.

"Do not blame yourself, Ylonya," Shaunan said. "It is my thought that the agent of the Prophet of the One has used some dark power to conceal the whereabouts of himself and Jacob. Such things are not unheard of in the Wayzenmoot."

"That may be. Nonetheless, I have failed you and failed Abigail. I do not know how she will respond to this news."

"As I said," Shaunan said gently, "the blame is not yours. I should have recognised how unhappy Jacob still was. But now I must go and tell Abigail. You two get yourselves something to eat, then rest. We will not be moving on until tomorrow."

Aidren was standing behind Ylonya, his face miserable.

"And you are not to blame either," Shaunan said to him. "Go, eat, rest."

With a heavy heart, Shaunan walked up the winding wooden stairs of the inn to find Abigail. Earlier, she had dosed her with a light sedative potion, but that would have worn off by now. She stood outside the door of the girls' room and listened. Silence. Raising the latch, she went in.

Ellyn was sitting on her bed watching Abigail, who was still asleep, her face pale, streaked with past tears. When she saw Shaunan, she tiptoed over to her. "Have they found him?" she whispered.

"No," Shaunan replied in the low voice she had learned carried less than a whisper, "Ylonya and Aidren have returned empty-handed. Thank you for watching her, Ellyn, you've done a good job. Now go down and spend some time with them. Try to stay cheerful, my dear, for their sakes."

Ellyn looked at her doubtfully, then squared her shoulders. "All right, I'll try."

"Good girl! Off you go."

When Ellyn had left the room, Shaunan woke Abigail gently. The girl sat up, her face full of hope. "Have they found him?"

"I'm so sorry, Abigail. They have not. I believe the Prophet's agent was using some dark power to shield himself and Jacob against being found."

Abigail's face went stark white. She brought up her knees and leant her forehead on them. Shaunan could hear the sound of muffled sobs. She put her arm around the girl's shoulders. Abigail stiffened, then clung to her, crying out her sorrow. Shaunan soothed her, sending feelings of calm and comfort to the girl's mind.

It took Abigail a while to regain any measure of self-control, but eventually she gulped once, and raised her tearstained face to look at her mentor. "What are we going to do? We've got to find him, somehow."

"I am sorry, but I do not know where we would start looking. Ylonya is one of the best finders in the whole of Veylindré, and if she cannot find him, none of us can. If he has been abducted by an agent of the Prophet of the One, he will be on his way to Talamdor by now."

"Then we need to go after him." Abigail withdrew from Shaunan's arms and stood up. "We need to leave now, straight away."

"Where would we go?" Shaunan asked. "There are many ways of travelling between Talmis and Talamdor and we do not know which one Jacob has taken. If we searched for him on the wrong one, we would only be wasting time.

"I am sorry," she continued, breathing deeply, knowing the girl would hate what she said next, "but I think the best thing we could do would be to continue our journey to Ranusheim and hope the Wayzenmoot can help us find him. I know of no other way of doing it."

"You're abandoning him!"

Shaunan winced inwardly at the accusation in the girl's tone. She kept her own voice soft and even, recognising how hard it must be for her to hear this. "No, I would never abandon him. We are just going to try another method of finding him." She touched her hand. "Please trust me. I want to find Jacob as much as you do but I honestly believe the only way which remains to us is to ask for the Wayzenmoot's aid."

Abigail stood with her arms crossed, hugging her shoulders, as though she was trying to contain her pain. Her face was bleak.

"I suppose I must trust you," she said in a bitter voice Shaunan had not heard before. "But you cannot possibly care about Jacob like I do. Do not expect me to be happy about this. I will come with you to Ranusheim because I have no alternative. Any hope of happiness has gone. Now please leave me alone. I need to pack."

"We will not be leaving until the morrow. Will you come down and eat with us or would you prefer to eat up here?"

Abigail shrugged. "I don't know." Her voice wobbled. "I don't know anything anymore."

"I will send Ellyn up to you presently," Shaunan said, leaving her, realising there was no point talking to her in her present state of mind.

When the company left Talmis the following morning, Ellyn could almost taste the pall of unhappiness over them, it was so visceral. Ylonya led Jacob's horse, with much of their baggage on its back, at the front of their small cavalcade.

They joined the Great South Caravan Route, a wide, well-maintained road with gentle, rolling farmland on either side, so different to Dagâran. It led to Céardochis, where they would turn north and head for Néartanis.

Ellyn watched Abigail as the girl sat listlessly on her horse, staring at the landscape as though she wasn't seeing any of it. Aidren was riding behind them all, his expression morose. She guessed he was still blaming himself for losing Jacob.

Even Ylonya was down, due, Ellyn supposed, to her failure to find Jacob. And the energy she had expended in the search had exhausted her, drained her normal ebullience.

Only Aunt Shaunan was her normal self. Thank the Six for that!

She didn't know what to do – she knew instinctively that trying to cheer up either Abigail or Aidren would go badly. And she didn't have the nerve to approach Ylonya. Her need to help, to make things better somehow, was making her stomach roil uncomfortably. She wasn't sure which one of her friends to try to comfort by the simple fact of her presence but knew that her aunt would be keeping a close eye on Abigail. So she dropped back until Aidren's horse drew level with her own.

They rode on in silence for a while.

Then Aidren burst out, "Why are you riding with me? Don't you know I've failed everyone? It's my fault Jacob is missing. I'm surprised the Waymage didn't send me home with my tail between my legs. It's what I deserve."

"You mustn't think that," she protested. "Truly, nobody blames you for Jacob going missing. You heard Aunt Shaunan say it was an agent of the Prophet of the One. How were you to know he was lurking in a corner, waiting to snatch Jacob?"

"I should have had a good look round before I left him."

Her heart sank. He was determined to blame himself. She didn't know this Aidren. Normally he was an even-tempered man. She couldn't understand why he was wallowing in this negativity. She'd try once more, then leave him to it.

"Aidren, *I* don't think that you are to blame and neither does Aunt Shaunan. Please believe me."

His head came up and he looked at her directly for the first time. "*You* don't think I'm to blame? Will you swear it by the Six?"

She reached across, put her hand on his where it held the reins. "I swear it by the Six and the Way, my friend," she said, wanting to say what was in her heart, but not quite daring to. "You are not to blame. This could have happened to any of us at any time."

She saw his eyes welling up. Did her good opinion mean so much to him? Maybe there was hope for her, after all. She looked away while he got his emotions under control.

When she looked back, he was smiling at her. Still not the Aidren she knew, but it was a start.

Abigail was adrift on an ocean of pain and grief. All the time she had been in Veylindré, Jacob had been at her side. With her. Without him, she did not know how she was going to cope with all the challenges ahead. She had lost him, like she had lost her mother, father, brothers and sister. She was alone. She had lost him. He was gone forever. How could she continue without him?

She rode on, barely conscious of Shaunan's presence at her side. Why hadn't Ylonya been able to find him? And why was the Waymage walking away from any hope of finding him? Surely she knew her heart was breaking?

"Abigail." The tone of Shaunan's voice told her this was not the first time the Waymage had tried to get her attention. She turned, waited for her to say something that would make any sense.

"Abigail," Shaunan said. "Talk to me, my dear. Tell me what is on your mind and heart."

Didn't she know?

Abigail then realised Shaunan had courteously refrained from dipping into her thoughts. That consideration for her privacy deserved an answer at least.

"I feel so lost. Without Jacob, I don't know who I am. Until now, he's been with me. I can't bear to think," she said, her voice dropping to an anguished whisper, "that I may never see him again."

The simple naming of her sorrow brought on tears. Sternly, she ordered them back. Tears helped no-one. Crying herself sick wouldn't bring Jacob back. She realised Shaunan was speaking again.

"...when we reach Ranusheim."

"I'm sorry – what did you say? I only caught the last few words."

"I was saying," her mentor said in a gentle voice, "as soon as we reach Ranusheim, I promise I will ask the Wayzenmoot to use all their powers to try to locate him. I know your grief is great, coming on top of all else you have suffered. I feel your sorrow. Tell me what I can do to help you bear it. We have long seisdags on the road ahead of us and you need to be awake and present for them."

Abigail bowed her head, recognising the truth in Shaunan's words. She gave her a weak smile. "Do you have a potion that will numb my sorrow?"

"I am sorry, Abigail," Shaunan said, "but I do not think that would be wise. I can give you something to help you sleep well every night, but any potion strong enough to numb your sorrow would also seriously weaken you, both mentally and spiritually. Anguish is a natural part of life, an essential component of love. If you want to grow stronger as a person, you will have to live through this. And," she added, "we are going to need your powers in the seisdags ahead."

"Yours is the knowing, Waymage," Abigail said formally. "I will do my best."

Chapter 20

Abigail sat bolt upright in the near darkness, starting out of her dream with the words of the prophet Joshua, spoken in her father's declamatory tones, ringing in her head.

"When ye have transgressed the covenant of the Lord your God, which He commanded you, and have gone and served other gods, and bowed yourselves to them; then shall the anger of the Lord be kindled against you."

The faint light of dawn was stealing in through the gaps in the wooden shutters. She could see the hump that was Ellyn's body, peacefully sleeping in the bed next to her, and hear her friend's gentle breathing. Lucky Ellyn – she still had her Aidren with her.

Oh my God! Was *this* why Jacob had been taken from her? Because she had bowed down before the Six? Shivering, she reached for her shawl and wrapped it around her. "When ye have gone and served other gods, then shall the anger of the Lord be kindled against you." It was clear enough. God was punishing her by taking Jacob away.

But would He, really? She remembered another text, one of which her mother had been fond, from the Gospel of John: "In my father's house are many mansions."

When Abigail had come to her one day, puzzled by her father's denunciation of anyone who was not Presbyterian, her mother had said, "Remember, my dear, what our beloved Lord told the disciples, 'In my father's house are many mansions'. I am sure all Christians and all good men will come to heaven in the end."

Abigail shook her head. Which text should she believe?

Her father had taught her that the Bible was the inerrant word of God. Yet it contained so many contradictions. It had seemed such a natural decision to follow the Six. She had found so much goodness in the people of Veylindré and in the Way.

Or had Jacob been right in his condemnation?

Whom could she talk to? Would anyone even understand? How could they? Only she and Jacob in this whole wide world were Christian. And now he was gone. She was alone. But the habit of sharing her troubles with Shaunan was well-established, and after long thought, she decided to talk to her after breakfast. If she could get her alone. She couldn't speak of this in front of the others. She bowed her head repeating her father's prayer softly, but for the first time, it did not bring her any consolation.

After breakfast, Abigail made her request. "Please may I speak with you alone?"

Shaunan looked up. "Of course. Ylonya, please would you and Aidren and Ellyn top up our supplies and prepare the horses for departure."

The three of them left the room.

"What do you want to speak with me about?"

"May we go to your room?"

"Surely," Shaunan said and led the way to the room she had been sharing with Ylonya. What was troubling the girl? She was trembling and as white as a sheet.

Shaunan sat near the fire, absently admiring the finely carved wood panelling on the walls. She gestured for Abigail to join her.

"I'm so frightened," Abigail blurted out as she sat. "What if Jacob being abducted was all my fault?"

What was this about? "What makes you think that?"

"I woke up with a text from the Bible in my head," Abigail said, "and now I can't forget it."

Then she shared her fears with Shaunan – that she had transgressed against her god, that Jacob's abduction was that god's way of punishing her. "What if it's true?" she wound up. "What if I've committed a great sin by following the Six and the Way and so God is afflicting me as a punishment for straying?"

The anguish was pouring from the girl in waves. Shaunan fought to close her mind to it, so she could listen with full attention. Mother Ranu, please help me to find the right words. "Is your god so stern?"

"I don't know!" Abigail wailed. "My mother didn't think so, but my father certainly believed we would be punished for our sins, forever and ever."

"Think of your mother, Abigail. If you had taken this problem to her, how would she have responded?"

"I tried that and remembered a saying of Jesus my mother loved. 'In my father's house are many mansions'. She… she believed that in the end, no-one would be locked out of God's love. That if we repented of our sins, we would always be forgiven."

"Your holy text seems to contain some contradictions," Shaunan said, feeling her way with care. "Which one does your heart believe is true?"

"It was one of the things I was struggling with, even before we came here. We are taught that the Bible is the inerrant word of God. But the differences between the God of the Old Testament and the God of the New seem so huge to me, even if I've never dared to share that with my father. He would have called me a heretic. The Jesus I love and follow would never shut us out from his grace and mercy, but the God of the Old Testament…" she shuddered, "…can be harsh and unforgiving. I do not know which one to believe in."

Again Shaunan asked, "Which one does your heart believe is true?"

Abigail was gazing into the dancing flames, fiddling with her hair in agitation. The silence in the little room was broken only by her uneven breathing.

"I'd like to believe I would always be forgiven. But what if following the Six is the one thing God cannot forgive? The words of Joshua are clear.

"And I feel so guilty I didn't recognise how much Jacob was struggling with worshipping the Six.I should have realised that. I thought he accepted the Way because he'd seen how much it would help him become a better smith. But he still found it hard to follow any other gods."

She sighed.

"It's different for me. The Six and the Way open doors in my heart. I can see no ill in following them. But what if I'm wrong? What if Jacob is right?"

Shaunan realised the girl was suffering a full-blown spiritual crisis. She had not fully understood how belief in the Six contradicted everything Abigail had been taught by the leaders of her own faith.

"I think," she said, treading cautiously, "there are two issues here. First, what you believe about sin, which we call wrongdoing and, second, what you believe about how your god responds when people fall short of their best selves. These are big issues you are wrestling with. Help me to understand."

"That's what I need – for you to hear me, then help me to understand what I need to do."

"So tell me about sin. What does it mean in your faith?"

"Oh, my goodness! Where do I start? There are so many things considered sin in our world. There are the big ones, which I guess any people would share – killing, lying, stealing, fornication. Catholics, who are a particular type of Christian, believe that there are seven Deadly Sins: pride, greed, wrath, envy, lust, gluttony and sloth. Which pretty much cover all areas of human wrongdoing, I suppose."

Shaunan nodded. "I see. That is a very comprehensive list. And your god would be angry if you committed any of these? Hmm. I think that in Veylindré we perceive such prohibitions as ethical values, which we try to follow, rather than what you call sins. Following the Way means behaving in the best way we can. But I do not believe the Six would punish us for falling short."

"Maybe our God wouldn't either," Abigail said in a small voice, "but that is what I was brought up to believe."

"Let me see. I wonder whether we can look at it another way. Does your god take our choices into account?"

"Oh, yes! Free will is very important. I was taught that sin is a choice we make, to move us away from union with God."

"Very well." Shaunan thought for a moment. "I would like you to consider these questions: Did you have any choice about coming to Veylindré? Or about deciding to become one of us, by following the Six and the Way, so that you could live safely here? And have you stopped praying to your god in your daily Immersion practice?"

Abigail gaped at her. "I hadn't thought of it like that. I had no choice about coming to Veylindré. The Way seemed so good and real to me that I chose freely to embrace it. And yes, I still pray to Jesus every morning."

"Then I do not see why your god would punish you for doing the best you can with the life you have been given. Do you?"

Abigail's faced cleared a little. "I suppose not," she answered. "But we are taught we have to follow God's commandments, or else we will not get to heaven but be cast into the fiery pit of hell."

"Tell me about heaven and hell."

"They are the two places our souls go to after we die. Jesus, who is the Great Judge, examines all the deeds and words of our lives, then decides where we should go. I'm terrified of going to hell."

"All right. Go back to what your mother told you, that your god would always forgive you if you repented. What about that?"

"This is where I get so confused. On the one hand, I believe that through God's grace, we will always obtain mercy. And on the other, I was told that if I fall into sin, I will suffer for it, both here and after death."

Mother Ranu, help me to lift this burden from her. "You have said you have to follow your god's commandments. What is the greatest commandment?"

A reluctant smile crept over Abigail's face. "A lawyer asked Jesus that question. I have always loved his answer. In fact, I loved it so much I learned it off by heart. 'Thou shalt love the Lord thy God with all thy heart, and with all thy soul, and with all thy mind. This is the first and great commandment. And the second is like unto it, Thou shalt love thy neighbour as thyself. On these two commandments hang all the law and the prophets.'"

In an instant, Shaunan saw her way clear. "Then as far as I can understand it, you are fulfilling both those – you are still following your god, and praying to him every day, and you do your best to be kind to others. I think," and here she smiled at Abigail, "you need to concentrate on the part about loving yourself."

Abigail blushed, then almost smiled. "You are so wise, Shaunan. I feel much better now. Thank you so much."

"You are welcome, my dear. I hope you will always bring your troubles to me. That is why I am here." She embraced the girl, then said, "I expect the others will be waiting for us. Come."

Ylonya's gaze followed the Waymage and her initiate as they left the downstairs room of the inn. "I wonder what that's about?"

Aidren shrugged. "None of our business."

"What do we need to buy?" Ellyn asked.

"Fresh bread would be good, cheese – one of those Néartanian round cheeses should keep well – and I fancy some of last year's apples, if we can find them."

"Do all three of us need to go?" Aidren asked.

Ylonya looked at him. "If you'd rather prepare the horses for departure, Ellyn and I can buy what is needed."

Then smiled to herself as Aidren's face brightened. Like most men, he did not enjoy shopping.

As Aidren headed for the stables, she said, "We'd better get moving, Ellyn. When the Waymage and Abigail are finished, we need to be on our way. The days are short."

The two women strolled down the main street of the village. Neat Néartanian houses, their wood gleaming with varnish, nestled cheek by jowl with neat Néartanian shops. their windows full of orderly displays.

They exchanged friendly nods with spotlessly attired Néartanians, bustling along, minding their own business. The only building of any distinction was the Temple of the Six and even that looked neat and tidy. And on the outskirts, Ylonya could see neat Néartanian fields.

She admired the thrift and industry of these people but could not imagine living like they did – quiet, unadventurous lives, one season much the same as the next. Events in the wider Commonweal did not seem to have touched them. She would be bored out of her mind inside a couple of seisdags.

Ellyn seemed excited.

This would be a good time to get to know her a little better. "Is this your first trip outside Dagâran?"

"It's my first long trip anywhere," Ellyn said, shaking back her dark, curly hair. "Aunt Shaunan has taken me to Myndorian a couple of times for festivals, but otherwise, I've spent the whole of my life in Nordvein." She laughed. "I already feel as though we have been travelling forever. I had no idea that the world outside Nordvein was so big, so… fascinating."

Ylonya felt a twinge of sympathy, mingled with an unexpected pang of envy. From her earliest years, she had travelled the length and breadth of the Commonweal, sharing her mother's trading journeys. What would it be like to be rooted in one community?

"Tell me more about your life in Nordvein."

"There's nothing much to tell. My father died in a mining accident and my mother died in childbirth shortly afterwards, when I was five. To tell you the truth, I hardly remember them. Aunt Shaunan has looked after me since then."

Ylonya looked at the leather bag slung over her young companion's shoulder. "Yet you are not a miner."

Ellyn laughed. "I thought my Waymark would be a miner's and was so surprised when I was called to be a Néartanian cordwainer. In the years since, I've been training with Master Raimun in Nordvein. When this adventure began, I was waiting to be assigned my journeywoman piece so that I could travel to the Hall of Clothiers in Céardochis to complete my training. It was wonderful to train with Master Markhan in Luvodican – I learned so much from him."

"And how long have you known Aidren?"

Ellyn blushed. "Most of my life. Why?"

"No reason. I was just curious."

"What about you?" Ellyn said. "Where did you grow up?"

Ylonya laughed. "All over the place. As soon as I was old enough, my mother took me with her on her trading journeys. We lived in our wagon. We only came home to Porusport to re-stock before taking to the road again. My father is Guildmaster Brickon, Master of the Hall of Traders, so he has to stay put."

"It must be so exciting to visit so many places," Ellyn said, "but don't you ever want to settle down?"

"No. I don't think I'd ever be satisfied, living in one place. If you continue on this journey, you'll be visiting a fair few yourself. When we get to Céardochis, I'll buy you a silver ring as a souvenir."

Ellyn's smile lit up her face. "Oh, Ylonya! That would be wonderful."

"You're welcome. But Ellyn," Ylonya said, moved by a sudden foreboding, "don't relax into it too much. Not everyone you meet will be kind or trustworthy. Be on your guard."

By the time Ellyn and Ylonya returned, Aidren had saddled up all the horses and loaded their baggage on to the packhorse. Shaunan and Abigail were waiting for them inside the inn.

Everyone mounted up, crossed the bridge over the River Clearwater, flowing deep and fast towards the Gulf of Dagâran, and joined the Great South Caravan Route. It was a fine cold day, good for travelling.

"How far is it from here to Céardochis, Ylonya?" Ellyn asked, excited about being on this journey, seeing new places, meeting new people, having new experiences.

"About another ninety miles, so probably another four days. The Caravan Route crosses the Central Plains of Néartania here, then carries on north-west all the way to Porusport."

"What is it like in Céardochis?" Abigail asked.

Ellyn glanced at her friend, who was looking less troubled now, if still pale. It was good to hear her joining in the conversation. She had been so worried about her yesterday; she had been so withdrawn. Whatever Aunt Shaunan had said to her must have helped.

"Céardochis," Ylonya said, "is one of the most important trade centres on the Caravan Route."

"Why?" Aidren chimed in.

"Mainly because of its location," Ylonya said. "It stands at the conjunction of the Caravan Route and the River Mistbourne, which rises in the mountains of Talamdor and flows north-east all the way to the Néartanian Straits. And there is a main road linking Céardochis to Néartanis, the capital city of Néartania. That is the route we will be following."

"What happens there?" Abigail asked.

"Céardochis is the main commercial centre of Néartania – it is possible to buy items made by all the craftspeople of the land there. If you know where to go, that is. Which of course, I do. Once a year, during the Season of Growth, it hosts an annual Craft Fair, which attracts traders from all corners of Veylindré. It is also home to two of Néartania's three chief Guild Halls, the Hall of Clothiers and the Builders' Hall."

"It must be a very busy place," Abigail said.

"It is indeed." Ylonya laughed. "I like the bustle of Céardochis. I feel at home there."

Ellyn looked around her. Here, the countryside was so different to the neat homesteads and villages they had seen so far in Néartania and to the Dagâran she knew and loved.

At home, her views were bounded by the great Dagâran Range, which marched down the spine of Dagâran all the way from the north coast to Luvodican and the forest in the other direction. But now they had left Talmis behind, they were riding through a wide plain of grassland, bordered by soft hills in the far distance, almost invisible to the naked eye.

Even though it was the Season of Dormancy, Ellyn could smell the green scent of things growing. And the sky seemed huge and boundless, stretching upwards forever.

"This is so different to the land south-east of Talmis," she said.

"Néartania is a huge country," Ylonya said. "These are the Central Plains, which run right across the land from the Talamdor Mountains in the west to the Gulf of Dagâran in the east. They are bounded by the River Clearwater to the south and the River Cristail in the north. The herders follow their cattle and horses all over them in the warmer seasons, only returning to their homes part way through the Season of Completion, depending on the weather."

She laughed. "If I had not been a trader, I would not have minding being a Néartanian herder – their lives are very free."

"Freedom is that important to you, then?" Ellyn asked.

"It is like bread and clear water. I could not live without it."

A surge of admiration for this self-sufficient woman rose in Ellyn's heart. It must be a fine thing to have no ties, to be able to go where you wanted, when you wanted, free of all obligations, except for seeing what lay beyond the next hill. But lonely, too. She could not imagine a life without close friends, without anyone to rely on, or who relied on her.

Aidren drew her aside. "Ellyn," he murmured, "I retrieved Jacob's sword from the Temple at Talmis before we left. Do you think Abigail would like to have it?"

"I think she would."

Chapter 21

When Jacob came to, he was on lying on a bunk, a blanket over him. It felt as though the storm was over. Good.

But it was unexpectedly silent. He remembered being with other people, people he knew. Where had they gone? He strained his ears and could hear the regular splash of oars in water. But the clean, salt smell of the sea, which had been such a part of his life in recent weeks, was no longer present. And now he thought about it, the cabin itself looked different – it was smaller, to start with. Where was he?

He sat up, swung his legs around in preparation for getting up and investigating. Then he noticed something of which he had no memory at all. Around his left wrist was a silver-coloured bangle, a full half-inch wide, set with a small, round stone, of a red so dark it was almost black. Like a very dark garnet – not that he had seen many. But even in this dim light, its facets sparkled.

He examined the bangle more closely. It was a beautiful piece of work, with fine engraving running all around it – a pattern of intersecting triangles. It fitted snugly on his wrist, but he could find no catch. He could not remember buying it – he would never have been able to afford such a fine piece anyway – nor being given it.

What was going on?

This vessel did not feel like, or sound like, the *Sweet Sarah* – that had been the name of the ship. Good, he had remembered it. He and a group of other people had been sailing across the Atlantic Ocean, travelling to the New World. Had he been injured in the storm? Lost consciousness? He was obviously no longer at sea. He checked himself over, stood up and stretched all his limbs. Nothing hurt. The only thing he could see that he didn't recognise, apart from the bangle, was a small puncture wound in the crook of his elbow. But it was not painful and had healed well.

He sat down again, tried to fill in the gaps in his memory. He was missing something. Something important.

He cudgelled his brains. Images of two people swam up into his conscious mind.

A girl, slight, beautiful, with blue eyes and masses of soft, blonde hair. He felt he knew her, that she was important to him.

And a man – tall, stern, angry, with a shock of grey hair and a deep voice. That memory wasn't so pleasant – he hadn't liked him, whoever he was.

Why could he not remember? Maybe he had banged his head during the storm. He had heard of such things.

So what *could* he remember?

He was Jacob, Jacob Wallingford. His father had been a blacksmith, and he, Jacob, had been his apprentice. But the reason he had left his village, left all the people he knew, eluded him. What was wrong with him? His mind was clear, he just had the uneasy feeling something was wrong, something was missing…

Then a hatch he hadn't noticed opened and he saw grey sky through it, blocked by the body of a man.

Jacob sprang to his feet.

Balancing a tray in his hands, the man climbed down the steps into the cabin. A thin, almost emaciated man of medium height and middle years with white skin, pale, dead eyes and, above them, a shock of bright red hair. He wore unremarkable black breeches and tunic over a white shirt, with a black cloak. The lining of his cloak was dark red.

Jacob fumbled for his knife.

"Be easy," the man said, in a soft, hissing voice, which made the hair on the back of Jacob's neck stand up. "My timing is good. I hoped you would be awake by now. Here is breakfast."

At the word "breakfast", Jacob suddenly realised he was ravenous. How long had he been unconscious? He fell on the food as though he had not eaten for a week. Thick slices of bread lavishly spread with honey and a mug of something warm to wash it down with. For a few minutes, he thought of nothing else. He had never tasted anything so delicious in his life.

Then wariness returned. "Thank you, sir – I'm sorry, I don't know your name."

"My name is Portak. I serve the Prophet of the One."

"The Prophet of the One? Who is that?"

"What do you remember, Jacob?"

"How do you know my name?"

"You have spoken long in your sleep, my friend."

That did not sound good. What had he said? Where was he?

"Where am I?"

"In a boat, moving upriver towards the border with Talamdor." Portak paused, then repeated his question. "What do you remember, Jacob?"

Jacob shrugged. He might as well answer. Better go along with what the man wanted until he knew where he was, what had happened to him. "Not much. The last I remember, we were on the *Sweet Sarah* and a great storm blew up. Did I hit my head?"

"Something of the kind," Portak replied smoothly. "But you feel better now, do you not?"

"I was on a ship, the *Sweet Sarah,* sailing to the New World, with some people. I don't remember why." He could feel the panic rising in his throat, almost choking him.

"What do you remember about that?"

"I can only remember two people and them only dimly. A girl with beautiful blonde hair and an angry man. Why can't I remember what happened?"

"These things happen sometimes with… blows to the head."

The man's voice was making him uneasy. There was something disturbing about him, something… not quite right. "What happened to the other people?"

"You can forget them. They failed to make it ashore."

A pang of regret filled Jacob's heart. He would not see the blonde girl again.

When Portak closed the hatch behind him, leaving Jacob in the cabin, he was well satisfied.

The bangle of control had worked its usual magic. The boy could not remember any of his time in Veylindré. Excellent. That would make life easier.

The Prophet would be pleased indeed with this one. He was sure the boy was one of the survivors of the raid. At any rate, he fitted the description that dolt, Oltan, had given him. It was a pity he hadn't managed to capture the girl too but the Prophet would surely forgive him. Surely.

And from what he had overheard in the tavern, half of his work had already been done for him – the boy already mistrusted the Six.

He had searched the boy thoroughly while he was unconscious and discovered he carried no Bloodstone. He hoped his master would forgive him for not finding it. He shivered – the Prophet of the One was not known for his gentle and forgiving nature.

But the encounter in that inn in Talmis had been a smooth piece of work. That would surely count in his favour. The boy had only looked away for a few seconds and he had dosed his drink. He had scarcely got him back to the boat he had hired when he had fallen asleep. And remained asleep for two full days and nights. Odd – the potion usually induced unconsciousness for only a few hours – where was this boy from?

Nevertheless, it had been useful. It had given Portak plenty of time to draw the blood from him, with which he imbued the clear stone of the bangle of control, turning it blood-red. Then he had used the Bloodstone, some of his last vial of blood, and the spell his master had taught him to seal the bangle around the boy's wrist.

Short of cutting a hand off, he would never be able to break free unless the Prophet himself released him.

And he had discreetly thrown Jacob's Goldstone into the fast-moving waters of the Clearwater. The boy would not be needing it again.

As a bonus, they were more than forty miles away from Talmis when the boy came round. Slow progress – but the current of the Clearwater was strong and fast flowing, and they were rowing upstream. There was nowhere for him to run.

Satisfied, Portak smiled. The boy was young and handsome, but not his type. At last, he would be able to return to Talamdor, see Balmak again. They would be on this boat for another three days, before the Clearwater became too shallow to navigate. Portak was sure he would be able to buy a couple of horses at the small town of Clearhaven. It would take a further three days to reach the secret tunnel through the

Talamdor Mountains. After which, the rest of the journey would be simple.

He had contacted the Prophet to let him know of his success, but had received no response, which was worrying. He wished he could use his Bloodstone to contact Balmak, let him know he was on his way home, but it was a one-track link to the Prophet, through Chief Messenger Tamin.

He shrugged.

He would be glad when he was off this boat. Although he had paid well for it at Talmis, he did not trust the captain or the crew. The feeling was mutual. He would have to be careful to keep them away from Jacob, his prize. No telling what they might do if they thought the boy was there against his will.

Now the boy was awake, Portak would befriend him. Or at least give the appearance of befriending him.

Most importantly, he would keep the boy docile. While the bangle would keep him from regaining his lost memories, it could not influence how he would react to new encounters.

Jacob was getting fed up with being cooped up in the small cabin. He tried the hatch, but it was locked. Was he a prisoner of this man, this… Portak?

"Hey!" he shouted. "I want to be let out of here."

He waited, listened.

Nothing.

He pounded on the hatch with the pommel of his knife. "Hey! Let me out of here! I want to come up on deck."

Footsteps overhead. Someone had heard him. Then the harsh scream of metal on metal as the latch was pulled back.

Finally.

As he watched, the hatch opened and Portak clambered down into the cabin.

"Why am I a prisoner?" Jacob demanded. "I want to go up on deck, feel some fresh air on my face."

The man's expression was mild but watchful. "Of course, my friend," he said smoothly, "whenever you wish. You had better wear a cloak. There is a cold wind."

Jacob grabbed his cloak eagerly, fastened it at the neck and followed Portak up the steps on to the deck of the boat. They stood at the prow. To keep out of the way of the crew, he supposed. It was so good to be outside again. But the man had been right – the wind was bitterly cold. He clutched his cloak around him.

"Where are we?" he said. "And where are we going?"

"We are on the River Clearwater in western Néartania, travelling towards the town of Clearhaven, which is where the Clearwater becomes too shallow to be navigable. We will reach it in two or three days, I suspect."

Jacob recognised none of these strange names. He fought down the feelings of unease and looked out over the landscape.

To the left-hand side – port, the sailors called it – grassland, with a great forest in the far distance. To the starboard side, more rolling grassland, stretching as far as the eye could see.

But ahead of them, almost filling the forward horizon, stark and beautiful in the winter sunlight, a formidable range of snow-capped mountains.

He did not recognise this place, this land, at all. And hadn't it been high summer? What was going on? "But why are we here? Where are we going?"

"We are returning to the great land of Talamdor. Or at least, I am returning, and you are going there for the first time. It is the land beyond those mountains ahead of us."

"I've never heard of it," Jacob snapped. "Why am I here?"

"Peace, my friend. You are here because I found you wandering after the shipwreck and rescued you. Your mind was confused and you had nowhere to go, no friends to succour you. So I have brought you with me, to start your new life."

Jacob thought about this. "Thank you, I suppose," he said slowly. "But your answers are meaningless to me. I have never heard of Néartania or Talamdor. Are we in the New World?"

"No," Portak said in a low voice. Jacob wondered why he whispered. "We are in the Commonweal of Veylindré, in the land of Néartania, as I said. It is fortunate it was I who found you and not one of the evil Veylindréan witches who inhabit it. Your fate would have been very different had you fallen into their hands."

"Witches? You have witches here?" His heart began to race as panic flooded through him. Where on earth had he ended up?

"Alas. Yes, indeed. They worship six goddesses, so-called, and work sorcery using golden stones."

Jacob shuddered. It sounded as though he had had a narrow escape. "This… Talamdor we are going to," he said. "Are there any witches there?"

"By the One, no!" Portak answered. "In Talamdor, we worship the One and follow the One True Way."

Jacob relaxed. This sounded much more like the England he had left behind. "Then I thank you, sir, for saving me."

"You are welcome. Come now. It is important for you to rest after such a nasty knock on the head. Let us go below and I will answer any questions you have about this new world."

Portak would be glad to get off this boat and on to horses. The last couple of days had been exhausting – trying to keep Jacob away from the Néartanian crew and giving non-informative or misleading answers to the boy's many questions. But they should be at Clearhaven in a few hours. Then he would be able to relax. At least a little.

"Are you ready to go?"

"I cannot wait to be off this boat," Jacob said, his dark eyes glowing with excitement. "You say it will take us another two days from Clearhaven to reach the border of Talamdor?"

"Yes, it is about sixty miles. I am sure I will be able to buy horses there. Once we are through the pass, we will be safe."

"You are generous, Portak," Jacob said. "I wish I had some money of my own."

"I am sure that once we are in Talamdor, you will be able to find work. You said you are a smith?"

As though he didn't know, as though the boy's Dagâran Waymark did not proclaim it for all the world to see.

Portak had been concerned that the crew would question them –would ask why two good Veylindréans were travelling towards the forbidden land of Talamdor. But he had much practice at deflecting unwanted questions, at giving uninformative answers.

His new cover story, having changed his glamoured Waymark to Yrusian, was that he was a trader from Garûnalonden, looking for new opportunities in western Néartania. Only to Jacob did he reveal the truth – that their true destination was Talamdor. Who could he tell, after all? Portak had ensured that he was with the boy any time he appeared on deck.

At last they reached Clearhaven. Portak paid the captain the balance of what was owing and strode down the gangplank, followed by Jacob. The Néartanian crew raised both anchor and sail and headed back down the Clearwater as fast as they could. Cowards! Their time would come.

Portak breathed a sigh of relief.

"It is so good to be back on dry land," Jacob said.

"Yes, my friend. The dangerous part of our journey is nearly over. In two days' time, we will be safe over the border and back among civilised people. Follow me and we will see about finding mounts for us both."

Half an hour later, they were on their way. They had found a hostler in Clearhaven who sold Portak a couple of horses, and for a few extra guilders, he had thrown in the tack and some provender.

They were all set.

Once clear of the town, riding on the smooth grassy track which led to the secret pass, Portak turned to Jacob. "Now that we are alone, Jacob, you may ask any questions you like."

The boy's face brightened. "Thank you. You have told me so little."

Portak smiled and nodded.

"Tell me some more about Talamdor. I know so little about it."

"Talamdor is the land of the free," Portak said, "where all people wishing to avoid coming under the dominion of the witches of Veylindré and their false goddesses dwell. Our ruler is the Prophet of the One, my master. It was he who led us in rebellion against the evil Havimi, who subjugated my people many years ago, and kept us in slavery. But our brave Prophet, guided by a vision from Holy Talamu, put the heart back into my people and we rose up and expelled them from our land."

"How long ago was that?"

"About thirty years ago. In the years since then, we have used our time well by building up our strength, rebuilding our economy and recruiting young people into our army. Now we are nearly ready."

Portak was expecting the boy to ask what they were nearly ready for, so was alost wrongfooted by his next question.

"Who is Holy Talamu? You have not spoken of him before."

"Holy Talamu is our goddess, whom we serve with all our hearts and souls."

"Your god is female?" The dismay was clear to hear in the boy's voice.

"She is as strong as any god," Portak replied sternly. "You would do best not to speak ill of her."

"I'm sorry. I was just surprised. My God is male."

"Your god?" Portak could not keep the surprise out of his voice. "The god of your world is male?"

"Yes. I have never heard of a female divinity before this."

"You must speak of this with the Prophet," Portak said. "It is beyond my knowing. Let us leave this subject now. Ask about something else."

"Where do I start? I know nothing of your land. You say it is the region beyond these great mountains?" Jacob nodded up at the snow covered crags ahead of them.

"Yes, we will have to go through the secret pass to get there."

"Why is it secret?"

"Because we do not wish any who do not believe as we do to find a home in our land."

"But you are taking me there?"

"Yes, because it is my home, and I've taken a liking to you," he lied smoothly. "I did not wish to leave you to the mercy of the witches of Veylindré."

The boy smiled at him in gratitude. "You have my thanks for that. Their ways sound so wrong to me. And magic is evil."

Portak started. Was that what the boy believed? Better tread carefully here.

"It depends on how it is used," he said. "Some magic can be used for good purposes."

"Such as what?"

"Did your god never use magic to cure the ills of your world?"

"Hmm," Jacob said. "We don't call that magic, we call that miracles. But I suppose you might be right."

"So it is not the magic in itself that is evil, but how it is used and what the consequences of using it are. If you wish to know more, I must ask you to wait until we reach Talamunem City and speak to the Prophet about this. I am a simple man. Such questions are beyond me."

A flicker of annoyance crossed the boy's face. "Then what can you tell me about?"

Chapter 22

Travelling across the Central Plains was a fresh experience for Abigail. Such a huge, open landscape. It seemed as though it stretched on forever – rich grasslands, threaded with a lacework pattern of little streams and small rivulets, and green plants growing even in this cold season. And the sky above, with its ever-changing cloudscape, extending from horizon to horizon in every direction. The air was full of birdsong. Every so often they passed a small encampment of the herders Ylonya had mentioned – clusters of leather tents, inhabited by sturdy, tanned men and women, dressed warmly in cloaks and furs. Their children running wild, shouting and laughing, playing wherever they liked. Ylonya was right – it must be a good way to live.

Her own life in England had been so very different. She had lived in a small, stable community, where there was a place for everyone and everyone in their place. From Squire Petty down to the smallest child, they all knew where they belonged. And their village was boundaried by neat fields, not this burgeoning wilderness. All at once, she was overwhelmed by the high skies and wide spaces around her. How had she ended up here?

Her grief for Jacob was tearing at her heart. Every step her horse took was moving her further away from any possibility of rescuing him. She had accepted Shaunan's reasons for continuing to Ranusheim in her head, but her heart was yearning to abandon the journey and search for him. He was the only person who truly knew her, knew her life before she had arrived in Veylindré. She was missing him so much, the pain was also physical – a dull ache in her chest.

The others were talking gaily around her, but she did not have the heart to join in.

"Ylonya," Ellyn asked, "how far do the Central Plains go on for?"

"For more than two hundred and fifty miles, from the Gulf of Dagâran in the east, to the Talamdor Mountains in the west, and for between eighty and a hundred miles between the two rivers which form their boundaries. So further than your Myndorian in the north, to Fionnan in south Dagâran."

Ellyn gaped at her. "Truly? They are as big as almost the whole of Dagâran?"

Even Abigail could not help smiling at her friend's astonishment, which she shared. Néartania was a huge country indeed. It helped to explain why Ylonya and even Shaunan had not known where to start looking for Jacob.

"Abigail," Aidren said, as they made their way down to the inn's taproom, "I picked up Jacob's sword from the temple at Talmis before we left. Would you like to have it?"

Her eyes filled with tears. "Thank you, Aidren, that was good of you. But I would have no use for a sword. You keep it and use it. It should belong to a warrior. Then, if we ever see Jacob again, you can return it to him."

That was not what he had expected to hear. He bowed to her.

"I will take great care of it, and hold it in trust for Jacob."

"Thank you, my friend."

Had it not been for his residual feelings of guilt, Aidren would have enjoyed this part of their journey. The great rolling grass-scape of the Central Plains was as unfamiliar to him as it was to Ellyn. But he was loving it – the wide, open spaces seemed to expand him, somehow. Anything could happen here. And probably would.

They were sharing their journey with others now. Until now, their small company had travelled alone. But the Great South Caravan Route was busy, even at this time of year. They met, or overtook, parties of traders, their mules and wagons laden with trade goods. The inns they stayed in each night were bustling, full of people from all corners of Veylindré. Or so it seemed to him.

Tanned Yrusian traders rubbed shoulders with sturdy Néartanian farmers. He saw dark-skinned people from his own land of Dagâran and the tall, pale folk of Garûnalonden. There were even a few brown-skinned Lèniumen – travelling musicians or storytellers, to judge by their bright clothing. Living along the Caravan Route must be like attending a permanent festival.

It was fascinating to listen to them. At the table next to them, a tall Garûnalonden man with blonde hair and startling green eyes was having a conversation with a Lèniumen – a storyteller perhaps, for he was not garbed as a healer.

"What brings you here, my friend?" the Lèniumen asked.

"I come," the tall man said, his accent throaty and rough to Aidren's ears, "with a consignment of wool for Lord Lesym and Lady Bélia in far-off Luvodican. In normal times, we would have sailed from Garûnashavn in the south of my land, down through the Yrusian Sea and the Néartanian Straits to the Gulf of Dagâran. But we have been hearing that Havimi pirates," and here he broke off to curse in his own guttural tongue, "have been seen in the Ranusian Sea. So I and my companions have taken the overland route from Mathven. And you? What are you doing here, so far from Lènium?"

In contrast, the Lèniumen's voice was light, almost musical. "Ah, my friend, we storytellers must travel all over the Commonweal, finding audiences for our tales. My company and I celebrated Dagârastide in Iascan, in northern Yrusian, and are also travelling towards Luvodican for the festival of Lèniastide, six long seisdags away. Perhaps we might travel together? For it is said there is safety in numbers."

"Belike you have the right of it," the Garûnalonden agreed. "I will speak to our trade master."

"Aidren!"

Aidren's attention snapped back to his companions. "I'm sorry, I didn't hear what you said."

"I could tell," Ellyn said, a twinkle in her eye. "You were miles away."

Aidren flushed. "I was listening to the people on the next table," he said in a low voice. "I've never met any Garûnalonden or Lèniumen before."

"We saw the Lèniumen storytellers in Luvodican," Ellyn reminded him.

"Oh, I know," Aidren said, "but then they were telling their story. It's fascinating to listen to all the different accents."

Shaunan smiled. "Yes, here on the Great South Caravan Route, you will encounter people from every land in the Commonweal. But now we must go to our beds. We still have two days more to travel before we reach Céardochis."

The sprawling trade centre that was Céardochis came as quite a shock to Abigail. One moment they had been riding through grasslands, the next, they were surrounded by bustle and noise. Andover, the only town she had visited back home, was nothing like this. Although the main part of the town appeared to be ahead of them, the other side of a wide bridge over the river, the settlement had spread over to this side too.

They were riding through a maze of what she realised were pens for cattle and other livestock. Although there were many empty pens at this time of year, the smell of the animals was rich and pungent. Their lowing and bleating filled the air.

"What is the name of the river?" she asked Ylonya.

"The Mistbourne. The old town centre of Céardochis is set within a wide loop of it. Once we have crossed the South Bridge, which you see ahead of us, we will have arrived. To reach the road to Néartanis, we will have to ride through the whole town and out through the North Gate. There is a wall which spans the width of the mouth of the loop, which closes the circle made by the river. And the port is at the bottom of the loop, just down the river from here."

"Thank you."

"Yes," Shaunan said. "Céardochis is one of the jewels of Veylindré. It is the principal commercial centre for the many crafts made by the Néartanians. Had we not met you and started on this journey, Ellyn would be travelling here in the fulness of time to undergo further training in her craft at the Hall of Clothiers. The Hall not only trains cordwainers but also other craftsmen and women who make all the things we wear – dyers, embroiderers, fullers, glovers, shoemakers, skinners and tanners, spinners, weavers and woolworkers."

Abigail shot a glance at Ellyn. "Cheer up, Ellyn. I'm sure when all this is over, you'll come back here to finish your training."

"I hope so. Ever since I got my Waymark, it has been the dream of my heart to train here."

Even in this cold season, the wide streets of Céardochis were crowded.

As Ylonya led the way, Abigail's eyes wandered everywhere, taking in the sights. The wooden houses were tall and, at three or four storeys high, loomed over them. Every so often, they passed a larger building built of fine, well-crafted stone.

People from all over Veylindré thronged the streets. Tall, blonde Garûnalonden, clad in wool breeches and tunics, with fur-lined jerkins over them. Shorter, brown-skinned Lèniumen with brown eyes, dark hair worn in braids and dressed in clothing of many cuts and colours. Less conspicuous people – lean and lithe, wearing neutral colours, the better to blend in – reminded her of Ylonya. She knew by their Waymarks they were Yrusian traders. More familiar were the dark-skinned Dagârans in their leather riding clothes of dark brown and all shades of red. And in among them all, the short, cheerful figures of Néartanians, quite at home in all the sound and commotion.

The noise was overpowering. It reminded her of Luvodican during the height of the festival. But even then, the city of Luvodican had had quite a different atmosphere – stately, austere, grand.

Céardochis buzzed like an enormous beehive. In spite of her heartache, Abigail could not help feeling excited.

Abruptly, they came out of the street they had been riding along into an enormous open square. There were grand buildings all around it and the central space was filled with a great market consisting of dozens of small, wooden huts from which, it seemed, you could buy anything you desired.

"Ah, I love Céardochis," Ylonya said. "I love its sprawling chaos, so different to the rest of Néartania. People come here from every part of the Commonweal, making it one of the best places to catch up on the latest news. When we have found somewhere to stay, I will go out and learn what I may."

"That would be well, Ylonya," Shaunan said. "We will await you in the inn. Unless you three," and she nodded at Abigail, Aidren and Ellyn, "want to go out and explore?"

"May we really, Aunt Shaunan?" Ellyn said, cheering up.

"Of course, so long as the three of you stay together and are back at the inn before dusk."

"Where shall we go first?" Ellyn asked as they left the inn Ylonya had chosen half an hour later.

"I'd like to visit the temple," Abigail said. "I noticed it as we rode past. I'd like to see what goes on when it's not Ranusdag."

"All right," Ellyn said. "And I'd like to have a wander round that huge market – I spotted some wonderful stalls. What about you, Aidren?"

He shrugged. "Whatever you like. The market is nearer, so let's go there first, then walk on to the temple."

Ellyn led the way to the central square. There was so much to see, so much to exclaim over. As Ylonya had told them, it seemed it was possible to buy anything here – from clothing and household goods to food and drink. And craft items of all kinds. Abigail seemed to be enjoying it as much as she was and Aidren didn't seem to mind tagging along.

"Look at this, Abigail," Ellyn said, stopping at a stall which sold leather goods. "I wonder what dye they used to make that leather such a beautiful yellow."

"Crushed yarrow," the stallholder said. "I make it into a paste and rub it in warm."

Ellyn blushed. "Thank you. I am a cordwainer myself so I am interested in such things."

"Are you from around here?" the woman asked.

"No, we are from Nordvein, in northern Dagâran."

"What brings you here?"

"We are travelling to Néartanis with my friend's aunt," Abigail broke in. "Visiting a sick relative."

Ellyn gaped at her. Why was Abigail not telling the truth? Aidren nudged her from behind, and said in a low voice, "It is wise not to reveal our purpose to strangers."

"That's right," Ellyn said, pulling herself together. "We must go now. It was good to meet you."

"I'm sorry, Ellyn," Abigail said as they wandered on. "But it seemed to me we should keep our destination secret."

"That's what Aidren said," Ellyn replied. She shrugged. She couldn't see why, but they both seemed convinced. Oh well…

"Let's go to the temple now," she said, leading the way down one of the many streets leading out of the square.

They had not gone far when they heard a shrill voice coming from a narrow, dark side alley. "Leave me alone! You're hurting me!"

Without hesitation, Ellyn ran into the alley. "What's going on here?"

Some youths were gathered around something – no, someone – on the ground, some with stones in their hands.

The victim was a young boy, Yrusian by the look of him, with a withered left arm, his pale face full of terror. A stone had cut him on the right cheek.

Ellyn charged towards them. "Stop it! Leave him alone. Pick on someone your own size!"

"What's it got to do with you?" one of the larger youths said, rounding on her.

"Yeah," another shouted. "Get out of here, Dagâran bitch. It's none of your damn business." He threw a jagged stone at her.

It hit her on the collarbone. The bright pain was agonising.

Then Aidren and Abigail were there. Abigail put her arm around her, drawing her away.

Aidren strode forward. "It is our business," he said, drawing his sword. "It is the duty of all good citizens to prevent bullies from preying on the weak."

Confronted by an angry Warrior of Dagâra, the youths fled.

Blackness.

"Aidren," Abigail said, "I'm going to call Shaunan. Look after the little boy. I'll see to Ellyn."

"All right," Aidren said, walking over to the terrified child.

Shaunan. We need you. There's been an accident. I think Ellyn's broken her collarbone.

Where are you?

Abigail closed her eyes and sent as clear a picture as she could. *In a side alley, off the street leading from the central square to the temple.*

We're on our way. Look after her.

Abigail wondered who Shaunan meant by "we" but that didn't matter now. She clasped her Goldstone and examined Ellyn carefully, using her healing sense. The collarbone was broken; that much was certain. Fortunately, she had fainted. Abigail hoped she would not come round before Shaunan arrived. She covered the girl with her cloak and tried to focus her healing sense to alleviate her friend's pain, murmuring, *"Gal ens bynn wellent, gal ens bynn wellent."*

She could hear Aidren talking to the little boy. "What is your name, child?"

The child's voice was high and thin, full of fear. "M-mekin, sir."

"Well, Mekin, you're safe now. Others will be arriving soon and we'll get you back to your people. Who are you here with?"

"W-with my father, Mardal. He's going to be so angry with me."

"Why's that, Mekin?" Aidren asked.

"I wasn't supposed to leave the inn," Mekin said, shivering in reaction. "But I wanted to visit the temple, to ask Lènia to heal my arm."

Abigail's heart twisted in pity. The poor child. Then she heard a voice in her mind, *Abigail, we're nearly with you. Which alley are you in?*

Once more Abigail sent her mentor the picture. Moments later, Shaunan and Ylonya appeared in the mouth of the alley.

"Well done, Abigail," Shaunan said. "What happened?"

"We were on our way to the temple, when we heard the voice of a child crying out in pain. Ellyn ran down here, and we found a group of boys tormenting that one," she indicated Mekin with her chin. "There was a confrontation, and one of the boys threw a stone at Ellyn. Then Aidren stood up to them, and they fled. It all happened so quickly."

Shaunan sighed. "Youngsters can be so cruel," she said. "Let me look at Ellyn. What have you done, so far?"

Abigail took a deep breath. Was this a test? "I used my healing sense to examine her," she said. "I think the stone has broken her collarbone. Then she fainted. So I've covered her with my cloak and tried to lessen the pain."

"Good. You have done the right things. Let me see her now."

Gratefully, Abigail moved aside.

Using gentle fingers, Shaunan examined Ellyn, who was showing signs of coming round. "You are right. Her collarbone is broken. We must take her to the temple so I may heal her."

"Can you heal the child's arm as well?" Abigail asked.

"I do not think so," Shaunan said with clear regret. "It is beyond my powers to heal that kind of disability. If his family took him to the Healer Hall in Berlysian, they might be able to do something. Only the very best healers can remedy such a maiming." She turned. "Bring the boy with us," she told Aidren and Ylonya. "We must go to the temple. It will be a refuge for him and a place of healing for Ellyn."

"I will carry her," Aidren said.

Ellyn opened her eyes. "What happened?" Then she moved and gasped in pain.

"Gently, Ellyn," Shaunan said. "Your collarbone is broken. If we help, do you think you can walk? The temple is not far."

Ellyn bit her lip, then nodded. "I think so." Then she cried out, "The little boy! What has happened to him?"

"We have him safe," Aidren said.

"Oh, thank goodness! Those horrible boys."

"Can you rise now?" Shaunan said. "Ylonya and I will help you."

With Shaunan and Ylonya supporting her on either side, Ellyn could manage to walk.

Abigail stepped over to join Aidren and the child. "Come," she said, holding out her hand to the little boy. "We are going to the temple. Word will be sent to your father."

Aidren was furious with himself. Once again, he had let everyone down. Why hadn't he stopped Ellyn from running into that alley?

The temple was as grand and awe-inspiring inside as any temple he had ever seen. Even the High Temple in Luvodican was no finer than this. The wide ceiling was supported by tall pillars and painted with images and symbols of the Six. The six altars were adorned with snowy-white cloths, on which stood silver candlesticks.

"We need assistance," Shaunan told the young Ranusian adept who came forward to greet them. "One of our company has been injured. We also have a young child here who has lost touch with his family."

"Please follow me, Waymage," the adept said. "I will take you and your companions to the infirmary."

"Abigail, bring Ellyn and follow me," Shaunan said. "Aidren, Ylonya, stay here with the child and see if you can discover where his father is staying."

Aidren wanted to protest. He wanted to stay with Ellyn to make sure she was all right, that her injury was not serious. But he knew there was no point in arguing. The Waymage's authority was absolute. With longing in his heart, he watched them leave.

"Now, Aidren," Ylonya said. "Can you explain to me what has happened?"

"It was as Abigail told the Waymage. Ellyn rushed into the alley when she heard Mekin," he indicated the boy, "crying out. Then it all happened so quickly, I didn't have a chance to stop it. So I left Abigail to look after Ellyn and confronted them. I think," he said, with a satisfied smile, "they were not expecting to see a Warrior of Dagâra."

Ylonya laughed. "Well done, my friend. You did well. There is no thought of blame here. We had better find out where this young man is from and who his father is."

"His father is Mardal, an Yrusian trader," Aidren said. "I was about to ask him where they were staying when you and the Waymage arrived."

"Mardal?" Ylonya turned to the child, who was watching her with big eyes. "Mardal from Porusport?"

The child nodded.

"I know him."

"You know my da?" Mekin said in surprise.

"Yes, child, we have travelled together in the past. Where are your party staying?"

"I don't know the name of the street but the inn has a great golden lion hanging outside."

Ylonya nodded. "I know it. I will fetch him at once. Aidren, you stay with Mekin."

Twenty minutes later, she was back, a tall Yrusian trader at her heels. "Mekin!" the man said. "Where have you been? I've been so worried about you."

"Da!" Mekin burst into tears. "I'm so sorry, I'm so sorry. I only wanted to come to pray to Lènia so she would heal my arm."

A shadow passed over the man's face. Of grief and remembered pain. His voice was gentle. "What happened?"

"There were some boys," Mekin sniffled between sobs, "big boys and they started to tease me about my arm. I tried to run away. But then I was in an alley with no way out. Then a big Dagâran girl came and started shouting at them and they threw a stone at her. This man," he pointed at Aidren, "drew his sword and frightened them away. Then the other people came and they brought me here. Da, are you very angry with me?"

The man, Mardal, Aidren supposed he was, swept his son up into his arms. "I'm a little angry you sneaked away without telling me, but of course I'm not *very* angry."

He turned to Aidren. "Young man, I do not know your name."

"I am Aidren of Nordvein."

"Then, Aidren of Nordvein, know that Mardal of Porusport is in your debt. This one's mother would have grieved indeed if we had lost him."

"Thank you, Mardal" Aidren said, his cheeks flushing. "But it wasn't just me. My friend Ellyn was the first into the alley. And now she is injured and the Waymage is healing her."

Mardal frowned. "Is the injury serious?"

"No, I don't think so. Abigail said she thought Ellyn had broken her collarbone."

"Who is Abigail?"

"She is Ranusian. She was with us when it all happened."

"Then my debt extends to all three of you. Please tell the others when they return. Mekin and I must go back to the Lion. We were getting ready to leave for Berlysian in the morning, when we realised that this one," he ruffled his son's hair, "was missing. Once again, I am in your debt."

"Berlysian?" Ylonya said. "What is the purpose of your journey?"

"Partly trade."

Ylonya nodded, as though this went without saying.

"But also to visit the Healer Hall, to see whether they can do anything about Mekin's arm. The Healer in Porusport told us he is old enough for something to be done, now."

"May the Way guard and guide you," Ylonya said.

"Thank you," Mardal said. "And may the Way be with you also. Ylonya, it was good to see you again."

Although Shaunan had healed Ellyn's collarbone, healing her spirit was another matter. She sensed the girl had lost some of the lovely, trusting innocence which, until now, had been a big part of her personality.

When she retreated to her room after picking at her supper, Shaunan drew Abigail aside.

"Would you talk to Ellyn, please? I need to know what is in her heart and mind. I think she might share her troubles more easily with you."

"Of course. I'll go up and speak to her now. Will we be leaving Céardochis in the morning?"

"I am not sure," Shaunan said. "It may be better for us to stay an extra day, both to allow Ellyn to recover and for Ylonya to gather the latest news."

"Do you think the healers in Berlysian will be able to heal Mekin's arm?" Abigail asked. "Aidren told me Mardal and the others were travelling there in the hope that they could."

"If anyone can, it will be the healers at the Healing Hall. They are the best in all Veylindré."

"Oh, I hope they can. Those boys were so cruel, picking on him just because he was different."

"That is the way of the world, I am afraid. It is natural for us to mistrust people who are different from us in some way. Although, I must say, I am surprised at those boys. Living in Céardochis as they do, they must encounter all sorts of people every day."

"I know how he must have felt," Abigail said. "It's not so long ago that I was the different one because of having no Waymark. I think Jacob…" Shaunan felt the pang of sorrow from the girl at the mention of his name "…and I were very lucky it was Aidren and Ellyn who found us, not people like those boys. When folk reacted to us with fear and mistrust on our journey to Luvodican, I often wondered how Aidren had the courage to stay alone with us, while Ellyn went back to fetch you."

Shaunan smiled. "I think his desire to prove himself as a Dagâran warrior helped him to conquer his fears."

"I suppose so. I'm so glad I belong here now."

"You most certainly do."

Ellyn was curled up on top of her bed, miserable. It was as though something inside her had broken. Oh, Aunt Shaunan and Abigail had mended her collarbone and, apart from a residual ache, it was as good as ever. But she felt like crying or screaming or both.

Those boys. She had never encountered anyone like them – so apt to violence for no good reason. Their behaviour had filled her with loathing – how could they act that way? Why did they act that way?

"Ellyn? May I come in?"

Abigail's voice.

"I suppose so. It's your room too."

The other girl came in and, kneeling on the woven rug in front of her, took her hands.

"I came up to see how you are feeling. Oh, your hands are freezing! You've let the fire die down. Snuggle down under the comforter. I'll see to the fire."

Her voice was warm, persuasive, kind. Bemused, Ellyn did as she was told.

Abigail busied herself feeding the fire. Then, when she was satisfied it was well alight, she sat on the edge of the bed.

"What's wrong, my friend? Is it your collarbone? Shaunan told me it had mended well."

Ellyn shook her head. "My collarbone is fine. I just feel… different inside." She glanced at the older girl and saw nothing but warm attention. Maybe she'd understand. "It was those boys. I've never met anyone like them before – they seemed to love violence for its own sake. They picked on that small boy just because he was different. Now I feel as though, all my life, I've been ridiculously naive. One thing's certain – I'll never trust a stranger again."

"Ah, Ellyn, I know how you feel. I felt exactly the same when Jacob and I returned to our settlement and found the Havimi had… had killed my family and everyone I knew." Abigail paused, then continued, "You said it well. They, too, seemed to love violence for its own sake. It made me sick to my stomach. Like you, I'd never seen such meaningless cruelty before."

"Oh, Abigail! I'm so sorry!" Ellyn cried. "That's so much worse than what happened to me. I feel so bad for letting it get to me like that."

Abigail put an arm round her. "Not at all. Your feelings are perfectly natural. I only told you about it so you would know that I do understand. I also felt like I'd never be able to trust anyone again. But then we met you and Aidren in the forest, then Shaunan came, and you were all so kind to us. Which helped me to understand that most people are naturally good and kind, and that evil people are the exception, rather than the rule. Don't let those boys destroy your faith in others."

"Do you really believe that?"

"Yes, I do. Jacob found it hard to trust you all but I didn't. I'm not sure why – maybe I *am* naive. But I'd rather risk being hurt again than close myself off from people."

Ellyn sat up and hugged her. “Thank you, Abigail. I’ll try.”

Abigail smiled. “Good for you. Now, do you want to come downstairs or would you rather rest up here awhile?”

“I think I’ll stay here for now,” Ellyn smiled, feeling unaccountably shy. “You’ve given me a lot to think about.”

“All right.” Abigail bent over, kissed her brow, like an older sister might. “I won’t be long.”

֍ Chapter 23 Δ

When they finally reached the high, snow-capped mountains after two days' hard riding, Jacob thought they had gone wrong somewhere. There seemed to be no way through except by climbing right up into them. He shivered. Even his good woollen cloak did not keep out the icy fingers of the penetrating wind. Why had Portak brought them here?

Portak dismounted. "Hold the reins for me."

He reached into his pack and brought out a triangular stone worn smooth with use, dark red, flecked with other colours, and a plump leather pouch.

Jacob could not identify what mineral the stone was made of. As he watched, Portak took a small, glass vial out of the pouch and emptied it onto the stone. The liquid was dark red – surely it wasn't blood? Then he held the stone aloft and muttered some words in a harsh, guttural tongue, quite unlike his normal, slightly hissing tones. To Jacob's astonishment, the mountain wall in front of them began to glimmer in the weak sunlight. A deep red light shone from it.

He rubbed his eyes, shook his head. What was happening? Witchcraft, that was what. But weren't Portak's people against witchcraft? When his vision cleared, there was a narrow path in front of them leading straight through the mountain. This must be the secret pass Portak had spoken of.

"Come," Portak said, climbing back on his horse. "The entrance to the pass is only there so long as the blood light is shining. We must be swift."

Blood light? What was that about? What was he getting into here? Jacob shrugged – there was nothing he could do about it.

The two of them entered the defile, which was only wide enough for one horse. Portak led, Jacob followed. What else could he do? The walls of the pass stretched high above them on either side. It was like being in a tunnel. The sky far above them had no colour at all. The only sounds were the clip clop of their horses' hooves and the whistling of the wind, which was blowing from directly in front of them. Yet how could that be? It was bitterly cold.

"How long will it take to get through?" Jacob asked.

"A couple of hours, if all goes well."

If all goes well? What did he mean? It seemed churlish to ask. After all, Portak was the only friend he had in this world. Jacob gritted his teeth, fought down his fear and followed, a length behind Portak's horse's tail. As they rode, the path steadily climbed. Time in here had no meaning. He had no way of knowing how long it had been since they had left the outside world. That was what it felt like – as though they were in a different place altogether. He felt stifled, breathless, as though there was not enough air for both of them. How long must he endure?

Finally the path began to level off, and then to fall. They must be nearly through by now. Then even the weak light of the sky was cut off as they entered a dark tunnel lit only by a sooty red light.

The only thing that kept Jacob from turning tail and fleeing was the certainty that he would find the mouth of the pass closed against him. The only way out of this nightmare was to keep on going.

"Portak, how much farther is it now?"

"Not far, my friend. We have only to pass the Guardians of the Pass and we will be in Talamdor."

"There are guardians? Why?" Jacob said, trying to keep a note of panic out of his voice.

"Because we do not permit just anyone to enter our land. Talamdor welcomes only those who believe as we do."

"What are these guardians like?"

"You will see. If you are pure of heart, you have nothing to fear."

As Portak spoke, they reached the end of the path. Before them was a wide cave, with a solid wall of stone at its end, roiling with the same dark red light Jacob had seen at the entrance to the pass.

"What happens now?"

"We await the Guardians."

They did not have long to wait.

Two gigantic figures, eight feet or more in height, clad in shining red armour from head to foot, emerged from the wall. Through the eye slot of their visors, Jacob could see yellow eyes flaming.

He shrank back.

"Who comes to this place?" The voice was deep, cold, malevolent.

Jacob could not tell which of the two had spoken and felt the hair on the back of his neck standing up.

But Portak was unafraid. He stepped forward. "I, Portak, trusted lieutenant of the Prophet. I bring a new believer. Our journey is urgent."

"You are known to us, Portak. You may enter. This other will need to pass the tests."

"What tests?" Jacob muttered.

"Peace, my friend. All will be well. Just answer their questions and do not resist."

"What is your name, stranger?" the voice demanded.

"Jacob."

"Full name?"

"Jacob Wallingford."

"Where are you from?"

"I am from England. It is… not in your world."

"You lie!" The voice rose in anger, harsh and discordant. "You have a Dagâran Waymark on your forehead. You are from Veylindré."

To Jacob's horror, razor-sharp claws sprang out from the ends of the creature's gauntlets as it reached towards his throat.

Portak leapt forward, putting himself between the creature and Jacob. "Honoured Guardian," he said, "if I might explain?"

The Guardian retracted its arm, but its claws remained out. "Speak, Portak."

"Honoured Guardian, the young man is telling the truth. He was shipwrecked on the shores of Dagâran. I found him wandering, lost and alone. We spoke and I realised he shared our beliefs. I have brought him here to meet the Prophet."

"Then why does he have a Dagâran Waymark?"

"I do not know, Honoured One. It is a mystery. Doubtless the Prophet will be able to discover the truth of it. But I will vouch for him."

"Very well. We will continue the questioning." The head of one of the Guardians turned to Jacob. "Whom do you worship?"

Was this a trick question? What if he answered wrong? "I worship the one true God."

"You do not follow the Six of Veylindré?"

"Absolutely not." That at least he could answer with a clear conscience.

"That is well. What is your purpose in coming to the sacred Land of Talamdor?"

Jacob glanced at Portak. What should he say? "I'm not sure I have a purpose, Honoured Guardian. As Portak said, he brought me here for my own safety. He is the only person I know in this world."

Silence. Jacob could sense that the two Guardians were conferring without words. What would his fate be?

"Very well," one of them said. "You may enter. But you will need to pay the price of passage."

"The price of passage?" What did they mean? He had no money – no means of payment.

"We must take your blood."

"Take my blood? Why?"

"Do not presume to question the Guardians of the Pass," the voice boomed.

"I'm sorry. Of course."

Jacob extended his arm – the one with the strange bangle on it.

The Guardians gazed at it, then nodded to each other. One of them drew a knife from a sheath at its belt, and a small, glass vial, like the one Portak had earlier. Nicking Jacob's arm with the knife, he? it? collected the blood in the vial and smeared it on the wall. The red light flared up, then died down.

To Jacob's astonishment, as a wide, tall archway formed in the wall, the wall itself melted into nothingness.

"Go."

The landscape they came out into was more extreme than western Néartania.

Jacob flung up an arm to protect his eyes, blinded by the orange-red light of the setting sun. When his vision cleared, he saw a deep snowscape overshadowed by the mountains behind them, the last of the light turning the snow into a glittering wonderland. When he looked behind, the mountains themselves were bathed in the sunset light, their cold grey blushing a warm pink. The archway through which they had come had disappeared. Turning back, he could see nothing that grew – only snow, ice, and bleak, bare rock.

"Welcome to the sacred Land of Talamdor," Portak said from behind. "Come! We must leave the horses here and continue on our journey."

Jacob was shivering uncontrollably. "Leave the horses? Do we have to walk the rest of the way?"

"No, indeed," Portak laughed. "Follow me." He led Jacob around a spur of rock jutting out from the base of the mountain. Ahead was a sturdy building, nearly invisible in the snow, painted white with a snow-covered roof. At one side was a stable block.

They dismounted, led their horses into separate stalls and took off their tack. There was deep straw on the floor, a water trough and a hay net for each horse. Jacob wondered idly where the owners of this place brought the hay and straw in from – it seemed clear that nothing could grow in this barren landscape.

"They will stay here," Portak said, "until it is time for me travel over the mountains again."

"But how will we get to Talamunem City?"

"Patience. You will see. We will spend the night here and be on our way in the morning."

As Jacob tried to contain his irritation at Portak's continuing refusal to answer his questions, he noticed that the mark on the man's forehead had changed from the pointy P with the diagonal line through it to a dark red triangle. But he knew from experience there would be no point asking about it.

They made their way towards the building and its main door – made of oak, blackened with age, banded with iron.

Inside, all was light and warmth. They walked into a large vestibule with white walls and a high ceiling criss-crossed by polished wooden beams.

A tall, thin man with a pale face and lank, black hair came towards them, his dark eyes alight with friendship. He had the same blood-red triangle on his forehead as Portak. "Master Portak! You have returned. Welcome once more to the Talamdor Border House."

And the same slightly sibilant voice.

"Greetings, Gamlon. I have brought a companion with me." He gestured Jacob forward. "He is to be taken to the Prophet."

Gamlon's eyebrows shot up, but he said nothing. "Indeed? Then we must make sure you are both comfortable before you continue your journey."

Jacob felt a frisson of unease. Portak was obviously well known and respected here. He hoped the man would keep his word, and not abandon him in this God-forsaken land.

"That was my hope," Portak replied. "We will need beds for the night and warmer clothing for our journey to the City."

"I will see to it myself. It is an honour to serve an agent of the Prophet."

Bowing low, he led them up some wide stone stairs on to a landing, which led off in either direction to corridors with multiple doors on either side. He turned left and showed them into adjacent rooms. "Rest, sleep, whatever you will. Supper will be served at twelfth hour."

"Thank you, Gamlon," Portak said. Then, to Jacob, "Rest now, my friend. I will knock on your door when it is time."

It was the first time Jacob had been alone since this adventure had begun. He stripped off his wet cloak and snow-stained boots and flung himself down on the bed.

A moment later, he was sound asleep.

And as he slept, he dreamed. He was riding through dark woods with Abigail and the others when a small woodland creature shot across the path in front of Abigail's horse, which bolted, throwing her off. His heart nearly stopped – she was injured! He leapt off his horse, knelt beside her. She looked so beautiful – her blonde hair scattered every which way. But pale now, and still. He could not lose her, could not lose the only person who knew of his life before they had come to Veylindré.

Then Shaunan was there, such a relief.

"Is she badly hurt?" he asked.

Shaunan shook her head. "I think not, but I will not know until I've examined her."

He watched the Waymage examine his beloved, fear for her filling his heart, then the welcome verdict. "I think she has just been knocked unconscious. I can perceive no deeper harm."

"Then why isn't she coming to?" he asked, gnawing an anxious lip.

"Give her time," Shaunan said. "She has knocked her head on this tree root. Come, my friend, help me to move her, so I can see more clearly what damage it has done."

He rode with Abigail soft and warm in his arms.

Two tall red figures loomed out of the gloom, their clawed hands reaching out for her.

"Abigail!" he cried and woke up. For a moment, he did not know where he was. Then memory returned. He was at the

Talamdor Border House with Portak, on his way to Talamunem City to meet the Prophet of the One.

He sat up, hugged his knees. Who was Abigail? Why could he not remember who she was? Was he going mad? Portak had told him that all his companions on the *Sweet Sarah* had perished in the shipwreck. So why did his dream tell him otherwise? That Abigail had survived. That they had journeyed together… somewhere… before he had ever met Portak… God!

He was so confused. Logic told him this dream was just… a dream. But it had seemed so real. His heart had been full of love for that girl. One thing he knew instinctively: he must not tell Portak. Even now, the details were fading from his mind. He could see only her face.

A knock on the door. Portak's voice. "Jacob? It's time for supper."

He sighed, a deep sigh from the bottom of his heart. "Give me a minute. I'll be there."

"How are we going to travel in this snow?" Jacob said the following morning. "It is too deep for the horses. They will founder."

"Come and see," Portak said.

He led Jacob around the back of the Border House, where a high-sided wooden sled was waiting for them. It was wide enough to seat two, its runners banded with a red metal Jacob did not recognise, drawn by a team of four pairs of large, fierce dogs with brindled fur and light eyes. Their breath steamed in the cold air.

The man in charge of the sled team was small, dark-skinned, his eyes nesting in wrinkles. He was dressed in fur-lined leather trews and hooded jerkin, with leather gauntlets on his hands and sturdy boots on his feet. He snapped to attention when Portak's eye fell on him.

Jacob wondered why… was it respect? Or fear?

"Here is our transport, at least as far as Kalthund on the eastern bank of the River Caethwas. After that, if the snow is shallow enough, we will travel by horse again."

Jacob took his seat on the left-hand side of the sled. The driver tucked the furs in well around him and gave him a warm hat with fur flaps and fur-lined gauntlets. Also, a pair of oval wooden circles with a vertical slit in the centre of each, held together with thin cord, which mystified him.

He shrugged a question at the driver, who took them back and mimed putting them over his eyes. Jacob realised they must be to shield them from the glare of the snow. He smiled his thanks. Portak obviously had some influence here.

The man nodded, then walked round to the other side of the sled and settled Portak.

Jacob braced himself for a bone-jarring jolt, but the dogs took up the weight of the sled smoothly and soon they were flying over the snow faster than he would have thought possible. The wind in his face, the sun sparkling on the snow, made the ride exhilarating. As the dogs' untiring legs ate up the miles, he had nothing to do but look at the passing landscape. The fur flaps on his hat and the noise of the dogs made conversation difficult. He was not ungrateful – he needed time to think.

This country was beautiful – harsh, but stunning. As they travelled away from the mountains' shadow, and the sun rose higher, he was grateful for the eye-coverings. They protected his eyes but also allowed him to see more than he expected. Without them, the glare from the snow would have blinded him. If he kept his eyes squinted almost shut, he could see where they were going. He had never before encountered such an expanse of snow. Where he came from – southern England – the winters were cold, but not permanent. He could not imagine this much snow ever melting completely away.

On either side of him, great rocks emerged and receded as the sled passed them, their granite tinged with pink in the morning sunshine. The track along which the dogs were running was well-established and continued as far as he could see. The landscape was wild – no human beings lived here. What lay ahead of him on this journey? This forbidding land was making him uneasy.

He recalled his dream from the evening before – about the blonde girl, Abigail, whom he was sure he had loved. He was positive his dream had not made her up; somewhere, she must exist. Did that mean Portak was lying about the shipwreck? But he had no other reason to doubt him, except for the fear he seemed to inspire in others. And the odd reaction of those Guardians – something about a "Dagâran Waymark", whatever *that* was. He wished he could remember how he had got here, who he had been before…

Before what? Before he had woken up in the cabin of the Néartanian boat and met Portak for the first time. Because he was fairly sure they had not been anywhere near a coastline. But what could he do? He knew no-one, apart from Portak, in this mysterious land. He had nowhere to run, no-one to run to. How he wished it were otherwise.

They stopped once along the way to water the dogs, steam rising from their coats, scrapping over the bowls of meat the driver put in front of them. Then the three men ate some lunch – a kind of loaf baked with meat in it. It tasted oddly familiar… where had he eaten this before? If only he could remember. Then the journey continued, and the memory was left behind.

They reached Kalthund in the early evening.

Jacob stepped stiffly out of the sled, stripped off his hat and gauntlets and removed the snow protectors from his eyes, passing them all to the driver with a nod of thanks. He stamped his feet, which were so cold he could no longer feel them.

"Come, we need to get inside." Portak said.

Jacob followed him with a shrug. What else could he do? But he was getting tired of blindly following this man, who was beginning to frighten him. He decided that, once they reached Talamunem City, he would apprentice himself to a smith and make his own way.

The rest of the journey to Crullfeld – wherever that was – took four long tedious days.

They crossed the River Caethwas and Portak purchased horses from a hostler in the smaller settlement on the west bank. True to his prediction, the snow had lessened here, so it was possible to ride once more. But it was a cold and dreary business.

"Portak," Jacob said, "can you tell me something about this land?"

"What do you want to know?"

"Everything, I suppose. We must have travelled sixty miles yesterday and met hardly any people. Are there so few people in Talamdor?"

"Not at all," Portak laughed. "The area of Talamdor between the mountains and the River Caethwas is not typical of the land as a whole. As we travel further west, you will see many more settlements."

"Where are we now?"

"We are in the most fertile region of Talamdor, between the Rivers Caethwas and Roillon. At this time of year, there is not much to see, but for most of the year the fields are full of growing crops and grazing herds of cattle and sheep."

As they rode on, Jacob found this was true. Every so often, they would pass through a small settlement inhabited by farming folk and others. When they passed a smithy, he felt a wave of longing and homesickness. Why had he ever left his home? He didn't belong here.

As the light faded from the sky on the first day, they stopped in one of these villages. The inhabitants were tall and swarthy in appearance, dark of hair and eyes, dressed in clothing of black and red. It seemed they didn't care much for their homes – he saw piles of refuse in the streets and the walls and windows of the buildings were grimy.

Portak strode into the inn. "Two rooms, and stabling for our horses," he said to the innkeeper.

As the man looked up, the colour drained from his face. "Master Portak. Of course, whatever you say." His eyes turned to Jacob and he shrank back in fear. "Who is this?"

"It is not your place to ask questions," Portak said harshly. "Show us to our rooms."

The man louted. "Yes, Master Portak. At once, Master Portak."

He was careful to keep as much distance as possible between himself and the two of them. When he opened the door to show Jacob to his room, he noticed the man wore a similar bangle to his own. What did it mean?

"Why do these people fear us?" he asked Portak. "Why are they so unfriendly?"

"Me, because I am an agent of the Prophet, and they are afraid their sins may be found out," Portak said. "You, because of your Waymark. Veylindréans are not welcome here."

"But I'm not from Veylindré. I don't know why I have that Waymark – whatever a Waymark is. I don't even know what it means."

"The Prophet will answer all your questions."

Jacob bit his lip, swallowing angry words. He was getting sick to death of being told this. He didn't know who this Prophet was and wasn't sure he cared. He was beginning to wonder whether going along with Portak had been a mistake. But what choice did he have? His memories between the *Sweet Sarah* and waking up on the Néartanian boat were… not there. He hated feeling so helpless, so not in control of his own destiny. Lost in anger and resentment, he realised Portak was speaking.

"… and on the third day we will reach Crullfeld, on the west bank of the River Roillon. After that, it should take us only three more days to reach Talamunem City. Where your questions will be answered."

Jacob shrugged but remained silent. He seriously doubted it.

Chapter 24

The following morning, Ylonya went out to gather news. How odd to meet Mardal here, of all places. She had trained with him, oh, it must be fifteen years ago. Why was he in Céardochis? On Guild business, or for some other reason? She must catch him before he left.

When she reached the Golden Lion, Mardal and the other traders were in the courtyard packing up, almost ready to leave.

"Mardal, may I speak with you before you go?"

He swung round in surprise. "Ylonya! What are you doing here? I thought you were staying with the rest of your party."

She lowered her voice. "I need to hear the latest news. Are you still active in the Guild?"

He looked around to check no-one was listening, then murmured, "Yes, but I have not been in contact with them for some time. My wife was adamant we should travel to Berlysian to see whether Mekin's arm could be restored."

Hiding her intense disappointment, Ylonya said, "So you've picked up some trade goods here to justify the trip?"

He grinned sheepishly. "How well you know me."

"Is our contact in Céardochis still Baldis, the innkeeper here?"

"Yes, that was why I chose this place."

"Then I will speak with him. Thank you. I hope the Healer Hall can fix Mekin's arm. May the Way guard and guide you."

"Farewell," he said, giving her a rough hug. "May the Way be with you also."

She ducked in through the inn door, into a low-ceilinged room full of drinkers taking advantage of the relaxed licensing laws of market day. She walked up to the long wooden bar, which ran the length of one side, and ordered a dark ale. The barman, a short, thick-set man with an apron that had once been white around his ample middle, had a Néartanian Waymark, so she knew he couldn't be Baldis.

"Is Baldis around, please?"

"Who should I say wants him, mistress?" the barman asked.

"Tell him it is a friend and show him this token." She took a bronze coin out of her belt purse and handed it to him.

"Fair enough, mistress. Gilda!" he called to the girl collecting mugs. "Mind the bar for me. I need to speak to Master Baldis."

He returned a few minutes later with an unremarkable man of middle height and middle years, with a ready smile on his face and an Yrusian Waymark on his forehead.

"I am Baldis. Come within."

When Ylonya returned around noon, her face was unwontedly grave. Abigail wondered what news she had heard.

"Shaunan, I need to speak with you alone," Ylonya said. She turned to Abigail and Ellyn and smiled. "I shall need to visit the market before we leave tomorrow morning. Do you want to come with me later?"

"Yes, please," Abigail said.

Ellyn said, "Yes, all right."

Aidren cut in, "As long as you all stay together."

Ylonya nodded. "Yes, we'll go together. You can come with us, if you like."

"I think I should, to protect you."

"As you wish."

Half an hour later, she returned. "Come on then, let's go."

Abigail wondered what her news for Shaunan had been but knew it was useless to ask. She sensed it had been serious but had not been able to overhear the import. Shaunan must have been shielding.

The inn they were staying in was only ten minutes' walk from the market square and Abigail was looking forward to another look round – there was so much to see. She hoped it would cheer Ellyn up a bit – the girl was still very subdued.

"I haven't forgotten my promise," Ylonya said to Ellyn.

"Which promise was that?"

"That I would take you to a silversmith I know and buy you a ring."

Ellyn's face brightened. "I'd forgotten about that. Thank you."

Ylonya smiled at her. "We'll stock up on provisions for the journey on the way back."

She led them through the busy market to a street off the square. Halfway down on the right was a small shop with the legend 'Céardochis Silver Emporium' in curly letters on a sign hanging above it. "Here we are. This is my friend Gadaria's shop."

As she opened the door, the two girls followed her in. Aidren remained outside, on guard.

The middle-aged woman behind the counter was Yrusian in appearance, but had a Dagâran Waymark, as befitted her vocation of silversmith. Her small shop was filled with display cases of jewellery and silverwork of all kinds.

"Ylonya!" she said, smiling. "I have not seen you for a long time."

"It is good to see you, Gadaria. I have two young friends with me who would like to choose a ring apiece."

"I have many to choose from," Gadaria said, gesturing to the ring trays beneath the glass counter. "What style were you thinking of?"

"That is up to them," Ylonya said. "I want them to have a memento of our first journey together."

The girls' eyes wandered from tray to tray. How to decide?

Then Abigail spotted a delicate ring she thought Ellyn would like. "There's yours, Ellyn. Look, the –" she counted down, "– fifth ring down on the second row. It's shaped like a leather belt with a buckle."

"Oh, that's perfect!" Ellyn said, her dark eyes glowing. "Do you have it in my size?"

Gadaria looked at her friend's slender fingers. "Yes, I think so. Here we are." She gave Ellyn a ring to try. It fitted perfectly on her middle finger.

"May I really have it?" Ellyn asked Ylonya.

"Of course," Ylonya said. "I always keep my promises."

"Thank you so much!"

Ylonya was a genius. This small kindness was exactly what Ellyn needed to help restore her faith in people. And to think of something that Ellyn would have on her hand, as a constant reminder. How thoughtful.

Abigail continued browsing the rings, trying to find one for herself. There were so many to choose from – thin, delicate ones, broader, more masculine ones, rings with stones of many colours, faceted and unfaceted, and rings without. Then her eye was caught by one particular ring set with a flat, oval, dark yellow stone on which the swirling circle of Ranu was engraved. That was it. That was it! Now, if Gadaria only had it in her size…

"I'd like this one, please," she said, pointing.

Gadaria's eyes flicked up to her forehead on which the Ranusian Waymark was clearly visible. "Most appropriate," she said, taking it out of the tray. "I hope it fits you," she continued, "it is the only one I have in that style."

Abigail held her breath as she tried the ring on different fingers. It fitted on the ring finger of her right hand. She gazed at it with joy. "It fits!" she said, beaming.

"Then we'll take both," Ylonya said.

"Thank you so much, Ylonya," Abigail said. "It's beautiful."

"You're welcome. Thank you, Gadaria. I knew you would have what we wanted."

The silversmith smiled. "It has been a pleasure to see you, my friend."

Before they left the shop, Ylonya asked, "Is there anything you want to buy? It will be a while before we're back in a place like Céardochis."

"I'd like to buy something for Aidren," Ellyn said. "May we wander round the market stalls? And could you distract Aidren so that he doesn't see?"

"And I'd like to buy something for Shaunan," Abigail said. "She has been so good to me."

After browsing up and down the aisles of the stalls, an increasingly disgruntled Aidren trailing along behind them, Ellyn found a leather cuff with an embossed Dagâran symbol on it at the same cordwainer's stall they had visited before. "Do you think he would like it?" she whispered to Abigail.

"I'm sure he would." Good, she seemed to have cheered up.

"Aidren," Ellyn said, "this is for you."

"For me? Thank you, Ellyn." He gave her a clumsy hug.

Abigail hid a smile. There was hope for them yet.

The gift for Shaunan took longer to find. Abigail kept getting distracted by the sight of her beautiful ring – it was so special. In the end, she decided on a wooden barette carved in the shape of a wreath of flowers, which she thought would contrast beautifully with her mentor's silver hair.

As they left Céardochis on the Great North Road heading for Néartanis, the pale sun on their right, Shaunan breathed in the scent of the fragrant pines around them.

While the road was well-maintained and tempting, it was not for them.

She looked ahead and behind to ensure they were unobserved, then guided her horse off into the woods. The others followed.

Half a mile in, she stopped in a small clearing surrounded by tall trees, with soft brown pine needles beneath and dismounted. The others did the same.

"Gather round. Now that we are away from prying ears, I have some… unsettling news to share with you."

"Is this the news that Ylonya came back with?" Abigail asked.

"Ylonya, would you like to tell them?"

"As you wish, Waymage," Ylonya said, then turned to the three young people, her mobile face unusually serious. "I spoke with a… friend of mine yesterday. He told me agents of the Prophet of the One have been seen in Néartania in recent seisdags. We fear that news has reached him about Abigail's and Jacob's arrival in Veylindré. How, we do not know. But we are wondering whether Jacob's abduction may have been planned and that the agents are also searching for Abigail."

"Searching for me?" Abigail said. "But why?"

"We do not know," Ylonya said, frowning. "Perhaps it is because you are not from Veylindré and he believes you have some quality he cannot find elsewhere."

"Who are this 'we'?" Aidren asked.

Ylonya was silent for a moment. Then she nodded her head sharply, as though coming to a decision.

"As we are on this journey together, I have to trust you. But you must promise not to speak of this to anyone else. Our lives and our safety may depend on your silence."

"You have my word, on my honour as a Dagâran warrior," Aidren said.

"I promise," Abigail and Ellyn said together.

"Very well." Ylonya took a deep breath. "I am a member of a secret guild – the Guild of Intelligencers. It was set up thirty years ago at the request of the Wayzenmoot when the activities of the Prophet of the One first began to cause them concern.

"We are based in Porusport and have one or two members in each town or city in Veylindré. Most of us are Yrusians of one kind or another, either traders or mariners. It is our job to gather information about what is going on in the Commonweal, then report our news either to the Wayzenmoot or to the Hall of Justice in Mirunan, through Mistress Margera, our Chief."

"Your mother is the head of the Guild?" Ellyn said. "Is that why you got involved?"

Ylonya smiled. "That was part of the reason. I couldn't help finding out about it when I journeyed with my mother as a young girl. And I believe it is the most important work in the world."

Ellyn turned to Shaunan, who had been watching their reactions. "So it will be like our journey from Myndorian to Luvodican when we had to stay off the main roads?"

"Yes, Ellyn, very like that. We are fortunate to have Ylonya with us. Her knowledge of the byways of Veylindré is unparalleled."

"So this friend of yours is a member of the Guild too?" Aidren asked.

"Yes. He is our contact in Céardochis."

"What happens now?" Abigail said, her worry plain on her face. "It sounds like they are hunting for me, that they want to kidnap me, like they did Jacob. How will we avoid them?"

"Fear not," Ylonya said. "After I had met my friend and reported to Shaunan, I bought enough provisions for us to get to Néartanis unseen by any agent of the Prophet."

"But where will we sleep?" Ellyn said. "It's too cold to sleep outside on the ground."

"The route I plan to follow has some farms along the way. With luck, we will be able to stay with them each night."

"But how do we know they won't give us away?" Aidren asked.

"Trust me, Aidren. Baldis has told me where it is safe to stay."

Shaunan sensed his determination to protect Abigail – and the rest of them. That he wasn't going to lose them as he had lost Jacob. She hoped his ardent devotion would not have to be put to the test.

So Ylonya was a spy. Abigail hadn't thought people of that kind would be necessary in Veylindré. Perhaps this world was not as idyllic as she had believed. Everyone she had met so far, apart from those horrible boys in Céardochis, had been kind and hospitable. Even those who had avoided her before she had her Waymark had reacted from their fear of the unknown.

But Veylindré had seemed to be blessedly free of the kinds of political intrigue which plagued her own world.

Wake up, Abigail. Someone abducted Jacob. Someone was after her. She would need to be alert to the dangers, on her guard.

The route Ylonya took them on meandered through the woods and fields of northern Néartania. They had left the broad grasslands of the Central Plains and were riding through a landscape which reminded Abigail intensely of the England she had left behind. Orderly fields divided by hedgerows or drystone walls, gentle hills, and streams which sparkled in the cold sunlight. Interspersed with clumps of trees and the occasional small village.

Each night, Ylonya led them to an isolated farmhouse and presented her bronze token to the owner. Their horses were hidden away in outbuildings. They were served a delicious, warming meal, then left to themselves. Sleeping space was often at a premium, and Abigail became used to sharing one narrow bed with Ellyn. It was a good thing neither of them were stout. Both of them were so tired at the end of each day that sleep came easily.

The following morning, they would be served breakfast and waved on their way with few words. Lunch, eaten on the road, comprised a loaf of *feolin*, washed down with water from the nearest stream.

Abigail sensed the journey was taking longer than Shaunan liked. Although she said nothing, Abigail could feel, as the days ticked by, her mentor's growing unease.

She drew her horse alongside. "Shaunan, what is wrong?"

The answer came into her mind. *I feel...* Shaunan paused, staring off into the distance, then continued, *Abigail, you have a Ranusian Waymark. Push your mind out gently. What do you sense?*

I don't know how to do that.

She heard a gentle laugh in her mind. *You do. It is done by using the same talent you used when you called Ylonya and I to that alley in Céardochis. Close your eyes, and focus on sensing the minds of others around you. Then gradually push the sensing out as far as you can.*

Abigail opened her mind to her surroundings, reaching out, searching. At first it was difficult to get past the minds of the others. She concentrated, trying to ignore them. Then she felt it. A sense of something malevolent, searching for something, or someone. For her, maybe. She closed her mind quickly.

Yes, I feel it. What does it mean?

I fear it means that we may not reach Ranusheim before the Prophet makes his next move.

His next move? What will that be? She could feel the fear gnawing at the edge of her mentor's mind and fought down her own feeling of panic.

Shaunan turned to face her. *I do not know. That is what is worrying me. We must get to the Wayzenmoot and tell our story before anything worse happens.*

But... Ylonya will keep us safe, won't she?

I have great faith in her abilities. But we are only five. Only two of us have any experience of fighting – Ylonya and Aidren.

Fighting? Do you think we will have to fight our way there?

I hope not. But I would be happier if we had a few trained and experienced warriors with us.

We need to warn the others.

I agree. We'll do that when we stop tonight.

"Waymage," Aidren said, "how much further is it to Néartanis?"

"Not too far now, Aidren. I think we may reach it by sunset tomorrow."

Then they heard it. The steady pounding rhythm of cantering horses coming up fast behind them. Although they were still out of sight over the brow of the hill, they were getting closer every minute.

"Aidren and Ylonya," Shaunan said, "be ready."

She didn't need to tell him. Gripping the hilt of his sword, he strained to discover who was pursuing them. The sun was close to setting, the trees casting long shadows to their right. Now he could see the dust rising from the footfalls of the pursuing riders.

Ylonya stepped up beside him, then they spread out to give as much cover as possible to the others She began to draw her sword but Aidren signalled her to stop. She frowned, her eyes questioning him.

He quoted the Dagâran Warriors' philosophy, which was also the law of the Commonweal, the law of the Way: "Never draw a weapon unless drawn upon, hostility comes from escalation."

Ylonya tilted her head towards the group behind them.

Aidren glanced back.

Ellyn, Abigail and even the Waymage were showing varying states of apprehension.

Ellyn, his little Ellyn, looked positively terrified, while Abigail trembled slightly but looked ready to defend herself.

Shaunan was as ready as he and Ylonya were but wary – warier than Aidren had ever seen her. He knew she was no warrior. If these riders meant ill, all her Waymagic could not help them.

It would be down to him and Ylonya. He hoped she was up to it.

He looked back at Ylonya and shrugged. "It is still the law."

She sighed and nodded, sheathing her sword once more.

The riders came into view.

Aidren braced himself for battle, then sighed with relief. He took his hand off his hilt and held it out and open in the traditional greeting. Two of the three looked like Garûnan Watchmen in their distinctive dark blue uniforms – tall muscular men with blond hair riding sturdy horses. No reason to die for the cause just yet.

Then his gaze locked on to the man flanked by the two Watchmen. He was a very different matter. Aidren had no idea what to make of him. Although he was dressed like them as a Garûnan Watchman, his hair was black, his eyes were dark and foreboding. A disfiguring scar stretched from cheekbone to hairline. He did not look like any Veylindréan Aidren had ever seen.

Instead of returning his greeting, they rode straight towards him, as though to mow him down.

"Aidren!" Ellyn screamed.

The rider closest to him had levelled his spear.

It was too late to get out of the way.

Everything he had learned at the Hall of Warriors clicked together. He leapt backwards but was caught by the point of the spear.

Had he stood still, it would have skewered him.

As he was thrown back into a tree, all the air left his lungs. Leaves fell all around him as he tried to heave in air.

The next moment he was rolling to avoid an axe which reverberated in a root behind him. His sword was in his hand as the rider loomed over him, his sabre darting this way and that, trying to land a killing blow.

The terrain was working to Aidren's advantage – the trees and uneven ground made it difficult going for the mounted man and easier for him to dodge away – or position himself so his attacker was forced to adjust in his saddle to line up another stroke.

As the overly eager rider lunged at him, his mare bucked. He whipped her furiously, pulling her back.

But that mistake meant Aidren was ready for him. He stretched upwards and grabbed the man, yanked him from the saddle, his sword clattering to the ground beside them. They fought on, hand to hand, rolling on the ground.

By the Six! The man was stronger than his lean frame suggested. He wrestled with Aidren, his long legs snaking round him, then rolled, leaving Aidren bottom-most. He gasped in pain.

Both of them saw the sword at the same time, just out of reach. Grunting and flailing, they both grabbed for it. While the man's filthy fingernails scratched at Aidren's left eye, making it smart painfully, his other hand reached for the elusive sword.

Aidren fought to pull those fingers away from his eye with one hand, while groping desperately with the other to get that sword first. Nothing else mattered. His eye was on fire as the grip got tighter – would he ever be able to see out of it again? He fought to grasp the sword with his other hand.

With a hoarse cry, his opponent grabbed the sword, held it high and swung. So this was how he would meet his end. He heard a crunch and a clatter as the sword dropped by his head. With his one good eye, he saw the man's puzzled expression as blood dripped from his forehead from an axe blade deeply embedded in his skull. Then he fell, burying Aidren beneath him.

Aidren heaved the body off. Who had killed him?

Ellyn was standing over him, tears pouring down her face. "Are you all right?"

He regained his feet, then, gripping her shoulders, kissed her hard on the lips. "Go back to Shaunan. I need to help Ylonya."

The Yrusian woman had managed to disable the horses by hamstringing their legs, which had worked well – up to a point. But one of the men had her pinned against a tree, a death grip around her neck. The other, the one who looked different, was limping towards them, one leg shattered from falling beneath his crippled horse, whose screams went through Aidren like a knife.

Ylonya's face was blue and desperate as the life was being choked out of her. Aidren roared a challenge and the limping man swung round to meet him. Aidren thrust his sword deep into the man's chest to the hilt and out the other side.

The man throttling Ylonya looked around startled. But it was far too late.

In one swift action, Aidren kicked the corpse off his blade, spun round, then swung with all his remaining strength. The man's head came clean off, bouncing off a tree and rolling to a stop.

The fight was over. They had won.

The others came racing towards them, as he and Ylonya exchanged a long look.

"Thank you, she croaked, "for my life."

Abigail walked over to where Aidren was sitting, Ellyn hovering over him, her face stricken, sobbing her heart out. "Where are you hurting?"

"It's mainly my eye," Aidren said. "That filthy devil was trying to gouge it out with his fingernails. If it hadn't been for Ellyn, he'd have got me for sure."

"I think I'd better leave it for Shaunan to look at," Abigail said. "I've never tried to heal such a serious injury before and I don't want to make it worse. Do you have any other wounds?"

"Only where he caught me with his spear." He pulled up his leather tunic to show her. "I don't think it's serious, but if you could heal it, I'd be grateful."

Abigail held her Goldstone, and murmured, "*Belannath Ranu, gal em bynn wellent, gal em bynn wellent.*" She held the words in her mind as she covered the bloody cut on Aidren's chest with her right hand. She sensed the power being transferred to his body and it began to close and heal, leaving only a neat scar. Thank God! Or rather, thank Ranu!

Ellyn had moved away and was being noisily sick. What was wrong with her?

Then Shaunan was by her side. "Well done, Abigail. I will tend to his eye. You go and see to Ellyn."

To be continued in Volume 2 *The Prophet and the Wayzenmoot*

The Stones of Veylindré – Glossary

Bangles of Control – Bangles made of talamunium, used to control all lower status Talamdorians.

Ceremony of Assignment – Takes place at each of the six Festivals, during which Waymarks are assigned to young people who have completed the Time of Testing.

Dagârastide, Festival of All Souls – Marks the end of the Season of Completion.

Dagârsdag – Fourth day of the Veylindréan seisdag.

Feolin – A loaf baked with meat and bread combined. Used as travelling food.

Garûnastide, Festival of Dedication – Marks the end of the Season of Awakening.

Goldstones – Tools used by Veylindréans to work the magic of the Way.

Golden Stone of Ranu – The master ranusfelsen stone, located in Ranusheim.

Lènia's Bruagan – A herb that can help restore lost memory.

Lènia's Nimbane – A herb which can counteract poison.

Lèniastide, Festival of Music and Storytelling – Marks the end of the Season of Dormancy.

Lethara – A drug used by healers to induce unconsciousness.

Néartastide, Festival of Thanksgiving – Marks the end of the Season of Thanksgiving.

Ranusfelsen – The mineral out of which Goldstones are made, and all Veylindréan temples built. It looks like a pale sandstone, but in the sunlight, hints of gold, green, red, orange, purple, blue and brown show through.

Ranustide, Festival of Wisdom and Lore – Marks the end of the Season of First Fruits.

Season of Awakening – Equivalent to early spring.

Season of Completion – Equivalent to late autumn.

Season of Dormancy – Equivalent to deep winter.

Season of Growth – Equivalent to late spring.

Season of First Fruits – Equivalent to summer.

Season of Thanksgiving – Equivalent to early autumn.

Season / Cycle of Proving – Time spent by a couple waiting to marry, to prove their commitment.

Seisdag – A period of six days, equivalent to our week.

Talamunium – A metal found only in Talamdor. Used as an alloy of silver, to overpower the will of any who wear the bracelet.

Temple of the Six – Seven-sided building which is a place of worship.

Test of Faith – Undertaken by all Talamdorians at the age of 12, to see whether they are worthy of becoming truebloods.

Time of Testing – A time of learning and testing undertaken at puberty by each person in Veylindré, to discern their goddess affiliation.

Truebloods – Talamdorians who have passed the Test of Faith, and are the ruling class of Talamdorian society.

Way of Veylindré – The magical / religious system of Veylindré.

Waymage – Local wise person / priest/ess of the Way. One in each community.

Waymarks – A special mark on the forehead of all Veylindréans, which shows their goddess affiliation.

Waystones – Pillars of ranusfelsen – one in each community. They help the inhabitants to access the power of the Way.

Wayzenmoot, The – Council of the Way. Located in Ranusheim.

Yrusiastide, Festival of Journeying – Marks the end of the Season of Growth.

The Stones of Veylindré: Characters

Characters from 17th century England:

George Crutwell – Witchfinder. Prophet of the One in Talamdor for 30+ years.

Richard Forster – A friend of Abigail's.

Mercy Paignton – Abigail's best friend.

Squire Petty – The gentry from Abigail's and Jacob's village.

Elder Sanderson – Presbyterian Elder. Pastor Winters' second in command

Matthew Sanderson – Son of Elder Sanderson. Pastor Winters sees him as a prospective husband for Abigail.

Thomas Winters – Presbyterian Pastor. Abigail's father and instigator of pilgrimage to the New World.

Mary Winters – Wife to Thomas, and mother to Abigail, **Isaac, Daniel** and **Faith**.

Captain Wood – Captain of the *Sweet Sarah.*

Characters in Veylindré:

Abigail Winters (Abi) – The heroine, from 17th century England. 17 years old.

Aidren – A young Warrior of Dagâra. Skilled with the sword. From Nordvein. Member of the Company.

Alaine – a weaver, wife of Rodis of Néartania.

Baldis – Agent of the Guild of Intelligencers in Céardochis.

Balmak – Portak's lifelong friend and lover.

Balon – A warrior who led the forces of Veylindré against the Talamdorians in ages past.

Barlan – An innkeeper in a village south of Myndorian.

Bélia, Lady – The ruler of Dagâran. Lives in Luvodican.

Bodan – A member of the Council of Nordvein.

Brann – A member of the Council of Nordvein.

Brickon – Guildmaster of the Hall of Traders. Ylonya's father.

Brunan – A servant at the Temple of Myndorian.

Donan – The former husband of Shaunan, now dead.

Ellyn – A young apprentice cordwainer, from Nordvein. Niece of Shaunan. Member of the Company.

Findoran – Waymage of Myndorian.

Gadaria – Dagâran silversmith, living & trading in Céardochis.

Gildon – Master Warrior of the Hall of the Warriors of Dagâra. Lives in Luvodican.

Gomlak – An agent of the Prophet, killed at the cove.

Grunen – A man of Nordvein.

Haldor – A young man of Luvodican, handfasted at Dagârastide in Luvodican.

Havimi – A race of pirates, living in Havim to the south of Veylindré.

Hedwin – Adept of Ranu, trained by Findoran, sent to Nordvein to cover for Shaunan's absence.

Jacob Wallingford – Abigail's boyfriend, from 17th century England. A talented smith.

Janissan – A young woman of Myndorian, handfasted at Dagârastide in Luvodican.

Jaradol – Messenger from Smithsport, to Lord Lesym and Lady Bélia.

Jordis – Son of Rodis, Néartanian farmer.

Kalen – A smith, living in Luvodican. Old friend of Shaunan's who takes Jacob on as his apprentice.

Kormak – Garûnalonden Watch officer (Portak in disguise).

Lesym, Lord – The ruler of Dagâran. Lives in Luvodican.

Lyma – A member of the Council of Nordvein.

Lymon – A boy at Ceremony of Assignment in Luvodican. From Myndorian.

Mardal – Yrusian trader and agent of the Guild of Intelligencers. Lives in Porusport.

Margera – Guildmistress of the Hall of Traders, and Head of the Guild of Intelligencers. Ylonya's mother.

Marinden – First Waymage of Dagâran. Lives in Luvodican.

Markhan – Master Cordwainer in Luvodican.

Mekin – Son of Mardal, has a withered arm. Encountered in Céardochis.

Meldar – Waymage of Nordvein before Shaunan.

Norin – A stable hand in village south of Myndorian.

Oltan – A guard of the East Gate of Myndorian.

Petan – The husband of Waymage Findoran.

Portak – Agent of the Prophet of the One. Uses the alias Kormak while in Veylindré.

Prophet of the One – The principal antagonist, ruler of Talamdor.

Raimun – Master Cordwainer of Nordvein.

Rewald – Waymage of Talmis.

Rodis – A Néartanian farmer on the road to Talmis, with whom the Company take shelter.

Sanderon – Sword Master at the Hall of Warriors in Luvodican.

Shaunan – Waymage of Nordvein. Abigail's mentor and member of the Company.

Shula – A girl at the Ceremony of Assignment at Luvodican. From Myndorian.

Tamin – Chief Messenger of the Prophet, responsible for sending and receiving messages from agents in the field.

Torlin – Trade Master at Smithsport.

Ylonya – An Yrusian guide and intelligence gatherer. Member of the Company.

The Stones of Veylindré – Places

Avarin – A mining village in northern Talamdor.

Berlysian – A settlement in the Vale of Berlysian, Lènium. Home of the Healer Hall and the Hall of Apothecaries.

Caethniss Castle – A border fort of Talamdor.

Caethwasim – A slave port of Talamdor.

Céardochis – The commercial centre for the many craft items made by the Néartanians. Home of the Hall of Clothiers and the Builders' Hall.

Chorich Castle – A border fort in Yrusian.

Claymont – A village in western Dagâran, on the River Redwater.

Coèdnis – Located in Néartania, on the edge of the Great Forest. Home of the Woodworkers' Hall.

Colaste a'r Teisen – The training school for Ranusian adepts, to turn them into Waymages. In Ranusheim.

Commonweal of Veylindré – A federation of six Lands: Dagâran, Garûnalond, Isle of Ranu, Lènium, Néartania, and Yrusian.

Cristail Keep – A border fort in Néartania.

Crullfeld – The location of a farming collective in Talamdor.

Dagâran – One of the six Lands of the Commonweal of Veylindré.

Deepwoods Keep – A border fort in Néartania.

Fenland – A substantial area of marsh and fen, which skirts the Inland Sea of Yrusian, to the north and west.

Fionnan – Centre of the wine-growing region in Dagâran. End of the Great South Caravan Route.

Fort of Ranu – The only entrance to the Isle of Ranu.

Garûnalond – One of the six Lands of the Commonweal of Veylindré.

Garûnashavn – The principal port of Garûnalond. Home of the Hall of Messengers.

Havim – Country of pirates and slave traders. Loose alliance with Talamdor.

Homing, The – The central settlement of the Fenland.

Iascan – The main centre of the fishing industry in Yrusian. Home of the Fisherfolks' Hall.

Inland Sea – A large inland sea in Yrusian, the southern part of which forms the border with Néartania.

Irnvein – A mining village to the north of Nordvein in Dagâran.

Isle of Ranu – One of the six Lands of the Commonweal of Veylindré.

Lèniashaven – The principal port of Lènium, where the shipbuilding industry of Lènium is based.

Lènium – One of the six Lands of the Commonweal of Veylindré.

Luvodican – The capital city of Dagâran. Home of the Hall of Weaponcraft and the Warriors of Dagâra.

Mathven – Located in Yrusian, a port at the mouth of the River Yrus. Home of the Hall of Mariners and Shipbuilders.

Mirunan – The capital city of Garûnalond. Home of the Hall of Justice and the Academy of the Watch.

Mistbourne Keep – A border fort in Néartania.

Mount Talamu – In Talamdor, mountain sacred to Talamu.

Muilléan – Located at the mouth of the Ranu River. Home of the Hall of Papermakers.

Myndorian – A town to the West of the Dagâran Range. Commercial centre for the mining industries of Dagâra. Home of the Hall of Metalworking.

Myner's Gap – A pass through the Dagâran Range between Nordvein and Myndorian.

Nailach – The northern port in Havim.

Néartania – One of the six Lands of the Commonweal of Veylindré.

Néartanis – The capital city of Néartania and its main port. Home of the Hall of Plenty.

Nellènium – The capital city of Lènium. End of the Great North Caravan Route.

Nordkeep – A border fort in Néartania.

Nordvein – A village to the east of the Dagâran Range.

Northern Range – A range of high mountains which divide the habitable parts of Garûnalond from the Northern Wastes beyond.

Plavin – A village in Lènium, home of Raewe.

Porusport – An inland port at the confluence of the Rivers Porus and Yrus. Start of the Great South Caravan Route. Home of the Hall of Traders.

Ranusheim – The capital city of the Isle of Ranu. Home of the Wayzenmoot and the Hall of Scriveners and Printers.

River Caethwas – Located in Talamdor.

River Choris – Located in Yrusian.

River Clearwater – Located in Néartania.

River Cristail – Located in Néartania.

River Elvan – Located in Garûnalond.

River Iascus – Located in Yrusian.

River Mistbourne – Located in Néartania.

River Porus – Located in Yrusian.

River Ranu – Located in Isle of Ranu.

River Redwater – Located in Dagâran.

River Roillon – Located in Talamdor.

River Yrus – Located in Yrusian.

Roillby – A village on the eastern bank of the River Roilldon in Talamdor, due east from Talamunem City.

Roilldon Fort – A border fort of Talamdor.

Rorschak – The location of a copper mine in Havim.

Rouliris – A town on the Great South Caravan Route in Néartania, north-west of Céardochis.

Ruslen – The capital city of Yrusian.

Silvin – A village in northern Talamdor.

South Plains Keep – A border fort in Néartania.

Taellingsford – Located at the southern tip of Lènium. Home of the Hall of Tradition.

Talamdor – The country of the enemy, ruled by the Prophet of the One.

Talamunem City – The capital city of Talamdor.

Tarrin – A village in western Yrusian.

Talmis – Centre of the agricultural region of Néartania. It hosts an annual Cattle Fair.

Ullmass – Site of the annual Wool Fair in Garûnalond. Beginning of the Great North Caravan Route.

Vale of Berlysian, The – Fertile area in the centre of Lènium.

Virunon – A village in south-west Yrusian.

Yrusian – One of the six Lands of the Commonweal of Veylindré.

Acknowledgements

I would like to thank my son, David, for suggesting, one day in October 2019, that I might enjoy writing a fantasy novel, for his many helpful suggestions and for his warm support throughout the process; Mike Richards for his encouragement and excellent advice; early readers Yvonne Aburrow, Stephanie Bisby, and Sue Jacznik; the members of Northampton Writers Group for their encouragement along the way; and Jon Davies for his efficient editing. And last, but not least, Maz, David and Becky Woolley, for being the best family in the world.

Printed in Great Britain
by Amazon

31779192R00185